THE DEAD PLAY ON

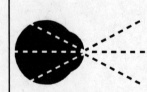

A CAFFERTY & QUINN NOVEL

THE DEAD PLAY ON

HEATHER GRAHAM

THORNDIKE PRESS
A part of Gale, Cengage Learning

GALE
CENGAGE Learning·

Farmington Hills, Mich • San Francisco • New York • Waterville, Maine
Meriden, Conn • Mason, Ohio • Chicago

Copyright © 2015 by Heather Graham Pozzessere.

A Cafferty & Quinn Novel.

Thorndike Press, a part of Gale, Cengage Learning.

Thorndike Press® Large Print Core.

The text of this Large Print edition is unabridged.

Other aspects of the book may vary from the original edition.

Set in 16 pt. Plantin.

LIBRARY OF CONGRESS CATALOGING-IN-PUBLICATION DATA

Graham, Heather.
    The dead play on / by Heather Graham. — Large print edition.
        pages cm. — (Thorndike Press large print core) (A Cafferty & Quinn novel)
    ISBN 978-1-4104-7979-2 (hardcover) — ISBN 1-4104-7979-X (hardcover)
    1. Large type books. I. Title.
PS3557.R198D433 2015
813'.54—dc23   2015008187

Published in 2015 by arrangement with Harlequin Books S. A.

Printed in the United States of America
1 2 3 4 5 6 7 19 18 17 16 15

Dedicated to our men and women in the military, past and present.

And to the USO and International Thriller Writers — especially Sloan D Gibson and John Hanson of the USO, Tom Davin and Chris Schneider of 5.11 Tactical and Kim Howe of ITW.

To those who work at Walter Reed, the hospitals and bases in Kuwait, Ramstadt and Mildenhall.

And to Kathleen Antrim, Harlan Coben, Phil Margulies and F. Paul Wilson — with whom I shared one of the most amazing experiences of my life, a USO tour to visit our servicemen and women.

We can never thank those who serve — who risk everything — enough.

■ ■ ■ ■

BOOK 3
CAFFERTY & QUINN

■ ■ ■ ■

PROLOGUE

Tyler Anderson knew the band's set list; hell, he'd been playing with the B-Street Bombers for years. They could change things up when they wanted, but it was a Wednesday night, and most Wednesday nights they just kept to the list. They played hard, and they played well, but the weekends tended to be way crazier, with bachelor parties, conventions and the crowds — mainly tourists — that thronged the French Quarter. Wednesdays they did their most popular songs, cover songs by Journey, the Beatles, the Killers and other older songs, along with some newer hits that had made the Top 40 list.

And then something happened.

He picked up his sax — his beloved saxophone, his one precious memento from his friend Arnie Watson.

Arnie was dead and buried now. He'd survived three tours in Afghanistan, only to come home and die of a drug overdose. Arnie's brokenhearted mother had insisted that Tyler take his saxophone. After all, they'd learned to play together on the sometimes mean streets of New Orleans, working their way up over the years from dollars tossed in their instrument cases to playing scheduled dates in real clubs.

And so Tyler had decided that he could keep his friend close by playing the sax.

But when he picked it up that night, something — he didn't know what — happened.

They were supposed to go into Lady Gaga's "Edge of Glory," but he didn't give anyone a chance to begin. He was suddenly playing — and he didn't know why. He wasn't even sure he knew *what* he was playing.

And then he did.

Out of nowhere, he realized, he'd started playing The Call's "I Still Believe," which had enjoyed a moment of glory in the vampire film *The Lost Boys.* It was a good song — a *great* song for a sax player, with a challenging arrangement. Arnie had loved to play it.

But he had never played the song himself. Didn't know it.

But he did now. It was as if the damned

sax was playing itself.

And as he played, Tyler felt as if the room was drifting away in a strange fog. And suddenly he was seeing things that Arnie might have seen. Sand and mountains and withered shrubs. He heard explosions and men shouting. There was blood.

But . . .

Arnie had returned from Afghanistan. He'd gone "down range" from his base in Kuwait three times, but he'd come back.

Then the sounds of the explosions dimmed and he saw a New Orleans street.

Rampart Street.

Where Arnie had died.

They'd estimated his time of death at about 5:00 a.m. There should still have been a few people about. Rampart was the edge of the Quarter; Treme was across the street, and while not the best part of town, it had been all right since the summer of storms and the television series. Yeah, there should have been plenty of people around. While a certain song might claim that New York was the city that never slept, everyone knew that title really belonged to New Orleans.

In the wake of his vision, Tyler felt as if he were being physically assaulted, and he found himself gripping the sax as he played as if it were his lifeline. And as he played,

11

the club began to fade again.

He felt as if he were with his old child-hood friend, walking down Rampart. They knew it well, having grown up in the Treme area. Not far from St. Louis #1. And churches! Hell, there were churches everywhere around here.

But Arnie was scared, and Tyler could feel it.

Arnie started to run.

It was the oddest damned thing. Tyler could vaguely see reality — the crowd in the Bourbon Street bar. And he could see somewhere else deep in his mind, where Arnie was. It was almost as if he *were* Arnie.

Beneath the sound of the music he heard a rumble . . . and a whisper.

"You're dead, buddy. You're dead."

Cold. Cold filled him. Cold like . . . death.

Then, suddenly, he wasn't playing anymore. The night was alive with the sound of applause. He blinked — and he was back at La Porte Rouge. His fellow band members were staring at him as if he'd turned pink.

The room was full, and people were pushing one another, trying to get a better look at what was going on. Jessica Tate, one of the waitresses and a good friend, was staring at him as if he'd just changed water into wine, and Eric Lyons, the head bartender,

12

was clapping loudly and — most important — looking pleased, because happy people tended to tip better. His performance had been good for business, Tyler realized.

He lowered his head, lifted the sax and waved to the crowd. And then, with his bandmates Gus, Blake and Shamus looking on, he turned and left the stage — *ran* from the stage. He had to get out. He had to get the hell out of there.

He ran down Bourbon to the first crossroad and headed toward Rampart. He made a right and came to the place where they'd found Arnie.

The needle still in his arm.

He fell against the wall of an appliance store and sank down, tears in his eyes.

Arnie hadn't been a junkie. Arnie hadn't even smoked weed. He'd been doing some heavy drinking since he'd come home, but that was all. His kneecap still pained him from the shrapnel he'd taken on his third tour.

Arnie's death had been hard — so hard — on everyone. The cops had been sorry, but Tyler had seen the look in their eyes when they'd talked to Arnie's mother. They'd seen it before when vets came home. They survived bullets and bombs and land mines, but then, away from the war zone,

13

they were unable to adjust. Maybe they lived with too many nightmares. Whatever the reason, the result was that their bodies might have returned, but their minds had been permanently damaged and never came home from the war. They had all tried to assure his mother that Arnie had been a good man. That he hadn't really been a junkie but had only used the heroin to enter a dream world where he could forget his pain — and then the dream had taken him on to eternal peace.

Tyler sat against the wall, the tears still glistening in his eyes. He slammed his fist against the ground. He cried out loud, sobbing for long minutes. He looked at the sax he was still holding.

And then he knew — somehow, he just knew.

Arnie hadn't ridden any dream into eternal peace.

He'd been murdered. And whatever the hell it took to prove it, Tyler was going to see that his friend got justice.

CHAPTER 1

Michael Quinn parked his car on the street in the Irish Channel section of the city of New Orleans.

There were several police cars already parked in front of the 1920s-era duplex to which he'd been summoned.

He headed up a flight of steep steps. The door to "A" stood open; an officer in uniform waited just outside on the porch.

"Quinn?" the man asked.

Quinn nodded. He didn't know the young officer, but the officer seemed to know him. He had to admit, being recognized was kind of nice.

"He's been waiting for you, but he wants gloves and booties on everyone who goes in. There's a set over there." He pointed.

"Thanks," Quinn said. He looked in the direction the officer indicated and saw a comfortable-looking but slightly rusted porch chair on the far side of the door. He slid on the protective gloves and paper booties.

"You're good to go," the officer said.

Quinn thanked him again then entered a pleasant living area that stretched back to an open kitchen. The duplex had been built along the lines of a "shotgun"-style house. It was essentially a railroad apartment; the right side of the room was a hallway that stretched all the way to the back door, with rooms opening off it on the left. He'd never been inside this particular building, but he'd seen enough similar houses to assume the second half of the duplex would be a mirror image, hallway on the left, rooms opening off to the right.

Crime scene markers already littered the floor, and several members of the crime scene unit were at work, carefully moving around the body.

Quinn noticed that one marker denoted the position of a beer can. Another, the contents of a spilled ashtray.

A third indicated a curious splotch of blood.

In the midst of everything, in a plump armchair with padded wooden arms and a pool of dried blood underneath it, was the reason for Quinn's presence. Dr. Ron Hubert, the medical examiner, was down on one knee in front of the chair, his black medical bag at his side, performing the preliminary work on the victim.

The remnants of what had once been a man sagged against the cushions. His throat had — at the end of the killer's torture spree — been slit ear to ear. A gag — created from a belt and what had probably been the man's own socks — remained strapped around the mouth. A drapery cord bound his left wrist, while the right had been tied to the chair with a lamp cord.

Both of the victim's arms had been burned — with lit cigarettes, Quinn thought. The man's face had been so bashed in, it wasn't possible to determine much about what he had looked like in life.

He had been struck savagely, making it look like a rage killing. But a rage killing was usually personal. The addition of torture suggested that the killer was mentally deranged, someone who reveled in what he was doing — and had probably done it before.

And torture wasn't carried out in a red haze of fury.

"Come around and stick close to the wall, Quinn," Detective Jake Larue said. He was standing behind the couch, his ever-present notepad in hand, slowly looking around the room as the crime scene techs carefully went through it and the ME examined the corpse. Quinn was surprised at Larue's directive; the detective knew damned well that Quinn was aware he needed to avoid contaminating the scene.

But this kind of scene unnerved everyone — even a jaded pro like Larue. Most cops agreed that when crime scenes stopped bothering you, it was time to seek new work.

Quinn looked at the walls as he walked around to Larue's position. He noted a number of photographs of musicians on display. He thought he recognized some of the people in them, although he would have to take some time to remember just who they were.

"What the hell took you so long?" Larue asked.

Quinn could have told him that he'd made it to the house in less than ten minutes once Larue had called him, but it wouldn't have meant anything at the moment. Frankly, after quickly scanning just the living area, he was wondering why he'd been called. The place was equipped with a large-screen television and a state-of-the-art sound system, so presumably the dead man had had money. There was drug paraphernalia on the coffee table to the side of the couch.

A bag of what he presumed to be weed lay out in the open. Glancing toward the kitchen counter, he saw an impressive array of alcohol.

People didn't tend to get stoned on grass and suddenly turn violent, but they were known to become killer agitated after enough bourbon or absinthe. Was this the result of escalating tensions between associates in the drug trade? There was a wad of twenties lying on the table by the bag of weed — which, he saw on closer inspection, looked to have been tossed carelessly on top of a spill of white powder that he didn't think would prove to be baking soda or talc.

Drug deal gone bad? Someone holding out on someone?

"Were you first on scene?" Quinn asked, reaching Larue's side. The detective stood still. Quinn knew he was taking in the room — everything about it.

Larue was a good-looking man with short-cropped hair. His face was a character study — the lines drawn into his features clearly portrayed the complexity of his work and the seriousness with which he faced it. He'd been a damned good partner when they'd worked together, and now that Quinn had been out of the force for several years and worked in the private sector as a PI, they got along just as well together when Larue called him in as a consultant. Even when they'd been partners, Larue had never really wanted to know how Quinn came up with his theories and conclusions. What he didn't know meant he couldn't question Quinn's credibility or his methods.

Larue gave him a questioning glance. "First on the scene were two patrol officers. Since it was pretty evident this man was dead and most likely Lawrence Barrett, who's lived at this address for several years, they steered clear of him and did their best to check the premises for the killer without touching anything. Then I arrived. Damned ugly, right? And no sign of a clear motive. It looks like drugs were involved, but you and I both know looks can be deceiving. It's about as ugly as anything I've ever seen, though."

It was possible to learn a lot about murder — and murderers. But no amount of profiling killers, studying the human mind — or even learning from those who had committed horrendous crimes and been caught — could fully prepare anyone, even those in law enforcement, for the next killer he or she might encounter.

"Ugly and brutal," Quinn agreed.

"What do you see?" Larue asked him.

"A dead man and a hell of a lot of liquor and drugs — not to mention a fat wad of money," Quinn said. "Doesn't look like the motive was robbery — or not a typical robbery, anyway. You have a tortured dead man. Hard to discern, given the extent of the damage, but he appears to be in his late twenties to early thirties. Caucasian, say six-foot even and two hundred pounds. From the bleeding, looks like death came from a slit throat, with the facial beating coming postmortem. Not a lot of blood spray — blood soaked into his clothing and pooled at his feet, but there *is* that spot on the floor near the entrance. There's no sign of forced entry, so it's my best guess he answered the door and let his killer in — which suggests that he knew his attacker or at least expected him. I doubt it was a drug buy, since so many drugs are still here. He lets whoever in. Whatever social discourse they engage in takes place there — four or five feet in. The attacker most likely disables his victim with a blow to the head, maybe even knocks him out. Dr. Hubert will have to determine what occurred, because the face and head are so swollen, I can't tell. When the victim is knocked out or too hurt to put up a fight, the killer drags him into the chair and ties him to it. What seems odd to me is that the

21

attacker did all this — but apparently came unprepared. Everything he used on the victim he seems to have found right here, in the house. And what happened wasn't just violent, it was overkill."

Dr. Hubert looked up from his work and cleared his throat. "Based on his ID, this gentleman indeed is — was — Lawrence Barrett, thirty-three, and according to his driver's license, five foot eleven. I'd have to estimate his weight, too, but I'd say you're right in the ballpark."

Just as Quinn considered Larue one of the best detectives in the city, in his mind Ron Hubert was the best ME — not just in the city, but one of the finest to be found anywhere. Of course, it was true that Quinn had a history of working with Hubert — even when Hubert had been personally involved in a bizarre case that had centered around a painting done by one of Hubert's ancestors. The more he worked with the ME, the more he liked and respected him.

Quinn turned to Larue. "How was he found? Anyone see the killer coming or going?"

"Barrett has a girlfriend by the name of Lacey Cavanaugh. She doesn't have a key, though. She came, couldn't get in, looked through the window and freaked out. The owner of the building, Liana Ruby, lives in the other half of the building, heard her screaming and called the police," Larue said. "Mrs. Ruby didn't hear a thing. But then, she's eighty-plus and was out at the hairdresser's part of the day. Not to mention there's special insulation between the walls, too — the former tenant was a drummer, who put it in to keep his practice sessions from disturbing the neighbors. She gave the responding officers the key, but she didn't step foot inside the apartment. She says she never does — says Barrett has always been good, paid his rent early, was polite and courteous at all times."

"So where is Mrs. Ruby now?" Quinn asked.

"Lying down next door. I told you, she's over eighty."

"What about the girlfriend?" Quinn asked.

"She's at the hospital. She was with the officers when they opened the door, and when she got a good look at . . . she went hysterical and tripped down the steps," Larue told him. "She was still here when I arrived, though, and I interviewed her. She said he didn't have any enemies as far as he knew. He might have been a coke freak and a pothead — and even an alcoholic — but he was a nice guy who was great to her and

23

tended to be overly generous with everyone." Larue held his notepad, but he didn't
so much as glance at his notes. He could
just about recite word for word anything
he'd heard in the first hour or so after
responding to a case.

"Okay, so. A nice guy with no known
enemies — and a street fortune of drugs
still in front of him — was tortured and
killed. Do we know what he did for a living?" Quinn asked.

"Musician," Larue told him. "Apparently
he did so much studio work that money
wasn't an issue."

Quinn looked over at the body again,
shaking his head. "No defensive wounds,
right?" he asked Dr. Hubert.

"No. I don't think he even saw the first
blow coming," Hubert said. "Of course, I
don't like answering too many questions
until I've completed the autopsy."

"For now, your best guesstimates are
entirely appreciated," Quinn said.

"So?" Larue asked Quinn as the ME went
back to examining the body.

"Hmm," Quinn murmured. "Even if he
made a good living, a drug habit is expensive. I don't know how far you've gotten
with this. Do we know if he'd borrowed any
money from the wrong people? Or, follow-

ing a different track, did Lacey Cavanaugh have a jealous ex?"

"She's in surgery for a badly smashed kneecap at the moment. Those are steep steps, you might have noticed," Larue said. "The hospital has informed me that we'll be able to talk to her in a few hours."

"Good. That could be important information," Quinn said.

This murder was, beyond a doubt, brutal to the extreme. And while Quinn, like most of the world, wanted to believe that every human life was equal to every other human life, in the workings of any law-enforcement department there were always those that demanded different attention. Larue was usually brought in on high-profile cases, cases that involved multiple victims, and those that involved something . . . unusual.

This murder, Quinn decided, was bizarre enough to warrant Larue's interest.

It struck Quinn then that he had missed something he should have seen straight off. He realized that the photos on the walls were all of the same man — undoubtedly the dead man — with different musicians and producers of note.

What he didn't see anywhere in the photos or the room was a musical instrument. Of course, it was possible Barrett kept his instrument in another room, but . . .

"What did he play?" Quinn asked. "Do we know that?"

"Half a dozen instruments. The man was multitalented."

Quinn was surprised to get his answer from above — the top of a narrow stairway on the left side of the room.

He saw Grace Leon up there and knew he shouldn't have been surprised. Jake Larue liked Ron Hubert's work as an ME, and he liked Grace Leon's unit of crime scene technicians. Grace was small, about forty, with hair that resembled a steel-wool pad. She was, however, energy in motion, and while detectives liked to do the questioning and theorizing, Grace had a knack for pointing out the piece of evidence that could cement a case — or put cracks the size of the Grand Canyon into a faulty theory. She was swift, thorough and efficient, and her people loved her. Larue had a knack for surrounding himself with the crews he wanted.

"Hey, Grace," he said. "Thanks. I take it you found a lot of instruments?"

"There's a room up here filled with them. But more than that — I've seen this guy play. He grew up in Houma. I've seen him at Jazz Fest — and I've seen him a few times on Frenchman Street. He played a mean harmonica, and I've seen him play keyboard, guitar, bass — even the drums."

"This is a competitive town, and he was obviously in demand, but why the hell kill a musician — and so violently?" Larue said thoughtfully.

"Did anything appear to be missing up there?" Quinn asked Grace.

"Not that I can tell," she said. "But you're welcome to come up here and look for yourself."

Quinn intended to.

"He definitely played guitar," Hubert noted. "I can see the calluses on his fingers."

"A musician. Tortured, brutally killed," Quinn said. "Drugs everywhere. And nothing appears to be missing."

"It's not the first such murder, either," Larue said.

"Oh?"

"We had a murder last week — this one is too similar to be a coincidence. A man named Holton Morelli was tortured then bashed to death with one of his own amplifiers," Larue said.

"He was a musician, too, I take it?" Quinn asked.

Larue nodded.

"What did he play? Was his instrument found in his place?" Quinn asked.

27

"He was like Barrett. Played all kinds of things. Piano, a couple of guitars, a ukulele — he had a whole studio in his place," Larue said. "No surprise. This is a city that loves music. Half the people here sing or play at least one instrument."

Quinn was well aware of that. He loved what he did and considered it as much a calling as a job, but he loved music, too. He played the guitar, though certainly not half as well as most of the guitarists in the city. But whether he was playing or not, he loved living in New Orleans and being surrounded by music pretty much 24/7, from the big names who popped down for Jazz Fest to the performers who made their living playing on the streets.

He forced his attention back to the case. Two musicians were dead, but nothing — including their instruments — appeared to be missing. But they'd both been tortured — which might mean that the killer wanted some kind of information from them before he finished them off. Or that the killer was a psycho who just liked inflicting pain.

"I have a feeling something has to be missing," Quinn said aloud.

"But what?" Larue asked.

"If not an instrument, maybe a piece of music," Quinn said. "Two musicians are dead, and there has to be a reason. I can't believe anyone was so jealous of someone else's talent that they resorted to murder. There has to be more going on here. If I'm right about something being missing, it's crucial for us to figure out what."

Larue nodded. "In Holton Morelli's case, it's not going to be easy. He lived alone. He was fifty-six and just lost his wife to cancer. His one son is in the service. He was given leave to come home, but to the best of his knowledge, nothing was missing from the house, but of course he hasn't been there for a while, so . . ."

"Same area of the city?" Quinn asked.

Larue shook his head. "Faubourg Marigny."

"Since I didn't see the other crime scene," Quinn said, "what else was similar?"

"Enough to point to there being one killer," Larue said. "Holton Morelli was bashed in the head after letting his murderer into his house. Then he was tied to a chair with electrical tape, tortured and beaten to a pulp with an amp."

"Tortured how?" Quinn asked.

"Burns from a cigarette," Dr. Hubert put in, nodding.

"I'll need to see his file," Quinn said. "The killer tortured those men because he wanted something. I can't imagine these guys weren't willing to give it up. They would have been ready to do anything to save their lives."

"Once they were attacked, the murderer had to kill them if he wanted to escape being accused of the crime," Larue pointed out. "Why not just give up the information before it got to that point?"

"Maybe they didn't know the information the killer wanted," Quinn suggested.

"Can we be sure the killer wanted something? Maybe he just enjoyed torture. There are sadists out there who do," Larue reminded him.

Quinn nodded. "That's true. But I'd bet *this* killer wanted something."

"You're probably right, and we'll have to discover what it is." Larue stared at Quinn assessingly. "I'm sure you'll find out what it is. Why the hell do you think I called you in?" He smiled. "Not to mention you play the guitar and have at least a passing familiarity with the local music scene."

Quinn lowered his head, grinning. "Thanks."

"You coming on up?" Grace called down to Quinn.

"Yep, right now."

He headed up the stairs. Larue didn't follow him; he was still concentrating on the body and the surrounding area.

"We're examining everything in the place," Grace said, "but there were no glasses out, no cigarette butts — I don't believe there was any socializing before the killer made his move."

"I agree. The way I see it, Barrett let the killer in, a few words were exchanged and then the killer decked him," Quinn said.

"Based on the evidence, I agree. That splotch by the door could have come from a facial wound. My guess is, analysis will show it's mixed with saliva," Grace said. "I suspect he was stunned by the blow, which the killer delivered right inside the door, or even that he was knocked out stone-cold. We're searching the place thoroughly. At some point the killer was probably in every room, looking for . . . whatever. Anyway, come in and check out the music room."

Quinn followed her through the first door on the upper level. A drum set took up most of one corner; two guitars and a bass sat in their stands nearby. A few tambourines lay in a basket, and a keyboard on a stand was pushed up against one wall. A tipped-over saxophone stand sat underneath the keyboard, but there was no sign of the sax itself or its case. There didn't appear to be room for another instrument, but there was no way to know for sure without asking someone who'd been there before.

"Sheet music? That type of thing?"

"Next room — it's an office. But it's neat and organized. There are papers on the desk, including sheet music, but the piles are all neat and squared up. It doesn't look like anything's been disturbed," Grace said.

"Curious."

"Maybe. Or maybe the killer squared up all the piles when he was done to hide what he'd been looking for."

Quinn looked through the other rooms. A closet had been left open, but if the drawers had been opened and their contents searched, the killer had put everything back the way he'd found it.

Judging by marks in the dust, the killer had definitely looked under the bed, though.

So had the killer been looking for an object of a certain size?

"Are we having the same idea?" Grace asked, interrupting his thoughts. "The guy was looking for something at least as big as a bread box."

"Looks like it. Well, I want to talk to the landlord. Thanks, Grace. And the usual, of course. Keep me posted, please."

She nodded. "You know I will."

"Your thoughts, as well as anything scientific," he said.

"You bet, Quinn."

He hurried back downstairs.

Larue was waiting for him. He stepped outside, and Quinn followed.

Larue turned to him. "We have a sadistic killer on our hands," he said.

"I think that's obvious," Quinn said.

Larue met Quinn's eyes, his own expression thoughtful. "The night of the first murder, there was a holdup in the street. A group of musicians was stopped at gunpoint late at night. All that was taken were their instruments — sax, guitar, harmonica, if I remember right. One fellow was hurt pretty badly, pistol-whipped."

"Did they give you a description of their attacker?"

"They said he was medium build. They thought tall. He had a 'plastic' face. And they're pretty sure he was wearing a wig."

"A plastic face?" Quinn asked. "Probably a mask. God knows you can buy any kind of mask around here."

"You have to admit, it does seem similar enough to hint at a connection, though. Assaulting a group of musicians in the street, and then two musicians murdered, the first the same night as the assault."

"Yes. Although as far as we know he left all the instruments behind in both murders."

"True. But it seems probable that it's the same person — someone with a hate on for musicians — and he's escalating."

"And at a fantastic degree. We're going to have dead musicians lying across the entire city if we don't get to the truth quickly."

"Okay, so we'll have a visit with Mrs. Ruby then get to the hospital and talk to Lacey Cavanaugh," Larue said grimly.

There was nothing like the sound of a sax.

Danni Cafferty stood just outside La Porte Rouge and listened to the music spilling from the Bourbon Street pub. It was delightful.

Somehow the addition of a sax seemed to make almost anything sound better — richer, deeper, truer.

Wolf, at her side, barked, breaking her concentration. "Hey, boy," she said, patting the hybrid's head. "It's okay, I'm coming. I just wasn't expecting to be so enchanted. Beautiful, isn't it? No, maybe cool or . . . mournful, in a way. There's something deep and passionate about a sax, huh?"

Wolf barked again as if in complete agreement and wagged his tail.

She looked into the club. From the side door she could see the band. It was darker in the club than it was outside, and it took her a minute to see the sax player. He was tall, lean and striking. She thought instantly that he was a New Orleans boy, born and bred, the way he played his sax. And there was something special about him. He was a beautiful golden color, with close-cropped dark hair, and he leaned into his music as if he'd been born listening to it, born to play. He wasn't playing alone, of course, but it seemed to her that he was amazing — even in a city filled with amazing musicians.

She couldn't listen all evening, she told herself. Quinn had called to tell her that Jake — Detective Larue, his ex-partner from his days as a NOLA cop — was coming by to see them that night. She was carrying takeout from her friend's new restaurant on St. Ann's, and she'd actually meant to head down the block to Royal but had decided to walk along Bourbon for a few blocks first.

She hadn't meant to get so distracted.

The song — something by Bruce Springsteen — ended. And then, despite the difference in the light inside and out, she realized that the sax player was staring at her. Well, she *was* standing in the bar's doorway with a giant hybrid wolf–German shepherd at her side. She told herself it was Wolf. That the guy was staring at the dog by her side. People always stared at Wolf. They were either terrified, or they wanted to cuddle him.

But the truth was, the man *wasn't* looking at the dog, he was staring straight at her. As if he knew her.

She frowned.

Did she know him?

She might. She'd gone to school here, along with a number of her high school classmates who had never moved away, and while they might all live in different areas now and do different things, they ran into one another now and then. The guy did seem familiar. He might have been one of the kids who, like her, ended up in a local private school after the storms had struck, since their own schools had been flooded.

But she wasn't sure. She lifted a hand and waved, then shouted, "Way to go! Wow!"

Then she left, still feeling a little uneasy.

She turned at the next corner and cut down to Royal Street, heading for her house and her souvenir and collectibles shop, The Cheshire Cat, that occupied a chunk of the first floor.

The front door was open when Danni reached the shop, which was just as it should have been. They didn't officially close until seven, and it was barely past six.

Billie MacDougall — who had been her dad's right-hand man and assistant until the day he died and was now hers — was behind the counter. Billie looked like a cross between an aging Billy Idol and Riff Raff from *The Rocky Horror Picture Show.* He was skinny as a beanpole, but his looks were deceptive, because he had a wiry strength. He was also the best employee — and friend — anyone could ever have.

"Dinner!" he said, grinning as he saw her, his Scot's burr coming out in the single word despite his decades in America.

She walked to the counter and set down her bags of takeout. "Figures I could help out a friend with a new place *and* have something wonderful to eat."

"Do I smell lasagna?" Billie asked eagerly.

She smiled. "You do indeed. When Adriana decided to open a restaurant, I suspected it would be Italian, since she's first generation herself. I'm sure it's excellent, too. I loved eating at her house when I was growing up."

Billie made a face. "You doona like Scottish fare, lass?"

Danni laughed. "Sure, I love it. Not that it's plentiful in New Orleans," she said drily.

"Plentiful enough in this house. If I've made it, it's Scottish. And you love my cooking."

"This is America. We love everything. But if you've suddenly discovered that you don't like Italian, you don't have to eat it, you know."

"Don't be cheeky, lass. I'll just take the bags to the kitchen and get things set up," he told her, grabbing the food. "I'll go ahead and have me dinner then watch the shop till closing so you and Quinn can take as much time as you like for dinner." He grinned at her. "That is, if there's any food left."

"I bought a salad, bruschetta and a whole tray of lasagna," she said. "I don't believe you could possibly eat it all."

"You never do know now, do you? Make fun of me and Scot's cooking, will you?" Billie said.

Danni grinned. "Is Quinn back yet? I don't know why he went to the station if Jake said he was coming here."

"He didn't go to the station," Billie said, heading toward the kitchen.

"Then why did you say he did when we talked this afternoon?" Danni asked.

"I never said that. I said he was on the phone with Larue and then he left," Billie called from the kitchen doorway. "You just assumed he was going to the station."

"Then where *did* he go?" she asked.

"Wherever he went, he had to leave quickly," Billie said. "And I don't ask the man for a schedule when he leaves the house, just as I don't ask you. When he's ready, he tells me. Which is after he tells you, most of the time, so I guess we'll both know soon enough."

"You're right. I just hope he gets back while the food is still warm," she said.

"We do own that thing called a microwave," Billie said.

"Ah, but is it Scottish?" she murmured drily.

"I heard that!" Billie called back.

Danni grinned, walking around the counter to take the stool behind it. Wolf followed her and curled up at her feet.

She glanced at the computer; they'd had a busy enough day for a Thursday. Billie had sold a number of the handmade fleur-de-lis necklaces one of the local vendors had started making. They were delicate and beautiful, and while only gold- or silver-plated, they sold for almost a hundred dollars because of the work involved. She was glad to see that people still valued craftsmanship.

She noticed, too, that he'd also sold

several of her own watercolors of the French Quarter. While the shop — and other matters — tended to take up a lot of her time, she had majored in art and actually had something of a local following. She loved visual art, and her favorite medium to work with was either watercolors or oils on canvas. Despite the fact their last case had involved a long-dead artist and a painting, she was determined not to lose her passion for her art.

The bell over the door gave off its pleasant little tinkling sound, and she looked up.

It was the sax player.

In fact, the sax was in his hand, its case in the other.

"Hello," she said, frowning slightly. He had followed her here, she thought. Still, it was early evening. There was still light in the sky and plenty of people out and about on Royal Street, many of them seeking restaurants and bars, but some of them shopping, as well.

And Wolf — though he had risen — didn't seem to expect any danger. Wolf, she had learned, had a wonderful ability to sense whether people were trustworthy or not.

He even wagged his tail slightly. Everything had to be all right.

The door closed behind the sax player.

40

For a moment he looked around the shop. Danni — as her father had — mixed souvenirs and affordable trinkets in with real antiques and collectibles. There was another "collectible" area in the house, in the basement, where she kept items too powerful and dangerous to be sold or even shown. Of course, the basement wasn't really a basement; the "ground" floor was actually built up above the street, and you had to climb a few stairs to get to it.

She loved the shop, just as her father had. She had grown up loving it. She had a couple of real medieval suits of armor as display pieces, along with the work of a number of local artists besides herself, both new and antique jewelry, busts, a few nineteenth-century vampire hunting sets, flags, weapons and more. She knew she was good at creating wonderful window displays and that the shop was as much a gallery as a showroom, to the point that sometimes people came just to look around rather than buy. She wasn't sure if that was good or bad. It was obviously less than ideal if they didn't buy, but having such wonderful word-of-mouth reviews had to be good.

"May I help you?" she asked as the man continued to stand just inside the door, looking around the room.

41

He met her eyes at last. "Danni? Danni Cafferty?"

"Yes," she said. "Forgive me, but . . . do I know you?"

He nodded. "You may not remember me. I'm Tyler Anderson. I was a few years ahead of you in high school."

"Tyler — yes!" She remembered him now. She hadn't thought of him in years. He'd graduated before her, and she hadn't seen him since. But she remembered. He'd been part of what a number of the magnet-school music students — who had been "adopted" by a Garden District school during the aftermath of Katrina — had called the Survivor Set. As an art student, she'd been dragged in as something of an honorary member.

It was good to see him again, and she smiled. He really was a beautiful man — he always had been. Almost like a golden god with hazel eyes.

She walked around the counter. "I haven't seen you in forever! It's wonderful that you found me. How have you been?"

"Fine . . . good. Mostly," he said awkwardly.

"I heard you playing earlier," she said. "You're incredible. You always were, but now . . . wow. You're *really good.*"

"Not that good."

"No, trust me. I just heard you, and you are."

He shook his head impatiently. "No, no, I . . ." He paused, looking around the store. "Is anyone else here?"

"Well, Billie — you remember Billie — is in the kitchen. And Quinn is due home soon."

"Quinn . . . Michael Quinn? The Michael Quinn we knew back in school?"

"Yes."

"Are you two married?"

"No, no. I mean, one day. Maybe. He lives here. Mostly. Not always." Danni stopped speaking; she was never sure how to describe her complex relationship with Quinn. But then again, she didn't really have to explain. She added lamely, "We're together. A couple."

"So is it true?"

"Is what true?" she asked carefully.

"That he was a cop and then became a private investigator. And you guys look into things that are . . . different. Bad things, odd things."

Danni shrugged uneasily. "I try to collect things that people think may be evil or haunted in some way. You know how people can be. Superstitious."

"Is it just superstition?" he asked.

"People can be wonderful or evil. I think we both know that. But things are just . . . things. Why? What are you talking about?" she asked.

"Murder. I think my friend was murdered — and that the saxophone he left me is haunted."

She stared at him and murmured, "Okay. Can you . . . ?"

"Do you remember Arnie Watson?" he asked quietly.

She did. She remembered his incredible talent, and she remembered seeing a piece written about him by a local columnist just a week or so ago. He'd died on the streets after coming home from the Middle East. After he'd survived three deployments. Somehow that seemed to compound the tragedy of his death.

"Yes," she said.

"Arnie was the best," Tyler said passionately. "An amazing man and an amazing friend."

"I believe you," she said then paused, remembering what she had read. He had died of a drug overdose. So sad, and such a waste of a good man.

What was even more tragic was that so many soldiers came home only to die by their own hands, their minds haunted by the demons of war.

"He died of an overdose, didn't he?" she asked.

"Damn you, it wasn't suicide!" Tyler said.

"I never said anything about suicide."

"And it wasn't an accident. He was murdered. You have to believe me."

"I'm more than willing to listen to —"

Tyler shook his head emphatically. "You have to help me. You have to prove that he was murdered. I know you can do it. And you will. You and Quinn will."

"We're not infallible."

"I know you can find the truth. You have to. Because if you don't, whoever is doing this will kill again. I know it."

"Tyler, you can't know that."

"I *do* know it. And he just might kill *me.*"

CHAPTER 2

Mrs. Liana Ruby wasn't as frail as one might have thought.

They didn't have to knock on her door; an officer had been keeping watch over her while the police worked in the other side of the duplex. She had been lying on the sofa, but she got up when they came in. She was a little thing, but she quickly offered them tea or coffee, and then, when they declined, she told them, "Well, you may be on duty, but I'm not. Excuse me while I get myself a big cup of tea — with a bigger shot of whiskey."

Quinn and Larue sat in her living room and waited. When she rejoined them, she was shaking her head with disbelief. "Sad, sad, sad. Poor man. He may have had his vices, but then, he was a musician. And as sad as it is, it's true sometimes that the more tormented the musician, the more powerful the song. Why anyone would hurt such a polite fellow, I don't know. Now, that just sounded ridiculous, I know. But he was courteous and kind, with a friendly word for everyone. Kids threw a football into his car and dented it, and he just threw it back. I asked him if he didn't want to call the police or file an insurance claim, and he shrugged and told me they were just having a good time. Said the dent gave his car character!"

"Did you see or hear anything at all unusual earlier?" Larue asked her.

"Son, I was sound asleep — without my hearing aid. If little green men had descended from Mars and blown up the Superdome, I wouldn't have heard it," she said.

"We believe he was killed around 5:00 a.m., Mrs. Ruby," Quinn said. "I'm not surprised you were sleeping, and certainly not surprised you didn't hear anything. Did you notice that you didn't see him later in the day?"

"Good heavens, he works nights. I *never* saw the man until well past noon," she said.

"What about anyone — his friends and acquaintances, not to mention strangers — you might have seen visiting him?" Quinn asked.

"Mr. Quinn, you may think I'm generalizing, even stereotyping, but musicians only come in strange," Mrs. Ruby said. "And so do some ex-athletes."

That drew a smirk from Larue as he looked at Quinn.

Quinn looked back at Mrs. Ruby. "You know me?"

"I followed your football career years ago, young man." She wagged a finger at him. "And I witnessed your downfall, saw you join the dregs of humanity, and still, like most of this city, when you died on that operating table and came back to life, I said a hallelujah. Yes, I know you. And I know you were a cop and became a private eye, and that you've been working weird cases with this one here —" she paused and nodded toward Jake "— and old Angus Cafferty's daughter. So let's establish this right away. You work the strange — and musicians are strange."

"Can you describe any of the friends hanging around in richer detail than just 'strange'?" Quinn asked her, grinning.

"Sure. I'm eighty-eight. Not much else to do. Traveling too far around the city tires me out, so I sit on the porch a lot. Lord, I do love watching the life around me. And lots of people come and go. A tall, beautiful black man came a lot. When he's here, the house is a'rocking. I mean, for real. The man is a drummer. Then there's a woman — let's see, early forties, pleasant, hardly strange at all, for a musician. Brown hair, brown eyes." She leaned toward Quinn. "She's got the hots for the tall black man. There's a pudgy fellow, about five foot nine. You got pictures? You show 'em to me. You want to get a sketch artist out here? I can have a go. But I don't think you're going to find his killer among them. I got a glance at what they did to him — no friend of the man did anything like that."

"The first you knew about this in any way was when Lacey Cavanaugh came to you?" Larue asked.

Mrs. Ruby winced. "That poor girl. When we looked in that window, we couldn't see clear. But he wasn't moving, and I knew . . . well, I wasn't giving anybody a key until the cops came. I'd give a lot to help you more. Whoever did this came and went. Guess he was with Larry for a while," she said quietly, her face grim.

"Mrs. Ruby, thank you for your help. If you think of anything else, anything at all, that could be helpful, you'll call us?" Quinn asked. Both he and Larue handed her their cards.

She studied the business cards and then looked at the two men. "How long do you think he was in there?" she asked. "An hour? Two hours?"

"One," Quinn said. Larue nodded his agreement.

"Still, six in the morning — someone should have seen the killer leave," she said. "I do watch television, you know. I am aware of how things go down."

"I'm sure you are," Jake told her. "And we're doing a canvass of the neighborhood. I have officers going door-to-door."

"We watch television, too," Quinn said gravely.

She gave him a swat on the knee. "Behave, young man. I'll be here, ready to look at pictures, describe people, whatever you need," she told them.

"Is there anywhere else you can go?" Larue asked her. "Crime scene techs will be coming and going, and there will be officers on hand for a while, but if you feel insecure . . ."

"I'm not insecure. At my age?" Mrs. Ruby demanded.

"Still, be careful when you open the door," Jake warned her.

"Detective Larue," she said. "I won't be opening my door without seeing who is outside, I promise you. And if I *do* open the door, I'll have my Glock in hand and a truckload of silver hollow-point bullets that will take care of *any* opponent, human or . . . otherwise. And don't you worry. I have a permit for it, and I know how to use it."

"Just don't go shooting the postman," Jake warned.

"Want to visit a shooting range with me?" she demanded sharply. "I won't go shooting any uppity cops, either, I promise. Though it may be tempting."

Laughing, Jake apologized as they rose.

They left the house and walked down to the street together, ready to head to the hospital in their separate cars.

"I think the old bird likes you best," Larue told Quinn.

"You acted as if she were senile. Telling her not to shoot the mailman."

"She's eighty-eight!"

"And Bob Hope was still performing for our troops at that age," Quinn reminded him.

Jake nodded thoughtfully. "It's all good. I'm glad she likes you. You can talk to her once we figure out which of the city's musicians she might have been talking about. But then, you were good with that charming old battle-ax from Hubert's case, and that god-awful painting-society matron,

Hattie Lamont," Larue said.

"Not as good as Billie," Quinn said, smiling.

"They're seeing each other?"

"Oh, yes. They fight like a pair of alley cats sometimes, but they can't stay away from one another," Quinn said.

"And Danni?"

"Danni is great," Quinn said softly. They'd agreed to take things slowly, which was almost a necessity, given that he was often asked to consult on cases outside Louisiana. But that was something else they shared. They both believed strongly that working to solve strange crimes was an integral part of who they were.

But he loved being back in town, loved being with her. She was a strikingly beautiful woman, five-nine, slim and agile, her every move graceful. Her eyes reminded him of the blue sky on a clear Scottish morning, and her hair was a rich deep auburn. She was deeply compassionate and possessed old Angus's steely courage and determination — and she was just as stubborn as her father, too.

"She's expecting you tonight," he told Larue.

"Yeah, well, I was just coming over with the files on the first case — wanted to see what you thought or what you might know, since you sit in at the clubs sometimes. But then . . . then we found Lawrence Barrett." He fell silent.

Quinn turned. The body of Lawrence Barrett was just being carried out.

Ron Hubert nodded to them. "I'll get you a report as soon as possible," he promised.

"Two in a week?" Quinn asked. "We'd better get over to the hospital and hope that Lacey Cavanaugh knows something we can use."

"Arnie wasn't messed up," Tyler told Danni. "Not like that."

The saxophone was in its case now, and leaning against the counter. She was glad that the shop was empty, because Tyler seemed too upset to care where they were or what was going on.

"Let's say you're right. That someone murdered Arnie. Can you think of any reason why?" she asked him.

"That's the problem," Tyler said. He leaned an elbow on the counter and looked reflectively into the distance as he spoke. "We're talking about a good man here. A black man from a poor neighborhood who went to church every week, loved his family, never stole so much as a dime from anyone

53

and did nothing but love his music. He did the right thing — he up and joined the military because he believed we had to support our way of life. When he came home on leave, he did nothing but hug people and play his music. He didn't talk much about what he'd done, just said that war was ugly, there were good people who were the enemy and some jerks who were on the same side. He believed he made a difference — he got to see schools being built, and people from both sides coming together to dig wells and feed starving kids. And enemy or not, he said it was hard as hell to kill a man. He survived bombs and gunfire and . . . came home to this. And I knew his death wasn't right. I knew it wasn't right from the get-go. He was happy ever since he got home — he came home to his music! His family loved him. They're good people. They never had much, but what they didn't have in money, they made up in support. And he never did drugs, not before he went overseas or after he came home. There was no reason for him to walk offstage one night and decide to suddenly stick a needle in his arm. Why can't anyone else see that?"

"They may question what happened, Tyler," Danni said. "But we all see the obvious and find it easy to accept, too. You said he was found on the street, a needle in his arm?"

"Yes."

"No one else around?"

He turned his gaze back to her. "Would you expect a murderer to hang around?"

"What I'm trying to figure out is how someone got him under control so they were able to stick the needle in his arm. There must have been an autopsy."

"There was."

"And there was nothing else in his system?"

"I don't know. It's not like I'm trained to read a death certificate. There were some chemical names in there I didn't recognize, but even if they were tranquilizers or something, the cops probably just thought he took them himself. And yes, he'd been drinking."

The little bell over the shop door rang. A couple of young tourists came in, and Danni excused herself, walking over to ask them if they needed any help. They were looking for a specific line of jewelry, and she carried it. She was glad it was in a display case to one side of the store, not under the counter where Tyler was standing as if unaware of her customers, though he managed a smile when they came over to pay.

55

But as soon as they were gone, he asked, "Well, what do you think?"

What did she think?

She didn't know *what* to think. She remembered Arnie. Like Tyler, he'd been a couple of years ahead of her in high school, but he'd played beautifully even then, and she could remember watching him play in the school band. He'd been a big guy, a solid, muscular six-two, at least.

And he'd had training when he joined the military. He couldn't have been an easy mark.

But she did find it strange that, if Tyler was right, he would begin with drugs by heading straight for a needle.

"I don't know what to think," she said.

Lacey Cavanaugh was out of surgery. In her horror and anguish, she'd pitched down the steep front steps and smashed a kneecap. The doctor warned Quinn and Larue that she was still under heavy sedation — probably a double-edged good thing. She would otherwise be in tremendous pain over both the loss of her boyfriend and the wreck of her leg.

Quinn was standing closest to her head. She opened her eyes when he took her hand.

"Miss Cavanaugh," Jake said, "we're so

sorry to bother you when I know you're hurting in every possible way, but I'm afraid we need to talk to you. I'm Detective Larue, and this is my associate Michael Quinn. We have some questions we need to ask you, because as I'm sure you know, time is of the essence as we try to apprehend whoever's guilty of your boyfriend's . . . death. So if you could just think back, when was the last time you saw Mr. Barrett?"

Lacey stared at him from her haze, tears in her eyes. "Oh, God. Larry . . ."

Quinn squeezed her hand. "We're so sorry," he said softly. "We know you loved him, and that he was a good man."

Larue stared at him; they didn't really know that he'd been a good man.

But the words had the desired effect on Lacey. She looked at Quinn with such grief and gratitude in her eyes that he almost regretted being quite so gentle.

"He was the best," she said softly.

"And we have to find out who killed him," Quinn said. "You want him punished for what he did, don't you?"

She nodded. "I last saw Larry . . . last night. I didn't stay, because my little sister had a piano recital."

"So last night at what time?" Quinn asked.

"Seven," she said.

57

"And you didn't go back to his house until this afternoon?" Larue asked.

She didn't answer. She was staring at Quinn, still holding his hand as if it were a lifeline.

"Lacey, did you talk to him again after that?" Quinn asked.

She nodded.

"When was that?" Quinn asked.

"Last night — well, early this morning. Somewhere around three. He was playing last night at the Old Jackson Ale House. I called him at three because that's about when he gets home."

"And everything was fine?"

"Yes. We were both going to sleep. And I was supposed to go over to his house in the afternoon. Which I did. He didn't answer the door. And then I looked in the window and I couldn't really see . . . but it looked like . . . but I thought he'd be okay, you know?"

She began to sob softly.

She really had loved the man, Quinn thought.

"I'm so sorry," he said again. "Lacey, can you think of anyone — from his past or maybe your own — who would have wanted to hurt him?"

Tears squeezed between her lashes. She

58

shook her head.

"An ex-boyfriend?" Larue asked.

She opened her eyes and glared at him.

"Lacey," Quinn said, "we have to ask."

"No," she said. "My ex married the girl he was cheating on me with — three years ago. We're actually all on fairly friendly terms. And he's in Detroit now, anyway, playing some backup gig there."

"Thank you, Lacey. I hope you understand, we have to ask. What about the drugs?" Quinn said.

Once again tears streamed from her eyes, silent tears that just ran down her cheeks.

"We argued about the drugs," she said softly. "I said the pot was fine, but the coke . . . we didn't need the coke. He didn't deal, if that's what you're getting at. He just shared with friends. He always shared everything with friends. He helped down-and-out musicians. You don't understand, *everyone liked him*!"

"What about his ex-girlfriends? Any crazy ones?" Larue asked.

"Crazy ex-girlfriends?" Lacey repeated. "Pretty much all of them," she said. "But mostly crazy in a good way. And none living in New Orleans. Suzanne Delmer is working on a cruise ship, and she's crazy like a happy puppy. Before her it was Janis Bruge, and she's out in LA now. This can't have been anyone we know — it *can't* have been. There's just no reason."

"Okay, so let me ask you something else. When you reached the house, did you see anyone around? Anyone at all?" Larue asked.

She shook her head, biting her lower lip. "There were some kids playing with a football in the street. A UPS truck down a block or so. It was just kind of a lazy afternoon. Typical," she said.

More tears fell.

"Lacey, can you give us a list of people he'd played with recently and the places he'd been playing?" Quinn asked her.

"Of course," she said. "You want his hangouts, too?"

"Yes, any place he might have come into contact with the person who hurt him," Quinn said.

She frowned and gave him a hazy look. He realized she'd been doing pretty well for someone who had just undergone surgery and was on heavy-duty meds.

"You know what I think?" she asked.

"What?"

"I think there's a crazy person in New Orleans."

There were lots of crazy people in New

Orleans, Quinn thought.

"No one who knew Larry could have done this," she whispered. "There's a madman out there, a vicious madman breaking into houses and torturing and killing people."

"Lacey, the killer didn't break in. Larry opened the door to him," Larue told her.

She began to sob in earnest. " 'Cause he was so nice! He would have opened the door to anyone who needed help. I don't . . . I just don't believe he knew his murderer. You have to catch him. He's a madman, and he'll kill more people if you don't catch him right away!"

"Danni?"

Danni was definitely relieved to hear Quinn's voice.

"In the shop!" she called.

"Whatever that is in the kitchen, it smells great. Can't wait to eat."

Quinn strode into the shop like a force of nature, though without any intent of seeming so. It was just that he was well over six feet, broad-shouldered and striking, and when he moved, Danni thought, smiling, he drew all eyes to him without even trying. Whenever she saw him — and that was often, since they basically lived together now — she felt a little flutter in her heart, especially if they'd been apart for more than a few hours. No matter how often they touched, he still electrified her. They slept together most nights, and when he was near her, he aroused her; no matter how often they made love, he still thrilled her.

Of course, she reminded herself, she was in love with him.

Even when she wanted to kill him.

He was bright, determined, compassionate and strong.

Also pigheaded and very annoying when she thought she was right and he disagreed. He'd worked with her father, something she hadn't known until after Angus Cafferty's death. That had been hard to take at first, but then, she'd never known that her father had been something of a secret sleuth, handling the same kinds of items she and Quinn handled now.

The Cheshire Cat had merely been the tip of the iceberg. Her father had dedicated his life to taking in or destroying items — old and new — with a reputation for being haunted, even evil.

"Oh, excuse me, sorry," Quinn said when he noticed Tyler Anderson. He smiled slowly, and Danni realized that she was actually a little irked. Quinn's memory was better than hers. He not only knew he had met Tyler before, he also remembered where and when.

Wolf naturally went trotting over to Quinn for a pat on the head. Quinn obliged absently, his attention on their visitor.

"Tyler Anderson. I know your music, man," Quinn said, walking forward. He shook Tyler's hand. "I watched you play years ago when you were at Paisley Park on Frenchman Street. I heard you were still playing around the city. I've been meaning to look you up. Great to see you."

"Thanks," Tyler said.

"So where are you playing? We'll come see you," Quinn said.

Tyler looked at Danni.

"Quinn, Tyler's here to ask us for help," she said.

Quinn looked at her, brows hiked high over his hazel eyes. "I . . . see," he said slowly. "So, Tyler, you hungry? We're having something wonderful. I have no idea what it is, but the whole place smells divine."

"I'll go see how Billie's doing," Danni said. "He should be done with dinner by now."

The house that contained her shop was one of the oldest in the French Quarter, having survived two major fires that had ravaged New Orleans in the early years. The ground-floor entry led straight into the store, and a hallway led back to the kitchen, dining area and Danni's studio/office. There were bedrooms upstairs, and a large apartment in the attic, where Billie and Bo Ray Tompkins, who also helped out in the shop, each had their rooms.

She would have called Bo Ray down to help, but he'd had his wisdom teeth extracted earlier that day. He was sleeping, and she didn't intend to wake him up.

The basement held Angus's old office, along with a number of items that never would be on sale.

"Tyler," she said, "come on with me and I'll introduce you to Billie. Quinn, can you watch the shop for me for a sec?"

He nodded, and she smiled her thanks.

"Billie?" she called, heading through the shop and back to the kitchen.

Wolf trotted after her.

"Just finishing up," Billie said as they entered. "Hello," he added, noticing Tyler's presence. He stood, dusting his hands with his napkin and then offering one to Tyler. "Nice to meet you. I'm Billie. Billie Mac-Dougall."

Tyler introduced himself in turn.

"Well, then. Table is set, though you'll need to grab another plate. The lasagna is wonderful. Italian food is delicious, though I assure you, you'll find many an excellent restaurant in Scotland," Billie said, looking at Danni.

She laughed and turned to Tyler. "I offended him somehow by liking Italian food," she explained.

Billie sniffed. "I'll be watching the shop," he said, excusing himself. "Wolf, come along with me. There'll be a treat for you when we close up, I promise, a few bits left over from a good Scottish leg o' lamb," he said, looking sternly at Danni before he left the kitchen.

A moment later Quinn walked in and looked at her curiously. "What's up with Billie? He looked upset, like you offended him or something."

"Didn't mean to," she said, reaching for another plate. "Tyler, please, have a seat."

Quinn dug into the refrigerator. "Tyler, what will you have to drink?"

"Water would be fine."

Quinn got another glass and poured them all ice water. Billie had already cut the lasagna into neat serving-size squares, which she dished out before sitting.

"So," Quinn said, meeting Tyler's eyes. "Tell us what's up." Then he took a bite and started chewing enthusiastically.

65

Danni lowered her head for a moment. Quinn had probably skipped lunch; he seemed to be starving. Tyler hadn't even glanced at his plate, and she wasn't sure whether to be worried about him and his fears or not.

Tyler pushed the food around on his plate. "I think my friend was murdered."

"Ah," Quinn said, without seeming surprised. "And your friend's name was . . . ?"

"Arnie — Arnold Watson," Danni put in.

Quinn sat back and took a drink of water. Danni saw his brow furrow as he considered her words.

"I read the obituary," he said quietly. "I thought it was a damned shame. He sounded like a wonderful person. A soldier who gave what he could to his country. It's hard, though, coming back, sometimes. I've known guys who believed they were fine then woke up in the middle of the night shaking and screaming, sweat pouring off them. Even with everything we know about post-traumatic disorders, sometimes . . . the depth of a guy's depression is invisible because *he* thinks he's all right."

Tyler Anderson put down his fork. "He didn't kill himself. And he wasn't an addict."

"Of course he wasn't," Danni said gently,

resting a hand on Tyler's where it lay on the table.

"No, you don't understand. I'm an addict — in recovery, but an addict all my life. I would have known if Arnie was into drugs, too, and he wasn't, not in any way."

Danni nodded. "But . . . I've seen things happen to men who come home from war. And maybe that was the problem. He wasn't an addict, but maybe he *was* in pain. His death was accidental because he only tried it once or twice, and —"

"He *tried* it once," Tyler said. "Only once. If you don't believe me, ask the police. There were no other track marks on him, just the needle mark from the one injection. But it sure in hell wasn't something he did, and it wasn't an accidental overdose. Someone did it *to* him. Someone *killed* him!"

"I don't disbelieve you," Quinn said. "But . . . how do you know? How can you be so sure? Things can happen overnight, things we don't expect. I've seen cops who can't take a case for whatever reason, and suddenly, they're ingesting every substance out there."

He'd asked the questions, Danni thought, but he already believed Tyler.

"The sax told me," Tyler said.

For a moment, just for a moment, Danni

thought she had misheard him. That he had said, "The *sex* told me," as if he had been referring to a girl he'd slept with or who had slept with Arnie.

But then she remembered what he'd said when he came into the shop and realized he was talking about the saxophone.

The musical instrument that now lay in its case by his side on the floor.

"The *sax* told you?" Quinn repeated.

Tyler nodded gravely. "I was playing . . . just the other night. It was his sax, you see. It's really old, some kind of an antique his grandmother bought for him. A silver-plated Pennsylvania Special. I don't know what it's worth or the rest of its history. I just know it's a damned good instrument and Arnie loved it. Said it was special. But the point is, I was playing *his* sax. And suddenly I was playing *his* song, and I could see his life — his life before he came home. I saw the war. I could feel the damned sand, it was so real. And then I heard his killer."

"His dealer?" Quinn asked.

He was really pushing Tyler, Danni thought. Testing him.

Tyler thumped a hand on the table. "His *killer,*" he repeated. "I heard him talking to Arnie just before he shot him up so full of poison that he died within minutes. I heard

68

him, I'm telling you. I heard him say, 'You're dead, buddy. You're dead.' "

Danni and Quinn turned to look at each other, silent for a moment.

"Are you saying the sax . . . talked?" Quinn asked.

Tyler closed his eyes, looking as if he was in pain. "No. I was playing the sax," he said quietly. "But while I was playing I saw what Arnie saw, felt what he felt, heard what he heard."

"You didn't happen to see the killer, did you?" Danni asked.

He stared at her. "Are you mocking me?"

"I swear, I'm not," she said softly. "But if you really believe that he was murdered, why didn't you go to the police?"

"The police?" Tyler asked drily. "Yeah, right. I wish you could see the way *you're* looking at me, and you're open-minded enough to believe me. The police . . . I can just imagine the snickers. I'm not sure they'd even *try* to keep straight faces. You both said you read the newspaper articles about his death, so you know what they're saying. The same crap you hear everywhere. 'He just hadn't adjusted. He was like so many soldiers. Strong, stoic, not about to admit to having nightmares he couldn't handle, nightmares so bad that he'd turn to

69

drugs to wipe them out.' Especially not a marine like Arnie. Admit it. That's all stuff you believed about Arnie when you read he was dead. And like everyone else, I bet you thought, 'What a waste, what a tragedy. A man comes back from the war and takes his own life. Makes you stop and think.' But no one stops to think, 'Hey, whoa, maybe he *didn't* kill himself.' "

Tyler was certainly passionate in defense of his position, Danni thought. Of course, he'd been Arnie's friend. His best friend, she imagined.

"Tyler, how long have you had the sax?" Quinn asked him. "You said it's special, but would anyone else know that?"

"Probably," Tyler said and then shrugged. "I don't know. He told everyone in the band back in high school it was special, that his grandma told him so. I've had it since about a week after he died. His mom said she had to give it to someone who would love it the way Arnie had loved it, would take care of it the way he did. She used to love to listen to him, and then she'd laugh. She told us both that Arnie got to be as good as he was because of the sax. His grandmother told him it was special, kind of . . . magical. But according to his mom, the magic was because he believed it. Plus he loved playing,

70

and he practiced all the damned time. And practicing made him the musician that he was."

Quinn nodded. "I read in the paper that the family intended to sell his sax, along with his other instruments, and donate the money to a foundation helping veterans."

"Arnie had a bunch of saxes. They planned to sell some of them, but not this one."

"What do Arnie's parents think? Would they tell you if they suspected he'd made any enemies?" Quinn asked.

"Arnie's parents think he was murdered, too. But there's nowhere they can go with that any more than I can. They know the police would think they were crazy, too, if they tried to convince them some random killer had hunted Arnie down and killed him with an overdose of heroin."

Quinn pushed his plate aside and leaned on the table, his attention focused entirely on Tyler.

"Were you with him the night he died? Do you know who he was hanging around with, what might have been going on in his life?" he asked.

Tyler shook his head. "I wasn't with him the night he died. Wish I had been!" he said fervently. "I was working in the Quarter that night, too. Arnie had been sitting in with

71

my band, getting back into the swing of playing. I was filling in with another group. A friend of mine was sick and needed someone to cover for him, and I figured Arnie was just getting used to my band, so I'd head over to work with the other group. My band didn't mind. They all knew Arnie was way better than me," he added without rancor. "Usually when we end a shift we're all hungry, so we go out for pizza or something. But that night Arnie told them he had something to do, so he'd see them the next night. And that was it. Sometime after he left the band, someone killed him.

"They were playing at the same place where you saw me today, Danni, La Porte Rouge. What the police didn't investigate, I did. Who was he hanging around with? Me. Other musicians. His family. What was going on in his life? Nothing. So yeah, I promise you, the cops would laugh at me if I tried to tell them some random murderer who didn't steal a thing from him just decided to off him by pumping him full of heroin. Believe me, I know what I sound like. Like I'm on crack myself. But I know what I saw and what I heard when I played that sax, and . . ."

"And?" Danni asked.

He looked at her with eyes as gold as his

72

skin and said, "I knew Arnie. And like most of us who grew up around here, he was exposed to his share of drugs and alcohol. He saw what it did to people — including me. Arnie wouldn't have touched the stuff. Hell, he'd have swallowed his gun before he stuck a needle in his arm. I know it."

He stopped talking and looked at the two of them questioningly.

Danni turned to Quinn. He nodded slowly.

"We'll look into it," he promised.

Danni almost fell off her chair.

How? she wanted to scream at Quinn. How the hell were they going to look into it? No witnesses, the body already interred, and they weren't likely to get any help from the ME or the cops.

Obviously, Tyler Anderson didn't want to accept the fact his friend had committed suicide, and maybe that was all this was: a man desperate to think the best of his friend. But then there was the vision he'd claimed to have had while playing the dead man's sax . . .

It was all just too damned tragic.

She winced, lowering her head.

And yet, was it any less a tragedy if he'd been murdered?

It was almost as if Tyler read her thoughts.

When she looked up, he was staring at her.

He shook his head. "The truth. The truth is what we all need. And if . . . if I'm right, it's not vengeance I'm after. It's justice. Justice for Arnie."

Looking back at him, she understood. She didn't know why, but she understood. Wondering, not knowing, those were the emotional upheavals that tore people to pieces.

"We'll need a lot from you," Quinn told him. "I need names — all the musicians he might have played with and anyone he might have been seeing. A one-night stand, a long-lost love — anyone. And," he said, "I'll have to talk to his family."

Tyler winced at that. "Yeah," he said. "I know."

"And," Danni added, "if the sax . . . says anything else to you, we have to know."

Tyler stiffened and stared at her. "The sax doesn't *talk*," he told her, irritated.

She smiled. "I didn't say it *talked*. But if it gives you anything else, another vision, anything else at all, we need to know right away."

He nodded and said, "Thank you."

"Of course," she said softly.

He rose, picking up the sax case.

"Oh, and . . ." He paused, looking at his

74

plate as if surprised. Somewhere along the way he'd actually finished his food. "Thanks for the lasagna."

"My pleasure. I just hope we can help you," she said.

"One more thing," Quinn said.

"What's that?" Tyler asked.

"The sax," Quinn said.

"The sax?" Tyler repeated, puzzled.

"That's the sax that Arnie's mom gave you, right?" Quinn asked.

"That's it."

"Leave it here," Quinn said.

"But . . . I'm a saxophonist. I make a living playing music."

"You have others, right?"

"None that I play like this," Tyler said.

"You'll play it again," Quinn promised. "For now, please, let us keep it. Let us try to figure out if there really *is* something about this sax that's special. But if anyone comes up to you threatening you for a sax, hand it right over. Any sax you happen to have on you."

Tyler looked puzzled. "You're talking about that holdup down near Frenchman Street, right?" he asked, then something dawned in his eyes.

"More than that, Tyler. Two musicians have been killed in their homes."

"Two?" Tyler looked shocked. "I saw something on the news a few days ago about a guy, but —"

"Another man was killed today. It will be on the eleven o'clock news, if you don't believe me. I think someone wants the sax you have right there. They just don't know where it is," Quinn said. He frowned, puzzled. "Didn't Arnie have his sax the night he was killed?"

"He must have, but I don't know if it was found with him or not, and I don't know what sax he had," Tyler said.

Danni looked at Quinn. He'd caught her by surprise with his mention of a musician's murder earlier that day. Clearly he knew much more, saw more connections, than she did.

Tyler looked as if he were loath to part with the instrument.

"It could mean your life," Quinn said quietly. "And while you're at it, when you're talking to people, make a point of saying you wish you had Arnie's old sax. Don't tell anyone who doesn't already know that you had it or where it might be. As far as you know, it went up for auction."

Tyler still looked doubtful.

"When you got here you told me you knew what Quinn and I did," Danni said quietly. "So let us do our job, all right?"

Tyler nodded and slowly handed over the sax. "Thank you." He reached into his pocket and produced his card. "This is me. If you need me at any time for anything, just call. Obviously, when I'm playing, I don't hear my phone. But I'll check it every break in case . . . in case I can help."

"Here are our numbers," Quinn said, and produced a card, as well. It had his cell, Danni's cell and the shop number.

Tyler took the card as if it were a lifeline. "Thanks," he said.

"Be careful, okay?" Quinn said. "I expect the police will be putting out a parish-wide warning for musicians, but it doesn't hurt to be reminded. Don't open the door when you're alone, even to people you think are your friends. And make sure you warn your band and anyone else you play with that someone has it in for musicians."

Tyler nodded gravely. "I'll do that," he promised.

"I'll walk you out through the front," Quinn told him.

Danni picked up in the kitchen while Quinn led Tyler back through the shop. When he came back he slipped his arms around her where she stood at the sink.

She spun in his embrace, staring at him, a

sudsy plate in her hands.

"Hey! What the heck is going on? You know way more than I do. Do you really think this has something to do with the incidents with those other musicians? And what about this second murder? Are you sure it makes sense for us to investigate this? Arnie's death must have been investigated, even if they just wanted to know where he got the heroin. He was a hero and a popular local figure, found dead on Rampart Street. They could be right, you know, and it really was an accidental OD."

He took the plate from her. Suds were flying, because she was waving it around as she talked, she realized.

"I'm sorry. I thought we'd think alike on this," he said.

"I'm not saying I disagree."

"What, then?" He moved away from her, and she was almost sorry she had spoken.

There was a sudden distant look in his eyes, as if he was remembering something she hadn't been a part of. She loved him so much, but she knew he'd had a life before he'd met her, a very different life. He'd once been a shining star, and then he'd crashed and burned, finally becoming the man he was today.

"You know," he said quietly. "*I* was messed

up. So messed up that I almost died. I *did* die, actually. They brought me back."

"I know that," she said softly. "I thank God constantly that you came through. And you're right. I believe Tyler. And I *don't* believe Arnie Watson just left work one night and decided to stick a needle in his arm."

"All these incidents are related — they have to be," Quinn said. "Larue was mistaken earlier when he told me about Holton Morelli, the musician who was killed in his home last week. He wasn't the first to die. Arnie Watson was."

CHAPTER 3

Quinn heard a knock at the side door, off the courtyard entrance, to the house on Royal Street just as he was returning to the kitchen.

He knew it was Larue or another friend. Only those in their close circle ever used the courtyard entrance.

He looked at Danni and saw the resolve reflected in her eyes. He lowered his head, not wanting her to see the bittersweet smile on his lips. He couldn't help but remember when he'd first gotten to know her. He'd worked with her late father many times. And when he'd been thrown into an "assignment" with her the first time — seeking a mysterious Italian bust — he'd believed he'd been stuck seeking help from a spoiled debutante.

Danni was beautiful, filled with grace and charm and a smile that could melt a man's heart — or ignite his libido. And Angus had never said a word to her about his special "collection." She'd been pitched almost blindly into a world where people killed over possessions that were more than they seemed, and where the sins of the past could thunder down upon the present.

And now, when he looked at her, he saw the resolve in her eyes, an implicit promise to find justice for Tyler's dead friend.

"I'll get it," he said. "It's probably Jake."

"You have a very odd smile on your face, considering the circumstances," she told him.

"I was thinking that I'm a lucky man," he said softly.

"Quinn, this is bad, isn't it? Very bad."

"Yes, but I have a luscious — and brilliant — partner," he told her. "One who comes with . . . benefits."

"Hmm. I confess I appreciate my co-worker — and eye candy — too," she said.

She was worried, though; he could tell. Her eyes had already fallen to the sax he'd been so determined they should keep.

There was another knock, and Quinn went to let Larue in.

He greeted Danni warmly. Over the past few years they'd gotten to know one another well. Although Larue preferred to believe in what his five senses told him, Quinn knew he respected the connection he and Danni felt to something . . . more. And all of them believed deeply in right over wrong, which meant together they were a crime-solving force that worked.

"Want some coffee?" she asked Larue warmly.

"I'll have something a lot stronger — if that won't bother you?" he asked, looking at Quinn.

"Not at all. One man's demon can be another man's friend," he said. He looked over at Danni with a questioning glance.

"I'll stick to coffee," she said.

Billie came into the kitchen from the shop just then. "Detective Larue, good to see you," he said then caught the serious vibe in the room and quickly added, "Or not."

"Billie, good to see you," Larue replied.

"Shop is locked up," he said. "I'm going to go catch up on some television, I guess."

"Stay, Billie," Quinn said.

"Yes, stay," Larue echoed.

Billie nodded. He had started working with Angus in Scotland, and after Angus's death he had cast himself in the role of Danni's guardian. They were lucky, Quinn knew, to have him in their fold.

Quinn poured Larue a good stiff scotch and set it in front of him. Larue told Danni that he would take a coffee "chaser," too, and soon the four of them were seated around the table.

Larue spoke first, telling them about the holdup in the street and progressing to the two murders. Quinn, in turn, explained everything that had happened with Arnie Watson and how Tyler Anderson was convinced that Arnie had been murdered.

Larue frowned and said, "The ME reported Arnie's death as an accidental overdose. Based on the circumstances, we accepted that finding. And I'm still not a hundred percent convinced his death is connected. These other murders . . . They were about as brutal and sadistic as you can get."

"The connection makes sense," Quinn argued. "They were all musicians. The holdup? Only their instruments were stolen. After that, things escalated. First you had Arnie's death. Maybe it was a gentler murder because the killer and Arnie were actually friends. But Arnie didn't have the sax on him. Not the right sax, anyway."

"I wonder why that was," Danni put in.

"What?" Quinn asked her.

"Arnie had been playing with Tyler's group that night. But he wasn't found with his sax, and his family had the . . . special sax after he died, when his mother gave it to Tyler, who left it here with us. So what happened to his sax that night?" Danni asked.

"Maybe he had a different sax and his killer *did* take it," Larue suggested.

"That seems like the most logical explanation," Quinn said. "The killer lured him to Rampart, where he killed him when no one else was around. He stole the sax from him. But then he discovered it was the wrong one and figured maybe Arnie needed money and had sold it."

"Could be," Larue said.

"But he stole all the instruments when he robbed that group of musicians, right?" Danni asked.

"He did," Larue answered.

"If he was looking for a saxophone, why take other instruments?" she asked.

"So that no one would know he was looking for a sax?" Quinn suggested. "Anyway, somehow the killer got Arnie to go with him. Maybe he was a friend, or maybe he preyed on Arnie's generosity, which seems pretty well-known, and pretended to need help with something. Maybe he even told him another vet needed help. When Arnie was dead, he took the sax then discovered later it was just a regular sax, not worth what a Penn Special is. Or maybe it wasn't the monetary value. Maybe he knew it supposedly had special powers and what he wanted was to play as well as Arnie played. And then he started trying to figure out where the sax had ended up, first hiding his goal by stealing a bunch of different instruments. Then he started targeting people he thought were likely to have ended up with it, and when Morelli and Barrett couldn't or wouldn't tell him, he got pissed off and killed them."

"Sounds like a good working theory," she said.

"Where is this sax you got from Tyler?" Billie asked.

Quinn pointed out the case where it was sitting under the table.

Billie picked it up and opened it carefully then took out the instrument.

"You play?" Danni asked him with surprise.

"If you can play a bagpipe, the sax is a piece of cake." He coaxed a few off-key notes from the sax. "I didna say I could play well," he said. "Give me a minute."

He began to play again. The sounds were suddenly clear and good.

"Nice," Danni said.

"Is it the sax itself? Is there something special about it?" Quinn asked.

"It's a good instrument," Billie said. "But . . ."

They all sat in silence for a long moment, staring at Billie and the sax.

"It's a sax," Billie said at last.

Quinn laughed suddenly. "Okay, so, apparently, the 'magic' doesn't come out for us."

"All right, no offense, guys, but I'm feeling like a fool — sitting here and waiting for a sax to do something," Larue said.

"We're not offended," Danni said and looked at Quinn. "We need to call Tyler and get him to take us out to meet Arnie's family. We have to know more about that sax."

"I've got to go home and study some files," Larue said. "I didn't handle Arnie's death, and obviously not the attack on the musicians, but now . . . with what you're telling me, maybe everything does all connect. At any rate, I'll call the night shift and have them set up interviews with those musicians starting first thing in the morning. Quinn, I'll give you a heads-up as soon as I have a schedule — figure you'll want to talk to them, too." He rose.

Quinn knew that Larue had knocked back the scotch in a single swallow and then nursed his coffee the rest of the time they'd been speaking. The man did look tired as hell, but then, he knew that Larue didn't believe in set hours, and that his life was pretty much his work. He loved New Orleans and considered himself a warrior in the city's defense.

Quinn followed him to the courtyard door and locked it thoughtfully after him. It was nearly ten. They should all get some sleep and start in the morning, he thought.

But when he returned to the kitchen he found Danni gathering up her shoulder bag, her keys in her hand.

"I called Tyler. The band's giving him the night off. I'm going to drive by and pick him up, and then he'll take us to meet Arnie's family. He says they're always up late anyway, and I figured we might as well make a start on things."

He smiled. Danni was her father's daughter. She wouldn't stop now.

After all, stopping could mean another life lost.

"Let's do it," he said.

"I'll be holding down the old fort," Billie said drily. "If Bo Ray comes to after all that pain medication, I'll bring him up to speed. And if he doesn't, I just might practice on that sax."

Bourbon Street was heading into full swing

when Danni drove toward it along St. Ann's to pick up Tyler Anderson. He was without an instrument and told them that, without him there, the band was only going to play songs that didn't require a sax.

The Watson family lived in the Treme area, just the other side of Rampart at the edge of the French Quarter. She was easily able to find street parking.

The house was in a line of dwellings that had mostly been built between the 1920s and 1970s. While the Treme area had faced some tough times with gangs and drugs since the summer of storms — Katrina, Rita and Wilma — Danni had a number of friends who lived in the area. True, some had left after the storms, never to return. But many had dug in, driven by a love for New Orleans so deep inside them that it would never die. There was crime here, as there was everywhere. But there were honest citizens here, too, just trying to get through life with work, family and friends.

The Watson house appeared to have been built in the early twenties, with porch and window arches reminiscent of the Deco Age. The yard was neatly mowed, and there were flower beds with lovely blooms lining the concrete path to the house.

"They're good people," Tyler said. "They

didn't deserve this."

"No one deserves this kind of thing, Tyler," Quinn said.

"No, but them more than most."

He'd let the Watson family know that they were coming. Before they reached the front door, it was opened by a tall, straight-backed elderly man with light mahogany skin. He smiled as they came up the path. "Welcome, and thank you, folks," he said. He had his hand out, ready to greet them. "I'm Woodrow Watson. Pleased to have you. Danni Cafferty, I knew your father. Fine man. Can't say as you'd know me. I was just in your shop a few times. Now, Michael Quinn, I *have* met you, sir, but I'll bet you don't remember me."

Quinn smiled. "You're wrong. Now that we're face-to-face, I *do* remember you. Your whole family showed up at football games. Arnie was a year or two younger than me, but he was in the band, and you all came out to see him every game."

"That's right, son, that's right. You sure could throw a football," Woodrow said.

"Well, that was then," Quinn said.

"Come in, come in," their host encouraged. He looked at Tyler. "Thank you for bringing us all together."

"Yes, sir," Tyler said.

They entered directly into a parlor with a comfortable sofa covered in a beautiful knitted throw and a number of armchairs set with covers to match the throw. As they came in, a woman, wiping her hands on a dish towel, came out to greet them, as well.

"I'm Amy Watson, and thank you all for what you're doing. Tyler says we're going to have some help with things at last."

"We're going to do our best, Mrs. Watson," Danni promised her.

"Please. I'm just Amy, and my husband is Woodrow. Sit, sit," Amy said. "It's a little small and tight in here, but please, make yourselves comfortable. Can I get you anything? We don't keep any spirits in the house here — figure you can find enough just about anywhere else in the Big Easy. But I have coffee, tea, juice . . ."

"We're just fine, Mrs. Watson, thank you," Danni assured her.

"We just finished dinner and already had some coffee," Quinn added. "Too much, you know, and we'll never sleep."

"Well, then, if you decide you'd like something, you just holler," Amy said.

"I promise, we will," Danni said.

"Let's sit, shall we?" Woodrow asked.

Danni, Quinn and Tyler took the sofa; the Watsons chose the chairs facing them over the carved wooden coffee table.

"I know this is a difficult time for the two of you," Quinn told the Watsons, "so I apologize in advance for any pain my questions may cause, but the more information I have, the better I can do my job. So . . . where was Arnie's special sax — the one you gave Tyler — on the night he was killed?"

The Watsons looked at one another without speaking. Amy had a look of gratitude in her eyes, and it mirrored her husband's. Woodrow was the one to speak. He looked at Quinn and Danni and said incredulously, "You said *killed.* You used that word. *Killed.* So that means you believe us — you believe our son didn't just suddenly stick a needle in his arm. Right?"

"We *do* believe you, Mr. and — I'm sorry, Woodrow and Amy," Danni said. "We *do* believe you. Some musicians were held up at gunpoint leaving work not long ago. And more recently two musicians have been killed in their homes. We believe that someone is out there looking for something, and it might be Arnie's sax."

Woodrow stood up and walked to the fireplace. He leaned an arm on the mantel and looked at his wife then back at Danni. "You think someone is looking for Arnie's *sax*? And that they're killing over it?"

"The sax you gave me," Tyler said. "And don't worry — it's safe. Danni has it at her shop, over on Royal Street."

Amy and Woodrow looked at each other again.

Finally Amy sighed. "We don't have his special sax — the one my mother gave him. We assumed he had it with him the night he was killed. We figured it was stolen."

"Then what did you give me?" Tyler asked her. "You made me feel . . ."

"That sax is just a replica. We wanted you to feel you had something special of Arnie's," Woodrow said. "And you always said he was so good and you were second-rate. We figured if you thought that was Arnie's 'special' sax, you'd feel like you could play just as well as he did. And I'll bet you have. Playing is believing. Living the music, son, you know that. So we gave you one of his other saxes, the one that looked like the special his grandmother gave him."

Tyler looked as if he'd been hit in the head with a two-by-four. "But you don't understand. It has to be that sax. I could see what Arnie saw. I could feel him when I played it."

"Magic in the mind, son, magic in the mind," Amy said. "And it was the best gift

92

we figured we could give you, though there's no gift out there that says a big enough thank-you to a real friend. And, Tyler, you were his friend. I think you believed in him so much in your mind that you saw his death so you could go out and fight for him."

"I believed it," Tyler said. "I believed that sax was magic, that I could play because of that magic — that I could almost talk to Arnie again," he finished softly.

"That's magic, son. Love and belief," Amy said. She looked back at Danni and Quinn. "I don't rightly know what else could have happened to Arnie's special sax besides whoever killed him taking it. Arnie was found with nothing except the clothes he was wearing. And," she added, her lips tight, "that needle in his arm. They even told me they couldn't find another single track line on him, but I think they wind up with a dead black boy on Rampart Street, and they just don't want to think anything else."

"I can assure you, Amy, the detective who's now on the case — Detective Larue — doesn't see the world that way at all. We'll find the truth," Quinn promised her.

"You know, I heard something about those musicians being held up," Amy said. "But they were only knocked around and hurt.

93

They weren't killed."

"Two people *have* been killed now, and as I said, right in their own homes. So don't answer the door to anyone — even old friends of Arnie's. The killer might come around here if he doesn't have the sax and I'm right that that's what he's looking for," Quinn said.

"We're not alone here," Woodrow said. "We got good friends. We got family around the area. Hey, we got Tyler."

"Always like a second son," Amy said fondly.

"Amen," Woodrow agreed.

"You may be in danger, though," Danni told them.

"Got a shotgun in the back. I always did protect my home," Woodrow said.

"Don't you worry none about us," Amy said. "Even I know how to use that gun. You just go out there and find out who murdered our boy."

"We plan to do just that, Amy," Danni told her, reaching out to touch the woman's shoulder reassuringly. "I'm not sure how we'll go about it, but I promise you, we'll do everything it takes."

"As will Detective Larue. He's a good guy," Quinn said.

"You know the man well?" Woodrow asked.

"I worked with him for years," Quinn said. "Since . . ."

"No worries, son," Woodrow said. "We know about your troubles. You been clean all this time now?"

"Yes, sir," Quinn said.

"You got an angel with you, boy," Amy said. "Don't you forget that."

Danni watched Quinn. New Orleans was a good-sized city, but that didn't mean that old-time citizens forgot anything. She knew Quinn's dark past, and she wasn't surprised the Watsons did, too. Both his downfall and his resurrection had been covered in the local media.

"I never forget, Amy, trust me," Quinn told her.

"Bless you, boy," Woodrow said.

"Thank you," Quinn said. "And you can't come up with any explanation of what might have happened to that sax?"

"None. None at all," Woodrow said. "We reckoned the killer took it that night, like Amy said."

They were back to square one, Danni thought. But if neither Tyler nor the Watsons had Arnie's special sax and they were right and the killer was still searching for it, just where the hell was it?

"You at a dead end already?" Woodrow asked. He was clearly trying to sound matter-of-fact, but there was a hopelessness in his voice that squeezed at Danni's heart.

"No, sir," Quinn said. "We're just at the beginning."

"Thank you," Woodrow said. "Thank you for what you're trying to do. But thank you most of all for believing in my son."

Quinn gave a reluctant grin. "Thank Tyler for that, Woodrow. He made us see the light, so to speak. Not that it was all that difficult — your son was a true hero. But because these days we recognize what soldiers go through, it was easy for people to think maybe he just couldn't shake the pain of the past. The killer was clever, I'll give him that. Thing is, by being his champion, Tyler gave us what we needed to get started. No one can promise they'll solve every crime, but we *will* promise you this — we won't stop."

"Good enough for me. Tyler, you know how we feel about you. And Michael, Danni, you call on us or ask us anything you need or want, any time, day or night," Woodrow said. "You got our number? Or numbers? Arnie made us buy cell phones. Said he had to get us into the twentieth century, even if

96

he couldn't quite drag us into the twenty-first."

"We'll put them in our phones right now," Danni said.

They took a minute to exchange numbers. Amy still had trouble saving a number to her own phone once someone had called her, but in the end they prevailed.

Once that was accomplished, Quinn told them, "We could use a list of the people he was hanging with the most since he came home."

"Us, of course. And the rest of the family. Tyler there. The bands he played with," Woodrow said. "I can tell you some of the names."

"I know most of them," Tyler said. "Like I told you, he was sitting in with my group, the B-Street Bombers, the night he died."

"At La Porte Rouge?" Danni asked.

"Yes," Tyler said.

As they spoke, Amy was scribbling on a pad she took from the phone stand by the door. Now she handed the sheet to Danni. "Those are the people he talked about most — the boys in Tyler's band, a couple of others. I'll keep thinking and make a list of anyone else," she promised.

Tyler glanced over at the sheet. "Yep, that's them. Gus Epstein, lead guitar.

Shamus Ahearn, drums and sometimes bass. Blake Templeton, keyboard and sometimes rhythm guitar. We have a steady gig at La Porte Rouge. The bartender runs the place, and he likes us. A couple of guys pinch-hit sometimes, like Arnie was pitch-hitting for me that night. The bartender, Eric — Eric Lyons — sits in sometimes. And one of the waitresses — Jessica Tate — sings with us when we can get her to come up and it isn't too busy. We work a heavy schedule, but we love what we do, and in this city you can be replaced pretty much at the drop of a dime, so we're glad for the gig."

"Want to go barhopping?" Quinn asked Danni. "Or, should I say, want to hop into one bar?"

"Seems like a good idea," Danni said.

They rose, but Amy stopped them as they turned toward the door. "Are you sure I can't get you anything first? We've got some leftover shrimp and grits, and that's a dish that gets better warmed up. Or a cola or something?"

"No, no, honestly, sounds wonderful, but we just ate," Danni assured her.

"Well, then, you just wait a minute. No one leaves my house without a little bit of hospitality," Amy said.

She disappeared into the kitchen for a brief moment and came back with a small white cardboard box.

"For when you're hungry or need a little treat," she told Danni.

Danni thanked her and they left, promising to keep in touch.

She drove back to Royal Street, and as they went, Tyler talked to them about his bandmates.

"Shamus, the lucky bastard, is right out of County Cork. I always thought that was cool, but he thinks growing up here would have been the coolest thing in the world. Goes to show you — the grass always does look greener. Gus was born in Miami Beach but his mom was from Kenner, Louisiana, so he's been coming up to New Orleans since he was a kid. Blake is from Lafayette, about two and a half hours from here. I met Gus at an open session one night, and the two of us met Shamus at — go figure — Pat O'Brien's. I knew Blake from a school competition years ago, and I'd heard he was moving here, so I gave him a call. That was years ago now. We've had the steady gig at La Porte Rouge for about two years." He was quiet for a minute. "You know, if one of these guys was a crazed murderer, shouldn't

I have seen the signs somewhere along the line?"

"Maybe not," Quinn said. "Lots of killers come off like the nicest guys in the world. Anyway, we'll meet the band. They can tell us about Arnie's last night with them. You never know, maybe one of them will say something that will trigger someone else's memory or give us something to go on."

When they parked near the house and got out, they could hear the mournful sound of a sax coming through an open window.

"That's Billie," Danni told Tyler. "I hope you don't mind."

"Fine with me. It's not even a special sax," he said. "I could have sworn . . . I mean, I played better with that thing than I ever played in my life."

"Like Amy said, maybe because you believed you could play better," Quinn suggested.

"But I saw scenes from Arnie's life."

"Things you knew because you were his best friend," Danni said. "Things that fit with the way you think he died."

Tyler offered them a dry half smile, tilting his head at an angle as if he could hear the music better that way. "He's not half-bad," he told them.

"He's also a bagpipe player — or was,"

Danni said.

"You're sure it's not *the* sax?" Tyler asked.

"Not according to the people who should know," Quinn said. "Do you want me to go in and get it for you?"

"No," Tyler said. "I have another — let him play. Go ahead and let him play."

"Come on, then," Quinn said. "Let's head over to La Porte Rouge."

They walked up the one block from Royal to Bourbon and turned to the left. Neon lights blazed from everywhere. Women in scanty outfits stood by doorways with placards that advertised dollar beers and cheap food. People with drinks in open containers — from those who were barely twenty-one, if that, to retirees — cruised along, checking out the various venues in search of one that drew their attention or just taking in the sights and sounds. Music flowed from every establishment. In the street, songs combined and created an intriguing disharmony. Strip joints vied for business alongside all-night pizza joints and white-tablecloth restaurants, souvenir shops, voodoo shops and, always, music clubs.

There really was, Danni thought, nothing quite like Bourbon Street — the good, the bad and even the ugly.

They reached La Porte Rouge and let Tyler lead the way in. The band was in the middle of a Journey number.

The bar was like many on the street. The building itself was about a hundred and fifty years old; the long hardwood bar was about fifty itself, she thought. The stage backed up to the front wall so that the music oozed out the windows and open doors to encourage those who walked by to step in.

Cleanliness was definitely not next to godliness, but the place wasn't particularly dirty, either. So many people flowed in and out; so many drinks were spilled by the clumsy and the already wasted, that there was only so much the staff could do to keep up. But tonight, while there were twenty or so patrons scattered at the tables or standing in front of the band, it wasn't particularly busy. It was a Thursday night, and there were no major conventions in town, plus it was still only about eleven or eleven thirty. Bourbon Street would pick up soon — the night was still young in New Orleans.

Tyler was immediately recognized by a pretty blonde woman in black leggings and a corset-style blouse that was white with red trim; Danni saw the same blouse on another woman and figured it had to be a waitress uniform. The blonde wore it well; she was pretty without looking as if she should have been working at one of the nearby strip clubs.

"Tyler!" she said, kissing his cheek and smiling at Danni and Quinn. "I thought you were taking the night off."

"I was — I am," he said. "I was just bringing some friends by." He introduced them all to each other.

The young woman was Jessica Tate. She seemed glad to meet them — "any friend of Tyler's . . ." — and especially enthusiastic when she discovered that Danni owned The Cheshire Cat. "I love that place. I haven't seen you there, though. There's a guy who looks like Billy Idol most of the time when I'm in — sweet accent on him, too," she said, smiling.

"His name is Billie," Danni told her.

"I'm talking away," Jessica said, "and I'm supposed to be working. What can I get you?"

They ordered soda with lime and took seats at a table near the band.

"The band breaks for a few minutes every half hour," Tyler said. "You can talk to them soon."

"Terrific," Quinn said. Danni watched him as he studied the group. Quinn loved music. She wondered if one day, far in the future, he would have a chance to go where he wanted, play when he wanted and revel in his guitar.

After a few minutes she turned her attention to the group. Shamus Ahearn definitely looked stereotypically Irish. His hair was strawberry-blond, his skin pale and his eyes were light. Gus Epstein had dark, curly, close-cropped hair and was thin and wiry. He seemed totally focused on his guitar as he played. Blake Templeton — dark-haired, dark-eyed — was on keyboards. He was doing the lead vocals, too, and had a strong, smooth voice with a tremendous range.

"Nice!" Quinn called to Tyler over the music.

Tyler grinned. "We're even better with a sax. I thought Eric — the bartender — might sit in for a few, but I guess it's just a little too busy."

"It's busier now than when we got here a few minutes ago," Danni noted, looking around at the growing crowd.

"Yep," Tyler said. "But tomorrow night at this time . . . Well, you two are from here. You know. Friday nights in the Quarter . . ."

They talked about the reemergence of the French Quarter since the storms. Jessica brought them their drinks, apologizing for having taken so long. Danni watched her as she headed back to the bar, stopping to take an order along the way. She saw the bartender come over to her and smile as he listened to her recite the drinks she needed. He seemed to enjoy his job; the sudden influx of customers didn't get to him. There were eight seats at the bar, and every one of them was filled. He was friendly, calling out to the guy at the end that he needed just a minute as he filled Jessica's order.

Danni turned back to watch the band. Shamus suddenly noticed Tyler in the audience and looked at him curiously then studied her and Quinn — and never missed a beat.

A few minutes later Blake announced that they were taking a five-minute break and turned on the music system so that Lana Del Rey spilled out over the speakers, and then the whole band headed to the table.

"What gives, Tyler?" Shamus asked, sliding into the chair next to Quinn. He quickly offered Quinn a handshake as he studied Danni. "Hi, Shamus Ahearn. Nice to meet you."

They went around the table making introductions. Then Tyler addressed his bandmates. "They want to ask you guys about Arnie's last night," he said flatly.

"Oh," Shamus said, studying Quinn again. He grinned. "I should have realized you were a cop," he said.

"I'm not a cop," Quinn said. "Private investigator."

"Oh. Okay," Shamus said.

The rest of the band looked at one another then all shrugged as one. Speaking for the group, Gus said sure, they would be happy to do what they could.

Jessica came by with a tray holding three glasses of water and set them down in front of the band.

"Thank you, love," Shamus told her.

"Pleasure."

"You going to sing with us tonight?" Blake asked her.

"Can't. It suddenly got too busy," she said. "You guys okay?" she asked Quinn and Danni.

"Just fine, thank you," Danni assured her.

"What about me?" Tyler teased, raising his eyebrows in a mock leer.

"I know you're fine — and if you weren't, you'd lean over the bar and pour yourself a soda," she said. "So don't get fresh with me, Tyler Anderson."

"Wouldn't dream of it."

Jessica moved on.

Gus Epstein was sitting next to Tyler. "I don't know what we can say that would help. We finished up here about 3:00 a.m.

on the night he died. And he was his usual self all night. Friendly, happy. He was just a great guy."

"Amen to that," Shamus said.

"Actually, we asked him to go for pizza with us," Blake said. "We were all starving, so we were going right down the street. But he said he was tired."

"Yeah, that's right," Shamus agreed. "He said he wasn't hungry, that he just wanted to go home and get some sleep. We all said good-night and went our separate ways. Oh, and if you're asking these questions on behalf of some cop, you can check out my story. Marianna Thomas — a cranky old witch if there ever was one — was waiting tables that night, and she'll vouch for us."

"Arnie didn't say he was going to meet anyone, did he?" Quinn asked.

"No. Like Blake and Shamus told you, he said he was going home to bed," Gus said. "When we heard about him being . . . dead, we were all . . ."

"Fookin' stunned!" Shamus said.

"And devastated. He was one of the good guys," Gus added.

"But they said —" Blake began then broke off at a look from Tyler. "You know how they found him," he said.

"So you're a private eye," Shamus said,

looking at Quinn. "I guess you don't think what they're saying is right."

"Nope, I don't," Quinn said. "Two other local musicians are also dead — Holton Morelli and Lawrence Barrett. Murdered. In their own homes."

Danni watched the three musicians closely as the conversation continued.

"I heard about Morelli," Gus said, his tone a dry thread. "But I didn't think . . . Well, he was kind of heavy into drugs. Never played straight that I saw. I figured that . . ."

"Larry Barrett *too*?" Blake asked. "You sure? I haven't heard anything about him."

"I guess it hasn't hit the news yet, but yes, I'm sure," Quinn said.

"I knew Larry, too," Shamus said. "I was jealous as hell of him — he did so much studio work he made a fortune. But he liked his coke, too, you know. Maybe . . . it's got to be the drug scene. And we don't do drugs."

"Neither did Arnie," Tyler said.

"Be careful," Quinn warned them. "Be really careful. It's looking like both men were killed by someone they thought was a friend. Someone they let in the front door."

They stayed a few minutes longer, until the band's break was over. The whole group seemed to be in shock that another musician was dead. They sounded just a little bit off when they returned to the stage.

They parted with Tyler at the club, too. He was going to stay and finish out the night with his band.

On the way back to Royal Street, they were quiet, walking hand in hand.

"What do we do now?" Danni asked.

He looked at her, a slow smile forming on his lips. "We go home, go to bed. Perhaps do something incredibly life affirming. Something distracting, so we can return to this dilemma with fresh minds and a new perspective."

Danni laughed. "So you want to fool around, huh?"

"I believe it's called 'making love,' " he told her. He paused on the street, looking down into her eyes. His were hazel, ever-changing. She loved that there was something serious in them, something that spoke to her of sanity no matter what was going on around them. They'd learned that they had to give themselves over fully to a case in order to solve it, but they also had to hang on to their souls in the process.

"Indeed?" she murmured, stroking his cheek. She loved the rough feel of his jaw-line and the way that just standing there, thinking about the very near future, sent a sweet rush of liquid longing through her. "Personally, I like the thought of forgetting what we can't solve in a night and fooling around."

"However you want to put it is fine with me," he told her. His strides grew longer as he caught her hand again and hurried her down the street. "By the way, what's in that box that Amy Watson gave us?"

Danni let out a sigh of ecstasy. "So good," she whispered.

"Oh, yeah," Quinn had to agree. "More?" he teased.

"I don't know if I can take any more," she said, but she rolled his way on the bed. "Delicious," she added.

"Like a touch of silk," he said.

"Melts on the tongue," she said. "I just can't get enough."

"I'm here, my love. You can have all you want."

"Then why are you hogging Amy Watson's homemade candy?" she demanded.

"Hey, I'm passing it right over whenever you ask," he protested.

She rolled closer and leaned over him, blue eyes dazzling, the fall of her hair sweeping erotically over his naked shoulders. "Actually, I'm done with chocolate," she told him. A wicked grin teased her lips. "I'm ready for the real candy now."

"I always try to oblige," he vowed seriously and took her into his arms.

Their days, he knew, were about to grow longer again, and moments of sweet intimacy might well become few and far between.

It was time to stock up for the future.

CHAPTER 4

Danni was sleeping when Quinn awoke and rose. He showered and dressed, not wanting to wake her.

He loved to wake up first in the morning and watch her as she slept, hair spilling wildly around her, the length of her body half draped in the sheets. He smiled, thinking that she was a genuine work of art.

Actually, he also loved waking up to find her already awake herself, propped up on one elbow watching him, a mischievous smile on her face and a sensual look in her eyes.

They'd both grown up in the city, but he was about five years older than she was, and their paths hadn't really crossed until Angus had died. He still kept his house in the Garden District, but the more they were together, the more he knew that he wanted them to be together forever.

He was tempted to crawl back into bed

and just move against her until she woke groggily in his arms. That was fun, too.

He loved to stroke the length of her back. She would keep her eyes closed at first, but finally she would begin to smile and then touch him in ways that seemed to rock the earth.

He steeled himself to look away and walked to the door, letting himself out.

It was early, but he was expecting a call from Larue at some point, and he wanted to be ready to head straight to the station to interview the musicians who had been attacked after their gig.

Wolf wasn't in his usual spot in the hallway. The dog had decided that he was Danni's protector whether Quinn was in the city or not. He was always outside their room standing guard — unless Billie was already making breakfast.

He headed downstairs and found that Billie was cooking and Wolf was indeed with him, sitting patiently in a corner and awaiting his chance at something delectable. Bo Ray was there, as well, and the news was playing on the small TV set in the kitchen.

"How are you feeling this morning?" Quinn asked Bo Ray, pouring himself a cup of coffee. He breathed in the aroma as he waited for Bo Ray to answer. Billie made a

113

mean cup of coffee. Of course, in Quinn's mind, the best coffee in the world was to be found in New Orleans. It was rich and dark, and Billie's coffee could probably put hair on anyone's chest. But at The Cheshire Cat, they all loved it.

Bo Ray turned to look at Quinn. He had the appearance of a chipmunk that had been attacked on both cheeks by a swarm of bees.

"Great," Bo Ray said — or tried to. His mouth could barely move.

Bo Ray Tompkins was a young man they'd hired to help out at the shop on the first case Quinn had worked with Danni. A good guy at heart, Bo Ray had fallen in with some bad people and taken up their bad ways. Thanks to the help of Father John Ryan — a priest who was prepared to go to war in their strange fight against evil — Bo Ray had come back to the straight and narrow. They'd taken a leap of faith when they brought him in, and their faith had proved to be the right choice.

"I'm sending him back up with his knock-out pills as soon as I've gotten a breakfast smoothie into him," Billie said.

Bo Ray said something Quinn didn't understand. He shot Billie a questioning look.

"He said he's been watching the news.

Larue gave a press conference at the crack of dawn, warning all musicians to be hyper-vigilant — even among friends," Billie said. "I brought him up to speed on what's been going on."

Quinn nodded and turned back to Bo Ray. "After you finish whatever Billie's cooking up for you, head back on upstairs so you can get some rest and get better." He looked at Billie. "Did the oral surgeon say how long he was going to be like this?"

Bo Ray said something. Once again, Quinn had no idea what.

"I'll send him up some ice packs. He should be well on the mend by tomorrow. I think he's not too happy that sax is here," Billie said.

"Well, that's what *here* is for, remember?" Quinn said softly. "Not to mention it's not the sax."

"What do you mean, it's not the sax?" Billie asked. "It has to be! I was playing like a pro."

"It's amazing what the human mind will do," Quinn told him. "You sounded great because you expected to sound great. But we saw Arnie Watson's mom and dad last night. They never had Arnie's special sax. It disappeared the night he died. And if we're right — and I'd lay you odds we are — that the killer wants it, then obviously he doesn't have it, either, which means it's still out there somewhere. Anyway, after breakfast I'm going to head for the station. Larue is interviewing the three musicians who were attacked on the street. I want to be there for that. He's going to call me with the time, but I'm up, so there's no point in my waiting around here if the call doesn't come."

Wolf padded over as if he'd understood what Quinn had said.

"You'll all be fine without me," Quinn said. "Wolf will be here. No one gets past Wolf, right, boy?"

He hunkered down and patted his dog. *His* dog. He'd rescued Wolf from the K-9 unit after he'd been so badly injured that they were going to put him down. But Quinn knew Wolf considered himself to be Danni's dog now, and that was more than all right with Quinn. The hardest thing he'd been forced to learn was that while it was his instinct to protect Danni at all times, she was his partner. Didn't mean he didn't still want to protect her with his life, but it *did* mean he had to let her follow her own hunches and intuitions. But he was glad Wolf would also protect her with his life, because she had a way of plunging in on a hunch that meant she sometimes walked into dangerous situations.

And sometimes dangerous situations found *them.*

It was good to have a protector like Wolf.

Bo Ray started to say something again, but Quinn lifted a hand and said, "We'll talk tomorrow. Get some rest." He grabbed a waffle off the plate where they were cooling, chewing a mouthful as he poured his coffee into a to-go cup. "Let Danni know where I am," he said.

"Will do. And I'll man the shop today," Billie said.

"Be careful," Quinn said.

"Not to worry. Wolf knows a bad guy when he sees one," Billie said.

Quinn waved and left. Larue's call came through just as he reached the sidewalk. Larue was on his way to the station in the Quarter, and he told Quinn to head over whenever he was ready. They were set up to talk to the three musicians at 10:00 a.m.

Danni first woke with a sense of well-being. She stretched her arm out across the bed and then realized that Quinn was gone.

Her sense of well-being vanished.

She hurriedly showered and dressed then ran down to the kitchen. Billie was there, alone with Wolf, who was chowing down on

117

a waffle. The dog wasn't really supposed to have so much human food, but Billie swore that he never gave Wolf anything that would hurt him. And if she was being honest, she had to admit that she could never resist the giant hybrid herself. Wolf was ready to die for them at any time. How could you refuse to indulge a friend like that?

"Quinn's gone to the station to see Larue," Billie said, taking a forkful of the eggs on his plate. "And Bo Ray is back up in bed. No worries, though. I figure I can keep an eye on the shop today."

"Thanks, Billie," Danni said, grabbing a plate and helping herself to waffles and scrambled eggs. "Nice breakfast."

She tried not to grin as he grunted something about it not being Italian and chose not to rise to the bait.

Billie finished before she did and went out to open the shop. She cleaned up in the kitchen, deciding to leave as soon as she was done to see Natasha Larouche, aka Madame LaBelle. Natasha was a voodoo priestess and a dear friend. She also owned a voodoo shop where she learned just about everything that was going on in the Quarter and the surrounding area.

Once the kitchen was clean Danni walked out through the shop, Wolf at her heels.

Billie was behind the counter with the newspaper. He hated reading anything on a tablet.

"Your murder made the front page," he told her.

She walked to the counter and checked out the headline, which read Second Musician Murdered in Search for Valuable Sax.

"It sounded as if Larue thought Arnie Watson was the first," Billie said. "Wouldn't that make three?"

"It would. And I think Larue does believe now that the killings started with Arnie. But you know how the police think. The less the public knows about the details, the better. Makes it easier to ID the killer. And as far as the killer is aware, the official theory is that he's looking for a certain expensive instrument."

Billie nodded. "Good to know. I'll keep my eyes and ears open."

Impulsively, she kissed his wrinkled cheek.

Wolf followed her to the door. Natasha loved Wolf, and they usually talked in the courtyard at her place so he could hang out with them. Today, though, Danni wanted him on guard duty at The Cheshire Cat.

"Gotta stay, boy," she told him. "Watch over Billie for me."

He wagged his tail and whined but trotted

obediently over to Billie and took up a position by the counter.

The walk to Natasha's was barely a couple of blocks. Danni had basically lived in the house on Royal her whole life other than college, but she'd never ceased to love its location. If she turned to her right and looked down the street, she could see the fabulously beautiful Cornstalk Hotel, built as a private home in the early eighteen hundreds and graced with a wrought-iron fence molded in the form of cornstalks, because the owner wanted his beloved wife to feel as if she were back at her home in the North. Nearby were the George Rodrigue Studios, where the shop was filled with the artist's famous Blue Dog pictures. Though Rodrigue had passed away a few years ago, Danni thought his Blue Dog art would live forever.

Her favorite wig shop was also on Royal, and she thought of the amazing pieces the stylists created, not only for everyday but for the elaborate costumes of Mardi Gras and the city's other festivities, wigs that added two feet to the wearer's height, wigs with whole ships on them, wigs to fulfill just about any fantasy. She could easily get to Community Coffee, her favorite. The jewelry and boutique shops were ever-changing but always fun. They all carried a lot of the same T-shirts and souvenirs, but every little boutique was also different and stamped with the personality of the owner. Hard to find in this day and age, she knew. Sometimes she could even hear the children's laughter from a nearby school.

And while the city boasted many voodoo and occult shops, each one was equally unique, and none more so than Natasha's. Customers entered through a wood arch, and various magical items, amulets and beads and more, adorned the door. Entering, the visitor was treated to displays of gris-gris bags, an altar with its various offerings of pennies, pictures, pins and candles, and — the specialty here — carved African and Caribbean island masks. The outer gallery was large, and there were rooms in back for private readings. Natasha read palms, tea leaves, tarot cards . . . If it could be read, Natasha could read it. She was a deep believer in many spirits but one great power, and the ongoing battle, in the world as well as in the human heart and mind, between good and evil. Danni always thought how it was the people she knew who helped to make the world feel sane even when it wasn't. Father Ryan was a Roman Catholic priest, but while he loved his church and his calling, he and Natasha were great friends. While the world might see them as drastically different, they saw each other as kindred spirits.

The store had just opened, but those tourists who were early risers had already found the place. Natasha also had a local clientele — she was a voodoo priestess — but those in her flock knew that they were welcome at all hours, and that she was just a phone call, or a knock on the door, away.

Danni didn't see Natasha at first, but she did see her assistant, Jeziah, at the counter.

Danni thought Jeziah was one of the most beautiful people she had ever seen. Mixed race, he seemed to be made of gold. His eyes were neither green nor brown nor even hazel but a gleaming amber. He was tall and carried himself with an easy confidence that was attractive in itself. He was as loyal to Natasha as Billie was to her, and he — like Natasha — had been Danni's friend for years.

She smiled, walking toward him, and he asked her, "Where have you been? I have to say, Natasha was wrong this time. She expected you last night."

"How does she always know I'm coming?" Danni demanded. "That woman really is complete magic."

Jeziah laughed, leaned over the counter and whispered, "She was always a big fan of Marie Laveau, you know. And Marie Laveau got most of her mystical wisdom from being a good listener — and having the wisdom to truly hear what was going on. This time, it's not so much of a secret. She heard about the musicians, and knew you and Quinn would be involved in the investigation."

"The newest murder wasn't even made public last night," Danni said.

"Danni Cafferty! Have you forgotten? This is New Orleans. There's public, and then there's public. You don't think the people in Lawrence Barrett's neighborhood noticed the cop cars and the throngs of police over there?"

Danni laughed. "You have a point."

"Natasha is in the courtyard."

"Waiting for me?"

"Actually, she's doing a reading out there right now. Give her five, then she'll be ready."

Natasha definitely did have spiritual powers. Danni had seen her at work often enough to know. But she was also, as Jeziah had implied, brilliant at reading the people around her and at zeroing in on a situation.

"There are some new masks from Haiti on the wall. You might want to browse those for a few minutes. Hey, where's Wolf?"

"Guarding the shop," Danni said.

Jeziah didn't ask why. He merely nodded.

The Haitian masks were beautiful, painstakingly hand-carved. Danni could easily have studied each one for a long time, but it seemed she had barely begun when Jeziah told her to head out to the courtyard.

Natasha stood to greet her. She "held court" at a wrought-iron table in the courtyard. Small trees and well-tended bushes planted long ago surrounded the courtyard, while delicate wind chimes and dream catchers hung in the branches around them.

Natasha deserved the title of queen. She was statuesque, with coffee-and-cream skin, and large dark eyes that seemed to read a person's soul. She usually kept her hair swept up in a scarf, much like the famous voodoo queen Marie Laveau. Natasha wasn't against using any trick that helped her.

She gave Danni a kiss on the cheek and told her to sit.

"What have you heard?" Danni asked her.

"Well, naturally I've seen the news, but my flock speaks, as well. Gary Carter plays with a group on Frenchman Street, and he was well aware of that attack on those musicians. When the news got out that Holton

Morelli had been killed it was upsetting, but it was easy to say it might have something to do with his involvement in the drug trade. But now . . . do you know more?"

"I do," Danni said.

She went on to explain about her conversation with Tyler Anderson about Arnie Watson, and their visit to Arnie's parents. Natasha listened attentively.

"I knew Arnie Watson, heard what happened to him. His parents are devout Baptists, so I can't say they've been in the store often, but they're not crazy anti-voodoo crusaders or anything. They've brought out-of-town friends by, and even though she's Baptist, Mrs. Watson loves to buy rosaries for an aunt of hers. She gets one every year. But I must say, reading between the lines, Arnie's death seemed suspicious. Never knew him to use drugs, and I think I would have heard if he did," Natasha said.

"According to his parents, friends and bandmates, you're right. They all said he never did drugs and was happy to be home. And according to Quinn, you don't just go out one day and inject yourself with a lethal dose of heroin right out on Rampart Street."

"He could have been moved."

"The ME doesn't think so, but thankfully we're on good terms with Ron Hubert, so if necessary, we could get more facts."

"Exhume the body?"

"If necessary," Danni said. "Meanwhile, I was hoping you might have heard something on the street."

"I've heard a great deal of fear. But even when they're afraid, people have to work for a living. And people always talk — especially when they're afraid. It doesn't take a psychic or a Sherlock Holmes for people to figure out that this killer isn't just after musicians, he's looking for something specific. And since we're talking musicians, that pretty much has to mean a certain instrument. Word is, Arnie Watson had a special sax. Is that true?"

"Yes."

"And no one knows where it is?" Natasha asked.

"Tyler Anderson, Arnie's friend, thought he had it and brought it to us. But it wasn't the special sax after all. That sax disappeared the night that Arnie died, and no one knows where it is."

"Well, someone knows where it is — the person who has it. But what will you do if you find it?"

"Once we find it, we'll set a trap. But how the hell do you find one sax in the city of New Orleans?"

Natasha smiled. "You join a band."

"A band?"

"Quinn plays guitar."

"Quinn does. I don't."

"You can fake some songs. Your father gave up on you learning the bagpipes, but I know you took piano. And if you can play the piano, you can master a keyboard. And if the band plays loud enough, no one will care whether you can play or not, anyway."

"Such faith! How will I live up to it?" Danni asked her.

"I'm telling you, that's what you need to do."

"Quinn *is* fairly decent on the guitar. My friend Jenny LaFleur — you know Jenny, she and her boyfriend, Brad, play with a group called the Nightwalkers — told me that he's actually pretty good."

"There you go. There's your opening. This city *is* music. You want to get into the heart of the music scene, join a band."

"I'll talk to Quinn when he gets back. But Natasha —"

"Give me your palm," Natasha said.

"You've read my palm before."

"Hand it over," Natasha said, grinning. "You heard me. Hand over the hand!"

Danni complied.

With an elegant finger and a long, manicured nail, Natasha traced the lines in her palm. "This . . . is your life line," she said. "You should have a long life. But see these? These little striations off the main line? They seem to be deepening. Danni, this is a dangerous situation. We don't walk away from these things, but you need to listen to what I'm saying. You need to find that sax quickly — *and* the killer. I'm telling you, do what I say. And don't worry. I'll come and clap for you no matter how bad you sound."

"Naturally there was no one else in sight," Jeff Braman said. "There's always someone on the street and plenty of cops around. But not that night."

Braman was about thirty-five and looked like a holdover from the sixties. His beard was long, and as he'd told Quinn earlier, his hair would have been long, too, but the doctors had needed to shave his head so they could treat the wound he'd received from the butt of the attacker's gun.

"It was late. We'd been clowning around with the waitstaff as they cleaned up," Lily Parker, an attractive woman with shortcut dark hair, told him. Quinn thought she was in her late twenties to early thirties.

The third member of the group was Rowdy Tambor; he was the oldest of the

128

three, as well, probably in his midfifties.

Lily leaned over and tapped the city map Larue had spread out on his desk. "We were there — right on the corner. The guys were walking me home. I'm on Decatur, so we always head there when we're done, and then Rowdy gives Jeff a ride home."

"I live in the Garden District," Jeff said.

"I checked the records, and a patrol officer was a few blocks over right when you needed him," Larue said, shaking his head. There was no way to have a cop on every block at all times, and everyone there knew it.

"Forgive me if I'm asking you to repeat details you've already covered in the past," Quinn said, "but this guy who held you up at gunpoint and demanded your instruments . . . How did he manage to wield the gun, beat Jeff and take your instruments? I'm trying to figure out the logistics," he added quickly, so they wouldn't think he disbelieved them. "Every little detail is important."

"It'll be easier if we act it out," Lily said. She didn't appear to be offended. She stood up, and though they looked a little surprised, her bandmates joined her.

"So," she said then paused. "You want to be him?" she asked Quinn.

"Okay." He stood, as well.

Larue leaned back in his chair and tossed Quinn a pencil. "Your gun," he explained, when Quinn shot him a puzzled look.

Quinn caught the pencil and pointed it at the three musicians. "Okay — give me your instruments."

"I'm glad you didn't go into acting," Lily said. "Never mind. Give me the pencil. You be me. I'll tell you what to do."

Quinn handed her the pencil, and they changed places.

"You three are walking down the street," she said. "I had my ukulele that night, so my case was small, and even though he took it, I don't think he was much interested in it, honestly."

"Not my guitar case, either," Rowdy said.

"Okay," Lily said. "You three are just laughing and joking, and suddenly — I'm there. In front of you. In a black trench coat. And my face is all weird, as if it's made of plastic, but it's really a mask. Then I say, 'Stop! Hand me those cases now — right now — if you want to live.' "

Lily had made her voice harsh, guttural — and muffled.

"He talked like that?" Quinn asked.

"Yeah. I think the mask made his voice funny. I don't really know how to describe it. It wasn't a cool Mardi Gras mask. It was like those featureless white faces you see in Venice at Carnevale, except it wasn't white. It was opaque and shiny, skin-colored, and it made him . . . faceless," Lily said.

"She's described it perfectly," Rowdy said.

"What about the gun?" Quinn asked. "How did you know it was real?"

"Because he fired it," Jeff said drily. "When he came up to us, I said, 'What the hell?' And the next thing I knew, he'd bashed me in the head and fired."

As he described the action, Lily rushed between them and pretended to slam her "weapon" against Jeff's head.

Jeff's reflexes were strong; he ducked even though he must have known that she wouldn't hit him. And even if she did, it was just a pencil. But Quinn noted the way that, the second she'd made her move, she hurriedly pointed the gun at them again.

Jeff cleared his throat. "He fired when Rowdy made a move toward me. Maybe he couldn't tell that Rowdy was trying to help me and not tackle him. I was about out. I didn't know what the hell was going on. I just heard the shots."

"Shots?" Quinn asked.

"Yeah, two of them," Lily said.

"I suspect he fired in a panic, thinking

Rowdy was going for him, especially because he shot twice, and he wouldn't have wanted to draw attention to his presence."

"Maybe, but he knew what he was doing," Rowdy offered. "He told us to put our instruments down and move. Lily was sobbing by then and asking him how Jeff was supposed to move, but he said we'd better get him up somehow or he'd never move again. So we dropped our instruments and headed toward Esplanade as fast as we could, dragging Jeff and screaming for help. A cop heard us and called an ambulance for Jeff, and Lily and I went to the police station."

Larue had the report on his desk. He looked at Quinn. "Officers were sent out right away to search the area, but they didn't find anything."

"You guys can take your seats again," Quinn said, sitting down himself and turning to Larue. "No bullets? No casings?"

Larue shook his head.

"We're not lying!" Lily said angrily.

"I'm not suggesting you are. How many shots, again?"

"Two," Rowdy said. "And I'm sure of that. As certain as I am that we're sitting here in this room."

"Okay," Quinn said. "I need to know

because I'm going to try to find those bullets and casings. I need your help, though. First, he took your ukulele, Lily, your guitar, Rowdy, and Jeff, your sax?"

"Yeah, he took my sax. How did you know?" Jeff asked.

"It's in the report," Larue said quickly.

"What about the gun? Do you know what make or model it was?" Quinn asked.

"It was a gun. It fired bullets," Rowdy told him. "I'm sorry, but I've never held a gun in my life."

"Me, neither," Lily said.

"I went skeet shooting once at a casino in Mississippi," Jeff said. "And I still couldn't tell a rifle from a water pistol."

"All right, big? Small?" Quinn asked.

"About the size of the one Detective Larue has," Rowdy offered, pointing to Larue's shoulder holster. "But different."

"Okay, let's go in a different direction. How tall was he?" Quinn asked.

"Tall," Rowdy said.

"Medium," Lily said at the same time.

Jeff laughed ruefully. "I thought the bastard was a short little shit. But then, he was on me like a bat out of hell, so I'm not a good judge."

"About how long was it from the time you were attacked to the time the cop found you and sent someone to the scene?" Quinn asked.

"Just a few minutes," Rowdy said.

"Felt like forever, though," Lily added.

"I couldn't begin to tell you," Jeff said. "Those two were half carrying me, half dragging me, and the world seemed to be a blur. Why?"

"I'm trying to figure out if he might have had an accomplice — someone to help him with the instruments, maybe someone with a car — or if he had a place in the area to stash them and himself," Quinn said. An accomplice could even have come back later to pick up the bullets.

"Oh!" Lily's brown eyes went wide. "Let me think. I wish I could be more helpful, but the whole thing happened so quickly. And we were afraid we were going to die. Once he went after Jeff, we just complied as fast as we could."

"You did the right thing. No instrument is worth your life," Quinn told her. "Were those the instruments you usually played?"

"I play drums, too, but they stay at the club," Lily told him.

"Harmonica — and I didn't even think of it. It was in my pocket," Rowdy said.

"Sometimes I play keyboards," Jeff said. "But the bar has a piano, and I never take that home with me, either — obviously."

"But you always take your sax home?" Larue asked, looking at Quinn as he spoke.

"Always," Jeff said.

"You're pretty friendly with a lot of the other musicians in the city, yes?" Quinn asked them.

"Sure," Rowdy said. "Have been for thirty years. You never know when you'll need someone to cover you, and you never know when work might go sour and you'll be looking to cover for other people."

"Did you know the two men who were killed? Holton Morelli and Lawrence Barrett?"

"I knew them both," Rowdy said quietly.

"I knew Holton," Lily said.

"And I knew Larry," Jeff told them.

"What about a musician named Arnie Watson?" Quinn asked.

"Arnie? Of course," Lily said softly.

"Sure. Great guy. Terrible thing," Jeff said.

"He would have known what the gun was," Rowdy said. He frowned, looking at Quinn. "They found him with a needle in his arm. Are you saying you think . . . ?"

"We don't know what we think," Quinn said. "We just know we have a lot of dead musicians."

Lily trembled and swallowed audibly.

"You think the guy who did this to us . . . that he's the same guy who broke in and murdered Holton and Larry?" she asked.

"Maybe," Quinn said.

"Shit!" Jeff said. "I'm lucky as hell I was just pistol-whipped."

"We're all lucky as hell," Lily said.

"Well, there's one bright spot," Rowdy said. "At least it wasn't someone who thought our music stank."

He was trying for levity, and the others tried to smile.

"Whoever he is, he's still out there," Jeff said.

"Let's not panic," Quinn said. "We're investigating every angle, and we *will* put a stop to this. But even though he's already taken your instruments, you have to be more careful than you've ever been. Don't let anyone into your house — well, unless it's your mother."

"And even then, be careful," Lily murmured.

"One more thing," Larue said. "Will the three of you work with a sketch artist and see if you can agree on what the 'faceless' man looked like to the best of your recollection?"

"Of course. We'll do anything. We want this guy stopped," Rowdy said.

"Hell, yesterday I just wanted my sax — and my hair — back," Jeff said. "Now I just want to stay alive."

Lily, sitting next to him, squeezed his hand.

"Come with me," Larue said. "We'll go see Sergeant Hicks, and you can describe the man to him."

Quinn thanked the three of them, and after they left the office with Larue, he read the report again. They had definitely heard shots, but no bullets or even casings had been found.

Had their attacker cleaned up the scene before he left?

In about ten minutes, Larue came back by himself.

He tossed a copy of the sketch down on his desk. Quinn stared at it.

The man was faceless and wearing a trench coat. His hair was dark and stuck straight up in wild, thick disarray.

"Wig," Quinn said.

"I imagine," Larue said. "And the face . . . ?"

Quinn looked at his old partner. "Mask. And yet, if he was walking with his head down, no one would even notice." He rose. "Thanks. Thanks for letting me in on this."

"This case is all over the place," Larue

said. "If this *is* all the same guy, he's versatile, no single MO. I mean, he somehow overpowers a guy who went through boot camp and military training, and shoots a needle full of heroin into his arm. Then he dresses up like some trick-or-treater and attacks those three on the street. Then he just walks up to two different doors and brutally tortures and kills two men. Given that there were no signs that either victim was suspicious in any way, he must have shown up as himself. I mean, look at that drawing. No one would open the door to that freak."

"I believe it *is* the same person. And his tactics are changing because he's growing more desperate. He wants that special sax," Quinn said. "Well, thanks again. I'm going to get moving."

"Keep me in the loop if you hear anything," Larue said.

"Will do," Quinn said, heading to the door.

"And try to keep it legal," Larue said.

"Don't worry. I have a little more freedom than you guys in blue."

Larue shook his head. "Yeah, yeah, yeah. You won't get the department into trouble. But keep it legal anyway."

"Absolutely," Quinn said.

"Liar."

"As legal as I can," Quinn promised.

"You're going to go back and search where the police already searched, aren't you?" Larue asked.

"I am. But I don't think I'm going to find anything," Quinn said. "I think the attacker did a good job of covering his tracks."

"But you're going anyway?" Larue asked.

"There's one thing you taught me that will make me do just that," Quinn told him.

"What's that?"

"No killer is perfect, and everyone makes mistakes. We have to figure out where he's making his mistakes. The last two killings haven't given us much to go on, so we certainly don't want to give him a chance to perfect his methods, do we?"

It was here somewhere, somewhere in the city. He was going to find it, though.

The whole thing could have been so easy.

He shouldn't have needed to try so hard, to go to such lengths.

To become the Man With No Face.

Arnie Watson had trusted him, trusted him and stared in disbelief, wondering what was happening, when he'd stuck the needle in his arm.

And he'd taken the sax Arnie had that

night. The sax that should have been *the* sax.

Except it hadn't been.

But that sax was in the city. Somewhere. Arnie had given it to someone, left it to someone, entrusted it to someone.

Arnie had given away the magic sax. Who the hell had he given it to?

Who?

He pulled out the picture again. Things could still be salvaged. They couldn't prove that Arnie's death had been murder. Neither Rowdy nor Lily nor that ridiculous Jeff had known who he was, had recognized him. He'd never known just how important the mask was going to be until he'd visited Holton Morelli and then Larry Barrett.

And he'd never known himself, really known himself. He'd been sure he could get the sax if one of them had it.

He'd never known how far he would really go, but now he did. And he *would* get that sax. Eventually one of the local musicians would make sure of it. Because everyone wanted to live. Of course, if the cops got involved they would make sure the current owner didn't just offer up the sax. No, the cops would try to arrange things so he would have to come for it, and then they would arrest him. He wasn't going to let that happen, though.

He would find the damned thing himself, even if he had to murder every musician in the city to get it.

He stared at the picture some more. It made him angry. There they were, all those musicians — a few years ago, of course. The beautiful, the brilliant and the talented. Lost and alone after the summer of storms, clinging to one another. Still, they had the look. Every one of them had the look. They were superior. And none so superior as Arnie Watson.

Because of his magical saxophone.

Well, oh-so-special Arnie was dead now. And *he* was going to have the sax. He would have expected the sax to go to Arnie's parents. And if that were true and they had passed it on to another musician, he would find out.

But he remembered Arnie the night he had died. Arnie had laughed before he'd known what was happening.

"The sax?" he'd said. "Well, of course it's special. To me — and the person I most adore, who will hold it dear for all the right reasons."

Who the hell was that person? He'd accidentally put Arnie out too fast to find out. But he'd been new to killing people then.

He'd had no idea how easy it was.

Now he was no longer himself. He was the Man With No Face. And he would be whoever he needed to be whenever the need arose. Murder, he'd discovered, was not just easy.

It was an art.

And he was just as magical as the sax. He could disappear. He could be — and not be. He could be himself or anyone else he wanted to be.

But he had to find that sax.

He studied the picture. It wasn't just deciding who he was going to kill next.

It was deciding just how and when his victim would die.

CHAPTER 5

For the last few years that Quinn had been with the NOPD, Larue had been his partner. He'd always been a good cop, and Quinn was glad they were still on the same side. There were way too many times when it proved beneficial to be in good graces with one of the city's lead detectives.

Of course, there were things he and Danni sometimes did that made him extremely grateful that they weren't cops themselves. Their unofficial status frequently saved them from struggling with a moral dilemma, not to mention from being fired for going where a policeman couldn't legally go.

At the moment, however, Quinn didn't have anything in mind that even remotely smacked of illegal behavior. He headed down to Frenchman Street and the block where Lily, Jeff and Rowdy had been playing.

The street was crowded with clubs and

restaurants; in Quinn's mind, it was the best place to find local talent and up-and-coming musicians. Blues and jazz spilled through open club doors, occasionally punctuated by folk music and experimental mixes. He'd seen the best drummer he'd ever encountered on Frenchman Street; the man's arms had moved as if they were propelled by the Energizer Bunny.

It was Friday morning and still early; workers were still out cleaning up from the night before. He stopped in front of the Blues Bear, where the trio had been playing, and then he retraced their steps as they'd described their route to him. Lily had pointed out a spot on the map where they'd passed a tree just before being attacked. It was right by a large alleyway where vendors often set up.

The tree grew in a square opening cut from the pavement, surrounded by concrete and old paving bricks. Their attacker might have made his exit through the alleyway, but he hadn't come from that direction, Quinn thought. He had met the three head-on just after they passed the alley. Reliving Lily's reenactment in his mind, Quinn pinpointed the direction the shots would have taken. He would have fired toward Esplanade.

Two shots. The casings should have fallen to the ground where the attacker had stood. And the bullets had to have made impact somewhere.

Quinn crossed the street and headed down the block, inspecting the walls of the buildings as he did so.

He walked up and down, up and down.

He knew the police had searched, but things would have been a lot more chaotic then, with Jeff being rushed to the hospital, and both Rowdy and Lily in shock, unable to speak with much coherency.

He walked down a couple of blocks and then walked back slowly. He did it three times. The attacker could easily have picked up his shells, but bullets didn't just disappear.

He returned to his original position.

Then he looked at the tree.

It was scrawny; he actually had no idea what kind of tree it was. He looked at the two square feet of dirt in which the tree sat in its oasis amid the concrete. Ducking down, he searched through the dirt with his fingers.

"What the hell?" a passerby murmured.

The man at her side whispered back, "It's New Orleans. Just keep walking."

There was nothing in the dirt. Quinn

slowly rose and realized that he was staring right at a bullet that had pounded its way straight into the trunk of the scraggly little tree.

He pulled out his knife and the handkerchief he kept folded in a pocket for just such occasions. In less than a minute he had the flattened bullet cut from the trunk, along with a few chips of wood. He kept searching and was soon rewarded; the second bullet was lodged higher and covered by the few leaves that sprang from the bony branches.

He had them both. The attacker had found his casings, all right. But not even he had known where to find the bullets.

"May you prosper and live forever," he told the tree then turned to hurry back across Esplanade to the French Quarter and then toward the station.

The Cheshire Cat was quiet, and everything seemed to be going smoothly when Danni returned from visiting Natasha. Wolf greeted her enthusiastically. There was no living being in her life — Quinn included, she thought — who greeted her with the same display of love that Wolf gave her. Dogs were the best, their love unconditional. Whether she'd been gone a few days or a few hours,

Wolf greeted her in a way that let her know how much he loved her.

"Anything new?" Billie asked as she bent down, scratching the dog behind his ears.

"We're going to become musicians," she said, one eye on the two women who were studying the Egyptian display.

"Overnight?" Billie asked politely. "And just what instrument will *you* be playing, Danni Cafferty?"

"I have no idea, but I'll be faking something," she said. "Natasha said we have to become part of the music scene. Anyway, I'm going to head down to the basement for a bit. You all right there?"

"If a horde walks in, I'll call for you," he assured her.

Danni headed out of the shop, Wolf trotting by her side. When she was there, he was always at her heels. She didn't mind. In fact, she liked it.

She passed her studio and glanced in; the canvas she was currently working on — a view of the river — sat on its easel. It would have to sit there for a while longer, she thought then paused, looking thoughtful. During their previous cases, her artwork had proved to be very important. She abhorred the fact, but she was known to sleepwalk — and sleep-draw or even sleep-paint. She didn't know if she illustrated what her subconscious mind was trying to tell her or what the inspiration was, and sometimes she had no idea what the resulting artwork meant. But sometimes, when she looked closely at what she had created, she could see what had been there all along that they simply hadn't noticed.

She decided to put away her watercolor of the river and set out a fresh canvas.

When she had done that, she headed on down the stairs that led to the "basement," which was really at ground level and the foundation of the house. Her father's private rooms were there; the rooms where he'd stored collectibles that would never be for sale, items that had been involved in bad things, that were supposedly — or really — cursed, along with those pieces he couldn't bring himself to part with. Angus Cafferty had been fascinated by all things Egyptian, and also all things pertaining to medieval Europe and the Victorian era.

There were a number of boxes piled up along one wall; she knew the contents of some but not all. One of her favorite items among the collectibles was a full suit of armor that stood in one corner as if guarding the room and its contents. Against the opposite wall was an upright Victorian coffin. No one had ever been buried in it; it had been a display piece for a funeral home that had once been in the city. The funeral home today was a private residence. When she'd been little, she'd found the coffin scary, because it held a beautiful mannequin, painted to look asleep to show just how one's loved one would look on display. Danni had always been terrified that the mannequin would suddenly open her eyes and look at her. Other oddities had also found a home there, including props and posters from a number of movies. It always amused her that one of her father's favorites had been a giant, openmouthed stuffed gorilla from the classic but never-completed *The Gorilla That Ate Manhattan.* He'd also kept his private stash of Egyptian artifacts down here, including masks, a mummified cat, a mummified raven and a number of funerary art pieces.

To a child, the basement had been creepy.

Now she loved being down here. It was as if she could be closer to her father.

The most important object in the basement, however, was the book.

The giant old volume had a special place on her father's antique desk, protected by a glass dome. Danni only took it out when she needed to peruse it and was careful to return it immediately as soon as she finished. Her dad's swivel chair sat behind the desk, and she remembered how she'd liked to sit in it. She'd curled into it many a time when he'd been alive to read or do her homework, or to be with him while he cataloged his collection or made notes on particular pieces.

If it weren't so special to her family, the book would have been worthy of the best antiquarian bookseller in the world. Though yellowed with age, the paper was heavy and intact, the edges of the pages gold-trimmed. The book was American, something that always filled her father with great pride, and had been written by a woman named Millicent Smith and printed in 1699 in Boston. It contained herbal cures for every ailment known at the time and read like a medicinal how-to for the sixteenth and seventeenth centuries, but it also contained curious texts about deflecting curses, how to rid the world of an "evil essence still upon the earth" and other occult know-how. The information was couched very carefully; accused witches had been executed in Salem not long before its publication, and there were still rather dubious laws on the books in many states that would lead to further persecution in the decades to come. Danni knew that certain texts only became visible when read through specially colored lenses.

It was sometimes difficult to read because it wasn't an actual occult book, and the chapters weren't always arranged in ways that made sense to a modern reader. There was actually a chapter on musical instruments, but instead she found what she was looking for in a chapter called "Secrets of the Mind."

" 'Music,' wrote the dramatist William Congreve, 'has powers to soothe a savage breast,' " Millicent's text read. "And how incredibly true; at its worst it is strident and discordant and painful to the ears. It brings to mind war and heartache, death and disease. At its best, it prolongs life because of the happy status it creates in our hearts. And there is the core of the would-be musician. There is magic therein, but magic springs from the heart, from the longing of that which he would play or sing to bring forth the beauty that gently caresses the raw heart and opens the mind to all things."

Danni flipped through more and more pages but could find nothing specifically on instruments, haunted or otherwise.

Yet, as she sat there, she mulled with a certain amount of amusement over how Tyler Anderson had been convinced that he had become a better player because he had Arnie's sax. Was the music in the believing?

She didn't know.

She wished she believed that *she* could play.

With that thought in mind, she called Quinn. He sounded winded when he answered the phone.

"Where are you?" she asked.

"On the street."

"Doing what?"

"Walking."

"Because . . . ?"

"I'm on my way to the station. I dug out some bullets from a tree. They're from the attack on the musicians the other night — gotta get 'em to Larue. They're pretty smashed. I'd say our guy has a Glock 19, which is, unfortunately, one of the most popular handguns out there. And, of course, we're in Louisiana — tons of permits and even more unlicensed guns. But still . . ."

"That's the first real break of any kind, Quinn. That's great," Danni said.

"I'll be back soon," he said. "But why did you call?"

"Natasha thinks we need to be playing with a band, so we can become part of the music scene and get closer to the killer."

He was silent a minute.

"Did you hear me?" she asked.

"Bands," he said.

"Pardon?"

"Bands," he said. "If we're going to become part of the music crowd, we need to play with more than one band. But we'll start with Tyler's group. That's where Arnie played his last gig — at La Porte Rouge."

"Quinn, that's fine for you, but I — I suck!"

"It will be fine."

Easy for you to say — you love your damned guitar.

"What will I do?" she asked. "Continual renditions of 'Chopsticks'?"

"We can always whip out a bagpipe."

"Funny."

"Every band can use a backup singer," he told her.

"Do you think Tyler's band will let us play horribly with them?" Danni said.

"I beg your pardon. I don't play *horribly.*"

"*I* do."

"You don't need to play. You sing backup, and stand around and look pretty. Besides, we'll bring Billie. He can really play. You heard him last night."

Billie *could* play, and that could prove to be a godsend, Danni thought.

Quinn was quiet for a minute and then

said, "Give Tyler a call, and ask if he can use an extra guitar player and a backup singer, along with Billie on sax."

"Billie will be a big help. And if he's there . . . well, you two can join the band. I'll sit in the audience and —"

"No, you're not getting out of it. We have to make a real effort to become part of the music scene. That's how you get musicians to talk to you. And remember, we'll just be starting at La Porte Rouge. We may need to play all around the city."

"And split up?" she asked.

"No way. If we don't know the groups or the venues, we're not splitting up," he said sternly. "We're at our best together. Always."

"Come home so we can figure this out," she told him.

"I'll be there soon."

Danni had barely ended the call when her phone began to ring. Glancing down, she saw that it was her friend Jenny LaFleur.

"Hey, Jenny," she said. She should have expected the call; Jenny must have seen the news, so she was bound to be nervous.

"They're warning musicians to be careful," Jenny told her. "Do you know anything? Are we in danger?"

"You need to watch out and steer clear of anyone you don't know, yes," Danni said.

"Especially if you're on your own."

"Can you and Quinn come watch the band tonight? Quinn could sit in with us," Jenny said hopefully.

"Actually, I think we're going to be at La Porte Rouge," Danni told her.

"Hey, I'm your friend, and I would feel a lot better if you were around."

"We'll get over there soon, Jenny. I promise. For tonight . . ."

"Is Quinn sitting in with another group?" Jenny demanded.

"That's the plan," Danni told her. "I'm going to sit in with them, too."

Jenny's dead silence did nothing for her confidence. Finally she said, "Oh. So you two are . . . involved in this."

"Half the city will wind up involved in this," Danni said quietly.

"It's awful! I'm so thankful that Brad and I work together. We'll be very careful. Brad has a gun, you know. He doesn't normally carry it, but you can bet he's going to start now."

The thought of dozens of people who had legal permits — and dozens more who did not — running around the city armed didn't bode well, Danni thought. "Just be careful with that, too," she said quietly.

"Brad isn't an idiot. He's not going to run

around shooting at shadows," Jenny said.

"I wasn't really thinking about Brad. I've seen a few people working late who I'd rather not see running around with a gun in the dark," Danni said.

"Well, until they catch this guy . . ."

"Jenny, did you know the men who were killed?" Danni asked.

"I can't say I really knew them. I'd seen them play — they were good, too. We'd spoken a few times. Larry Barrett even came to see us play once or twice."

"Did you know Arnie Watson?"

"Arnie?" Jenny repeated curiously. "Of course. He was a few years ahead in school. He could play really well then, and he only got better and better. We had him sit in with us any time we could, once he got back from the military. Poor Arnie. It was heartbreaking to hear about him. Why are you asking about Arnie? How could this have anything to do with him?"

"I was just asking," Danni said. But she felt a shiver of unease slip along her spine. Arnie had played with her friends. That could mean they were in danger.

"I really wish you could come play with us tonight," Jenny said.

"You really can't wait to hear my keyboard playing?" Danni asked.

"I was actually thinking about Quinn doing the playing, but not to worry — we can give you a tambourine. Not even you can do too much damage with that! But, seriously, come play with us as soon as you can, okay?"

"I'm sure we will, Jenny," Danni said.

They said their goodbyes. Danni realized that she'd told Jenny they were playing with another band tonight, but she hadn't even asked Tyler yet. She called him immediately.

Speaking with him was great for her confidence as an investigator but not so much as a musician, since he, too, suggested a tambourine. "And wear something sexy, Danni. No one will care what you do onstage as long as you look good up there."

"What about your band? Will they mind?" she asked.

"Everyone is spooked now. They won't mind at all."

"Will they know what we're doing?" she asked, and thought, *Will they know that they're all suspects as well as potential victims?*

"I'd say most people have heard about the two of you, yes, so they'll know why you're really there. But that will help the situation, you know?"

"When should we be there?"

"Whenever you want, so long as you make it by nine thirty, when we go onstage."

"We'll show up between eight and nine," she promised.

He told her that would be fine. Then before hanging up he said, "And, Danni, thank you."

There was an unexpected depth of emotion in his voice, and she knew that however embarrassed she ended up feeling on that stage, it would be worth it.

When she hung up that time, she tapped her fingers on the table. There was one person they hadn't spoken to yet, the last member of their unique unit that dealt with the unusual aspects of the criminal element.

She dialed Father John Ryan.

It didn't surprise her that he expected her call.

"Danni," he said, answering without a hello. "I've been watching the news and waiting for your call. Bring me up to speed."

"First, Father, I need you at a bar on Bourbon Street tonight."

"Lovely," he said. "I can have a word with a few of those crazy people who carry signs saying 'God hates this one' or 'Christ hates that one.' I've been waiting for an opportune moment. I'm going to slip right up beside them, collar and all, and tell them,

'Excuse me, my child, but God and I just had a lovely conversation, and He's just fine with whoever, but He has a slight problem with you.' "

"No fighting in the streets tonight, Father. You're going to come and rouse the audience to applause whenever I'm onstage," she said.

She could almost see the grin on his face. "Well, bless you, girl. Bless you. Now, tell me what's going on, and how you and Quinn are involved."

Larue looked at the flattened bullets Quinn set on his desk.

"Well, damn. You *did* find them."

"No fault of the officers at the scene that they missed them," Quinn assured him. "They were embedded in the one tree in the area. The killer couldn't find them, either."

"I still find it curious that he's got a gun and only threatened people at first, and then hasn't used it whenever he actually killed someone."

"Maybe he realized he got lucky no one heard the shots and came running, and that the next time he tried something like that there could be a cop or someone else around."

"Maybe. Still . . ."

"You come up with anything?" Quinn asked Larue.

"I have someone putting together a list of local saxophone players," Larue said. "It's not easy. So many people in this city play so many instruments. But these . . ." He paused and pointed to the bullets. "I'm willing to bet on a Glock 19, though forensics can let us know for sure. We can throw data into a computer and see what matches we come up with for who plays sax and owns a Glock."

"The gun may not be registered."

"No, and it's popular as hell, besides. But we've got nothing else except for a picture of a man in a mask — the kind of mask that's sold in a hundred places. All we really have is that our killer's a musician, and hell, we don't even know that for sure."

"A musician or a wannabe, or even someone in the entertainment or hospitality field," Quinn said.

"Because of the hour?"

"The attack and all three murders occurred in the wee hours of the morning — the time when musicians are finished with their gigs, have packed up all their gear and are heading home."

"I'm going to hang out at the site of

Holton Morelli's last gig tonight, and I've got men going to Lawrence Barrett's last venue, as well. I figured you'd be going to the last club Arnie played."

"I'm going to sit in with a band I know. I've played with them before."

"And Danni?"

"Danni will be with me," Quinn assured him.

Danni's cell buzzed the second she got off with Father Ryan; it was actually hot, she'd been on it so long.

It was Billie, calling her from the shop. "There's someone here to see you," he told her.

"Oh?"

"A pretty young lass. She's been in before but says she just met you last night."

"Jessica?" Danni asked.

"That's her name."

"I'm coming right out," Danni said.

She hurried up the stairs, Wolf at her heels.

Jessica was at the case that displayed the Egyptian pieces. She turned and offered Danni a broad smile and then saw Wolf.

"Oh!" she said.

"He's friendly as can be — just big."

"He looks like a wolf!"

"Only part wolf," Danni said.

"Nothin' but a big old cuddly bear," Billie said, walking over. "Come meet him. Best dog in the world, and knows a friend right away."

Jessica looked nervously at Danni.

"Honestly, he's a doll. I promise."

Jessica went to the dog and patted his head. "Hello, Wolf."

Wolf wagged his tail.

Looking at Danni, Jessica smiled. "He *is* gorgeous. And nice. I don't know why, but I've always been afraid of big dogs. Maybe he can cure me."

"You have to watch out for any dog you don't know," Danni said. "Don't just go petting the next Rottweiler you see. Always ask."

"I will, I promise. Anyway, I was just really stopping by to say hi, since we met last night and I've been here so many times without seeing you," Jessica said. She lifted the shopping bag she'd been carrying. "I had to run down to the corner store before work. I have a little one, and I have to make sure my mom is set before I leave each night."

"A toddler? How nice," Danni said. "Boy or girl?"

"I have a little boy. Cutest little thing you've ever seen, if I do say so myself," Jessica said, blushing.

"Congratulations," Danni said. She smiled. "I'm surprised none of the band has mentioned him to me. He must be adorable."

"Oh, the guys have never seen him," Jessica said. "I don't want to bring my child to a bar. I keep a low profile, you know. Sad to say, but you make better money when frat boys and businessmen see you as a cute young thing instead of a mom. My son is my real life, and I like to keep it separate, you know?" She smiled. "Anyway, I just wanted to stop by. I'm on Royal, too, but closer to Esplanade. It was just so nice to meet you and Quinn. And of course I already knew Billie. He always makes shopping here a pleasure."

"I do my best," he said.

"Well, hope to see you again soon," Jessica said.

"Actually, you'll see us very soon. We're going to come and sit in for a few numbers with the band tonight," Danni told her.

"Cool," Jessica said. "That's really great."

She seemed genuinely enthused. In fact, she sounded relieved.

Danni didn't press her for a reason, since Jessica was already heading to the door, suddenly seeming anxious to get going. "I'll see you there, then," she called.

And then Jessica was gone.

"That was interesting," Billie said. "A more transparent setup for a conversation I've never seen. That girl certainly wants you and Quinn there tonight — badly, so it seems to me."

Danni looked at him. "You're going to be there, too."

"I am?" He sounded suddenly nervous.

"Suck it up, Billie. You can play, and you know it. So you'll definitely be in the band. Now if you'll excuse me, I've got to go figure out what I'm going to wear."

"Now, wait a minute, Danni Cafferty! I just happened to be okay on that instrument last night. Bands practice together, and I haven't practiced with this group."

"I've heard musicians who've never even met before just start jamming together, and it was magic."

"Not me. I'm a practice man."

She paused to grin at him. "Stop complaining — you're going to love it!"

"You'd best be careful," he told her. "Put me on the spot, will you? Careful, lass, or I'll be bringing me bagpipes."

CHAPTER 6

Danni, Quinn thought, was just one of those people graced with natural beauty. She could wear an old raggedy T-shirt, worn jeans and no makeup then smile and seem to be the most sensuous creature on earth. He wondered if there really was such a thing as "inner beauty" and if that was shining through whenever he looked at her.

Dressed to the nines, she was absolutely stunning.

The bands that played the clubs on Bourbon and Frenchman were often very casual in their attire, although some of the jazz trios often wore suits to entertain the diners at The Court of Two Sisters, Muriel's and some of the other fancier venues.

Danni had hit just the right mix for the evening. She was wearing a strapless dress that lightly hugged her form and fell to just above her knee. It was appropriate for the beach or a candlelit dinner. She wore sandals that added two inches to her five-nine frame, emphasized the muscles of her calves and complemented her already-statuesque posture. Her long auburn hair hung free, creating a wavy frame around her face.

Quinn stood with Billie at the foot of the stairs, waiting for her to appear. She looked at the two of them and flushed. "Too much?"

"Ah . . . no," Quinn said.

"Perfect, just perfect," Billie said. "We'll be needing to leave the house now, though, before lover boy can't make it out the door. Quinn, grab your guitar and let's go."

Quinn grinned at that, winking at Danni. "Billie, you could run ahead and —"

"Way more than I want to be thinking about," Billie said. "Come on, let's go. Before I *do* pick up my bagpipes."

Billie had the sax that Tyler had left the night before. Quinn had his guitar. Danni had . . .

Looks to kill.

She paused before they left, though, turning to Wolf. "You protect the store and watch out for Bo Ray, okay, Wolf?"

He whined. He would do as he was told, but he wanted to go with them.

"Come on, let's see how this goes," Quinn said.

It was only a few blocks' walk to the La Porte Rouge. It was early for a Friday night, but already Bourbon Street was booming. Couples, groups, the old and the young, wandered down the street. Some were three sheets to the wind already; this was a city where alcohol flowed freely. Some locals moved along briskly, going to or from work, long jaded when it came to the sins of the city they loved and going about their daily routines. A man in a white T-shirt and apron leaned against a wall that divided a pizza restaurant from a strip club. A sexy, scantily clad hostess leaned next to him, chatting as they took simultaneous cigarette breaks. A hawker passed them, advertising one-dollar beers.

When they arrived at La Porte Rouge, the band was already setting up. And, just as Tyler had promised, none of them seemed to mind that they would have company on-stage for a few numbers.

Until they went on at nine thirty, new talent worked the stage as an "open mike" night. Between their sets, canned music played over the loudspeakers. There were already a dozen patrons in the bar, and Quinn knew the crowd was going to get heavy — it was a Friday night, after all.

Tyler left the other band members — Shamus, Blake and Gus — to finish setting up while he went over the list with Billie, Danni and Quinn. Tyler pointed out three numbers for which he thought "dueling saxes" would be fantastic. Quinn was set to play for the majority of the set. Just as Tyler turned to Danni with a deep grin, Shamus came walking up with a tambourine trailing colorful ribbons.

"You can be up there with us the whole time, Danni," Tyler said.

"The backup mike is stage left," Shamus told her. "You'll have a sense of when to come in. Do it even if you're faking it half the time. You'll know the songs. We cover the most popular groups from the last few decades, a lot of eighties stuff. You'll be fine."

Danni looked at Quinn. He smiled.

Tyler and Shamus left them to do a sound check.

"Quit grinning at me," Danni said to Quinn, sounding more than a little panicked.

"Hey, this could be a good tryout for us," he said. "When all else fails, we may have a backup career here."

Gus Epstein came over and slid onto a

stool at the small table where they sat waiting. He must have heard Quinn, because he smiled at him sheepishly. "Great — more musicians in the city. Like we don't have enough competition."

"Trust me, *I'm* not competition," Danni said.

"Trust me, all you have to do is stand there and you're competition," Gus said. He looked at Quinn and said, "Sorry — you have to manage the request list, make sure we're all aware of any audience requests that come in, whatever."

"I'll deal with it," Quinn assured him.

"And you . . ." Gus said, looking at Billie.

"Yeah? What about me?" Billie demanded.

"You've got style," Gus said.

Billie grinned, and they all laughed.

But then Tyler wandered back over, looking serious. "We're glad you're here."

"Really glad," Gus said quietly. He looked around, as if he was afraid they might be overheard. "I mean, first we lost Arnie, and now, two musicians killed, right in their homes. Hell, yeah, I'm glad we've got a cop here," he said, meeting Quinn's eyes.

"I'm not a cop," Quinn said.

"You're like a cop, you *were* a cop, and it's good to have you onstage looking out for us."

As they sat there, everyone suddenly silent, Jessica served another table and then came up to them. Quinn noted that Danni greeted her warmly, as if they were old friends. Jessica's eyes were bright, and she told them with a pleased smile that all soft drinks and bottled water were on the house, and that Eric, the bartender, had told her to tell them that they were welcome to domestic draft beers, as well.

Quinn thanked her and waved to Eric. He was pouring a shot for a customer at the bar, but he smiled and nodded.

"Well, this is it — time to do or die," Tyler said.

"Don't say *die,*" Gus told him.

"Does 'break a leg' work?" Jessica asked, grinning.

Shamus joined them. "Tyler, you doing the intros?"

"I am," Tyler said, getting up.

Just as they were about to walk onstage, Quinn smiled broadly as a rather odd couple walked into the bar. Father John Ryan and Natasha Larouche.

Natasha was wearing a brightly colored turban that drew attention to her face beneath it. The woman had some of the most majestic features Quinn had ever seen. She wore a peasant blouse and long skirt.

Father Ryan had decided to doff his priestly collar for the night. Still, he was in black, and somehow — though maybe it was just in Quinn's mind — he still looked like a priest.

"Hey," Quinn said, greeting the two newcomers. "Thanks for coming."

"We've got to get you two off to the right start, eh?" Father Ryan said.

Danni had come up and swept past Quinn to give Father John Ryan a hug and a kiss on the cheek, then greet Natasha the same way.

"She's a little scared, huh?" Natasha asked Quinn, nodding toward Danni.

"I think *terrified* is the word you're looking for," Quinn said, smiling at Danni. "Give her a good old evil spirit to face down and she's fine. Put her on a stage, and . . ."

"I'm not that bad," Danni said indignantly. "I've got my tambourine."

"Hey, Gus!" Tyler called.

Father Ryan made the sign of the cross in Danni's direction. "Blessings," he told her.

"Ditto," Natasha said, grinning.

Quinn set a hand at the small of Danni's back and urged her toward the stage. A moment later he had his guitar, and he and Danni had taken their places. Billie would join them later, so for now Father Ryan and

171

Natasha joined him at the table.

Quinn kept his eye on the crowd as they went into the first number, a song by Journey — a staple on Bourbon Street. They moved from Journey to Def Leppard, and then to Deep Purple, Led Zeppelin and Billy Joel. By the time they reached the Billy Joel number, he noticed, Danni had gotten into the beat of the music. He smiled; he'd thought she might. She had a nice knack for being able to hit just the right harmonies at the right time — and she'd never even rehearsed with the guys. Billie came up when they did a jazz number, and Tyler, with the natural ability of a true entertainer, introduced him. He took that time to introduce Quinn and Danni, as well.

Granted, the members of the growing crowd were mostly inebriated, but he was pleased with the reception they got. Of course, he had a feeling that if Tyler had sneezed at that moment, he could have drawn applause.

There was nothing out of the ordinary going on at the bar, but then, Quinn hadn't really expected anything to happen. What they needed to do was get in tight with the music scene, meet more musicians and find out what the word was on the street about Arnie and his sax.

After a few more songs Tyler announced that the band would break briefly then come back with more standards and some newer hits. He asked who in the crowd liked country music, and that drew another wave of enthusiastic applause. He promised they would also do some old Johnny Cash and Willie Nelson tunes when they came back, and after that, some Leonard Cohen.

"Half of them don't even know who Leonard Cohen is," Tyler said to Quinn as they left the stage. "But this is still a good night."

"Good, I'm glad," Quinn said.

"You don't see anyone here who looks like he might be a homicidal maniac, do you?" Tyler asked. Quinn realized he was only half joking.

"He's not going to look like a homicidal maniac. But no, I don't think he's in the crowd. I don't think he gets off work himself until late," Quinn told him.

He turned around to look for Danni. She had been accosted in a friendly but slightly drunken manner by a group of frat boys as she'd left the stage.

"If you'll excuse me, I need to go rescue Danni," Quinn said.

"No need." Tyler pointed to a very tall black man with heavily muscled arms and shoulders. "You didn't get a chance to meet

Max yet. Max enforces the age limit here and removes those who get too feisty. You'll love him."

"So long as he saves Danni from her teenage fan club, it will be great to meet Max," Quinn said.

It would probably be great to meet Max under any circumstances, he thought. Despite his size, the man didn't come on as a bully. He walked up to the group and spoke in a friendly manner. The canned music was playing, so Quinn couldn't hear his every word, but he heard enough to know that Max was nicely telling the guys that the lady needed a break.

A moment later Danni was at his side and they headed back to the table together, the band in their wake.

To make way for her to sit, Father Ryan rose. "Not bad," he told her. "Not bad at all. Of course, I wouldn't want to suggest that my pleas to God above allowed for any heavenly intervention."

They all laughed; then Quinn introduced Natasha and Father Ryan to Gus, Shamus and Blake.

Quinn saw that Jessica was running around taking and delivering orders, along with two other waitresses they had yet to meet. He excused himself and went to the bar, where a young female bartender was assisting Eric, who was at the far end handing a pitcher of beer to a customer. Quinn headed in that direction, and Eric saw him and lifted a hand as Quinn reached him.

"What can I get you?" Eric asked.

"I guess we'll take six waters. Looks like things are pretty crazy here."

Eric grinned. "Busy night. You guys are like lucky coins or something. People generally come and go, checking out a dozen clubs in a night. But we've got people staying tonight, and they're all drinking. I gotta admit, I was doubtful about how all this would work out, but you all sound good together."

"I admit, I was doubtful, too," Quinn admitted, raising his voice a little to be heard.

"We haven't been this busy since —" Eric broke off and looked down at the bar.

"Since?" Quinn prodded.

Eric looked back up at him ruefully. "Since Arnie Watson was sitting in with the band. That guy could play like . . . like he was magic or something. God, I love it when the music is good."

"You play?" Quinn asked him.

Eric laughed. "I dabble. New Orleans is the Hollywood of the South, you might say.

In Hollywood, every server is an actor. In New Orleans, every server is a musician."

"We're all something else at heart, huh?" Quinn asked. He thanked Eric for the waters, balanced the bottles between his hands and made his way back to the table.

By the time he reached it, Jessica was there, apologizing for being so busy and not getting to them earlier.

"Go for the money every time," Tyler told her. "Hey, haven't I seen you get up onstage sometimes?"

"Yeah, but not tonight. It's wild in here tonight," she said. "Too busy. Which is good — making money is nice."

"Can't argue with that," Tyler agreed.

"So you're having fun?" Jessica asked Danni and Quinn.

"Actually, yes," Danni admitted.

"I'm glad. I have to tell you, it's good to have you here. I feel safer."

"Don't forget Max," Quinn told her. "Max even makes *me* feel safe."

"Max is the best," Jessica agreed. "Anyway, it looks like you're all set, so if you'll excuse me . . ."

Father Ryan and Natasha said goodbye at that point, too, saying they were going to go barhopping.

"A voodoo priestess and a Catholic priest,

176

barhopping together," Quinn said. "Gotta love it."

"Natasha knows a lot of the local musicians. So does Father Ryan, actually. You'd be surprised how many musicians are Catholic and flock to his church," Danni said.

"Including me."

Quinn looked up quickly at the sound of Shamus's voice. He hadn't realized that Shamus had stopped talking to the other members of the band and was studying them.

Shamus had gotten himself a beer. He lifted his plastic cup to them. "Best priest around. No bullshit with him. He tells it like it is and lives in the real world. I'm not saying he tells everyone to go off and sin or anything like that. He just recognizes real life for what it is and accepts everyone just as she or he is, gay, straight, white, black or whatever."

"He's a good guy," Quinn agreed. "He must be pleased to have you as one of his parishioners?"

"Hope so."

"Back onstage," Tyler announced. "Break time is over."

The night passed, and everything went well, Quinn thought. It was a pity, really, that they were only there hoping to catch a killer, because it kept him from losing himself in the music as much as he wanted to. By the time the crowd thinned out and Friday night was just a memory, Danni was in her element, joking around with Tyler onstage, and harmonizing easily no matter which of the two lead singers — Tyler or Shamus — took a song.

It was after 3:00 a.m. when they quit for the night. As the rest of the band packed up their equipment, Tyler walked over to them. "The guys want to head down to Café du Monde. You guys game?"

"Sounds great," Quinn said, and Danni nodded in agreement.

In another half an hour they were heading through Jackson Square and on to Decatur. Most of the night's partyers had gone on to their homes, hotels or bed-and-breakfasts, but a few people still straggled along the street. Quinn looked back toward the square and the cathedral rising high in the night sky. There was something peaceful about the scene. The equestrian statue of Andrew Jackson grandly guarded the center of the square as usual. He always loved to find the right position in front of that statue just as the sun was falling and see the cathedral rising majestically behind it.

The carriage drivers had called it quits for

the night, as well. Everything seemed especially serene.

He hoped no one else had died that night.

He walked with his arm around Danni's shoulders. Billie was ahead of them, walking with Shamus and arguing the beauty of Scotland to Shamus, who let him know in no uncertain terms that there was a reason why Ireland was called the Emerald Isle.

Tyler came up behind Quinn. "You're armed, right?" he asked.

"Always," Quinn said.

"This could be the night the killer strikes again," Tyler said nervously.

"We're good," Quinn assured him. And, he thought, they were. He closely watched everyone who walked by — especially anyone who was alone and looked as if he was trying not to be noticed.

This late, the area was devoid of the street "statues," performers who posed without moving for hours on end, as well as the tarot readers and artists who so often worked in and around the square. But just as they were about to cross Decatur Street over to Café du Monde, Quinn paused.

"A street entertainer," he said softly.

"Pardon?" Danni asked him.

"I know where I've seen the kind of mask the guy who attacked Jeff, Lily and Rowdy wore. I saw one on a guy performing down here once. He was working with a ballerina 'statue.' Their act was pretty cool. He was like an animator who made her come to life. Their tips bucket was pretty full."

"We know those masks are sold all over," Danni reminded him.

He nodded.

"But you're thinking the killer might be accustomed to wearing one?" she asked softly.

"I am," he told her.

This late, there was plenty of room to sit at Café du Monde. The weather was beautiful, so they chose to sit outside. Other musicians in the city began to join them, eventually taking up a half dozen tables. As Quinn had hoped, they were all talking about what had happened.

"Someone out there is jealous," a young brunette said. "I mean, think about it. Holton and Larry were both phenomenal musicians. They could play so many instruments it's ridiculous — and all of them well."

"Yeah, but when it came to a sax, they reigned supreme," her companion, a man with long dark hair, said. Then he looked at Tyler and hastily added, "I mean, they weren't better than you, Tyler. You're just as awesome." A stricken look crossed his face. "Oh, wow, man, maybe that's not good."

"I'm ready to head to another city. New Orleans is home and I'll always love it, but it's not worth dying to play music here," a man two tables away said.

Quinn spoke up. "Remember, Holton Morelli and Larry Barrett let their killer in. So don't let anyone in unless it's your mom, your spouse or your kid."

"What about the holdup on the street? Think it was the same guy?" a woman asked.

"With a gun," someone muttered.

"We're all going to need guns," the brunette said. She rose suddenly. "I've got to go home, get some sleep," she said. Then she paused. "Um, can someone come with me?"

Her companion rose. "Of course. But I'm going to be on your couch. I'm not leaving till it's bright daylight, preferably sometime after noon," he said.

Soon after they left, others started to head out, everyone sorting themselves into groups of at least two so as not to be alone.

"Was this any help?" Tyler asked Quinn.

Quinn nodded.

"I'd be mad if it had been a waste of time," Billie said, yawning. "We'd better hope Bo Ray is doing better, because he's going to have to open the store tomorrow. These old bones are worn to shreds. And if you want me to play again tomorrow night, well, I'm going to need my beauty rest."

"I'm sure Bo Ray will be fine tomorrow, Billie," Danni assured him, touching his arm. "You should play all the time. Seriously."

When it came down to their group leaving, Shamus, Gus and Blake decided they would all stay at Blake's place. Shamus encouraged Tyler to join them.

"Can't. Promised some old friends I'd hang out at their place now."

"It's almost 5:00 a.m.," Shamus reminded him. "Who hangs out at 5:00 a.m.? Well, other than musicians."

"I'm good — promise."

"I don't know where he's going, but I'll see that he gets there," Quinn said.

The walk back to Danni's was almost surreal. Tyler offered to flag down a cab to get where he was going, but Quinn told him to forget that, and they would pick up the car when they got back to the house. There were very few people out, though when they passed one man coming out of his apartment, Quinn felt his muscles tighten. But he realized quickly that the man was in scrubs and reminded himself that for a lot of people, the day was just beginning. The big street scrubbers were all out, washing away the garbage and vomit that always accumulated heavily on a Friday night.

At the house, Wolf greeted them all excitedly. Danni ran up right away to check on Bo Ray, who, she said when she came back down, was sleeping deeply.

"How did he look?" Billie asked.

"I didn't wake him up to look at his cheeks," she said. "Don't worry. I'll be up by ten. You get your beauty rest."

"I won't be long," Quinn assured Danni. "I don't think. Where am I taking you?" he asked Tyler.

"Just over to Treme. I'm staying with Arnie's folks — trying to keep an eye on them," Tyler told him.

"Sounds good," Quinn said, then turned to Danni and smiled. She was obviously tired. But she still looked stunning. "I'll be right back," he told her.

She grinned. "I'll wait up," she said huskily.

"You don't mind?" Tyler asked. "I mean . . . leaving here?" he asked, looking at Danni.

"Wolf will let me know if anyone is around who shouldn't be," Danni told him. "Go on, both of you — leave!"

"I really will be right back," Quinn said with a wink.

"Oh, Lord. I'm going up to bed," Billie said. "Really, you two, get a room."

Danni laughed as he headed up the stairs. "We intend to," she promised him.

Billie just kept going, waving a hand in the air. Quinn told Tyler, "Let's go. Danni, even with Wolf —"

"I'll lock the door and not dream of opening it for anyone but you," she assured him.

Quinn led Tyler back out to the courtyard and his car.

Danni meant to wait up; she really did. The night had been a strange kind of high, and when she first came in she felt as if she was wired and would be up all night.

But she headed up the stairs to change, and before she knew it, barely having kicked off her shoes, she crashed down on her bed.

Billie didn't have to worry about what was going on in the house that night, she thought drily. She wasn't going to make it another two minutes.

She had no idea how long she had been sleeping when her phone rang.

With Quinn out and everything that had been going on in the city, the sound of it put her into a raw panic, and she answered it immediately.

Caller ID told her that it was Jenny, but all she could hear was shallow, rushed breathing.

"Jenny?"

"Danni!"

"Yes, what's wrong?"

"He — he was here."

"Who was there? Where are you?"

"Home. Brad is driving the guys. I was all locked in and then . . ." Her voice dropped. "Then I heard the door."

"I can barely hear you, Jenny. Are you okay?"

"He was at the door, Danni. He was at my door!"

"Who was it? Is he gone? You didn't answer, right? You just pretended you weren't there?"

"Yes," Jenny said in a whisper. "I think he's gone, but . . . Danni! He had no face. No, he had a face. He had a weird face. Like Jason from those slasher movies. No, not like that, not exactly. Jason's face is a hockey mask. This was a face, but —"

"You *saw* him?"

"Of course I saw him. I looked through the peephole."

"But he's gone now, right? You didn't answer the door and he's gone?"

"Right. I'm just scared. I need Brad to get back."

"You should call the police."

"And tell them what? There was a man at my door but now he's gone?"

"Call them. Tell them exactly what happened. They can see if there are prints on the door. They can look around the area for him. He could still be in the neighborhood and still wearing that mask."

"I don't want to hang up. I want you to keep talking to me. Brad will only be another ten minutes or so."

"Jenny, you need to call the police."

"Oh my God!" Jenny exclaimed suddenly.

"What?"

"He's back!"

"If he's knocking at the door just ignore him, hang up and call the police."

"He's trying to break it down, Danni! He's slamming something against it."

"Call the police! Hang up now. I'm on my way, but you need to dial 911 *now.*"

"Danni!"

Danni heard a tremendous crashing sound.

Then the line went dead in her hand.

When they reached the Watson home in Treme, lights were on. Quinn could see

Woodrow Watson's silhouette through the blinds.

"Someone waited up for you," Quinn said. "Or just woke up, I guess."

Tyler grimaced. "I feel like I have to be here for Arnie. And I'm pretty sure the Watsons feel like they have to watch over me for the same reason, for Arnie."

"Nothing wrong with that, Tyler. Well, I've got to get back. I'll see you tomorrow. Remember not to open your door to anyone you're not one hundred percent sure of."

"Oh, trust me. I won't," Tyler assured him.

It was an easy drive back at that time of the morning. Bourbon was open to traffic, the street cleaners were still out, and people who worked at the hotels and breakfast establishments were pretty much the only ones out, hurrying to work or leaning against walls on their smoke breaks.

Just after he hit the clicker to open the gate to the courtyard at Danni's house, he saw her bursting out of the house with Wolf on her heels.

He frowned as she veered in his direction, racing toward the car. She opened the door and jumped in, telling him, "Drive to Jenny and Brad's place — and hurry. You know where it is, right? We have to get there *now*!"

He did as he was told, but as he drove he

glanced at her, concern ripping through him. "What happened?"

"He was there — the killer. He showed up at her door *with the mask on!*"

"She didn't answer, right? Did she call the police?"

"No, she didn't answer the door."

"Where was Brad?"

"Doing what everyone is doing, taking their friends home."

"So did she call the police?"

"I don't think so. She called me because she was scared, but she thought he'd gone away. I kept telling her to hang up and call the police. But she kept talking, and then she said he was back and trying to break in, and then I heard a bang. And then her phone went dead."

"Tell me you dialed 911?" he said.

"Yes, immediately."

"But you were going over there, weren't you? Are you crazy?"

"I was with Wolf, and the police were on the way."

"But you knew I was coming right back!"

"Quinn, he was there. In Jenny's house."

"He has a gun!"

"And I had Wolf!"

"Damn it, you know better than to —"

"Just drive!"

188

He wasn't going to win an argument at that moment, Quinn knew, but he was still angry — and scared. The danger was really hitting home.

Jenny and Brad lived on Conti, on the other side of Bourbon. It took him next to no time to get there, and he thanked God that there were no street closings or parades to block the way. He drove up to the old Spanish residence where Brad and Jenny lived. It was wedged between two businesses. If she'd screamed, there wasn't a huge likelihood that she would have been heard.

He was glad to see police cars were pulling up in front just as he and Danni arrived. He hadn't even gotten the car into Park before Danni tore out of it.

"Jenny!" he heard her cry.

"Damn it," he swore, leaping out himself.

He saw that the door to the house was swinging open. And as he rushed to the door behind Danni, officers in uniform were already heading up the walk. An officer moved to stop them, but another one said, "It's Quinn. Let them be."

Quinn kept going. He wanted to catch Danni before she found her friend.

Before she found her friend dead, as he had found Lawrence Barrett. As Larue had found Holton Morelli.

But Danni shoved past everyone and was the first one inside. He came through the doorway behind her and nearly crashed into her back.

"Jenny!" she cried.

CHAPTER 7

"Jenny, where are you?" Danni called out frantically.

Quinn looked around the parlor of the modest home. Music stands were everywhere, and there was an upright piano with sheet music piled high on top. There were even more sheets of music mixed in with the magazines on the coffee table. A cup still half-filled with tea was there, as well, as if Jenny had been sitting there waiting for Brad when the knock had come at the door.

He caught Danni by the shoulders and spun her around. "Wait here," he said firmly.

Just as he spoke, Brad Henderson came tearing through his front door. He screamed Jenny's name, too, then saw Danni and Quinn, and strode toward them, hysteria rising in his voice. "Jenny, where's Jenny? What happened? What's going on?"

Quinn could see that he was shaking so badly his knees were going to give out. He caught Brad when he started to fall and pushed him toward the comfortable old sofa, where he collapsed. The officers were already moving through the house.

While he was helping Brad, Quinn realized he'd lost Danni. She was heading deeper into the house on the heels of the two patrolmen who had arrived first.

"Brad, just breathe," he ordered.

One of the officers who had been heading down the hall returned to the parlor.

"Who is this?" he demanded.

"Brad Henderson," Quinn said. "It's his house."

He heard Danni call out again. "Jenny! Where are you?"

And then he heard Danni choke out a sound like nothing he'd ever heard before. "Sit," he told Brad.

The officer who had come out nodded, obviously as afraid as Quinn was of what Danni and the other cop might have found and equally unwilling to let Brad head farther into the apartment to see the potential horror for himself.

Quinn raced along the hall that led past the dining area and kitchen and to the two bedrooms in back. His heart seemed to climb into his throat as he ran, and when he reached the door to Jenny and Brad's room, he realized he hadn't even been breathing.

He let out a breath. Everything was all right.

The second officer was leaning against the wall as if he had collapsed in relief.

Danni had found Jenny. She had found her beneath her dressing table, where she had hidden behind the decorative table skirt. With Danni's coaxing, she was emerging from her hiding place, which had barely been big enough to contain her.

Jenny was shaking uncontrollably. Danni was trying to help her get up without cracking her head. Quinn turned quickly and called down the hallway, "It's all right. Let Mr. Henderson through, please."

Brad came running down the hall. Jenny turned from Danni's arms into his, sobbing uncontrollably.

Quinn left the room and headed down the hallway to talk to the officer who had waited with Brad.

"This isn't just your average break-in," he said. "I'm calling Detective Larue and —"

"Already done, Mr. Quinn," the officer said. "Our sergeants have been drilling us every morning. We know what's going on."

"Thank you," Quinn told him. He was relieved that even the patrol officers were aware of what was happening. It wasn't that New Orleans hadn't seen its share of violence before; after the summer of storms, things had been very bad for a long time. Not that New Orleans had become a hotbed of evil, it was just those with evil intent would always take advantage of a bad situation. At that time, there had been a big difference in petty crime, as well. It was one thing to break a window and steal electronics; it was another to break into a grocery store for bread.

"Detective Larue should be here momentarily," the young officer told him. He cleared his throat. "Sir, I have to ask you and the others to be careful, this being a crime scene and all."

"Yes, of course."

Quinn's phone rang. Larue.

He was moments away, and he wanted them all to sit tight until he arrived.

That wouldn't be too hard, Quinn thought. When he returned to the bedroom, Jenny, Brad and Danni were seated at the end of the bed. Jenny was sobbing on Brad's shoulder.

Brad tried to soothe her. "I won't leave you again, not for a moment. I'll never leave you again, Jenny."

"You were so smart to hide," Danni said.

The second officer was still sagging against the wall, watching them uncomfortably.

"Larue is on his way," Quinn said.

As if he'd been relieved of a giant burden, the officer nodded, found the strength to stand straight and headed out to the parlor.

"Brad, did you notice in the parlor — was anything missing?"

"What?" Brad said.

"Was anything missing?"

"I — I don't know. I was thinking about Jenny. I didn't really look."

"We should do that now," Quinn said.

The two men left the room, and Danni held on to Jenny, trying to soothe her.

With Brad out of the room, Jenny clung to her. She had a strand of Danni's hair caught in her fingers and it hurt, but Danni didn't say a word. She just waited until Jenny felt ready to speak.

"The face!" Jenny said. "It was so . . . He made my skin crawl."

"He's a man, Jenny. Just a man. And if you saw that same mask during Mardi Gras, you wouldn't think anything of it."

"But I could see his eyes," Jenny said. "They were . . . awful."

"What color?" Danni asked.

Jenny was silent for a minute. Then she

195

said, "I — I don't know."

"You just told me you saw them."

"Yes! And I saw . . . I saw brutality and evil and . . ." She trailed off and turned to Danni. "But I can't remember the color at all. They might have been brown. Or gray. Dark, I think. But there seemed to be a strange light in them. Like fire, like . . . death."

A chill rippled down Danni's spine.

Just then Brad and Quinn walked back into the room. Brad sat by Jenny again, his arm around her shoulders.

Jenny loosened her death grip on Danni — and her hair.

Quinn had the ability to impose a sense of order and security on a situation. Danni realized that she still felt frozen, numb, herself when he came over and hunkered down before Jenny. "Detective Larue is on his way, Jenny, and we'll get everything down on paper. You were incredibly smart to hide."

"I should have been here. I have a gun," Brad said angrily.

"I have a feeling that this man knew you were gone. I suspect he's started watching and waiting, aware that no one is going anywhere alone anymore and that the word is out that people shouldn't open their doors, even to friends," Quinn said quietly.

"He was here — in our room!" Jenny said, sounding on the verge of hysteria. "He touched our things! I'll never be able to sleep here again."

"You will, but you don't need to sleep here tonight. You can come home with us," Danni said. "My dad's room is empty, and Billie and Bo Ray are both up in the attic."

"Thank you, Danni," Brad said. "And we will take you up on that for now." Brad looked at her. He clearly recognized that the two of them coming to her house wasn't the permanent solution he knew he was going to need.

Detective Larue came striding into the room. Quinn rose quickly and said, "Jenny, Detective Larue is here now, so we need you to think hard and tell us everything that happened."

"He's out there," Jenny said. "He's out there . . . in our city. He's killed and killed . . . and he was here. In our house. In our *room.*"

"From the beginning, Jenny," Quinn said.

Larue glanced at Quinn. "It will be easier if we do this down at the station. Jenny, we're going to let the crime scene techs come through and see if they can find any evidence. He was in here, right? He might have touched something. He might have left some evidence. It's best if we leave that to them, and we can go to the station and sit, have some coffee and let you tell the story as it happened, okay?"

"I'll get you a jacket, baby," Brad said.

Jenny suddenly stood and squared her shoulders. "No — he was in the closet. I heard him, and I peeked and . . . he was wearing gloves, Detective. Even I know that means there won't be any prints. But he was in the closet, so I don't think we should touch anything in there. God knows why. Oh! I saw his hair. He had this dark kind of punk-crazy hair. God! He was creepy. How he can walk down the streets and not be seen, I just don't know."

Danni said quietly, "Because he gets rid of the mask the second he's away. And the hair is probably a wig that's easily removed. And there aren't many people out when he's . . . when he's attacking people. He operates in the one sweet spot when New Orleans is fairly quiet, partyers worn out and early people just getting up."

"Let's head out, shall we?" Quinn said.

They'd already been up all night. By the time they reached the police station, the sun was well on its way up.

Danni's phone rang. She answered it and

198

was greeted by Billie swearing, which didn't happen often. But despite his exhaustion of the night before, he'd gotten up early when he heard Bo Ray moving around, and they had seen Wolf sitting by the backyard door and not holding sentinel in front of Danni's room. They'd immediately realized that Danni and Quinn weren't there and started looking around for an explanation.

"A note!" Billie was saying now. "A phone call, a text message!" he chastised her. "Don't you know that this old ticker has already taken quite a lickin' with the Cafferty clan, eh?"

Danni apologized, trying to explain without missing what was going on around her.

"I'm grateful as hell that your friend is safe," Billie said. "But next time you remember to phone home, girl, you got me?"

Danni caught Quinn watching her. When she hung up, he said softly, "I overheard. And he has a point. But then, I have a few words for you, too, when the time is right."

She glared at him. He wouldn't have done any differently — and they both knew it. But she didn't say a word.

Larue had arranged chairs in a conference room. He had a tape recorder going, and he identified himself and those in the room, explaining that Jenny LaFleur would be

199

describing an event in which her home had been broken into by the suspected killer of Holton Morelli and Lawrence Barrett. Then he added, "And possibly the murder of Arnold Watson, as well."

Jenny went through what had happened minute by minute. "Brad had just left," she said. "He'd only been gone a minute or two. Then I heard a knock on the door. I thought it might be Brad, that maybe he'd forgotten something, but he has a key, so to be safe I looked through the peephole. I saw the man there, and it was like he had no face. Later I realized it was a mask, but right then he was just this scary faceless person, so I backed away and pretended no one was there. A few minutes later I went back to the door to check, and he was gone. I called Danni to tell her what had happened. She told me to call the police, but I felt stupid then. What was I going to say? A creepy freak had knocked at my door? Then . . . then I heard something slam against the door while I was still on with Danni, and I jumped and dropped the phone. I saw the wood start cracking around the bolt, so I ran to my room. I thought hiding under the bed was too obvious and that he would definitely look in the closet, so I wedged myself under the dressing table."

"A very smart spur-of-the-moment plan, Miss LaFleur," Larue told her. "What then? You saw him in your room, right?"

Jenny trembled. "A little. I heard him — heard his footsteps. I saw him at the closet, and I'm pretty sure he looked under the bed. I saw his hands when he was at the closet. He was wearing gloves."

"What kind of gloves?" Larue asked.

"Flesh-colored, or maybe clear. They made it look like he had mannequin hands," she said. She sat back suddenly. "I heard the sirens, and I think he left then. I just froze there. The next thing I knew, Danni was there in my room."

"Okay, let's go back a step," Larue said. "You looked through the peephole at him. You saw the mask. Can you tell me anything else?"

"No," Jenny said.

Larue produced the drawing the police artist had done.

"That's him," Jenny said.

"Do you remember the color of his eyes?" Larue asked.

"No. He was on the step," Jenny said. "The light was bad. I remember they . . . they seemed to glow. I couldn't see the color, though. I told Danni that. I remember that they scared me to death. I kept think-

201

ing they were demon eyes, filled with malice and hatred and evil . . . but I can't remember a color."

"That's all right," Larue said. "Maybe it will come to you later."

"He was like a freak, like a mannequin. He must have been obvious. How come no one saw him? How come the police couldn't find him?"

"Our officers started looking for him as soon as we got Miss Cafferty's call, Miss LaFleur," Larue told her.

"But they didn't catch him," she whispered.

"Jenny, the police did their best," Quinn said. "I'm sure he strips off the disguise as soon as he hits the street. And there are courtyards and alleyways everywhere. I'm certain that before he ever knocks on someone's door he's scoped out exactly how he's going to get away."

Jenny looked at Brad. "What are we going to do?" she said desperately.

"Get some sleep," Quinn suggested. He looked at Larue. "We're taking them back to Danni's house. After a few hours of sleep, maybe Jenny will remember something else."

"All right. That's reasonable," Larue said.

"Before we go, though, there's one more

thing," Quinn said.

Danni looked at him in surprise.

"Brad Henderson, for the record, please tell Detective Larue — and the recorder — what you found to be missing when you looked around the parlor."

"My harmonica, a tambourine, some sheet music and my sax," Brad said.

"Thank you," Larue said, meeting Quinn's eyes with a curious look.

Jenny spoke up again, her voice hard. "He left our place in a mask and gloves, carrying all that stuff — and no one caught him?"

"Jenny," Brad said gently. "You're alive, probably thanks to Danni calling the police and their sirens scaring him away. Let's be grateful."

Jenny began to shake again. "Oh, I am, I am grateful. But still . . . that freak is still out there. What if he comes back?"

"He won't come back," Quinn said.

Larue looked at Quinn questioningly.

"He took what he wanted. He'll move on to someone else next. But we do have to catch him — quickly. The next person might not be so smart or so lucky."

When they got back to the house, Quinn was pleased to see that Bo Ray was doing much better. His chipmunk cheeks were down to slightly puffy, and he was even managing to down some soft scrambled eggs. He hadn't shaved, so he looked a little the worse for wear, but not too bad. Bo Ray was a good-looking young man in his early twenties, and in much better shape in every way than when they'd met on the first case Danni and Quinn had worked together. He'd committed no crimes himself, but he'd become involved with some very dark characters because of his drug addiction. Father John Ryan had seen to it that he went to rehab, and Bo Ray had proved to be a valuable asset ever since. He was brave in the best way, Quinn thought. Even when he was afraid, he still did what needed to be done. To Quinn, that was real courage.

Billie had cooked, but he looked both aggravated and exhausted, his white hair going every which way. He was clearly still angry with Danni; Quinn could tell by the way he looked at her. But she would weather the storm. When you got right down to it, Quinn thought, he was still angry with her himself. Given what they knew about this killer, it had been insane for her to run out in the night, even if she had called the police first.

Bo Ray forgot his breakfast when Jenny and Brad followed Quinn and Danni into the kitchen. Luckily it was still a few minutes before opening time and they were able to sit comfortably in the kitchen while Jenny told her tale again. Wolf sat with his big nose on her lap, as if he knew she was upset and was trying to make it better.

"I'll call Father Ryan and Natasha and bring them up to speed," Billie said. "Then I'm taking a nap. You four, go to sleep and let Bo Ray open the shop. Night will come again soon enough."

"Night . . . how can I play again tonight? Or any night?" Jenny asked, looking at Brad with terrified eyes.

"It's how we make our living," he reminded her.

"I — I — Danni, you have to forget about playing that other place. You have to. You're my friend, and you have to come play with us. I need to work to survive, but I'm . . . I'm terrified. I can't go back out in the dark, not without you there to keep me safe."

Danni turned to Quinn. "She's right. We can divide and conquer, you know. I can sit in with Jenny and Brad, and you can go to La Porte Rouge."

It made sense, of course. But while he prided himself on not being a chauvinist, he couldn't help but think that he wasn't letting Danni go off alone to the Midnight

Royale Café with Brad and Jenny.

"Let's think on it, shall we?" he asked. "But don't worry — we'll come up with something."

"Why don't we do it the other way?" Billie asked. "You go with Brad and Jenny. Danni and I will stick with La Porte Rouge. I won't leave her, and we'll ask Father Ryan and Natasha to come again, too. Not to mention that nothing happens until after the set, when things go all to hell."

Quinn still didn't like the suggestion, though he had to admit it did make sense, and that if he weren't so ridiculously in love with Danni, he would freely admit it was the best plan.

He could also get Larue to assign a man to La Porte Rouge. Besides, what Billie had said was true: the killer seemed to attack around five, after closing, when he knew the local musicians would just be heading home. He attacked when he could wear a mask and pretty much count on going unnoticed.

"That's even better," Jenny said cheerfully.

Danni looked at her. "Oh?"

"No offense," Jenny said. "But Quinn just . . . well, he looks a lot fiercer than you, that's all."

Brad shrugged. "So Quinn is fierce-

206

looking, huh?"

"Safety in numbers," Quinn said quickly.

"So that's the plan?" Jenny asked.

"Temporarily," Quinn said. "Probably."

"Go to bed," Billie said. "And I mean to sleep."

They all rose as one and headed up the stairs. Danni and Quinn showed their guests to Angus's old room and gave them towels and whatever else they might need, including sweats to sleep in, since they had left Brad and Jenny's house without thinking to pack anything, and no one had been in the mood to stop there once they left the police station.

Once they were alone in the bedroom they shared, Quinn tried not to jump down her throat in anger, but he had to say something. "What were you thinking? This guy is a *maniac.* First, you ran out of the house without letting anyone know where you were going. Second —"

"Quinn! I didn't act foolishly — I called the police. I knew we would get there at pretty much the same time. You would have done exactly what I did."

"Danni, I've been in the military. I've been a cop."

"And you taught me how to shoot."

"Did you have a gun on you?"

She drew in a breath and stared at him. "We can't do this — argue like this."

"You can't risk your life that way — not even for Jenny!"

"Shh! She'll hear you."

"I'm speaking as quietly as I can. And then you suggest we split up. Are you crazy?"

"No, I'm just doing what my father would have done. Quinn, you can't always be the conquering hero. We're in this together. And right now I really am exhausted," she said. "We can talk about this more when we've had a few hours' sleep."

It was true. He had to shut up.

"Fine," he said quietly then removed his clothes neatly, pulled back the bedcovers and crawled in.

A moment later he felt her slide into her side of the bed. She didn't touch him.

He lay there for a while, knowing he needed to sleep, his mind racing. He didn't like to go to sleep when they were upset at each other like this. It hurt. At the same time, he kept thinking about the things Jenny had said.

Demon eyes?

Was the killer actually some kind of a demon, and was there really something special about the missing sax?

He didn't know. The killer sounded like flesh and blood.

And the greatest evil in the world could exist in the human psyche.

He hated lying here like this, next to Danni, yet so far apart.

Apparently Danni did, too. She rolled closer, as if unconsciously trying to get more comfortable. But she had come to bed naked, as had he. And her flesh burned against his body, soft and silken.

He waited a moment, smiling to himself. She'd made the first move.

He rolled over, taking her into his arms, feeling the firm pressure of her breasts against his chest. He kissed her lips, and his mouth grew more forceful, his tongue pressing deeper as he was instantly aroused by the mere taste and feel of her.

It was all she needed. She crawled atop him. The soft tease of her hair fell over his flesh as she leaned down, planting slow, lazy kisses on his chest. The length of her body rubbed erotically against his as she rose to find his lips again.

"Danni, I just —"

"You really don't know when to shut up, do you?" she asked softly.

He was afraid she was going to move away, so he quickly said, "I do . . . trust me," as he gathered her in his arms, rolled with her and took the lead, returning every kiss she'd delivered to his flesh with a kiss of his own to hers. Never a passive lover, she arched and writhed and rose against him, and soon they were locked together, the world around them disappearing as they made love. By the time they reached a searing climax they were panting and damp, lying side by side, truly exhausted in the best way. He pulled her back into his arms.

She started to arch away from him. "Quinn . . ."

He pulled her back down to him and nuzzled her ear softly. "You really don't know . . ."

She laughed softly and whispered in return, "Oh, but I do."

They made love again, and it was beautiful. Finally they slept, bodies completely entangled.

Danni knew that Quinn worried about her when he wasn't with her, but she didn't intend to give an inch on what she had done the night before. She really hadn't behaved stupidly; she'd made sure to call the police. In retrospect, she should have called him, too, and told him to head straight to Jenny and Brad's, but still, he would have done the same thing in her shoes.

She knew, too, that Billie's suggestion of who should go where tonight made the most sense. She was sure Quinn knew it, too. He just wasn't great at admitting it when he had to accept a solution he didn't wholeheartedly embrace, so she didn't say anything to him later, when he simply let the plans for the evening ride. He had, however, she learned, called Father Ryan and Natasha, who had both promised to come to La Porte Rouge and stay there. Both had been appalled to learn that Jenny had nearly been attacked, and Father Ryan — being a fighting man's priest, for certain — was doubly determined to keep an eye on Danni.

Maybe, she mused, that was enough to allow Quinn to accept the situation.

There wasn't much of the day left by the time they were all awake, had made some kind of meal that was breakfast, lunch and dinner rolled into one and gotten dressed and ready for the night.

That took longer than usual, since Brad and Jenny had to borrow from Quinn and Danni, since neither of them had much of an appetite for going back to their house just yet.

Danni was much taller than Jenny, though,

and Quinn had several inches on Brad, as well as a bigger build generally. Bo Ray and Billie both offered up whatever they had, and in the end Brad settled on a pair of jeans from Bo Ray and a T-shirt from Quinn. Danni had a dress she didn't wear often, because she considered it too short, which made it perfect for Jenny.

Bo Ray assured them that he had the store under control, but despite his confidence, they had no intention of leaving until the shop was closed, the house was all locked down and Wolf was prepared to guard Bo Ray and the premises while they were out.

Quinn left first with Brad and Jenny. Before Danni was ready to head out with Billie, she paused to ask Bo Ray, "You're sure you're fine? You know not to open the door. I'll be just a few blocks away, up on Bourbon. Well, you know that. If anything happens —"

"I'll call 911 and then you," Bo Ray said. "And I'm fine. Well, I'm fine 'cause you're leaving me Wolf. I wouldn't be so fine if you weren't."

She smiled, hunkered down to give Wolf a big hug before leaving and then kissed Bo Ray on the cheek, as well.

Billie — despite his grumpiness of the morning — was in a good mood as they made their way through the Saturday night crowds that already thronged Bourbon Street. He didn't even complain when a slightly inebriated young woman leaning over a balcony above them managed to pelt him almost in the face with a strand of brightly colored Mardi Gras beads.

At least she called down an apology.

When they reached La Porte Rouge, a folksinger was entertaining the crowd. The young woman had a lovely voice, Danni thought, but her songs were slow, and people weren't paying much attention. When she finished one number, Danni nudged Billie, and they both made a point of clapping enthusiastically, drawing the attention and finally the applause of the other patrons.

Tyler was alone, sitting at one of the round high-top tables near the stage. Danni claimed a stool beside him and explained that they were down one guitarist, and told him what had happened.

Tyler listened gravely. "Well, I'm glad we have you," he said cheerfully.

"Really?" she said disbelievingly.

"Yeah, really. Jessica was saying the other night that there are a few numbers she'd like to do with you if there's a chance for her to join us onstage. Now, that would be great — the two of you up there together. All those hormonal frat boys would go crazy."

"Great," Danni murmured.

"Frat boys pay with good money for lots of drinks," Tyler said.

"Speaking of, I'm getting a soda to keep the old pipes wet," Billie said, walking over to join them. "Danni?"

"Water, Billie, thanks," she said.

When he had gone, Tyler looked at Danni worriedly. "Are you guys sure it has something to do with a sax? Maybe this guy is after a song. You said he took some of their sheet music."

"And a sax," Danni reminded him. "You have no idea where the special sax could be, right?"

He shook his head. "And I was his best friend. Well, here, of course."

"What do you mean, *here*?"

"He was close with a bunch of guys when he was in the service. He was a staff sergeant and squad leader. He had three fire team leaders under him, who each had three or four men under them. His best friend in the service was Corporal Kevin Hart — one of his fire team leaders — who hailed from Houma. I can't imagine that Arnie kept secrets from me, but if anyone else knows anything, it would be Kevin."

"So he would have been discharged about the same time as Arnie, right? Is he back in Houma? We can take a ride out and talk to him."

"He's not in Houma," Tyler told her.

"Oh?"

"Kevin stepped on a mine. He's been up at Walter Reed getting his prosthesis and working on his physical therapy."

"Oh," Danni said softly. "Maybe we'll have to take a trip up to see him."

Tyler smiled. "Maybe we can get a friend with one of the veterans' organizations to send the band up for the day. We could play for the patients. And I'd like to meet Kevin, too. Any friend of Arnie's, you know?"

"We could just call him," Danni suggested.

"You want a dead man's secrets from one of his best friends?" Tyler asked. "A fellow soldier? You need to see him face-to-face."

Billie came back with his soda and Danni's water. In a few minutes Blake, Gus and Shamus came in, as well. They were disappointed that Quinn wasn't coming, but Shamus said, "Not to be crude, darlin', and forgive me, but I believe we're lucky we got the eye candy."

Jessica had come by with her tray on her

hip, checking whether she could get anyone anything. "Now, now, Shamus. Quinn is the eye candy to some of us, you know."

"Big talk from a little girl who never goes out," Shamus said.

"Ah, but I have a child, remember?" Jessica said.

Gus laughed. "And you turned us all down before that, too. But fine. To you, Quinn would have been the eye candy. I'm just glad it worked out so I'm the happy one, no offense intended."

"None taken," Jessica assured him. "Danni, did Tyler tell you? There are a couple of duets I'd love to do with you. I'll give you a list. Of course, I can only go up when the other girls are on the floor and it's not too busy, but if you don't mind . . ."

"I'd love it," Danni told her.

Jessica went back to work, the folksinger left the stage and the band went to set up. Danni discovered she wanted more water and walked up to the bar. It was still relatively early, but people were flocking in. The female bartender who had been on the other night came up and introduced herself to Danni. She was Sharon Eastman, and she said she worked weekends and sometimes Thursday. Danni asked for her water then stayed at the bar to watch as the band continued to set up.

"On your own tonight?" someone asked from behind her. "Well, not totally. I see that Billie is here. Where's Quinn?"

She turned around. Eric Lyons was leaning on the bar, smiling at her.

"Quinn is sitting in with friends at another bar tonight," she told him.

"Ah. Well, it's fun to have you all. Hope he comes back, too," Eric said.

"I'm sure he will. He and Billie love to play together."

"And you?"

"Well, I don't really play."

"You're good at harmony — not everyone is. Trust me, I see — and hear — it all here," he said.

"Thanks."

"I love to watch," Eric said. "People in general. See, watch Gus and the way he looks at Jessica."

"She's a pretty girl."

"He has a thing for her — he always has. Unrequited love."

"She's not married?"

"No, never was."

"Maybe she's still in love with the child's father."

"Maybe," Eric said with a shrug. "Who knows? None of us ever met him. Anyway, she's a great worker with a great voice."

Just then Blake waved to let her know they were going on. Before she could get up, Tyler said something to him then walked over to her.

"Jessica is going to do a song while it's still not too crazy," he said.

"Wonderful!" Danni said.

And it was. Jessica sang a popular Adèle song, and she hit every note with clarity and beauty.

When she came down from the stage, Danni was grateful that they only expected her to do backup — and that Shamus or Tyler would be singing lead.

"You're phenomenal!" Danni told her, stopping on her own way to the stage.

Jessica blushed. "Once upon a time I thought I'd be singing for a living. Not that long ago, either. Well, life has a way of getting you, you know?"

She walked on to pick up her tray, still blushing as customers complimented her and asked for their drink orders.

He studied the picture again. So it wasn't the LaFleur girl. Oddly enough, he admired the way she had eluded him. Brad might have been tougher to deal with, but he'd watched and waited till Brad was gone. He knew what Brad was doing and just how long it would take him to come back.

He thought about Jenny LaFleur. One of the beautiful people. One of the inner circle. And more clever than he had imagined. He smiled slightly, thinking that he would have enjoyed actually getting his hands on her.

It was changing. All changing. He'd been timid at first. Of course, he'd thought he could trick Arnie and kill him without ever being suspected — and get the sax. Unfortunately, it hadn't worked out that way. But he felt as if he was evolving, as if he was becoming a better killer, even if he'd had to run tonight.

They were afraid. They were all growing more and more afraid. They were grouping together; they were being careful never to be alone. That was because Danni Cafferty and that has-been football hero she was with now had gotten involved. That bastard Quinn knew there would be safety in numbers.

Eventually, though, they would be like rats. Rats in a cage. Arguing and growing impatient.

They would have to give up eventually and start acting normally again. They would go crazy; they would want their freedom and their own lives back again.

And now . . .

Now he knew there were other places to look.

There was Danni Cafferty's place. It would bear study and time.

There was the Watson house . . .

He had time.

He just had to wait and continue to do what he was doing, observe then take advantage of whatever opportunity came his way. It didn't matter to him; he had time.

Because they didn't see him. Because he was invisible.

Invisible, as he had always been.

And would always be.

Unless he had the sax.

Yes, he could wait and watch. And grab opportunity wherever it showed itself.

He smiled, because he knew. He was gaining power. He was after a magic sax — and that made *him* magic, too. Because he knew the city and he knew the night, and he knew how to blend into the darkness and the crowds so he could carry out his search.

He was invisible. He was invisible even when he was in plain sight.

CHAPTER 8

Because either Jenny or Brad had been targeted, Quinn knew it was important that he was where he was, but he still chafed with worry at not being with Danni. Every chance he got, he texted Father Ryan.

Father Ryan texted back every time that all was well.

During a break, Quinn sat with Jenny and Brad, along with Steve and Luis, their fellow bandmates. He didn't have to bring up what had happened. Brad and Jenny did that for him.

"I was working on a song," Brad said. "And it was in with the music that was taken. Not that it really matters. The song is in my head just as much as it was on paper." He looked at Quinn. "None of the big labels are tripping over themselves to sign us, but Jenny and I have a small indie label, and we make a little money each year off our sales. Thanks to iTunes and Amazon and other avenues, we do all right."

"So you think this guy has been after songs all along?" Steve asked. "Not that special sax of Arnie's?"

Quinn looked at him. "You know that Arnie had a special sax even before the murders, right? Did most people?"

"If you grew up around here, yeah," Steve said. He smiled a little awkwardly. "Anyone who was part of the Survivor Set knew all about it."

"The Survivor Set?" Quinn asked.

"The high school was flooded during the summer of storms," Brad said. "You're older than us, so you'd graduated by then. But we were shipped all over the country so we could finish high school. There were a couple of places that didn't close, though, like one private school in the Garden District, and they took in some of us. They — whoever *they* are — chose who got to stay because we lived in the French Quarter or Garden District or other areas that were still above water. There were about twenty of us, and by some weird coincidence, every one of us had some kind of musical or artistic ability. Most of us were musicians, but there were a few dancers and actors and actresses in there, and one or two artists. Danni was part of the group, so you probably know most of this already. We lucked out and got to stay, but a whole lot of kids did have to leave the area or just lost a year and graduated late."

"So everyone in this group knew about Arnie's special sax?" Quinn asked.

"Sure. In fact, there's a picture of Arnie holding it above his head while he ran across a flooded street. It made the papers all over the country."

"So all of you became close friends?" Quinn asked.

"We were the fish out of water, I guess. Public school kids suddenly in pretty elite private schools. So, yeah, we hung around with each other a lot," Steve said.

"But you know how it goes," Brad said. "Eventually things got back to normal. Well, almost back to normal. Some families never returned after that summer. New people moved into the city. We graduated and all kind of drifted apart. Even those of us who stayed in the city didn't necessarily stay friends. And remember, Arnie was a few years older than we were. The oldest guys graduated soon after the summer of storms."

"And I wasn't one of them," Luis said. "I met these goofballs later."

"So Arnie was in this group. And Tyler,

too, I take it?" Quinn asked.

Jenny gasped suddenly. "Quinn, Holton Morelli was a guest lecturer when we were there," she said. "And Lawrence Barrett was a teaching assistant." She met his eyes, and there was real fear in hers. "Is this person killing off people who were part of the Survivor Set?" she asked, her face pale. "If so, he won't stop. He'll come back for Brad and me."

Quinn didn't really know what this new information meant, but he quickly said, "Remember, Morelli and Barrett weren't really part of your set — they were teachers. And I don't believe these killings have anything to do with surviving the storms. I think they have to do with Arnie's sax. A sax was taken during each holdup."

He doubted his words afforded her any kind of reassurance when she said, "But still . . ." and looked as if she was going to collapse into her chair.

"It would be nice if you could give me a list of who was in that Survivor Set," Quinn said. "And if you can think of anyone else still playing in the city who was part of it."

Jenny looked at him with wide eyes. "I know who else was part of it," she told him thickly. "Someone who was actually in Arnie's class. One of the musicians who was attacked on the street. Jeff Braman."

They were trouble, Michael Quinn and Danni Cafferty.

She didn't remember. No one remembered. Because he'd been no one.

He hadn't known then that he was magic. He'd been invisible, always invisible even in plain sight. But Danni Cafferty . . .

She hadn't even been one of them.

But they had wanted her. She had been beautiful even then, and courteous. Old Angus would have strung her up if she hadn't been courteous.

But she'd never even seen him.

He liked to think now that it had been because of his power. Back then he hadn't realized he was magic, that his invisibility was good, something he would need to use at the right time in his life.

But even when she was courteous . . .

She didn't really see him. She'd never seen him. She didn't see him now.

She didn't have the sax, though.

Neither did Quinn. But there was that old skeleton who lived with them . . .

That didn't even matter. There was a slim possibility that the old Scot had the sax, though it might be difficult to discover whether he did or not. Still, there were always chances. Things to be done.

Danni . . . she thought she was magic, too. Like old Angus.

He smiled to himself. She needed to see his magic. He would have to show her.

Oh, yes. He was, one way or another, at one time or another, going to show her.

He'd always been in awe of her. Watching from a distance.

But now he was going to find a way.

He would force her to see his magic. And then he would never have to look at her again and admit that she'd never seen him, invisible or not. He didn't know if he still coveted her and was in awe of her . . .

Or if he hated her beyond all measure.

It didn't matter. He had to deal with her.

He had to make sure that she saw him — and then that she never saw anything again.

Danni found herself relaxing onstage this time, and she enjoyed seeing Billie enjoying himself, whether he was playing a solo sax part or duetting with Tyler.

Natasha and Father Ryan were there, just as they had promised. They seemed to be having a great time, listening to the music and talking animatedly between songs. It was almost midnight when Danni was shocked to see an elegant older woman walk into the club. It was Hattie Lamont, the socialite they'd worked with on the case concerning the Henry Hubert painting.

Being Hattie, she was dressed to the nines. Her iron-gray hair was cut short and curved under her aged but elegant chin. She was in jeans and a ruffled blouse that was both casual and ever-so-slightly elegant. Danni was idly keeping the beat with the tambourine when Hattie walked in and looked around for a minute, and then Father Ryan rose to greet her and lead her to the table.

Billie was in the middle of a soulful tune; his eyes were closed as he felt the music.

Danni smiled. Billie and Hattie had not begun their relationship as friends. Now, however, the two "spent a wee bit of time together, here and there," as Billie put it.

When the song ended the applause was almost deafening. Tyler and the other band members bowed, accustomed to the approval of crowds. Billie blushed and did the same, and then noticed that Hattie had joined Father Ryan and Natasha, and his blush turned darker than a barrel of boiled crawfish.

He was due to sit out a few numbers, and Danni grinned at him as he left the stage to join the others. It was fun to watch him head for the table and greet Hattie.

During the next break she went to join them. Because the table was small, the band headed to the bar for the break.

Billie was sitting close to Hattie, looking just a little awkward. Hattie didn't seem to notice, but then, Hattie could manage herself in any situation.

"Dreadful, what's going on," she whispered to Danni, and Danni was suddenly certain the woman had come not to see Billie but because she'd heard that Danni was playing. Apparently, Father Ryan had the same impression.

"Anything here that I'm not seeing?" he asked Danni.

She kept her voice low. "No, or if there is, I'm not seeing it, either. But last night the killer stole some things from Jenny and Brad's house. Instruments and sheet music. One of the instruments was a sax. I'm sure the killer is looking for Arnie Watson's special sax."

"And Tyler really has no idea of where it is?" Natasha asked.

"Not a clue," Danni said.

"Strange, when you consider Tyler was his closest friend," Father Ryan mused.

"He mentioned that Arnie was close with one of his army friends. Kevin Hart, a guy from Houma. Unfortunately, we can't just drive over and talk to him. He's at Walter Reed."

"Injured?" Father Ryan asked.

"Severely. He lost a leg, so he's being fitted for a prosthesis and getting physical therapy. He's been there six months. He rotated out with Arnie," Danni said. "Tyler said that he'd like to see Kevin, too. Actually, he thinks the whole band should go and play for the patients. I don't know if that's possible, but it's certainly one way to make the trip seem casual. But I don't know if we need to make it casual. Although if he doesn't believe we're all really looking out for Arnie's reputation, he may not talk to us."

Hattie waved a dismissive hand in the air. "I've been there many times. As you know, my late husband and I were quite fond of giving his money away. I could never see a better cause than helping those who fought for our country. If you wish to go and entertain them, just let me know." She offered Danni a wry grin. "I know all the right people. No doubt you could find the right people yourselves, but I can speed things up for you."

"I don't know," Danni said. "I'll have to talk to Quinn."

"Just let me know, dear," Hattie said.

Tyler called to Danni, and she headed back up onstage. When Billie came up for his next number, he definitely looked nervous. Danni loved that he cared so much now that Hattie was in the room. She whispered to him, "Just believe that it *is* Arnie's special sax."

He gave her a smile, then played beautifully.

The night wore on. Bit by bit, the crowd thinned, though Father Ryan, Natasha and Hattie were still hanging in. Finally Tyler announced the last song.

The waitresses and Eric were trying hard to clean up quickly, so as soon as she was done helping the band, Danni quickly collected all the glasses her group had used and brought them up to the bar. Eric offered her a smile of gratitude. "I never mind the hours," he told her. "But when it's time to leave . . . well, it's time to leave."

"I don't blame you," she told him, looking around. "You here alone now? I don't see Jessica or any of the other waitresses."

"I always let them go as soon as I can," he said. "See you tomorrow?"

"I think so," she told him.

"But no Quinn?"

She laughed. "Probably not — status quo for a while, I think, and then we may start sitting in somewhere else. But who knows? We aren't real musicians, anyway."

He laughed. "Define *real* when it comes to anything in the arts," he said. "You look and sound real enough to me up there. And your man can play a mean guitar. Your friend is really good, too."

"He is, isn't he? He learned the bagpipes first — guess that explains why he's full of hot air," she joked. Eric grinned, and she told him good-night.

When she returned to the table it was empty. Max had just come in, leaving his post at the door. She bade him good-night, too, and realized that Billie and the rest of her friends, along with the band, were standing outside on a litter-strewn and rapidly emptying Bourbon Street. Here and there people still laughed and walked — or staggered — along, off to get pizza or beignets, or heading back to wherever they were going to rest their heads.

"You hungry, love?" Shamus asked.

"Not tonight. I think I'm just going to head home. What about you all?" she asked anxiously.

"We're covered," Tyler told her. "We're going for pizza tonight, and I have my car, so we'll eat, then I'll drop everyone off and head on to the Watson house. What about you all? No one alone, right?"

"We're good," Danni assured him. There were goodbyes all around, and then the band headed down the street in search of food.

"All right, down to us," Father Ryan said. "Billie is going to see Hattie home, and I'm your escort, Miss Cafferty — well, I shall be seeing you to your house, and then Natasha on to hers, where I will retrieve my car."

"Wonderful," Danni said. "Except that . . ." She hesitated, remembering what Eric had said about Billie and how well he played.

What if the killer had seen Billie play and thought the same thing? Would he have thought Billie was so good that he just might have been playing a very special sax?

"You be careful," Billie told Danni.

"I'm with a man of God and a priestess for the universe," she said. "I'll be fine. But Billie, I don't like this. I say we all walk to my house, I'll get the car, and we'll get Hattie home."

"But Danni dear, it's a matter of only a few blocks to my home," Hattie protested. "I got here all on my own, you know."

"Honestly, Hattie, at this moment I think you might be fine other than bumping into a run-of-the-mill mugger — which would be bad, too, of course. But Billie has been playing with the band."

"First time ever on a stage here, Danni, so who'd be after me?" he asked.

"I'd rather not find out because he attacks you," Danni told him.

Billie let out a deep sigh and wagged a finger at her. "This from the one who took off like a bat out of hell just last night!"

Father Ryan lifted a hand and looked toward the night sky. "Lord and Mother Mary, help me. Both of you listen to me. We will all walk Danni home. Then Natasha. Then we get in my car, and Billie and I drop Hattie off, and then I drop Billie and head on home." He looked firmly at each of them in turn. "And there will be no arguments."

There were none.

Billie and Hattie took the lead. Behind them, Danni walked between Father Ryan and Natasha.

As they walked, Father Ryan asked Danni, "What's your feeling on this case? You and Quinn would know . . . Are we looking at greed and obsession or cold-blooded murder? Or is there really something . . . special about that instrument?"

"I don't know, Father. I tried to find something relevant in the book my father left me, but . . . I just don't know."

"Can it be one person? Just one person doing this?" Natasha asked. "I keep my eyes and ears open, both to those I know and those who come for readings. And all I've heard so far is fear."

"Just one person can cause nations to fall, remember," Father Ryan said. "And the police can hardly go door-to-door demanding to know if someone owns a Mardi Gras mask and a trench coat — and if they've been brutally murdering musicians."

"That person might have killed Jenny last night," Danni said. "But now, of course, she'll never be without Brad — and they're both staying at my place for now."

"Evil is such an elusive quality," Father Ryan said thoughtfully. "And I can't say I begin to understand it. Some say that it can and does reside in inanimate objects, and we've seen how a malignant soul can linger on. People believe in residual hauntings, when, say, a Civil War soldier fights the same battle over and over again. But no matter how you slice it, the earth itself isn't evil, and neither is the sky or the sea. Evil always begins and ends with man."

"Amen, Father," Natasha said quietly.

They'd reached Danni's house; Quinn's car wasn't back yet.

"Guess I beat him home," Danni said.

"So we'll see you in, check everything out and make sure Wolf is on duty," Natasha said.

Wolf was indeed on duty. He was waiting by the courtyard door, and wagged his tail and wriggled his massive body as he greeted Danni and said hello to the others. Bo Ray, bare-chested with his jeans thrown on, came down the stairs to meet them. He seemed happy to see everyone, but it was obvious that the noise they'd made had awakened him. He was especially pleased to see Hattie, whom he hadn't seen in a while.

After a few minutes' conversation, Billie sighed and pointed out the hour.

"Everything fine here?" Father Ryan asked Bo Ray.

"Yep. Fine. I fell asleep about two, but there's nothing going on here. And I'd know, because Wolf would let me know, and he hasn't made a peep," Bo Ray assured them.

"Then we'll lock you two and Wolf in," Billie said. "I'm going with the good Father to see Hattie home."

"Okay," Bo Ray said, grinning knowingly.

Billie looked away, blushing. Hattie gave Bo Ray a tap on the arm. "Behave, young man. They're all just very politely seeing an old lady home."

"You'll never be old, Hattie," Danni told her.

"Of course not. She's way too mean," Father Ryan teased.

"What was it you said earlier, Father? Lord and Mother Mary, help me," Hattie said, rolling her eyes. "Let's move it now, children."

"Anything new?" Bo Ray asked Danni anxiously after the others had left.

She shook her head. "No. Earlier today Tyler mentioned another old friend of Arnie's, and I'm curious if that's something we should pursue. He's an army vet, wounded and still at Walter Reed. Maybe he knows something about the sax. I have to talk to Quinn first, though. And speaking of Quinn, have you heard from him?"

Bo Ray nodded. "Oh, yeah. I left you a note on your bedroom door. He said not to worry if he came in a bit after you, said they were stopping by Jenny and Brad's place to pick up a few things."

"That's fine. Everyone wants their own things. I'm not sure I can wait up for Quinn, though. I'm beat."

"I know just how you feel," Bo Ray said. "I'm going back to bed, since I have a feeling I'll be the one keeping The Cheshire

Cat going for the next . . . whatever. Night, Danni."

"Night, Bo Ray."

It was still dark out, not quite 5:00 a.m., and Danni decided to give staying up a little longer a try. She made herself a cup of tea and laced it with milk and sugar — "comfort food," as her father had called it — and sat down at the table.

But after she nearly fell asleep with her face in her teacup, she gave Wolf a dog treat and told him, "Say hi to Quinn for me. I'm out."

Wolf barked. She would swear the dog understood her words. As she headed for the stairs, Wolf circled a few times and then lay down in front of the courtyard door.

Up in her room, Danni shimmied out of the dress she had worn and into a long sleep T. She lay down on the bed, tired in every pore of her body.

But she kept thinking about Father Ryan's words, wondering whether evil really could reside in objects, in buildings, even in the air.

Her eyes began to close as she lay there. Just when she was beginning to drift off, she heard Wolf begin to bark.

At first the noise was just irritating. In her still half-asleep stage, she figured Quinn had gotten home and the dog was happy to see him.

But then she jumped out of bed. That wasn't Wolf's ecstatic Quinn-was-home bark. It was one of his warning barks.

She heard the dog bounding up the stairs; he was coming to stand guard over her, she knew.

When she opened the bedroom door she heard Bo Ray hurrying down from the attic. Obviously he had heard the dog, too. Wolf reached her side and barked with new fervor then bounded back down the stairs to the courtyard entrance.

"What is it?" Bo Ray asked tensely.

"I don't know. Wolf doesn't like something."

"You got a gun, right?"

"In the drawer by the bed."

"Get it," he said.

Danni did. She hated guns, but Quinn had taught her how to shoot, and she had a Glock 19 he had gotten her just a few months back.

She paused in her room, walking over to the window and looking out to the street.

There was someone staring at her house. Someone wearing a trench coat and who had what appeared to be a wild shock of dark hair.

And no face.

"We really do need to move back home, Jenny," Brad told her as Quinn drove. Jenny was in the front, and she lowered her head slightly. Brad, in the back, couldn't see her expression, but Quinn could.

It was clear to him that the last thing Jenny wanted at the moment was to go home, away from the protection of Danni's house and everyone there. Back to the scene of her terrifying close encounter with a killer.

"Soon, Brad," Quinn told him. "But not yet. Things are still too dangerous at the moment."

"I don't think he's coming back to our house," Brad said. "He already took what he wanted. He can't possibly be afraid that Jenny would identify him, because no one can identify him. Quinn, you know how much I appreciate what you and Danni are doing for us, but . . . I have a gun, you know."

Quinn was sure Brad was hurt that Jenny didn't believe he could defend her. He wasn't an idiot; he wouldn't push things to the point that might get her hurt, all for the sake of his pride. But he also had logic on his side.

Quinn didn't think the killer would head back to Brad and Jenny's house. He would move on to another musician — and another saxophone.

"For Danni's peace of mind," he said, knowing that Danni wouldn't care in the least what ploy he used to keep their friends safe, "it would be great if you would stay with us a few more days. I know she feels much safer with you two in the house."

"Brad, please, for Danni," Jenny said quietly.

"All right, fine — and thanks, Quinn," Brad said.

Jenny flashed Quinn a quick glance. Her gratitude and relief were obvious, and he smiled back and lowered his head in a small nod.

He'd reached Royal Street and hit the clicker to open the courtyard gate. But even as he pulled the car into its spot next to Danni's, he heard Wolf barking.

He was drawing his gun from the small holster tucked into his waistband even as he exited the car.

"Stay behind me," he curtly ordered Brad and Jenny.

He moved quickly across the courtyard, with the two of them following him. But as they walked between its umbrella-shaded tables, the door to the house opened.

Wolf came bounding out to greet him.

Danni stood at the door, with Bo Ray right behind her.

"He was here," she said softly. "I saw him in the glow of the streetlight. I saw him there — and then he was gone. Just gone. As if he'd disappeared into thin air."

"I think that, in an odd way, it's good that Danni saw the killer on the street. It means that he was going to come in here, but then he heard Wolf," Quinn said.

He'd gone out and searched the streets, but he hadn't found a man in a trench coat or a mask. Then again, he hadn't really expected to; he'd just been going through the motions. He'd taken Wolf with him, but whatever scent the dog had started out following had gotten lost in the mixture of odors once they got to Bourbon Street.

By the time he returned to the house, Billie was back, too. Natasha and Hattie had been safely returned to their own homes, but Father Ryan was sitting with the rest of the group around the table. Danni had brewed a pot of coffee and set out beignets and Danish; it was getting close to breakfast time.

"Why is that good?" Jenny asked Quinn. "It just means that he's still out there."

"It means that we're after a person," Quinn said. "One real-live person who can be warned off by a barking dog, and that's an advantage for our side. His whole MO has been based on taking people by surprise. When he killed Holton Morelli and Lawrence Barrett, he just walked up to their houses and knocked on their doors, and they let him in. At least that seems logical, since there was no sign of forced entry, which means he's almost certainly someone they knew. Someone they would just let in. But by the time he got to your place," he told Brad and Jenny, "he was back to wearing his mask. He didn't want anyone knowing who he is, which means he's aware that people are being cautious and that you wouldn't open your door to just anyone, even someone you knew." At Jenny's stricken look he hastened to add, "Calm down. I'm not saying you knew him, just that you might, and so might other people he passed, so he was making sure no one could recognize him."

Jenny breathed an audible sigh of relief. "Everyone in the city knows to be cautious now," she said.

"He's got to be after the sax," Danni said.

"He's after every sax in this city. And maybe a particular song, but mostly I think it's the sax."

"Yes, I believe that's true," Quinn said.

"At least partially true," Father Ryan said.

"What do you mean?" Quinn asked him.

"There's a sax in this house, and Billie's been out there playing and calling attention to it. But there's more than that here, Quinn. You and Danni are here. You've been playing music in public. You've been snooping around. The killer might have come here after the two of you," Father Ryan said.

"Or a two-in-one," Danni said softly. "The two of us — and a sax. But Father, he came when Quinn wasn't here. What if he's really after me?"

"Or maybe he thought it would be easier to take you out one at a time. Get in and get you, and the dog and Bo Ray if he had to, then wait to jump Quinn." Father Ryan turned to Jenny. "I'd guess he was well aware that Brad wasn't home last night. He was either trying to get in and get out before Brad got back or take you down one at a time because that would be safer and easier for him."

"Maybe he doesn't even want Quinn. I mean, he's not part of the Survivor Set," Jenny said.

"No, of course not," Danni said then frowned. "What about the Survivor Set?" she asked. "How does that fit in?"

"Everyone who's been killed was part of the Survivor Set, Danni, or they had something to do with it," Jenny said. "We just realized that when we were talking tonight. You were into art rather than music, but you were still part of the group. Even Holton Morelli and Lawrence Barrett, they taught us. Jeff was part of it, too."

"So was Arnie Watson," Brad added.

"So this person is trying to kill all of us . . . why? Because we were friends or at least knew each other years ago?" Danni asked.

"I really don't think so," Quinn said. "Every time something has happened, the common denominator has been a sax."

"Where is Arnie's damned sax?" Jenny asked. "We need to find it and give it to him, so he'll stop killing."

Quinn looked at Danni and weighed his words carefully. "We need to find the sax," he agreed. "But we also have to find whoever is doing this and stop him."

"Maybe he's not real. Maybe he's a monster. We think it's a mask, but maybe it's his face," Jenny said. "But," she added anxiously, looking at Quinn and Danni, "you kill monsters, don't you? Oh, Lord. Listen

244

to me," she said. "I sound like a crazy person." She laid her head down on the table and groaned.

"Everyone should get some sleep," Quinn said. "Being overtired doesn't help anything."

"Yes," Jenny agreed. But she didn't move. She looked at Quinn and said, "We're safe, right? I mean if the killer were to come back, well, you've got your gun?" She looked at Brad. "And you have yours, too, right? And you're ready to use them on that creep if he does come back?"

"We're armed, Jenny," Quinn assured her.

"I even know how to shoot," Father Ryan said. He smiled grimly and told Jenny, "God's warrior, you know. Don't get the wrong idea. I *am* a man of peace. But sometimes the innocent need to be protected."

"But you're going home, Father," Jenny said.

"We've always got another bed," Danni offered.

"Thank you, dear. But I think I will head back to the rectory. Mass later, you know? And I have never had a sax. I can't play a sax — trust me, you wouldn't want to hear me try. So . . . time for me to go now."

"Alone?" Jenny asked him.

"I wasn't kidding when I said I can shoot. And I have a permit for a concealed weapon, which I have on me, under my jacket. I'll see you all tomorrow night," he assured them.

He told them all good-night, and then Quinn walked him to the courtyard door and watched until he was in his car and on his way. Quinn didn't really know much about the priest's past other than that he'd been in the service as a young man and after, as a priest, served in some of the most viciously war-torn areas of the world. He truly was "God's warrior" in many ways; spiritually or physically, he was ready to go to battle for innocence and the good of mankind.

When Quinn walked back into the kitchen, he heard Jenny telling Danni, "I wish he wouldn't leave."

"We'll be fine, trust me," Danni said. "Please."

"*I* certainly trust you," Quinn said. "Why don't you all go on up to bed. I'm going to call Detective Larue."

"At this hour?" Danni asked softly.

He nodded. "Yes, I'll wake him. He'll be irritated, but he'd be more irritated if I didn't report in on what happened here tonight."

He pulled out his phone and called Larue, expecting that the others would leave, but they didn't. He looked at Danni as he spoke, making sure that what he told Larue was right.

Larue did sound tired, but he didn't say a word about the hour. Quinn figured that he'd been ready to get up and face the day, anyway.

After he rang off with Larue he assured the others that every officer on every shift would be on alert for anyone in a trench coat. The mask was secondary, since the killer was unlikely to wear it where he might be spotted, but of course they would keep it in mind, too.

, "He's just like Jack the Ripper, don't you think?" Jenny asked, shivering. "He commits horrible crimes then just disappears into the streets. He even manages to disappear while he's loaded down with musical instruments."

"Because he knows the city," Quinn said. "He's local, either born here or, at the least, he's been living here for quite some time. He knows the alleyways, what courtyard gates are left unlocked and where he can find easy access to hidey-holes. He's smart, so we'll just have to get smarter."

Quinn could hear the street sweepers

outside, cleaning up after another night of the usual mayhem in the Quarter.

"It's morning, guys," he said. "And I can guarantee you nothing happened during the night. Since this house was targeted, we don't need to be worried about anyone else. Not till tonight, anyway."

Jenny slapped Brad lightly on his shoulder. "We are not leaving — not until this is over," she told him.

Brad looked at Quinn and Danni apologetically.

"Hey, you're welcome to stay here as long as you like, you know that," Danni said.

"Absolutely," Quinn agreed, knowing Brad was still feeling awkward. Maybe some primeval sense deep within made him feel he was infringing on another man's castle.

"Thanks," Brad said awkwardly.

Finally Quinn realized that no one was going to bed until he did. "Wolf, you're on duty, boy. And don't worry about waking me up. Bark at anything you want."

Billie groaned softly. "We're opening in just a few hours."

"Not to worry. I actually slept awhile," Bo Ray said. "And I'll get in my last few hours now. Good night, all."

He headed up the stairs. Brad and Jenny followed him. Billie looked at Quinn. "Want me to stay up?"

"We're good. We've got Wolf," Quinn said.

Billie nodded and went on up. Danni looked at Quinn. "Wow. Can we really go up and sleep?"

"We can really go up and sleep."

"The funny thing is, I was exhausted before, but now I've got so much adrenaline going that I'm not sure I *can* sleep," she said.

He smiled and slipped an arm around her. "I can take care of that for you," he told her.

"Really?" she said, a curious smile on her face.

"Physical activity is known to relieve stress and make it easier to fall asleep."

"That's incredibly romantic."

"I can be romantic," he promised.

She laughed. "No, I meant it — that's incredibly romantic. At this moment, anyway. Makes me want to strip my clothes off as I run up the stairs — Oh, wait! The house is full of people. Guess I'll have to control myself till I make it to our room."

She turned and ran up the stairs. He followed.

She left a trail of clothing from the bedroom doorway to the bed. He tried to do the same but couldn't match her grace. He tripped over a shoe then remembered his gun. He saw the amusement on her face as he stopped to handle it with care, but he finally got down to bare flesh and made a dive for the bed then rolled carefully atop her.

"Mock me, will you?" he said in a mock growl.

She shook her head, still smiling, her eyes alight. "Never. Not when the finale is so . . . fine."

She ran her fingers along his back, and he felt arousal sizzle through him. He caught her hands and threaded his fingers through hers then leaned down low to kiss her lips.

And then lower. To kiss all of her.

It was, as promised, a wonderful way to relieve stress.

It was quite a while before they slept.

CHAPTER 9

When Quinn awoke, Danni wasn't next to him. A fleeting moment of panic swept through him. He couldn't help it; maybe it was some instinctive macho thing. It worried him that she'd moved and he hadn't wakened.

The panic subsided quickly, but another fear quickly arose. Danni was a sleepwalker — and a "sleep-sketcher." When things didn't make sense, when she didn't have a ready answer rolling through her mind, she had a tendency to rise and walk down to her studio and start to draw — all while she was dead asleep.

And she did so nude, since that was how they slept.

Quinn bolted out of bed.

The rest of the household might not be sleeping. Worse, Danni's studio was a short hallway down from the main gallery of the shop.

He slid into his jeans but didn't bother with shoes, shirt or even his gun. Bursting out of the room, he raced down the stairs. Wolf wasn't in the kitchen, he discovered, taking a hasty look inside.

Brad and Jenny *were* there, however. Brad was reading the paper Billie insisted on having delivered every day. Jenny was making coffee.

"Morning," he said to them. "Have you seen Danni?"

"We just came down," Brad said. "Do you want some breakfast? We'd like to help out."

"No, thanks," he said. Smiling — and aware that they'd both noted with interest that he was in nothing but his jeans — he hurried on to Danni's studio.

To his vast relief, he saw that she was clothed.

Their line of work called for strange hours sometimes. He hadn't glanced at the time yet, but it had to be eleven or twelve. Not only were Brad and Jenny in the kitchen, but he could hear voices from the shop. Bo Ray was talking to a customer. He was talking about a local craftsman and how each piece was one of a kind. No hard sell at The Cheshire Cat, just the kind of information that helped unique items sell themselves.

Danni wasn't aware of him at first; she

was seated on her stool and staring at the newly drawn picture on her easel. Wolf was by her side. The mammoth dog thumped his tail as he saw Quinn.

"Danni?" he said.

She turned to look at him, awake and aware.

"Hey," she said. She smiled, examining him from head to toe. "Like the outfit."

"Thanks," he said, leaning against the door frame. "I was worried, so I wasn't really thinking about my wardrobe."

"I'm sorry I scared you," she told him.

"I can't believe I didn't hear you leave. At least you didn't sleepwalk."

Her smile faded slightly. "I did. But apparently I had the sense to sleep-dress first. I woke up here, dressed and drawing."

"A psychiatrist would have a field day with you, you know?"

She grinned at that. "It is somewhat worrisome, but . . ."

"So what did you draw?" he asked her.

"La Porte Rouge. It's pretty good, actually, if I do say so myself. But it doesn't really tell me anything."

Quinn walked over to her, setting his hands on her shoulders as he studied the drawing. He saw the bar as if he were standing in the cross-street entrance. To his left

253

was the bandstand, and to his right was the bar. Jessica was there, and Eric Lyons was setting drinks on her tray. The place was crowded, but most of the faces in the crowd were indistinct, faded. He could see that Billie was offstage, sitting with Hattie, Father Ryan and Natasha. He and Danni were onstage with Shamus, Gus, Blake and Tyler.

Tyler's saxophone seemed to be the focal point of the drawing. It was slightly oversize.

"Great drawing," Quinn told her. "Wish I could draw a tenth so well wide awake, much less in my sleep."

"What do you think it means?" she asked him.

"I don't know. It looks like it's just a picture of where we've been, but your mind must have been trying to tell you something about it, since you drew it," he said carefully.

"You're not being honest," she said.

He glanced at her quickly. She could read him so well.

"I'm never quite sure what it means — your sleep-drawing. But I think this picture means that *you* think the murderer was in the bar the night when we both were playing. And that he's one of the people whose faces you've drawn."

254

Danni frowned. "I don't. Or maybe I just don't want to. I like the guys we were playing with. I like everyone there."

Quinn hesitated, well aware that things could be hitting too close to home. One of Danni's trusted employees had once proved to be involved in what could best be described as demonic rites.

"Still, not a bad place to concentrate," Quinn said. "It's the last place Arnie was before he was killed."

She stood up suddenly. "Arnie," she said.

"Is gone."

"Yes, but Quinn, the killer hasn't gone after his parents' house yet. But he will. He's bound to."

"Tyler has been staying with them."

"Staying with them, yes. But he doesn't get there till morning. What about all night, before he shows up? Why doesn't the killer show up before Tyler gets there? Or, if it's Tyler he wants, why doesn't he get there early and then ambush Tyler when he shows up? I can't believe we haven't thought about protecting them yet."

"I'm guessing the killer doesn't think they have the sax. He's convinced that a musician somewhere in the city has it."

"And there's what's frightening. Tyler is a sax player. The player most likely to have

Arnie's special sax if the killer figures Arnie's parents would have been as likely to give it to one of Arnie's friends as sell it with the rest of his stuff," she said. "And if the killer can't find it with any of the Survivor Set, eventually he'll think Arnie's parents must have it after all and go after them."

She was right, he realized, feeling irritated he hadn't thought things through that way himself.

"I can head over and talk to them now," he said. "See what I can do to convince them that they need to take special care."

"Special care? They need to stay somewhere else altogether," Danni said.

"And you think they can afford that? Or that they'll even consider leaving their home?"

"If they like living, yes!"

Quinn looked at Danni's drawing again. Her subconscious didn't steer her wrong. It was time to start looking at Tyler's bandmates, who just happened to be the last people who had been with Arnie on the night he died.

"There's also Arnie's friend," Danni said.

"Which friend?" Quinn asked.

"I didn't get to tell you. There was too much going on last night."

"Okay. Tell me now."

"Arnie had a close friend in the military. His name is Kevin Hart — Corporal Kevin Hart. He stepped on a mine, and now he's up in Walter Reed, doing rehab after getting a prosthetic leg. Hattie said she can help us get to see him. If Arnie was as close to this guy as Tyler says, he might have told him things he didn't tell anyone else, maybe things about people here in town. Maybe he even entrusted his special sax to him."

"That's a long shot."

"What else have we got?"

"Following up on the musicians around here, on people who knew about the sax. Maybe following through on that Survivor Set connection."

"All right, I agree with you that we have to do all that, but I think it's important that we talk to Kevin Hart, too."

"But we can't be here and also there."

"I could go," Danni said.

"I don't want you going anywhere alone," he said quickly. Maybe too quickly, and a little too harshly. He saw her bite down lightly on her lower lip.

Her tone, in turn, was cool. "Fine. You could go."

"I'm afraid to go. Too much is happening here, most of it dangerous. I need to keep an eye on things."

"You mean keep an eye on *me.* Quinn," she said, walking to the door and shaking her head, "you have to have faith in other people sometimes. You can't save the world on your own, you know. I have Wolf, Billie, Bo Ray and now Brad and Jenny."

"I do have faith in you. I just don't think either one of us should leave here. Not even for a night."

"And *I* think it's important to talk to Kevin Hart. One of us can stay, and the other one can go."

"No."

"Then we both need to go."

"No."

"You have to have some faith in me."

"I have tremendous faith in you."

"So you don't think I can take care of myself, even with a houseful of people?"

"I didn't say that. We're a team."

Danni sighed in aggravation. "Not much of a team if you don't have any faith in me or my judgment."

"Wait a minute, Danni. Just wait. Even if Arnie spilled his heart out to this guy, why think he'd have anything to say that would help? The guy isn't from NOLA. He wouldn't have known any place or person Arnie was talking about. Not to mention the guy is in bad shape, so we could just be adding bad news to what he's already going through."

"I'm sure he already knows that Arnie is dead. The military grapevine is pretty efficient. And I'm sure he'd want to help in any way he can to catch Arnie's killer. He knew Arnie, and that's what's important, Quinn. He might know something about Arnie that Tyler doesn't, that his folks don't — maybe something Arnie was keeping from people here on purpose. The point is, we're not getting anywhere, and people keep dying. I'm going to check on flights. You can come with me to see him or not."

As she walked out of the room he called out after her, "Hey! That's not teamwork. That's being a dictator."

Wolf looked at him and barked, obviously unhappy about a family argument.

Danni was probably right again, and he knew it. But that didn't change anything. He didn't like the idea of leaving town when people were still in danger and when they were just starting to associate themselves with the music scene.

He definitely didn't like the concept of leaving Danni in those circumstances, though he wasn't any happier about letting her leave on her own.

Irritated, he walked into the kitchen, where Danni was sitting at her computer and apparently chatting casually with Brad and Jenny, both of whom looked at him with uneasy expressions. They'd undoubtedly heard the argument.

"Coffee?" Jenny asked him, her voice pointedly cheerful.

"No, thanks," he said.

He strode quickly up the stairs and back to the bedroom to get dressed.

Back downstairs, he went straight to the courtyard door, but Danni saw him as he passed the kitchen, because he heard her jump up and come after him, calling, "Quinn!"

"What?"

"Where are you going?"

"To see Arnie's parents."

He didn't wait for her to suggest that she come with him.

Wolf had trotted along with him to the door. "Watch her, boy. Watch her and watch the shop, okay?" He scratched Wolf's ears, his other hand on the doorknob.

"You're being unreasonable," she said.

"Really? When you went rushing over to Jenny and Brad's the other night without thinking?"

"I *did* think. I called —"

"Whatever," he said.

He walked out the door, pulling it closed behind him.

As soon as he was in the car, he realized she was right. He *didn't* have enough faith in her to leave her on her own. That wasn't bad — not really. It meant he cared, that she had become everything to him. He simply didn't want her to be alone. No, not alone — without him. Maybe that meant he didn't really have faith in *anyone,* anyone but himself.

Or maybe it just meant he was afraid. The killer had come to their house and would have broken in if not for Wolf.

Wolf, as incredible as he was, was still a dog. But Quinn told himself he could leave now because . . .

Because the murderer wasn't killing by day. He was stalking at night or very early in the morning, when he had the least chance of being seen, or, if he was, of being noticed.

Or maybe that was when he was off work himself. Off work, and quickly wrapped in his coat, his mask hiding his identity.

That gave rise to another thought, and he called Larue. When the detective answered he said, "How do you feel about a press conference?"

Larue groaned. He hated press conferences.

"What did you have in mind? Shouldn't we at least discuss this first? And why now? You have something? A lead? A solid clue?"

"No, sorry. I'm thinking of the city. I think we need to tell people what we know about the killer's appearance, what they need to be on the lookout for. Can you call it for about five this afternoon? I need to make a call and then go shopping."

"Shopping?" Larue asked.

"Show and tell. You'll understand. I'll meet you at the station by four thirty."

Danni sat back from the computer, satisfied.

It was possible to catch a flight at eight in the morning and be in Washington by eleven local time. An hour for traffic would bring them to Bethesda and the hospital by twelve or twelve thirty. Two hours there, then an hour back to the airport, and they could catch a five-thirty flight that would land them back in New Orleans by seven thirty. Even if it took them an hour to get back into the city, there would be no problem. They could still sit in with the band.

"You found what you wanted?" Jenny asked her.

"I did. It's all possible," Danni said.

"What's possible?" Brad asked.

"Getting in a quick trip to Walter Reed."

"You're going to go away *now*?" Jenny asked, clearly upset. She turned to Brad with panic-stricken eyes.

Danni knew they had heard her arguing with Quinn, so she quickly said, "We'll only be gone about twelve hours, all of them in daylight."

She picked up her phone, ready to call Quinn. But then she hesitated, thinking about the way he'd walked out on her. She'd wanted to go with him to Arnie Watson's house, but he had left without her.

She excused herself and walked back into her studio to decide what to do next.

Wolf, following at her side, whined.

"You know what, boy? I have my own car. I can hop right in it and follow him on over there. And you know what else? I'm going to do just that!"

As she spoke, Billie stuck his head in to ask what was up.

"I'm going to be gone for a bit. I'm heading over to the Watson house," she said. "I'll take Wolf with me."

"Wolf should stay at the shop," he said.

She let out a sigh of frustration. "Well, if I don't take Wolf, I'll be in trouble for leaving on my own when a maniac is loose. I'm damned if I do and damned if I don't."

"Where's Quinn?" Billie asked.

"Already on his way."

"Why didn't you go with him?"

"He left too quickly. I had something I had to check on."

"Why not just wait for him to get back?"

"Because I want to talk to the Watsons myself. You stay here with Bo Ray, and I'll take the dog."

"How about we leave the dog with Bo Ray and I come with you."

"Is Bo Ray going to be all right with that?" she asked.

"He's done it the last few nights. And, besides, it's afternoon. Nothing is going to happen in the daytime. I'm not half as worried about Bo Ray as I am your friends. They seem to be really on edge, especially Jenny."

"All right," she said. "Tell the others what we're doing. I get you, and Bo Ray gets Brad and Jenny and Wolf."

Quinn decided he felt a little better about the Watsons when he arrived at their house. Amy didn't let him in without confirming his identity, and when he walked through the door he found Woodrow sitting in an armchair with his shotgun at his side.

Amy offered him coffee, which he gratefully accepted. Within a few minutes they all had coffee in front of them, Woodrow and Amy on the couch and Quinn in an armchair facing them.

"So," Woodrow asked, getting right down to business, "do you know who the killer is yet?"

"No, and that's why I'd like you two to consider leaving here. Just for a while," he hurried to add. Seeing Woodrow's silent but firm shake of the head, he took another tack. "Then think about having someone else here at all times, someone who can fight hand to hand if it comes to that."

"Arnie was a trained soldier. He knew what he was doing," Amy said. "And he was taken by surprise by someone anyway."

"There's safety in numbers," Quinn told her.

"That's a fact. We have family coming by during the day, and we have Tyler by night. I have my shotgun and my Good Book by my side. Amy and I are going to be all right," Woodrow said firmly.

Before Quinn could think of another argument, there was a knock at the door. Amy rose, and Quinn rose with her, drawing his gun.

"Now, young man, don't go panicking," she said. "I don't just open the door to anyone. But neither do I go shooting right off the bat when it might very well be a friend."

She walked to the door and, as she had said, she carefully looked through the peephole. A smile lit her face, and she opened the door.

"That's the problem. We all open the door right away to friends and people we *think* are friends," Quinn began, but he stopped when he saw who it was. As Danni walked in he found himself admitting that she did have a way with people; he had to give her that. She and Amy immediately embraced. Then Billie walked in behind her, and he, too, was greeted with a hug.

"Well, now, I'm betting you two are here to tell us the same things Michael here just did. So you sit down, too, and give us your arguments, but I'll warn you, they'll fall on deaf ears. We've thought this through. We're staying right where we are," Woodrow said.

Danni glanced over at Quinn. He wasn't sure what he thought of her following him here; he did know that she was as worried about the Watson family as he was.

And so far he had struck out, so he could only hope she would do better.

266

"I'll get more coffee," Amy said.

As she left the parlor, Tyler made an appearance, rubbing his eyes sleepily as he walked in. "Hey," he said, casually at first. Then, "Hey! Did something happen? Is anyone else . . . dead?"

"No, no one else is dead," Quinn said.

"We're pretty sure the killer tried to get into my place last night," Danni said. "But Wolf started barking and scared him off."

Amy came back into the room, cups dangling by their handles from one hand, the coffeepot in the other. "Now, wait a minute, young 'uns," she said, her tone a combination of affectionate and chastising. "Your house was nearly attacked, but you think Woodrow and I should get out of this one?"

"Because you might be next," Danni said.

"You think the killer will just give up on you and try us?" Woodrow asked.

"You think they should leave here?" Tyler asked. "I come stay with them."

Quinn just sat back to see what Danni would come up with. "But you're not here at night, when things are most dangerous. Look, Mr. Watson —"

"Woodrow, please," he interrupted quietly.

"Woodrow. I know you're all intelligent and competent. But my friend was smart, too, and the killer went to her house knowing just what time she'd be there alone. He's watching us. He knows us, knows our habits. The strongest guy in the world can be brought down by the right kick, the smartest man can be tricked. I believe . . ." She hesitated for a minute, glanced at Quinn then plowed on. "I believe *he* believed Arnie had his sax that night — his special sax. But he took that sax the night he killed Arnie, using a heroin overdose to make it look like Arnie had turned to drugs because of PTSD. The killer thought he could get away with it, and he almost did. Then he discovered it was the wrong sax, so now he's looking for the real thing.

"I think something in him snapped, the longer he went looking for the sax without finding it. First he just held up musicians on the street and stole their instruments. Then he realized he was going to have to start taking more drastic measures. He went after top sax players with enough money to have purchased Arnie's special sax if you had put it up for sale. Now he's killed three times — Arnie, Holton Morelli and Lawrence Barrett — and he broke into my friends' apartment and tried to break into my place, too. I don't know what would have happened if not for Wolf. But you don't have a Wolf. And like I said, Tyler isn't here most of the night, so you're on your own. When you're sleeping, you're vulnerable, and Tyler could easily be in danger if the killer broke in and waited to ambush him when he came home."

Danni stopped speaking, her cheeks flushed, and looked earnestly at Woodrow and Amy, who looked first at one another and then at Tyler.

"I never thought about the fact that we could be risking Tyler's life, too," Amy said.

"So it's settled?" Danni asked. "You'll discreetly move out of the house, at least for a little while?"

They still seemed hesitant.

Quinn decided it was time to speak up. "Please," he said earnestly. "The killer is not only escalating the level of violence but also his timing. Jenny was attacked one night, and the next he was outside our place. He's bound to make a mistake, and then we'll catch him, but let's let him make his mistake without losing any more lives."

Amy looked at Woodrow. "Where will we go? I will not go to any of the children's houses, because I won't bring danger down on them. And I don't think we can afford —"

"Come to my place," Danni said.

Quinn looked at her, startled, trying to figure out just where they would put everyone.

But Danni had it covered. "There are three bedrooms on the second floor, and there's a tiny third room up in the attic, next to Billie's and Bo Ray's rooms. It was once just storage, but there's a bed in it. We'll get it fixed up for Tyler. How does that sound?" she asked cheerfully.

"Like a lot of trouble," Amy said.

Like a very strange frat party, Quinn thought.

"No trouble at all. We love company," Danni said.

"The more, the merrier," Billie added, looking at Quinn.

Quinn glanced at his watch; it was getting late. If he wanted to get the word out the way he wanted to at Larue's press conference, he had to get going, and Danni did seem to have things covered here.

He rose. "I'll let you all work out the particulars," he said. "Thank you for the coffee, Mrs. Watson."

"Amy, please — especially if we're going to be living in the same house," she said.

"Yes, ma'am. Well, excuse me, but I have to go. Please lock the door behind me," Quinn said.

He could feel Danni's stare boring into his back as he headed for the door. She'd proved her point, and now she thought he was upset. He was, though he couldn't explain why. She'd managed to do what he hadn't, but that didn't bother him.

He just wondered if they were making a mistake, gathering so many people together in their house. If the killer decided to change his MO, maybe go for arson, they could all be wiped out in one fell swoop.

No, he decided. He agreed with the safety in numbers.

He turned back, intending to smile at Danni before leaving. He would even give her a thumbs-up.

But she wasn't watching him. She was studying her coffee cup.

He left the house and hurried to the one costume rental shop on Magazine that he knew carried almost everything possible and was open every day of the year except Christmas.

But he just didn't feel right, leaving Danni there with things so unsettled between them.

Billie and Danni hurried back to The Cheshire Cat to make room for their newest guests. She was glad to have Jenny and

Brad there to help get everything ready.

"This is great," Jenny said. "Does it mean you won't be leaving?"

"I'm still going to leave, Jenny, but just for a day," Danni explained to her. "I'll be back before dark."

"Is Quinn going, too?" Jenny asked.

Danni was glad she and Jenny were alone in the spare room on the second floor, and Brad was helping Billie in the attic. No point in hurting his feelings yet again.

"I don't know, but even if he does, you'll be fine. Wolf will be here, Billie knows how to take care of himself and Brad and Woodrow both have guns. In fact, I hope we catch this killer before Woodrow finds out who he is and goes looking for his own justice."

"The killer should die. I'm pretty liberal, but this guy really needs to die," Jenny said.

"That's up to the courts. I just don't want to see Woodrow locked up for murder," Danni said, going back to making the bed.

"What if your plane is delayed?" Jenny asked a minute later.

"It won't be," Danni said, growing exasperated. Honestly, she really didn't know if Quinn was going with her or not, and she still had to call Hattie and see if she could set something up for the next day. It was short notice, but now that she had decided to go, Danni wanted to go *now.*

"Danni, do you think —"

Jenny never finished her thought, because Billie and Brad had apparently finished up in the attic and Billie called loudly from the ground floor, "Hey, come on down here!"

The two of them hurried down the stairs to find that Billie had turned on the news on the small set in the kitchen. Larue was on, with dozens of reporters facing him. Quinn was there, as well, standing just behind Larue.

"Oh my God! That's him!" Jenny breathed, turning pale.

As Larue described the costume worn by the man they were seeking, one of his officers donned a similar mask and a trench coat. The warning was now out all across the city: if anyone saw anyone dressed and masked like the officer, they were to notify authorities.

"Is this how the Sax Murderer has been getting around unseen?" one of the reporters asked.

Danni saw Larue wince; he hated it when killers were given names. It upped their importance, in their own eyes.

"Yes. This is the costume described by several witnesses," Larue explained.

The conference continued for a few more

273

minutes before the station's regularly scheduled programming returned.

"That will get him," Jenny said hopefully. "That creep won't be able to run around in that sorry mask anymore. The bastard."

"Here's hoping. Meanwhile, we should get dinner going," Danni said. "Tyler will be here with the Watsons soon, and we all need to get ready to head out to work."

She had to hand it to Quinn; she was impressed by the way the press conference had gone. Descriptions went out as a matter of course, but there was nothing like seeing something with your own eyes to make an impression.

She hoped it would make a difference and the killer would be caught soon. If not, sax players would soon be leaving the city in droves.

Not good for a city that thrived on jazz.

She excused herself and called Hattie, who assured her that she would get round-trip tickets for both Danni and Quinn, though there was no way to send the whole band to play for the vets, as Danni had hoped.

"Thankfully," Hattie said, "it's spring, so you shouldn't have any trouble getting home before dark."

"You're keeping yourself safe, right?"

Danni asked her.

"Sweetie," Hattie told her, "I couldn't play a saxophone if you tried to teach me from now until doomsday."

"I'm not sure that matters now that you've been seen with us."

Hattie laughed softly. "Don't you worry, Danni Cafferty. I learned my lesson last time I worked with the two of you, and I never count on anything. But I have a brand-new and foolproof security system for the house, not to mention I have Billie to see me home."

"About that," Danni said. "There's safety in numbers, and you're always welcome over here."

"And y'all can escape over here whenever you desire," Hattie said. "But I know you stubborn people. You're a little army unto yourselves, and you see The Cheshire Cat as your fortress."

"You're part of that army, Hattie," Danni assured her.

"Well, thank you. I like that. I'll email you the flight info as soon as I have it."

Danni thanked her and walked back out to the kitchen, where the evening news was replaying the press conference.

She prayed it would help.

More than anything, she hoped the visual

would keep someone alive.

She had complete faith that the Sax Murderer would be caught and brought to justice. She just didn't know how many people would have to die before that happened.

Quinn wished Jenny didn't see him as the ultimate weapon.

He also wished their household hadn't gotten so big.

When he returned to the house on Royal Street, Jenny was overexuberant, Danni was overly quiet, Billie seemed to be perplexed and the Watsons were so busy trying to be helpful he felt as though he was constantly tripping over them.

"No one knows you're here, right?" Quinn asked Woodrow.

"No, sir. We just locked up and left, even brought our things out in grocery bags," Woodrow assured him.

"Good. I've asked Detective Larue to see to it that patrol keeps an eye on your house," Quinn said. "Meanwhile, make yourselves at home here. Bo Ray and Wolf will be on guard through the night while we're gone, but if anything troubles you — anything at all — don't be afraid to call. I keep my phone in my pocket and tuned to vibrate, so I won't miss a call."

He kept looking for a chance to talk to Danni alone, but with everyone getting ready to eat and head out to their respective gigs, there never seemed to be a chance.

He was pretty sure she was angry with him, but just as he was about to head out with Brad and Jenny, Danni stopped him.

"We have reservations for tomorrow," she told him.

"What?" Quinn asked.

"What?" Jenny, standing nearby, echoed.

"I called Hattie," Danni said, looking at Quinn rather than Jenny. "We have reservations to fly to Washington and from there —"

"Danni, I don't think we should be gone at night. That's when he strikes."

"We're not going to be gone at night. We leave in the morning, and we're back by seven thirty." He could tell she was trying to keep her voice level. "Quinn, I'm going."

With or without you . . .

She didn't speak the words, but he heard them anyway.

He nodded. "Send me the details," he told her, disturbed that she had made arrangements without settling the situation between them first. He was sure she knew just how he felt, too, but they were surrounded by people, so this was neither the time nor the place to have it out.

He walked out. Brad and Jenny followed him.

"I still don't see why it's so important that you guys have to go to Washington *now,*" Jenny said.

"Jenny, stop second-guessing," Brad said.

"But . . . there's so much going on *here,*" she said. "People need to be kept safe *here.*"

Quinn had reached a stop sign. He turned to look at her. "No one is going to be safe — no matter where they're staying or what precautions we take — until this killer is caught, and this trip could help us catch him. I hadn't thought of going up and back in a day — it's actually brilliant. That way no one has to be alone at night."

"Feels like we're afraid of vampires," Brad muttered.

"A killer who comes out just before dawn," Jenny agreed. "Do you think he's some kind of supernatural monster? I know you and Danni collect weird things. I know what you two do."

"The killer is not a vampire, Jenny. I was joking," Brad said. "*He* doesn't even think he's a vampire. It's not like he's drinking blood or anything. He's flesh and blood, right, Quinn?"

Quinn moved through the intersection, heading toward Canal and on to Magazine. "The killer is flesh and blood," he said. "But that doesn't make him any less evil."

CHAPTER 10

Sunday nights were usually slow — slower than Friday and Saturday nights, at any rate — unless there was a festival in the city or a major convention.

But when they took their breaks, Danni realized a lot of people in the audience were talking about what was going on.

A table next to where she sat with Billie during their first break was filled with young men who had just arrived in town for a "bachelor week." Danni listened to them talking while she sipped her water.

"It's terrible, a serial killer on the loose. Think we should be worried?" one of them asked the others.

"No. None of us can play anything but a computer keyboard," the groom-to-be, Harry, said.

"I guess not. Scary, though. He's killing off sax players," another said.

"What if all the musicians get scared and

leave?" the first man asked.

"Well, if there are no musicians, what will we do?" someone else pondered.

"Well, hell, there are still strip clubs!" one said, and they all laughed.

"A good stripper needs music, too," Harry said indignantly.

Danni felt Billie's hand on hers. "It will be all right," he told her. "You and Quinn will catch this guy."

"Am I crazy, Billie? To be so determined to speak with Arnie's friend Kevin? What if Quinn decides not to come with me?"

Billie shook his head. "No. You're a Cafferty, girl. Your instincts are good. And don't worry about Quinn. Mark my words, he'll be on that plane."

"You think so?"

"I do."

"Hmm. Think I'm going to order a beer."

"Jessica will come by to see what else we need," Billie said.

"She's busy. I'll just go to the bar," Danni said, and stood.

"I'll take something dark on draft, Danni."

She waved a hand to acknowledge his request. At the bar, Eric Lyons was working alone. "Hey there," he said. "What can I get you?"

"Two dark drafts of whatever," she said.

"Really?" He laughed. "Going from water to the hard stuff?" he asked, getting cups and pulling on one of the taps.

She was hoping the beer would help her catch a few hours of sleep before heading to the airport, though it seemed unlikely. Maybe she could sleep on the plane.

"Going wild tonight, what can I say?" she said.

"You never go home alone, right?" he asked her.

"Never. Why?"

"Oh, I was just watching the news today. Jessica was worried. I'm going to take her home. And I was talking to Blake Templeton. He said the band members all hang together until they get home. Apparently, musicians all over the city are seeing each other home, even staying at each other's places. I wonder if it's going to be like a blackout and in nine months we'll wind up with a slew of musically talented babies?"

"Well, that would be better than a lot of other outcomes, right?" Danni asked.

"Sure would."

"You're careful, too, right?"

He nodded. "Very," he assured her, and handed her the drafts. "And I play horribly, anyway. I'm sure no one is after me."

"The killer doesn't care about talent, only

instruments."

"In that case I'll just ditch everything I own," Eric said.

"Hopefully, that won't be necessary. No one's seen you playing onstage, right?"

"Well, they might have seen me, but I've never been asked to join a band," he said, grinning as he nodded toward the stage, where the band was playing a couple of songs without her and Billie. "Now, those guys — those guys are good. And your friend is amazing. He can really play the sax."

"Billie," Danni said. "And I never even knew until recently. His specialty is the bagpipes."

"He should play those one night," he said, still smiling, and then he grew serious. "All of them can play. But Arnie, now, he was special. Don't get me wrong, Tyler is good. But Arnie . . . there was just something about the way he played . . . He could make you cry."

"I remember."

"You do?"

"I knew him back in school," she said.

"Were you into music, too?"

"Art, back then. Still am. I love music, though."

"Who wouldn't? When it works, it's like

magic. Like Arnie and his sax."

"I guess someone is after that magic," Danni said.

"Hey, I think you're about to go back up."

"Thanks," she told him, hurrying back to the table. She and Billie barely had a minute to take a few sips of their beer before it was time to head back up onstage.

A few minutes later, Natasha and Father Ryan appeared. On their next break, Danni hurried over to thank them for coming again.

Tyler joined her. "Not only does Danni look great onstage, she brings her own fans."

"Tyler's staying at my house, along with Arnie's parents," Danni told the newcomers quietly.

"Good. No one knows, right?" Father Ryan asked Tyler.

Tyler shook his head. "Not even the rest of the band. I'll go with the guys to make sure they get home safely, and then I'll go back to Danni's. I guess you two will see that Billie and Danni get there?"

"Of course," Natasha said. "It's Billie I really worry about."

Billie cleared his throat. "Excuse me?"

"You play the sax, so of course I'm more afraid for you than I am for Danni."

Billie muttered something in Gaelic beneath his breath. They all grinned.

Just then Blake, Gus and Shamus strolled over to say hi and thank Father Ryan and Natasha for being there. Danni studied the three of them while they chatted. The more she worked with them, the more she liked them. She didn't want to believe any of them could be the killer. Shamus was fun and flirty, not to mention very good-looking. Gus was more of an academic. Blake, like Tyler, was even-keeled. They all loved their music and couldn't help grinning while they played. She was so comfortable with them that sometimes she forgot why she was there and actually had fun.

She left them at the table and headed to the bar; she wanted water again. She couldn't decide whether to try to sleep a few hours at the house or just stay up until it was time to head to the airport. She wouldn't even have a carry-on, but Quinn wouldn't leave unarmed, she knew. He would have to check a suitcase.

If Billie was right and he was going with her. She had texted him the flight numbers before she'd left the house. All he'd texted back was Thanks.

Danni didn't make it all the way to the bar. Jessica swooped in front of her, offering her a large glass of water with lime.

"Hey, did you have a chance to look at those duets yet?" Jessica asked.

"Oh, no. I'm so sorry. I'll get to it, I promise," Danni told her. "Hey, when they go back up, why don't you go sing something? It's slow tonight. I can serve drinks for a few minutes."

"No, no, that's all right."

"Please?"

Jessica seemed flustered. "Okay. Thank you."

When the band went up, Jessica joined them and did a Carole King number. The woman had a voice like silk, Danni thought. She should have been singing full-time.

"Wow," one of the men at the bachelor table said as Danni went by. He looked at her and flushed. "I mean, you're wow, too, of course."

She laughed. "Not to worry. She *is* wow."

It was after two when Tyler announced the last number. After that people said their good-nights. Danni assured Tyler quietly that someone would be waiting up for him.

She, Billie, Father Ryan and Natasha began the short walk back to her place. Natasha was tired, so they said good-night outside, and then Father Ryan and Natasha headed toward her house.

When Billie and Danni headed into the

kitchen, they found that Woodrow had waited up for them. He was sitting at the kitchen table, Wolf at his side — along with his shotgun.

"Ready for anything, you know?" he said.

Danni smiled. "Thank you."

"I let Bo Ray and Amy go up to sleep. The dog hasn't barked, so I figure no unsavory characters have come around the place," Woodrow said.

"That's good. Thank you. I'm going to head up, too, if you don't mind waiting a bit longer for Tyler to get in," she said.

"I can wait, if you want to get some sleep," Billie told Woodrow.

"No, sir, you go on up. I can rest by day. I don't mind being on guard — not with a dog like this one at my feet," Woodrow said.

"Thank you again," Danni said. "Quinn should be along soon, too."

"Then we'll batten down once everyone's in and accounted for," Woodrow told her.

"Oh!" she said. "I'll be gone during the day tomorrow. Quinn, too, I think. But please, the two of you need to stay in the house or the shop while we're gone. Larue will have an officer watching, especially if Quinn goes with me. But for your own safety, stay inside, all right?"

"If that's what you want," he said.

"It is. I worry, you know?"

Billie set a hand on her shoulder. "Everything will be fine," he said.

With Billie behind her, Danni started up the stairs. "I have to be awake by six. The plane is at eight, but I can be ready in fifteen minutes and there's not much traffic that time of day. But you should get some sleep. You're not —"

"If you're about to say I'm not a young man anymore, *don't*!" Billie told her. "I'll see to it that you're up and out on time."

"You don't have to."

"It's what I do," Billie said. "I looked after your father. Now I look after you."

Danni smiled at that and kissed him on the cheek. "Good night, Billie."

She went into the bedroom that had always been hers. She'd grown up thinking life was a lark. She'd never had any idea that her father collected evil objects, or objects that at the very least made men behave in evil ways. He'd been involved in dangerous situation after dangerous situation, and she'd never even known.

Her bedroom was comfortable. It was filled with old oak furniture and lots of art, a few pieces of her own, and many more paintings, large and small, by artists she admired.

She'd always loved this room . . .

Now, though, it seemed empty and cold. Just because she was at odds with Quinn.

They'd wondered at the beginning of their attraction if they could make it as a couple *and* as a working team. Now she found herself wondering about it all over again.

They weren't really arguing, she told herself. They were just having a difference of opinion.

She had to stop thinking about him and the situation. She really did need to sleep, if only for a few hours. Tomorrow would be a very long day.

But when she lay down, her eyes were stubbornly wide open and sleep was far away.

Over on Magazine, the Midnight Royale Café was far busier than usual for a Sunday night.

A local organization had chosen the café for their monthly get-together, and apparently none of them remembered that Monday was a workday.

Quinn chafed at being there. At first it had seemed logical, given that Jenny had been attacked.

But now he doubted there was any further need for him to protect Jenny and Brad.

The killer had already taken whatever he'd wanted from them. Quinn knew Jenny wanted him around, felt reassured by his presence, but he felt strongly that he needed to be back at La Porte Rouge — where Arnie Watson had played his last set.

Danni had messaged him earlier with the flight info and a link to his boarding pass. Despite the current chill between them, he intended to be on that plane.

On a normal Sunday night they would have finished by two; they might have even been packed up and ready to go. But the members of the group were in a party mood, and bars that were hopping were loath to close down, and Quinn really couldn't blame them. It was after three when the band announced they were on their last number, and even then, the bartender wanted them to keep going.

Quinn was helping with the equipment when his phone vibrated in his pocket.

At that hour he instantly felt his heart beat too hard, his muscles tighten.

Danni.

But he caught the caller ID as he answered and realized it wasn't Danni, it was Larue.

"Quinn," he answered tersely.

"You need to join me in Treme," Larue told him.

"What happened?"

"You beat the bullet by the skin of your teeth," Larue said. "I'm at the Watson house. Someone's been here. The place has been trashed."

"I'll be there as quickly as I can," Quinn said. He'd driven, but he had Brad and Jenny with him, and the band was still coiling amp cords and securing the system. "Can you send a patrol car for me? I'm at the Midnight Royale Café on Magazine."

"Give my man five minutes," Larue said and rang off.

Quinn hurried over to Brad with his keys. "Listen, I have to meet Larue ASAP. Here are the keys to the car. Go straight to the house once you leave here. I'm willing to bet someone is waiting up."

Jenny stepped up to him, her eyes wide with concern. "What's going on? Oh, God, is someone else dead? Quinn, how can you leave now? What about *us*?"

"As far as I know, no one else is dead. There's just a . . . situation."

"But —" Jenny began.

"Brad, you're armed, right?" Quinn asked.

Brad nodded. "And it's legal. I have a concealed carry permit, but even if I didn't, with everything that's going on . . ."

"We're almost ready to go," Jenny said. "If

291

you just drop us off, you'll have your car and —"

"Jenny, have some faith in Brad," Quinn said. "You're going to be all right."

He didn't wait for her to respond, just turned and hurried outside. Magazine was almost empty at this hour. Even their rowdy crowd had quickly dispersed. While he waited for the squad car, he pulled out his phone then hesitated. If Danni was sleeping, he didn't want to wake her. She could use some rest before getting on the plane.

He sent Billie a quick text message, telling him that he was fine, no one was dead, and he was heading out to meet Larue about a "situation." Of course, anyone who was still up would know he was with Larue as soon as Brad and Jenny got home, but he figured a message was always a good thing.

The patrol car arrived just as he finished texting.

"Thanks," Quinn said, hopping in.

"Nicest assignment I've had in a while," the young officer driving told him. He looked over quickly and flushed in embarrassment. "I was on patrol in the area. I rode by the Watson house every fifteen or twenty minutes. The guy got in and tore the place apart without me ever seeing a thing."

"How did you find out he'd been there?"

"In addition to the drive-bys, a patrolman was doing a walk-around once an hour. He saw that the back door was open." The officer shook his head in self-disgust. "I got sloppy, too predictable in my drive-bys. He must have waited for me to pass, and then he went in. The place is . . . Well, you'll see." He was quiet for a long moment. "Thank God no one was home."

It didn't take long to get to the Watson house, since there was very little traffic on the way. Even Bourbon had wound down to just a few people closing up or heading out. A couple of lone establishments still had customers nursing drinks, their doors open, their lights on.

When they arrived, Quinn leaped out of the car and hurried up to the front door, where he quickly slipped paper booties over his shoes. Larue was standing just inside, staring around the living room.

Quinn remembered having coffee in this room, which had been spick-and-span at the time.

Now it was as if someone in an absolute rage had torn through on an adrenaline binge. The comfortable couch had been ripped to shreds. Pictures had been torn from the walls, furniture thrown and broken.

Larue looked at Quinn. "It gets worse."

"How the hell can it be worse?"

A crime scene unit was already on the job. As Larue headed across the living room, Grace Leon, hands gloved, walked in from the back of the house, where the bedrooms were.

"Good to see you, Quinn. I think this guy wears gloves, but we're trying for a print or a hair or something — anything." She paused, looking at the two of them. "Good thing what this guy did, he didn't do to a person."

"I can't wait to see the rest," Quinn said drily.

Larue led him to the first room on the right. Lights were ablaze in there now, so it was easy to see the damage that had been done.

Pillows had been ripped to ribbons, the bed itself stabbed and ripped repeatedly.

There was a hole in one wall. The television had been thrown from the dresser. Clothing had been pulled from the closet and ripped into unidentifiable shreds.

"This is Woodrow and Amy's room," Quinn said.

"We're assuming there were pictures of the kids on the dresser. The frames are shattered, and the pictures are destroyed. Come on into the next room, which was Arnie's, when he was home," Larue said.

The next bedroom. Not only were the bed and the pillows slashed, the walls pummeled, and what looked like every piece of clothing in the closet and the dresser ripped and torn and trampled, there was something on the bed.

Raggedly torn pieces of paper. The shreds of a photograph.

Grace Leon stepped up behind Quinn.

"I think I know what it is," she said. "As soon as the photographer finishes, I'll show you."

Quinn went through the rest of the house with Larue, who showed him that the intruder had gained access by breaking in through the back door.

"Could this have been done by just one person? In only twenty minutes?" Quinn wondered aloud.

"He might have been in here longer," Larue said. "He probably left the lights off. My guess is he was expecting the Watsons to be home. When they weren't — and he didn't find what he was looking for — he just went nuts on the place then left through the back, same way he came in."

"Woodrow Watson had his shotgun with him wherever he went in the house. Who knows, maybe we made a mistake. Maybe Watson would have caught him tonight," Quinn said.

Larue shook his head. "This guy definitely carries a very sharp knife, and we know he's got a gun, too. And Watson had to sleep sometime."

Quinn shook his head. "On the plus side, I don't think there's anything paranormal about this. He knows the city, he's obsessed, but he's human. And oddly enough, there's a hopeful sign in all this — though I doubt the Watsons will think so."

"What's that?"

"He's starting to lose it. This destruction is maniacal. At first he was crafty — the way he killed Arnie. He nearly got away with it. Then he held up those musicians, but he didn't kill them. Even when he started torturing people and murdering them when they didn't give him what he wanted, he was rational. They would have died even if he'd found what he was looking for, because he didn't intend to leave any witnesses, but there was nothing wanton in the way he searched their places. Or Jenny and Brad's. But now he's losing it, and the more he loses it, the more likely he is to make a mistake, and then we'll have him."

"Well, we don't have him yet," Larue said.

"And we can't watch every musician in the city. Seriously, do you know how many there are?"

"I think we need to start watching La Porte Rouge more closely."

"Danni has been playing there every night. I'm sure if she'd seen anything suspicious, she would have said something."

Quinn nodded. "Still, it's the last place Arnie played." He looked at his watch. He couldn't believe how much time had passed. "I have to get to the airport."

"You're leaving town?" Larue asked. He didn't sound disturbed, just surprised.

"Only for the day," Quinn said. "Danni and I are going up to talk to a friend of Arnie's from the service. She's convinced this friend may know things Arnie didn't divulge to his local friends or family."

"Guess that means I get to talk to the Watsons about the destruction of their house. It's a good thing they're staying at your place."

"I hope they see it that way," Quinn said.

Grace came out of one of the bedrooms and walked over to them. "I've collected the pieces of the photo the killer left on Arnie's bed. I'll put them together at the lab, but I can tell you what I think they are — a picture of Arnie. A picture of Arnie playing his sax at La Porte Rouge."

Despite everything, Danni did fall asleep. Her alarm went off just as she heard Billie's tap at the door.

She jumped out of bed and turned to see if Quinn was going to get up and come with her.

He wasn't there.

She was glad she'd worn a long T to bed, because without thinking she burst out into the hall, leaping over Wolf in the process, her heart pounding.

Billie was just heading down the stairs.

"Quinn isn't here!" she said breathlessly.

"He's all right," Billie told her quickly. "Larue called him in on something just as he was getting ready to leave the club. He let me know. He gave Brad and Jenny his keys and left in a patrol car. He's fine."

"But . . . what happened? Was there another murder?"

Billie shook his head. "No, he said no one was dead and there was just a 'situation.' "

"Oh, okay. Thanks. Sorry you had to get up so early."

"I'll take a long nap this afternoon. Right now, I'll go down and get you some coffee."

Danni thanked him and hurried back into the bedroom. Wolf whined softly as she passed. She stopped to pet him and said, "Come on in, make yourself comfortable. You're the best dog in the world."

Back in her bedroom, she picked up her cell to check for messages. Quinn hadn't tried to reach her.

She was torn between anger and a sudden compulsion to throw herself back down on the bed and cry. But she couldn't take the luxury of wasting time feeling hurt and insulted. She had to make that plane. "Macho ass!" she said.

Wolf barked.

"I'm sorry, Wolf, but he *is* a macho ass!"

Showered and dressed, she hurried downstairs, Wolf at her heels. Billie had coffee for her and a small bag filled with PowerBars. "Most of the time they don't even toss you a bag of pretzels on planes anymore," he told her. He kept his voice low.

"Everyone else sleeping?" she asked.

He nodded. "I took over from Woodrow. He was on guard with Wolf until about five. I figured I'd just get up so I could wake you and sleep later, when Bo Ray's up and minding the store."

"Thanks, Billie," she told him. "Any more word from Quinn?"

"You could call him."

"I've got to go. Hattie went to a lot of

trouble to make this meeting happen, whether she'll admit it or not. And Wolf, you be a good boy. Guard everyone here. I'll be back soon."

Danni left the house. It was barely light. For a moment, just outside the door, she paused.

Was it still early enough for the killer to be stalking his next victim?

She couldn't play the sax to save her life, she reassured herself. But she couldn't help remembering that she hadn't packed the little Glock Quinn had gotten her and taught her how to shoot because she didn't have any baggage.

"Wolf and I are watching, Danni," she heard Billie say from the doorway. "Go on, get in your car and go already."

She smiled. It was good to be part of a team. Feeling safe and secure, she headed to her car, hopped in, waved then opened the gate to the street and eased out.

As she'd hoped, the traffic was light. She wondered about the "situation" that had taken Quinn away so early this morning.

At least he'd said no one else was dead.

She arrived at the airport early and discovered Hattie had booked her in first class. Hattie had proved to be a good friend, and she went out of her way to help them. For her, buying a last-minute first-class ticket might not have seemed extravagant, but it was a big deal for Danni, and she was very grateful.

She hesitated before boarding, hoping Quinn would show up, then wondering why he hadn't. She worried that something terrible had happened, despite what he'd told Billie.

She could just call him.

She couldn't bring herself to do it. The two of them didn't seem to be much of a team at the moment.

She told herself to stop wallowing and boarded.

First class was beyond comfortable. The flight attendant offered her a choice of drinks, and she opted for orange juice then gave her order for breakfast, as well. She thought about the PowerBars now stuffed in her purse. Billie was a good guy, and he and Hattie definitely had something going on. But they were from very different backgrounds. Billie never would have paid for a last-minute first-class ticket. What would he think about Hattie's generosity? Danni suspected he still had a lot to learn about Hattie.

Maybe no one ever really knew someone else.

The announcement to turn off all electronic devices came over the loudspeakers. They were getting ready to close the doors.

She could try to sleep, since it didn't appear as if anyone would be sitting next to her.

It was ridiculous, but she fought the sting of tears that teased her eyes.

Quinn had worked with her father for years, respected him, believed in him. Danni knew she'd come a long way from the girl who hadn't known what her father did — hadn't known what she'd inherited in The Cheshire Cat. And she knew Quinn loved her. So why couldn't he trust her instincts the way he'd trusted her father's?

A fasten-your-seat-belt reminder flashed on the screen overhead, and a flight attendant came on the loudspeaker to tell them they were about to close the doors.

Just when Danni had given up all hope, Quinn walked onto the plane and hurried to take his seat next to her.

Everything in the world seemed to change for the better.

He looked exhausted. Haggard. Five o'clock shadow darkened his chin.

He looked at her, still breathing hard. He'd run through the airport, she thought.

"Hey, made it," he said.

She nodded. "Yes, I see that." A moment later she added softly, "Thank you."

"You were right," he told her.

"About seeing Kevin Hart? We don't know that yet."

"No," he said, and gripped her hand as the plane backed away from the gate. "About the Watsons. If they hadn't been at your place . . . well, they would almost certainly be dead now."

CHAPTER 11

Their takeoff was smooth. By the time they were in the air, he'd told her about Larue's call and going out to the Watson house, and the violence visited on the furniture and everything else there, including Arnie's picture. She was upset for the Watsons, he knew.

As soon as they were in the air, their flight attendant came by offering drinks. They both asked for coffee.

The flight attendant asked if they wanted champagne. Quinn could barely keep himself from laughing, and he saw Danni looking at him in curiosity.

"Sorry," he murmured, when the attendant had moved on. "I was just thinking that we're both so overtired, one sip of anything would probably put us under our seats."

Danni smiled. She knew he never drank more than a few sips of beer just so it looked as though he was drinking. He'd died and been resuscitated because the adulation he'd received as a star football player in school had led to overindulgence in too many ways.

He hadn't known Danni then, and he was glad of that. He liked the man he was now, and when he looked back, he didn't like the man he had been.

"I slept a few hours," she said.

"I'm glad. But man, these hours are going to catch up with me soon."

"Did you learn anything helpful at the Watson place?" Danni asked.

"Not really. Grace Leon — you know Grace. She heads Larue's favorite crime scene unit — was there, though. If there's something to find, she'll find it. Thing is, once she starts dusting for prints, she'll find lots of them. Arnie had lots of friends, musicians mostly, and then there are his parents' friends. And of course our prints will be there. It's a nightmare, for sure. I feel terrible for the Watsons."

Danni leaned back, wincing as he spoke. "We're not there," she said. "Who's going to tell the Watsons what happened?"

"I talked to Father Ryan on my way to the airport — Larue sent me by squad car, so it was easy to make a few calls. Larue will stop by your place with Father Ryan, and they'll tell them what happened together. Their place is going to be even more of a mess when the crime scene unit finishes. Trying to return that house to any semblance of normal is going to take tremendous effort and expense."

"We can all help them."

"Of course."

"I just . . ."

"What?"

She looked over at him. "Well, I'm the one who thought going to DC today was so important, but now I'm wishing we were there with them."

"I'm sure it *is* important."

"But I probably could have gone alone," she said softly.

He sat back, remembering how aggravated he had been with Jenny for her dependence on him and the way it had upset Brad that she had so little faith in him. And he'd realized soon afterward that he owed Danni the same kind of faith. He cared about her so much that his love was keeping him from trusting her judgment. And he couldn't be that way — not if they were going to make it.

"You probably could have gone alone," he said, nodding. "But who knows? Maybe it will take both of us to figure out the right question to ask. And Father Ryan is the perfect person to talk to the Watsons. It's part of his job, after all." He turned and smiled at her. "We're going to be all right," he said softly.

"Hattie took care of everything. We're being met and taken straight to Walter Reed and then straight back to the airport," Danni told Quinn. "And to think you didn't even like her when you two first met."

"Have to say, I'm loving the woman at this moment," Quinn said, grinning. Then he grew serious. "She really has come through for us so many times in so many ways."

"She really has," Danni said. "I mean, I know we could have gone to see Kevin without her, but not so soon, and she's made it all so easy. In fact, we're being picked up by one of the surgeons who's been on Kevin's case from the time he returned to the States, a Major Victor Johnson."

"Really nice of him to take time out of his schedule, but I guess he wants us to be prepared for Kevin's challenges, physical and maybe mental, too."

As soon as they landed and stepped out of the security area, they spotted Major

Johnson, standing ramrod straight and looking distinguished in his uniform. He wasn't holding a placard, but the way he was keenly observing the crowd told Danni he was looking for them. He must have been given a description of them, because he walked right up and introduced himself.

Quinn explained that he had to hit baggage claim before they could leave, and Danni realized he had indeed brought his gun.

"You served?" Johnson asked after Quinn explained that he needed to reclaim his weapon.

"Private first class, US Army," Quinn said. "Then I was a cop, and now I'm a PI."

"Then you know what you're doing," Johnson said, and pointed toward the sign that directed passengers down to baggage claim. "I can hold on to that for you while we're at the hospital."

Once they were in Major Johnson's Jeep and headed to Bethesda, he asked them what they knew about Kevin Hart. Danni told him what Tyler had told her, and Johnson filled in the gaps.

Kevin had been severely wounded by a land mine. He had been fitted with a prosthetic leg and had extensive surgery on one side of his face. He was doing well. He was a solid individual who wanted to make it back to his old life, but he didn't like being seen in his hospital room. They were going to meet up with him at the cafeteria.

"May I ask why you're here?" Johnson asked Quinn. "From what I understand, you're not friends with Kevin. Hattie just told me that it was important that you talk with him."

Interesting, Danni thought. Hattie was on a first-name basis with the major.

"We're looking into a series of murders in New Orleans," Quinn said. "Kevin was close with one of the victims, Arnie Watson."

"Watson?" the major asked sharply.

"Yes. Did you know Arnie?" Quinn asked.

Major Johnson shook his head. "No, but I remember talking with Kevin about him. He said there was no way his friend OD'd. But I'm not sure what Kevin can tell you. They kept in contact. In fact, I understand that Watson was one of the few people Kevin allowed in to see him when he returned about six months ago. Arnie was with him when the mine blew. He was the one who pulled Kevin back to safety. Kevin doesn't want anyone feeling sorry for him. He's a strong guy, but the day he heard about his friend dying . . . well, it was a bad day for him."

"He knows we're coming to see him?" Danni asked. "And he's okay with it?"

"He does," Johnson said.

After that, Quinn told Johnson more about the case and how Tyler Anderson had come to them and that had led to the discovery that Arnie's supposedly accidental death slash possible suicide had been anything but.

Danni listened and watched the scenery as they drove. The foliage around DC and into Maryland was beautiful. It was truly spring.

Finally they drove up to the security checkpoint outside the hospital complex. Johnson knew the guard, and was quick to exit the car and allow it to be inspected. Then they parked and were on their way to the cafeteria.

On their way in, they passed a group of World War II veterans handing out pamphlets on veterans' centers across the country.

"Our servicemen and women look after their fellows," Major Johnson told them.

As they walked through the halls, Danni immediately noticed the number of men in wheelchairs, walking on prosthetic legs and gesturing with prosthetic arms as they emphasized their conversational points.

"The cost of war. We hear about numbers when it comes to death," Quinn said softly to her. "We don't always hear the tally when it comes to those who come home missing body parts or unable to walk."

"This is the place, though," Johnson told her. "This is where they come for the finest help they can possibly receive. Most of us . . . most of us don't see this as work. It's a matter of dedication."

In a few minutes they entered the cafeteria, where people were getting food, sitting around dining and talking. Some were civilians, but judging by the number of uniforms, most were in the service in one way or another.

A harpist was playing softly in one corner, and Danni remembered that Tyler had talked about coming, too, and about entertaining the injured.

"That table with the reserved sign on it is ours," Major Johnson said. "I don't see Kevin yet, but I'm sure he'll be right in. I'll go get coffee. Want something to eat?"

"Thank you, no. Thanks to Hattie, we had plenty to eat on the plane," Quinn told him.

Johnson smiled. "Her late husband enlisted just out of college," Johnson said. "And Hattie herself started an organization called Civilians for Soldiers to raise money for the Wounded Warrior Project and the USO. Too bad there aren't more of her in the world."

"Amen," Danni told him. She knew that Hattie was a true philanthropist, quietly supporting a number of worthy causes, but this was one she hadn't known about.

Danni headed toward their table, but Quinn obviously didn't feel like sitting yet; he walked back and forth near the entrance then paused to listen to the harpist.

Danni's eyes were caught by a small beautifully — but also uniquely — set table, with a small metal frame in the center that held a typed sheet of paper. She moved closer to read what it said.

The Fallen Soldier's Table

This table, set for one, is small, symbolizing the frailty of one prisoner alone against his or her oppressors.

The tablecloth is white, symbolizing the purity of their intentions to respond to their country's call to arms.

The single red rose in the vase signifies the blood they have shed in sacrifice to ensure the freedom of our beloved United States of America.

This rose also reminds us of the family and friends of our missing comrades who keep the faith, while awaiting their return.

The yellow ribbon on the vase represents the yellow ribbons worn on the lapels of the thousands who demand with unyielding determination a proper accounting of our comrades who are not among us tonight.

A slice of lemon on the napkin reminds us of their bitter fate.

The salt sprinkled on the plate reminds us of the countless fallen tears of families as they wait.

The glass is inverted — they cannot toast with us this night.

The chair is empty — they are not here.

The candle is reminiscent of the light of hope that lives in our hearts to illuminate their way home from their captors, to the open arms of a grateful nation.

Reading the beautiful words, Danni felt the sting of tears at her eyes.

Real ones, she thought. Not the petty tears that plagued her when her feelings were hurt or she was worried about things that might not even be real.

She tried not to look around at all the men and women in the room who were in wheelchairs, who were fitted with prosthetics. She knew they didn't want pity.

"Danni!"

She turned gratefully to see Major Johnson walking her way, balancing three cups of coffee. She hurried over to grab one. "Oh, thank you. I could have stood in line with you," she said.

"That's okay. I want you to meet Corporal Kevin Hart. Kevin, Danni Cafferty," Johnson said, stepping aside.

For the first time she could see the man who had been standing behind him.

Kevin had been gorgeous. His hair was the color of wheat, his eyes a brilliant blue. He had the look of a Midwestern farm boy with Scandinavian antecedents. He was tall, and he seemed to manage well on his prosthetic leg. He smiled as he shook her hand, and the smile almost reached the half of his face that still bore the scars of the explosion and surgery.

"Thank you so much for seeing me — us," she said. "Quinn is right over there. He hears music and he's suddenly lost."

Kevin's smile turned rueful. "Like Arnie. He was the only guy who didn't mind being woken at the crack of dawn by a bugle — as long as it was played well."

"I'm not sure how I'd feel about a bugle in the morning," Danni said. "But that harpist is really good."

Hart nodded. "The USO takes care of us. Even here, they bring in all kinds of people to entertain us. But you came to talk about

314

Arnie. I loved him. I'll help you in any way that I can."

Quinn had apparently noticed that Johnson was back and was with Kevin Hart, because he headed right over.

"You want anything, Kevin?" Johnson asked as Quinn approached.

"Nope. And you know me, Doc. If I wanted it, I'd go get it. Part of the therapy," he explained, looking at Danni. "So tell me. I wrote letters, you know. I wrote to Arnie's parents. I wrote to the New Orleans police. I knew Arnie didn't leave work one night and suddenly decide he was going to pick up a heroin habit, much less commit suicide."

"Why don't you three take the table?" Johnson said after Quinn reached them and introduced himself. "You can talk while I go over and see how Private Osborn is doing."

"Will do," Kevin said, heading for the table. Quinn and Danni followed.

"We don't believe he committed suicide or that it was an accidental OD, either," Quinn said. "What we do believe is that someone was after his sax. Unfortunately, if you wrote a letter to the police, some poor first-year file clerk probably just filed it away, given that there was already an official cause of death."

"Someone killed him for a sax?" Kevin asked incredulously.

"Him — and two other people," Danni said. "But I guess he gave up on trying to make the deaths look accidental. The others were tortured and killed."

"Over a sax," Kevin said, shaking his head. "You face all kinds of hell in a war, and then someone sticks a needle into your arm and you're dead on your home turf. That's bitter."

"Arnie's folks are good people. I know they want the truth. But more than that," Quinn said, "we don't want anyone else to die. We want this killer to face justice."

"Justice," Kevin murmured. "Forgive me. Justice to me would be to see the bastard skinned alive. I guess it's a good thing I'm not judge and jury. You didn't know Arnie. He went into every situation, no matter how bloody and gruesome, when he had to. But he played with the kids over there, and he believed in making a better world. He could make an instrument out of anything — drums out of pots and pans. Hell, he could play a paper bag and make it sound like a symphony."

"Danni and I both knew him back in high school. He was a musical genius even then,"

Quinn said.

"Damn, this sucks," Kevin said. "And I'd do anything in my power to at least catch whoever killed him. But I've never even been in New Orleans, you know?"

"We were hoping that maybe he had told you about someone who was jealous of him, someone he had some kind of beef with, especially someone who was part of the music scene," Danni said.

"Arnie wasn't a fighter. Well, that sounds odd — he was a great soldier. I mean that he didn't like to pick fights. If someone had a problem with him, he wanted it out in the open so they could talk it out. He didn't harbor resentments. If they disliked him, well, he was sorry, but they didn't have to hang with him. In the service you're with who you're with, but you learn to get along." He frowned. "You don't think it was someone he served with, do you?"

"No, we don't," Danni told him. "We're as close to certain as it's possible to be that it has to be someone who lives in New Orleans and knows the city backward and forward. Whoever is doing this disappears into courtyards or down alleys, or blends in with the crowd so quickly you'd barely have time to blink. It has to be a local."

"That's good to hear," Kevin said. He

shook his head. "Arnie made a point of getting along with everyone. I do know one thing, though, that he wasn't telling anyone else."

"What's that?" Danni asked.

"He was in love."

"With who?" Quinn asked.

"That I don't know. He said I would be the first to know, if and when he found out if she loved him, too." He shrugged. "He told me, 'Kevin, I found the girl I want to bring home to my mama. In my family, that means a lot.' I guess he thought anybody knowing about her would jinx him. He said he never mentioned it to anyone else — not even Tyler."

"So he liked her but didn't know if she liked him?" Danni asked.

"I'm not sure she had any idea Arnie was crazy about her. I think he'd been admiring her from afar for a long time. But I don't think knowing her name would help you any. If Arnie was in love with a girl, I don't think she'd be a homicidal maniac. Anyway, who the hell kills people over a sax?"

Danni glanced at Quinn. He didn't respond. She didn't know everything about his police work or some of the things he'd been involved with before they met, but she did know that he'd seen people kill for what most of humanity would consider ridiculous reasons.

Kevin answered the question himself. "How can I ask that, coming back from war? People get crazy things in their heads — ideas, beliefs, customs — and then they kill."

Danni set a hand on his. "We're trying to stop this killer," she said. "And anything you can do to help . . ."

"Of course," Kevin said. "Ask me anything you want. And I'll give you my cell number, too. If you think of anything at any time, feel free to call me."

"We will, thank you," Quinn said. "What about the guys in the band Arnie usually played with? Did he ever talk to you about any of them?"

"Tyler's band?" Kevin asked. "The B-Street Bombers?"

"Yes," Danni said. "So you know them? Well, about them, I mean."

"Sure. Arnie talked about them all the time. I could practically see them just from his descriptions, but he had pictures, too. He said Shamus was a massive flirt. I think he liked Gus Epstein the most, after Tyler. Said he came at music with a quiet wonder — that was his exact phrase." He paused, frowning. "I guess if he ever had a problem with any of the guys it was Blake. Blake was like Arnie — could play almost anything. Arnie said Blake took his sax from him once to show him how he thought something should sound."

"So they fought?" Quinn asked.

"No, I told you, Arnie wouldn't have fought over something like that. He mostly thought it was funny. He said everyone just kind of stared, 'cause when it came to the sax, no one was better than Arnie. Supposedly he had a magic sax." Kevin was quiet for a minute, smiling at a memory. "Arnie said it did have magic — the magic of the love his grandmother gave him."

"Whether it's true or not, our killer thinks the sax is really magic, the kind of magic that makes everyone who plays it better," Danni said. "That's our theory, at any rate. Do you have any idea what he might have done with that sax? Did he have a hiding place? Could he have given it to one of the men he served with?"

"No. Arnie had the sax overseas, but he took it home with him. To the best of my knowledge, at least." He paused for a moment then nodded toward the harpist. "She's good, but nothing can touch Arnie's smooth jazz."

"Well, no one can ever be Arnie or play

like Arnie," Quinn said. "But the B-Street Bombers are good. A friend of ours is playing sax with them now, along with Tyler. You've got to hear them sometime."

"I'd like that," Kevin said.

"You've met Tyler, right?"

"Sure. When we were on base in Kuwait, the USO set up a bunch of Skype calls for us. I've talked to Tyler. I even said I'd be coming to New Orleans to hear him play one day."

"You've still got to come. I have a big house," Danni said.

"We even have an extra house. I have a place in the Garden District. Barely use it anymore," Quinn said.

"Maybe I'll take you up on that one day. I have to visit Arnie's grave, you know?" Kevin said. "Pay my respects. But for now, while I'm stuck in this place, don't hesitate to call." He gave them his cell number.

"We appreciate it," Quinn said. "And we *will* call if we think of anything else."

Major Johnson seemed to know that the conversation was finished. He came over and told Quinn and Danni, "Just in case we get caught in traffic, I'd better get you to the airport. Hattie made me promise not to let you miss your plane. Kevin, you need any help with anything?"

Kevin shook his head. "I'm good." He stood up and shook their hands. "You call me. For anything."

"Thank you," Danni said.

As they left the cafeteria, she turned back to wave to Kevin and saw him staring at the harpist, a smile on his face. He must have sensed her attention, because he turned to her, still smiling, and waved.

She thought there was something infinitely sad in his smile. On impulse, she ran back and gave him a kiss on the cheek. "Thank you," she said.

"I told you I would do anything to —"

"No, I mean, thank you for serving our country. Please do come visit. We'd love to show our appreciation."

"Will do," he promised her.

Danni hurried to catch up with Quinn and Johnson. Quinn was looking back, and she saw him meet Kevin's eyes. The two men saluted at the same time, and Danni realized they shared something she would never really understand.

"Maybe I was crazy to think it was so important to talk to Kevin," Danni said. "I'm not sure what we learned."

She was looking out the plane window. Quinn reached over and touched her cheek.

"Sometimes what we didn't learn is as important as what we did."

She laughed softly and drew a pattern on the window. "And what didn't we learn?"

"Well, we can be sure that sax is somewhere in New Orleans."

"Are we really sure of that?"

"Okay, maybe it's more of a theory, but every investigation has to operate on theory until there's proof. But from everything we've learned, Arnie was a really good guy. He was friends with everyone. He liked the guys in his unit, and he was best friends with Kevin. But he didn't give the saxophone to anyone he served with, so that means it's most likely in New Orleans."

"Do you think that sax can really be magic?" Danni asked him. "And what if that magic can be used for evil?"

He was thoughtful. "Even if it can, whoever is after it doesn't have it yet. And you and I have seen enough to know that sometimes there are things we can't really explain. But some magic . . ." He paused. "Some magic may be nothing more than our belief in something — an outcome, an ability — manifesting as reality."

"You're talking about self-fulfilling prophecies," Danni said.

"In a way," he told her. "I'm just saying

323

that in this case, I think we're talking about belief. Arnie became such a phenomenal player because he *believed* his sax was special, even magic. It's pretty astounding what we can do when we believe in ourselves."

She gave him an enigmatic smile and turned back to the window. He squeezed her hand, and she looked back at him curiously.

"And each other," he added softly.

She lowered her head, nodding. "I've always believed in you."

"That is a bald-faced lie!" he reminded her. "You hated me."

"*Hate* is a very strong word. I merely thought you were . . . different."

"And now?"

She grinned. "Now I *know* you're different. But so am I," she added softly. Then she said in a very businesslike tone, "What else didn't we learn?"

"Actually, now we're on to what we *did* learn," he said.

"That Arnie was in love?"

"Exactly. No matter what Kevin said, we have to consider the possibility that she's guilty. We need to find out who Arnie was in love with."

"Right. In a city filled with women."

"I'm assuming we're looking for someone in her midtwenties to early thirties. And since he spent most of his time playing music when he was home, I'm also going to assume that he met her while he was working."

"He played several places."

"But mostly La Porte Rouge."

"You're thinking Jessica?"

"Yes."

"You think Jessica killed all those people? She couldn't have. Everyone said it was a man."

"How could they tell? The killer was in a trench coat and mask. They couldn't be certain."

"She has a toddler."

"So having a child means you can't be a killer?"

"I just can't believe it."

"I don't really believe it, either. But we have to take everything into consideration. Anyway, somehow I have to get out of babysitting Jenny at night. I need to be back at La Porte Rouge," he said determinedly.

"Babysitting?" Danni protested.

"I'm sorry. I know she's your friend, it's just that she's so . . . needy. Anyway, I'll go with them tonight. I know you'll be all right, with Billie, Tyler and Father Ryan, but I'm becoming more and more convinced — call it a gut instinct — this all goes back to La Porte Rouge."

"What about the woman who was attacked with her bandmates?" Danni asked. "The timetable has Arnie dying first, and then the attack on the musicians leaving Frenchman Street. Maybe the killer knows something we don't. Maybe she's the one Arnie was in love with, and that's why the killer was convinced that she had the sax."

"Lily Parker," Quinn said, remembering his interview with her, Jeff Braman and Rowdy Tambor.

In his mind's eye he could see the day at the police station when he had questioned them. Lily was pretty. Arnie might have been drawn to her.

"Lily Parker, right," Danni said.

"Maybe, but I'm still betting we're looking closer to home."

"Home being La Porte Rouge?"

"Yes."

"There's the other woman," Danni pointed out. "Eric Lyons's part-time bartender."

"Good point," Quinn said. "Try talking casually to her tonight or whenever she's in next. Talk to Jessica, too, and find out how they felt about Arnie. And talk to the band

and to Eric and anyone else you can. Eventually, if I'm right, and the killer is someone associated with La Porte Rouge, someone will say something — even if inadvertently — that will give us what we need. I'll make sure I'm back at La Porte Rouge by tomorrow night."

CHAPTER 12

Home was even more of a "Full House" than it had been when Danni had left that morning.

The Watsons, Tyler, Bo Ray, Brad, Jenny and Billie were all there, as she had expected. But Natasha was there, as well as Father Ryan — and a man Danni didn't know.

Father Ryan was quick to introduce him as Pastor Ben Cooke of the Baptist church the Watsons attended. Father Ryan had called on him to come over because the Watsons were in need of a little spiritual support.

Danni was embarrassed to realize that when she had been at Walter Reed, she had entirely forgotten the turmoil that was going to be part of the Watsons' next months — even years — as they tried to put their home and their lives back together.

To her surprise, though, they were in better shape than she had expected.

While doling out paper plates for the pizza they'd decided on so that everyone had something to eat before heading out for the night, Danni assured Amy Watson that everyone she knew would help once the crime scene tape came down and it was possible to start fixing the house.

"Oh, honey, I know we'll get the house taken care of, don't you fear none. A house don't mean nothing. Losing my boy, now, that will take some learning to live with. I don't say 'getting over,' because you never get over it. You just learn to live with it because you're still on the journey with other people you love and who love you. And we're lucky. We have our other children, and we're blessed with a bounty of friends."

"Amy, we will find the man who did this," Danni swore then wondered if it really could have been a woman. But witnesses had said it was a man. People could pull off all kinds of disguises, she knew. And the stereotypes of the past were going away. But biology remained the same, and some of the things the killer had done had taken a great deal of strength.

Father Ryan walked over. "Come on, darlin', let's get those plates moving."

Amy laughed, took the plates from Danni

and started handing them out. Danni smiled at Father Ryan. "I didn't know you were friends with the Baptists."

"And why not? We're not so different." He shrugged. "One of my best friends is a voodoo priestess, why not a Baptist? And if that throws you for a loop, I'll bring over Rabbi Abramson next time I come."

Despite the fact that she was so tired she felt as if she had a hangover, and despite the fear gripping the city, Danni found the evening strangely pleasant. They talked about sports and movies and art as they ate pizza, and drank water and beer and soda.

Then it was time for the musicians to head off to their respective venues. Quinn, Brad and Jenny headed out first in Quinn's car. Then Danni got up to leave with Billie, Tyler, Natasha and Father Ryan, and, as they headed to the door, she realized that Pastor Cooke was joining them, too.

Tyler, walking by Danni's side, said jokingly as they left the house, "What's this world coming to? We're heading to work accompanied by a voodoo priestess, a priest and a pastor. Everyone at La Porte Rouge is going to be afraid to sin!"

Soft laughter followed his words.

Billie was in the lead, his head bowed in deep thought. Behind them, Natasha, Pastor

Cooke and Father Ryan were involved in conversation. And Danni realized that Tyler had been waiting for his chance to talk to her.

"How was Kevin Hart?" he asked her.

"He's overcome so much. He's an amazing guy," she said.

"I'd like to meet the man face-to-face one day. I feel close to him, you know? We shared a best friend."

"We invited him to visit sometime, when he's ready, of course. So maybe you'll get your chance."

"You know someone like him, and you just want to help them, you know?" Tyler said. "But I guess what's most important at the moment is, was he able to help at all?"

"Yes and no," Danni said. "He didn't know anyone who didn't get along with Arnie. But there is one thing. Did you know anything about Arnie being interested in a woman? Someone he might have been falling in love with?"

Tyler looked surprised and shook his head. "Arnie liked to flirt, but he was never obnoxious about it. He was a good-looking guy in great shape. A lot of women gave him that look, you know? But if there was someone . . . he didn't tell me. Damn. Why didn't he tell me?"

"He didn't tell Kevin who it was. He just told him that there was someone. It sounded like he had a massive crush on someone and didn't think she felt the same way about him, so he hadn't said anything to her."

"He could have told me anything," Tyler said.

"Did he sneak off a lot? Hide what he was doing?"

Tyler laughed at that. "We were friends — I wasn't his keeper. He was living at his parents' house, but he was a grown man. You'd have to ask the Watsons whether he came home every night or not."

"Thanks," Danni told him. "I will ask them."

They'd reached La Porte Rouge. A small, sluggish crowd was in. Monday nights didn't tend to be wild, but since the city had begun its laborious comeback after the summer of storms, every night meant that someone was in the city, barhopping along Bourbon. The hawkers on the street had to work harder on Monday nights, but there were usually enough people to keep them busy, just with more breaks between spiels.

Shamus, Gus and Blake were setting up when they arrived. Before they could even say hello, Shamus greeted them with, "Did you hear what happened to Arnie's house last night? It was all over the news. Place totally trashed. Man, someone had a vengeance bone out for him or someone in his family."

Tyler nodded. "Yeah, I know. I've been with Arnie's folks most of the day."

"They doing okay?" Blake asked.

"Yeah, as much as anyone could after everything they've been through," Tyler said.

"Must be another maniac in the city," Shamus said. "I mean, whoever it was couldn't have gone there to kill Arnie, 'cause Arnie's already dead. This is getting bad, really bad."

"Worse and worse," Blake said.

"But at least his folks are all right. They are, aren't they?" Shamus asked anxiously.

"Yeah, yeah, they were out staying with friends. Didn't know a thing about it until the police told them," Tyler said.

Danni watched the band members as they spoke, and she wondered if she should be worried *for* them or *because* of them.

Kevin had said that Blake had taken the sax from Arnie to show him how something should be played but they hadn't fought, because Arnie didn't fight.

At that moment, at least, Blake appeared to be just as concerned about the Watsons as everyone else.

"We need to stay together, just like we've been doing," Blake said. "See each other home, watch the damned door. Hey, I wonder if that police press conference about the killer dressing up in a trench coat and a mask scared him off from breaking in, at least when people are home."

"Maybe," Tyler said.

"Maybe he'll just change his mask," Gus said.

They all looked at him.

"Hey, this is Mardi Gras town — the guy could dress up as the Statue of Liberty and no one would notice him."

That was probably true, Danni thought. "Let's hope he doesn't," she said.

Father Ryan, Natasha and Pastor Cooke had already found themselves a table a little distance from the stage, so she walked over to sit with them for a minute.

Jessica arrived at the table just after she did. She looked at Danni, her eyes wide, and asked the same question Shamus had. "You heard what happened to the Watson house?"

Danni nodded.

"So awful. They're such nice people. It's horrible. I guess not as horrible as —" She broke off, shaking her head, and tried to smile. After all, Bourbon Street was synonymous with having a good time, and waitresses weren't supposed to be grim and shivering. She teased about them not being much of a drinking crowd, seeing as there were two clergymen in the mix, and Father Ryan laughed and told her that he liked wine, just not that night.

Then Jessica turned to Danni. "Did you have a chance to work on those duets yet?"

"No," Danni apologized. "But I will. I swear." That gave her a great opening, so she hopped up and followed Jessica to the bar.

Startled when she realized Danni was right behind her, Jessica turned. "Did I forget something?" she asked.

"No, I just . . . I wanted to ask you a few questions about Arnie," Danni said.

"Arnie?" Jessica repeated, her voice soft and something cloudy in her eyes. "What can I tell you? He was a great sax player, a great musician. And one of the nicest guys I've ever met."

"Did you ever go out with him?" Danni asked.

Jessica blushed and set her tray on the bar. "Arnie? No, no, we were friends, just friends. Did someone tell you we were dating or something? I don't think anyone would say that. Because we weren't. Why?

Why do you ask?"

"Oh, I talked to a friend of his today, and apparently there was someone special in his life," Danni said.

"I never saw him with anyone, but . . . Eric?" Jessica said. The bartender was just placing a glass of seltzer with a squeeze of lime in front of a customer at the bar. "Did you ever see Arnie in here with a woman? Did he have something going on that maybe you knew about?"

Eric turned their way. "Arnie was a good-looking guy. He had that bad-boy smile, even though he wasn't a bad boy at all. Lots of girls liked him."

"But no one special that you know of?" Danni asked.

Eric and Jessica looked at each other then shook their heads in unison.

"Sorry, Danni. I don't know of anyone," Eric said.

"What about Sharon Eastman, the woman who helps you out on the weekends?" Danni asked him.

Once again, Eric and Jessica looked at one another.

"I know she liked Arnie," Jessica said.

"And Arnie liked her," Eric said. "But not like that, as far as I know." Eric shook his head. "You'll have to ask her, though, and she's not back in until Thursday night."

"Thanks," she told them.

"Danni!" Tyler called to her.

They were about to go on for the night, she realized.

Being backup, she spent a lot of time just moving to the music or shaking the tambourine. She prayed that her eyes wouldn't close and that she wouldn't fall asleep onstage.

As the night went on, the neon lights in the bar began blending together, and the music became a sonic blur.

"Hey! You all right?"

Danni started. It was Blake.

She smiled. "Yeah, I'm fine. Why?"

"We're taking a break."

"Oh. Oh!"

She walked off the stage. Tyler caught her by the arm and walked her to the table. "Danni needs to get home," he told Father Ryan.

"No, I'm fine, really."

"It's no problem," Tyler said. "It's a Monday night, quiet as a graveyard, and I know you haven't slept. Father Ryan, why don't you and Pastor Cooke go on ahead with Danni? We'll be cutting things short tonight, anyway."

"And what about me, Mr. Tyler Anderson?" Natasha demanded indignantly.

"My deepest apologies!" Tyler said dramatically. "You're young, so I figure you're accustomed to keeping later hours."

"I'll have you know I'm not about to move into senior housing yet!" Father Ryan said.

"No, no, it's just that you've been such a trouper, and I'm sure you're not usually up so late this many nights in a row," Tyler said, desperately trying to talk his way out of the verbal mess he'd made, albeit with the best of intentions.

Then Father Ryan laughed, setting them all at ease.

"I'm more worried about Billie than I am about myself," Danni said. "I can't play an instrument for love or money, but Billie is an amazing musician."

"I'll make sure he gets home safely," Tyler said. "And Natasha, too, if she needs an escort."

"No need. I'll leave when Danni does," Natasha said.

"All right, then, thanks," Danni said. She looked toward the bar. Eric Lyons was busy filling a tray of drinks for Jessica. Despite what Jessica had said, she couldn't help but wonder about her relationship with Arnie. And yet, as she watched Jessica's body language with Eric, they seemed to be close.

His fingers brushed Jessica's hands as he dropped swizzle sticks into glasses.

She hurried over to the bar. "Jessica, you don't walk home alone, do you?"

"No, no," Jessica said, her cheeks flushed. "Eric sees me home, and if he can't, one of the guys in the band always does. And when I get home —" she shrugged with a smile "— my mom is there."

She realized that they had to consider the possibility that the murderer could be a woman, even the unknown love of Arnie's life. But as she looked at Jessica's big blue eyes and guileless smile, she told herself that she just couldn't be the Sax Murderer.

"I will always make sure she's safe," Eric said.

Danni nodded. "Good. So . . . good night."

"Don't forget to look at those songs," Jessica said.

"I won't," Danni said, and hoped she wasn't lying.

Father Ryan, Pastor Cooke and Natasha were waiting for her at the table.

They reached the house on Royal Street without incident. Wolf greeted them joyously, and Woodrow Watson once again sat on guard duty with his shotgun by his side.

When it was time to quit for the night, Quinn told Brad that he was going to move over to La Porte Rouge the next night. Brad nodded gravely, understanding.

Jenny heard and came over. "You can't!" she gasped.

"We're pretty sure everything's tied to the group over there," Quinn explained.

"But I was attacked!" Jenny said, incredulous and angry.

"Yes, and thank God you're all right. But the killer has already been to your place. He's after something Arnie had, and he knows you don't have it," Quinn explained. "He's moved on, and he'll keep moving on until he finds what he's looking for."

"Jenny," Brad said. "I won't leave you alone again, I promise."

Their bandmates had come up by then, and Steve said, "Jenny, we'll all leave here together, and we'll all make sure you two get to Danni's place safely."

Quinn just hoped that with everyone so on edge, an innocent bystander wasn't going to get shot. But he knew that Brad knew how to use a gun, and his head was noticeably cooler than Jenny's.

"That will work," Quinn said.

"But —" Jenny began.

"Do you want this guy caught or not?" Brad asked her, aggravated. "Just let Quinn do what he does best — investigate."

Jenny fell silent. "Right," she said. "I'm sorry."

Quinn felt his phone vibrate. He quickly took it from his pocket.

"Quinn?"

It was Danni's voice. He glanced at his watch and realized that it was after three. He felt himself tense up. He couldn't help it. He would always be afraid when he heard her voice in the night that way.

"You all right?" he asked her.

"I'm fine. But he was out there again."

"He — you saw him?"

"I saw a . . . a *dottore*."

"A what?"

"You know, someone in a black cloak and a birdlike white mask. The kind people wear a lot during Carnevale in Venice. Like the doctors wore in Europe during the plague. We have them here sometimes."

"Where did you see him?" Quinn asked.

"Under the streetlight near the wig shop."

"What was he doing?"

"Just standing there, watching the house. Wolf was on edge, so I went out to the shop.

I didn't turn the lights on, and I went and looked through the window across the street. He was just standing there, staring at the house. It had to be the killer again."

"I'm leaving now." He motioned to Brad that they needed to go. Brad nodded, and the others gestured toward the stage and nodded to indicate that they would see to the rest of the equipment.

As Quinn listened, with Brad and Jenny following closely behind him, he headed out to the street and his car.

"I'm telling you, I saw him there. He was watching the house."

"Is anyone else up?"

"Woodrow is with me. He followed me into the shop and saw him, too."

Was it really the killer in a new costume? Even though it wasn't Halloween or Mardi Gras, when every second person on the street was in costume, people here dressed up year-round. They were painted and gilded. They were clowns. They were comic book heroes and supernatural creatures, and most of the time, they had a hat out for tourists to throw bills into.

"We're leaving the club now," he said. "Is he still out there?"

"No. He just . . . disappeared."

"Disappeared?"

"He was there one minute, Quinn, and then I blinked and he was gone. Quinn, we need to go over there and see if we can figure out how he's disappearing."

"I'll be there in just a few minutes. Don't go out there, Danni. Please don't go out there."

"Just hurry, okay?" she said then hung up.

By then they were in the car.

"I think our guy has a new costume," he said.

"Did something happen?" Brad asked.

"Danni saw someone watching the house from across the street again. This time he was dressed up in a Carnevale-style costume."

"Oh my God! What are they going to do?" Jenny asked. "Outlaw every street performer? *In New Orleans?*"

Quinn didn't answer. He knew that Jenny really was terrified. He wasn't sure he could blame her. She had nearly been a victim of the killer.

"Did they go after him?" Brad asked.

"No. They're waiting," he said. Or so he hoped.

While he was pretty sure it was going to be a fruitless effort, Quinn called Larue. He was grateful his old partner was equally determined to get the killer off the streets.

Larue agreed to direct people out to look for the killer right away. By the time Quinn reached Royal Street, there were police everywhere.

He ran inside to find Danni, who was looking thoughtful.

"This is wrong," she told him quietly. Once again, though it was the wee hours of the morning, everyone was awake, gathering in the kitchen or moving quietly out to the store to look through the windows to the street.

"What's wrong?" he asked her softly.

"Police everywhere — he'll see them. He'll know we're onto him. He'll hide. He'll slip into another alley. Or he'll just disappear completely."

Quinn shook his head. "He didn't just disappear. He's using the alleys and the courtyards of the French Quarter. He knows this city the way only someone from here can know it. Come on, let's go out and take a look ourselves."

Wolf went with them. Woodrow assured them that he would stay at the kitchen table, shotgun at the ready, until they got back. Jenny sat at the kitchen table with him, while Brad paced. Amy and Bo Ray stayed in the shop to keep an eye on the street and wait for Billie to come home.

"Show me where you saw him — as exactly as you can," Quinn told Danni.

She headed straight for a streetlight and said, "He was here. Right here. And then he was just gone — in a blink."

"Through that gate," Quinn said, looking behind him. He knew the street, knew there were several gates that led to private courtyards much like their own.

By day, this gate opened to a narrow alley that led to a courtyard surrounded by a few small boutiques and a café.

"It's always locked at night," she said.

He tried the gate, which opened easily. Wolf barked and started into the alley. Quinn had him on leash, but now he unclipped the lead to give the dog freedom to move ahead on his own then followed closely behind him.

It was dark; only a few small lights glowed inside the shops. Danni stayed close behind Quinn as they moved in. When they reached the center of the courtyard and stopped to look around, Wolf began to bark excitedly.

He ran for the door to the café. Quinn tried that door, too.

It was open.

He didn't stop to call for police backup. He went in, glad that Danni was staying close. Inside the café, chairs were piled on tables. He looked around, seeking a rear door.

He didn't need to look for long. Wolf whined and led him behind a counter and through the kitchen. Spotless stainless-steel sinks and counters and workstations were illuminated by a half dozen night-lights.

Wolf barked and ran through. Quinn hurried to catch up, relieved to hear Danni's footsteps behind him.

There was a back door leading out to Chartres Street.

Like the front door, it was unlocked.

Unsurprisingly, there was no sign of a man in a bird mask. In fact, the street appeared to be completely empty.

He turned to look at Danni. "He could be anywhere by now," he told Danni.

"Yes, he could be. But here's my question. Why wasn't that gate locked — and why was the coffee shop unlocked, too?"

"We'll get Larue on that."

Danni looked down Chartres Street toward Jackson Square then turned to look in the direction of Canal. She could see cars moving on Canal, as they just about always were.

She let out a sigh. "Why does he come and just watch the house?" she asked.

"He's waiting," Quinn said.

"For?"

"His chance. And we're not going to give it to him."

He pulled out his cell and called Larue then told him where they were and what they had found. Larue promised that within the next few hours he would contact every shop owner and find out how and why the gate and the café doors had been left unlocked.

"Go to bed," Larue told him. "I'll get on this. But . . ."

"But?"

"I know you. You look after your own. Mostly, you try to do it all by yourself. Sleep or you'll be worthless. I'll station a patrol car out in front of your place, but make sure someone is awake and watching at your place at all times."

"Will do," Quinn promised him and rang off.

"What now?" Danni asked.

Quinn smiled. "He told me to go to bed. I'm all for that suggestion."

"Don't grin at me like that. We're both keeling over."

"I'm not grinning. I'm contemplating bed."

She laughed. "And I'm contemplating sleep!"

"Let's do it, shall we?" he asked her.

"Sex or sleep?" she countered.

"Both?"

"We'll see, but let's get home first, okay?"

Wolf barked in agreement.

They returned to the house, where they told the others what they had discovered and what Larue had said. Bo Ray said he would open the shop in the morning, so he was going up to bed, and Woodrow promised to stay on guard until morning. After that, everyone said their good-nights and dispersed.

In the bedroom a few minutes later, Danni threw her arms around Quinn's neck. "I'm surprised you didn't give me a hard time about going with you just now," she told him.

"No," he said. "I didn't. So do I get a reward?"

She twirled away from him, strewing clothing behind her as she made her way to the bed.

He sat on the bed, grinning, to take off his own clothes.

But when he turned around, he saw that Danni had only gotten so far.

She was sound asleep, shoes and jeans off, shirt and underwear still on.

He pulled the covers up around her. His

head barely hit the pillow before he was sleeping himself.

Larue and Quinn were back at the courtyard the next morning, talking to the owner or manager of every shop. Everyone had been vague; they were each responsible for locking up their own shops. The last person out was supposed to lock the gate. So far, none of them seemed concerned. If someone had been in the courtyard, so what? Their shops had all been locked. And nothing had been taken, so they couldn't understand why it was so important to the police that someone had forgotten to lock the gate.

They'd left the café for last.

"Who's responsible for locking the café each night?" Quinn asked Rafael Payne, manager of the Courtyard Café. "Someone was definitely in here. That should concern you."

"Well, of course it concerns *me,*" Payne said. "I just don't know why *you're* so concerned. Nothing was taken."

"Someone got away through your café, and I'm pretty sure he knew he'd have an escape route," Quinn said.

Payne lifted his hands in exasperation. "Who? Why? And since nothing was touched, what makes you so sure anyone was even in here? This is like — like police harassment!"

"A killer might have escaped through this café and you don't care?" Quinn asked, aggravated.

"Was someone killed last night?" Payne asked, a worried look on his brow at last. He was in his midthirties, with well-muscled arms and a harried expression.

"Not last night," Larue said.

"Then what are you talking about?" Payne asked.

"A suspect was seen on the street, and he escaped through your shop," Larue said.

"Look, I don't know how or why it was left open. Someone got careless, that's all I know. Really. At the end of a day . . . we're tired. We make mistakes. And we're not the last ones to leave the area, you know. The boutique in front closes late — really late. Their stuff is high-end. They wait for a lot of people who work downtown to come after they get off. That shop is open until at least nine most nights. Why don't you harass them?"

"We need to know who left *that* door open," Quinn said, pointing to the café's front door.

Payne hesitated and then exploded. "*Me,* it was probably *me,* all right? But I'm not

350

the one who left the gate to the street open. You'll have to find someone else to blame that on! What, am I under arrest or something for forgetting to lock up?"

"Did you do it on purpose?" Quinn asked him.

"No!" Payne said.

"It's aiding and abetting, if you did," Larue said.

"It is not — there was no crime last night," Payne protested.

He was right, of course. It was stretching to think there could be any charge against this man.

Quinn looked at Larue.

"Thank you for your time," Larue said. "But if you think of anything . . ."

"Yeah, yeah, I'll call the police right away."

Larue looked aggravated. Quinn caught his eye, and Larue shook his head in disgust. Quinn gave it a try. "No one asked you to leave your doors unlocked?"

"No. It was a stupid mistake. And I probably wouldn't even have noticed if you hadn't come and made a big deal out of it."

"You don't have an alarm system or security camera?" Quinn asked.

"I'm back here in a courtyard, not right on Royal," Payne said. "I have to advertise just to let people know I'm here. I'm making it, but just. Hell, no. The cheap bastard who owns the place lives in New York City. He would laugh if I asked for a security camera or an alarm."

"Thank you," Quinn told him. He turned to go, and Larue followed him out.

"Asshole!" Larue exploded angrily. "Wait for the day the guy *does* get robbed then goes on the news crying that the police do nothing for the city."

"He's an asshole, but I think he's telling the truth. He just forgot and left his doors open. Thing is . . ." Quinn paused, looking at Larue. "I think Payne really *is* just a disgruntled jerk, but while he may not know the killer, I think the killer *does* know him. He knows he's a fool who doesn't bother much when it comes to locking up."

"You're giving the killer a lot of credit," Larue said.

Quinn shook his head. "He's not stupid, but I don't think he's a genius. He's just been watching, maybe for a long time, and storing up information that might be useful someday."

"Maybe you're right. So . . . any leads on the sax from your end?"

"No. Anything pan out on the trace evidence from the crime scenes?" Quinn asked.

"Nothing. It's as if this guy really does

just disappear," Larue said.

"In plain sight."

"So how the hell do we catch him?" Larue asked then shook his head in frustration before looking at Quinn grimly.

"I don't know, but we have to catch him before he kills again," Quinn said.

CHAPTER 13

Danni was in her father's old office when she heard Jenny calling her name. Her friend must have just woken up, she thought, and been afraid that she was alone. In fact, only Quinn was out. He'd met up with Larue at the courtyard so they could go from shop to shop and ask about the unlocked gate.

They would finish up at the café, she knew.

"I'm down here, Jenny. I'm coming up," she called.

She clasped the book she had been looking at to her chest and hurried back up the stairs and into the kitchen. Jenny was standing by the coffeepot. It looked as if she wanted coffee but was too paralyzed by fear to pour herself some.

"Hey," Jenny said, and awkwardly reached for the pot.

"Hey," Danni said.

"I was just . . . just wondering where

everyone was," Jenny said.

"They're all around someplace — well, except for Quinn. I was digging up the scrapbook from our year at the school in the Garden District," Danni said.

"Oh! That reminds me, I told Quinn I'd make up a list of everyone in the Survivor Set."

Danni nodded. "He reminded me when he left." She lowered her head, hiding a little secret smile. Quinn had woken her up with a kiss. He'd said she looked just like Sleeping Beauty, only he wasn't sure he was much of a prince. Then, of course, the mystical fairy-tale moment had been over, and he'd told her where he was going and asked her about the Survivor Set.

Danni put the scrapbook on the table and opened it as she and Jenny sat down. "There's a shot of the whole group of us who stayed. I think my dad actually took this picture. I remember it wound up in the papers, but he had a stack of copies made for whoever wanted them. Look, there's Lawrence Barrett next to the principal — I think his name was Hardwick. He passed on a few years ago, if I remember right. There, on the left side, that's Holton Morelli. He was a guest lecturer there that year, teaching music theory."

"You're right. I can't believe he wound up in the picture," Jenny said, and shivered. She pointed to a tall boy standing in the back row. "And there's Arnie. All three of them are in this picture. And look, there's Tyler in the back on the left, and next to him is Steve, our drummer. And right next to Steve, that's Jeff Braman."

"So," Danni murmured, "Arnie dead, Jeff attacked, Holton and Lawrence killed. And you attacked, too, of course."

"There you are," Jenny said. "Off to the side."

"We all look so lost and scared."

"We *were* scared. Most of us didn't know each other till we were sent to school together. Half of us didn't even have houses after the storm. But I don't get it. What's the connection?" Jenny said.

"I'm not sure the Survivor Set really means anything. I'm positive the killer is after Arnie's sax and doesn't care who has it. There just happened to be a lot of talented people in our class, but none of us knows about Arnie's sax," Danni said.

"None of the other B-Street Bombers has been attacked, right? Just Arnie. And then his parents' home was trashed."

"And the killer obviously didn't find the sax there."

"So his parents don't have it and don't know what happened to it?" Jenny asked. "I mean, they really don't?"

"They would tell us if they did, Jenny. They don't want more people dying," Danni said.

"We should just buy some weird sax and say that's it," Jenny said. "Maybe he'd never know. Except . . . is the sax really magic?"

Danni looked at her. "Music is magic in itself, don't you think?" she asked lightly. "Amy says that believing that sax was magic made Arnie believe in himself. Maybe that's the real magic."

"I believe lots of things — or try to. Doesn't make them so," Jenny said.

"That's because you don't really believe. You're just doing what they call 'wishful thinking,' " Danni told her. "When you really believe . . . I think it makes a difference." She looked at the picture again. "There's Amelia Addison, she's a dancer. Carrie Merrill, she was in theater arts. I think she's working in one of the shows they're filming here now," Danni said. "Do you see any of the other local musicians?"

Jenny studied the picture. "I don't think so, but I'm not sure. Some people change a lot. Some of the kids in the group left after graduation. So do you think the survivor connection means anything or not?"

"I don't know, but we have this picture now. If you can remember everyone's name, you can make that list for Quinn," Danni said.

"All right, I'll do it right now," Jenny said.

Amy Watson walked into the kitchen just then. She was in a hat and an attractive flowered dress, her handbag over her arm.

"You're going out?" Danni asked her.

"I visit my boy's grave nearly every day," Amy said.

"I know, Amy," Danni said. "But I'm not sure this is a good time for you to be out on your own."

Woodrow, in his Sunday best, followed her into the kitchen. "She won't be alone. I'll be with her, and anyway, I don't think we need to worry none during the day, Danni. The killer is a coward. He attacks in the darkness. You've said that yourself."

"And," Amy added, "no hell-spawn crazy-jealous killer is going to stop me from visiting my boy's grave. That's all there is to it."

Tyler came in behind them. "We all go once a week, Danni," he said.

Danni stood up quickly. "I'll go with you. Quinn is out, but Billie and I will go with you. Just to be safe, we'll create a crowd I'm sure he won't dare to take on."

"You're all leaving?" Jenny asked Danni anxiously.

Danni turned to her. "I'll wake Brad. And Wolf will be here with you, too. He'll know if anything is wrong. Plus Bo Ray is up front in the shop. Jenny, please. You'll be all right. It's midafternoon."

Jenny bit her lower lip and nodded. "I was just asking," she said.

"I'll go up and get Brad," Danni told her. "You're going to be all right. It's broad daylight, and the street is filled with people."

Jenny looked up at her and smiled. "You're right. I'm going to be fine."

Danni called Quinn to tell him what they were going to do.

"They have to go to the cemetery *now*?" he asked her.

"Quinn, I can't stop them unless I shackle them to the furniture," she told him.

"You're probably right. Give me a minute and I'll go with you. Larue and I are finished, so I guess a trip to the cemetery is in order."

Quinn was surprised by the size of the mausoleum in the "City of the Dead" where Arnie was taking his final rest.

He had been entombed in the Garden District, where narrow walks led a visitor through rows and rows of beautifully crafted tombs, box tombs, barrel-vaulted tombs, coping graves, parapet tombs, monuments and more.

Arnie had been entombed in a "society" vault — one that was actually a small mausoleum — for musicians. It was one of the few in the cemetery with an iron gate and a little altar inside, along with a single concrete bench where mourners could sit and remember their loved ones. The tomb was beautifully decorated; musical instruments had been crafted into the design of the pyramid-shaped building. New Orleans was known for its cemeteries and its unique mausoleums, but this tomb was one of particular beauty.

Amy and Woodrow took a seat on the bench; the others stood respectfully behind them. Danni had purchased flowers from a vendor on the street, and she placed them in the vase before the seal that noted Arnie's name, dates of birth and death, army rank, and that he had been a "Dearest and most beloved son."

When they stepped back outside and started back to the cars, Quinn was startled to see Danni stop and then go walking off around a gated family plot marked with an obelisk.

"Danni!" he said and hurried after her.

He quickly realized that she was following someone. When he caught up with her, he saw who it was.

Gus Epstein, Eric Lyons, Jessica Tate and the part-time bartender, Sharon Eastman.

Danni was hugging them one by one, and they were talking animatedly as a group of tourists passed them.

"We came with Amy and Woodrow Watson to visit Arnie's grave," Danni was explaining.

"We're here to visit my mom," Sharon said. "I lost her about a year ago, to cancer. This cemetery is so pretty. We figured we'd bring her some flowers then grab something to eat that wasn't prepared in a Bourbon Street bar," she explained then rolled her eyes. "We live in a city with some of the finest restaurants in the world, but we never seem to get a chance to eat at any of them. We wanted to do something different."

"Like visit a cemetery," Gus said. "Wait, sorry, didn't mean that, Sharon. I know how much you still miss your mom."

"I never mind a trip to one of our cemeteries," Eric said. "They're so beautiful."

"You have a family plot anywhere in the city?" Quinn asked him.

Eric nodded. "We do, actually. One day

I'll get to rest in the old family pile of stones way over there in the back."

"Hopefully not too soon," Amy said.

Quinn turned in surprise to see that she, Woodrow and Tyler had joined them.

"Mrs. Watson, Mr. Watson," Gus said. "It's good to see you. We're all so sorry. We heard about what happened to your house."

"Material things, my boy," Woodrow said. "Material things mean nothing."

"And a son means everything," Jessica said, walking over to the Watsons. "Everything in the world. I'm so sorry about Arnie."

"Thank you, child," Amy said. "And once we're back home, don't you young people be strangers, you hear?" she said.

Jessica flushed and nodded; she seemed uncomfortable, almost as if she felt she had been too familiar.

"Arnie will always be with us," Sharon said gently. "Any of us who knew him. And we can all still listen to his music, since he played on so many recordings."

Quinn realized that Sharon seemed to be there with Gus. Not just as a friend, but *with* Gus. Were Eric and Jessica a couple, too? He'd never seen Jessica appear to be particularly close with Eric, but the four of them were there together.

Amy smiled. "Yes, we have his music in the computer, and we're grateful for that," she said. She looked at Quinn. "I'm feeling a little tired right now. Can we go?"

"Of course, of course," Danni assured her. "See you soon," she said to the others.

They left the cemetery. Danni, her arm around Amy, walked just ahead of Quinn. He heard Amy tell her, "That girl gives me the willies."

"Really? Which girl? Jessica?" Danni asked.

"No, not Jessica. That other girl, that Sharon. I don't know what it is — she just makes me shiver. Jessica, now, she's a sweet thing. Don't know what she's doing with Eric Lyons, though. That no-account . . . He's not going nowhere but a bar all his life. Well, that's just me, and I'm sorry, don't mean any disrespect. But they should want more, you know? Like a real life."

"Well, it's an honest living," Danni told her.

"I know, but they can do better. Eric, he can really play. And Jessica is a little lark. All of them except for that Sharon. That girl . . . there's something not right about her."

"Well, we'll keep an eye on her," Danni promised.

She turned around and looked at Quinn. He nodded then turned himself to look at the group they had just left.

Gus and Sharon, Eric and Jessica.

And I'd been thinking Blake Templeton, he thought.

And maybe he hadn't been wrong. As Danni had said, they would keep an eye on Sharon. He would mention her to Larue, as well.

They would keep an eye on the others, too.

Everyone at La Porte Rouge.

When they returned to the house, Jenny and Brad were at the kitchen table, and Wolf was on guard and not sure whom to go crazy over first.

It was almost closing time for the store, so Danni excused herself to head into the shop area and check on Bo Ray. He told her all was well, and that Natasha and Father Ryan had been in. He grinned and told her that he knew they'd only been by to make sure he was okay.

When Danni returned to the kitchen, she discovered Jenny pointing out people in the picture to Quinn, while Brad looked on. Everyone else was gone.

"Danni has this mortified look on her

face," Jenny said. "It's pretty funny."

"Anyone else have a picture like this?" Quinn asked.

"My dad took it and had a bunch printed, so yeah. It also appeared in the newspaper," Danni said.

"Do you think it will help?" Jenny asked.

"Yes, thank you, I think it will," Quinn said. He looked at her.

Danni straightened the scrapbook so that Quinn could see more easily and said, "Here are your victims, the three who were killed, Holton and Barrett, and there's Arnie. And here are Jeff and Jenny and Brad. And there's Steve. And Tyler."

"Who else do we know in this picture?" Quinn asked.

"Well, let me see," Danni murmured, studying the photo. "Millie Arliss is a violinist in New York City now. I know because she's my friend on Facebook."

"And Gail Wicker," Jenny said, pointing out another woman. "She's teaching music at the University of Miami."

"George Hensen is currently touring with a production of *The Lion King*," Brad offered, pointing at another student.

"And Kyle Mason still plays somewhere in Austin, but he went on to law school and became a maritime attorney," Danni offered, seeing another friend she chatted with now and then on social media. "David Dumfries went to California and Gig 'Peewee' Mason wound up being a host at a casino in Las Vegas."

"That's it, that's everyone," Jenny said.

"Except there are some kids with books in the background talking to each other," Quinn pointed out. "And a dog-walker over there."

"But they weren't part of the Survivor Set," Jenny said. "We called ourselves the Survivor Set, but in a way, we were really the Outsider Set."

Quinn, Danni saw, was frowning. "Who is that by the tree?" he asked.

She peered closely at the picture. There was someone just behind a big oak that was dripping with Spanish moss. He was barely visible, and his face was turned away. "I have no idea."

Brad and Jenny strained to see the picture more clearly, but they couldn't identify the mysterious figure, either.

"Do you remember anyone hanging around, watching you, that day?" Quinn asked.

"No," Brad said.

"We were just kids," Jenny reminded him. "Kind of clinging to one another. And I guess we weren't all that observant."

"He's young, whoever he is," Quinn said.

"How the hell can you tell that?" Danni asked him.

"The stance. Looks like his body was long and lanky, like a typical teenage boy. The shoulders are a little hunched. Kids stand like that. Especially boys who grow tall fast and are often thin and awkward. I'd say he was your age or maybe a year or two older — closer to Arnie's age," he said.

Danni studied the picture again then looked at Quinn and shook her head. "I still have absolutely no idea."

"I'm sorry, but I don't, either," Brad said.

"We might be looking at the killer," Quinn told them quietly. As he spoke, his phone rang. He excused himself to answer it.

The rest of them looked at one another. "So none of us has any idea who the kid in the picture is?" Jenny asked.

"I don't," Danni said, and Brad shook his head, as well.

Quinn walked back into the kitchen. "That was Larue with some ballistics info. The gun the killer used when he robbed Lily, Jeff and Rowdy fired 9 millimeter bullets, which we suspected. Larue thinks it was a Glock 19."

"That's what you got me," Danni reminded him.

"It's a very popular gun," he said. He looked knowingly at Brad.

"Yes, I own one, too," Brad said.

Quinn nodded. "You own one, Danni owns one. And so do Gus and your own bandmate Steve," he said, looking from Brad to Jenny.

"Yes, but the night Jenny was attacked, I was driving Steve and Luis home," Brad reminded him.

"Where does Steve live?" Quinn asked.

"Treme, just the other side of Rampart Street," Brad said.

"And Luis?"

"Farther up in the Garden District."

"That could have given Steve time to hop in a car and get to your place," Quinn said.

"It could have, but it didn't," Jenny said passionately. "Steve would never hurt me or Brad."

"Someone is doing this," Quinn said.

"Then look at Gus," Brad argued. "He's with the B-Street Bombers. He would have been closer to Arnie, would have known all about Arnie's special sax. He could have followed him after the bar closed for the night. Why aren't you thinking about him?"

"Oh, I *am* thinking about him," Quinn

said. "We have to follow every possible lead."

"Yes, well, you can follow Gus really easily now, since you've decided to leave us for the B-Street Bombers and La Porte Rouge," Jenny said, a subtle note of reproach in her tone.

But Quinn didn't seem to be bothered by it. "Do you know who's seeing whom home now that you've both been staying here?"

"No," Brad admitted.

"Then maybe we should find out," Quinn said.

Truthfully, Quinn's gut led him to believe — as Brad had suggested — that Gus Epstein was the more likely suspect. Still, he intended to make sure that someone kept an eye on Steve.

Not long before it was time to leave for the night, he received another call, this one from Father Ryan, who told him that he would be stopping by the house. He said he wanted to talk to Quinn before Natasha joined him for a night at La Porte Rouge.

Quinn met Father Ryan outside on Royal Street. The priest appeared to be gravely concerned.

"Not sure how to do this, because anything I learn in the confessional is strictly confidential between man and God," Father Ryan told him.

"If a priest learns about a murder or a possible murder, I believe there's a way for him to get around that," Quinn told him.

"But I didn't learn about a murder," Father Ryan said.

"What if I guess?" Quinn asked.

"I don't know. Okay, I didn't hear about a murder or a proposed murder, but I think it would be a good thing if you started hanging around with the B-Street Bombers again."

"You saw one of them today?" Quinn said.

"I can't answer that," Ryan said.

Quinn looked up. Natasha was coming down the street. He and Father Ryan both fell silent. She arched her brows questioningly as she reached them.

"What's going on?" she asked. "There wasn't another — I mean, everyone is all right, yes?"

"Everyone is fine, Natasha," Quinn told her.

"Maybe the killer's lying low," Father Ryan said. "Letting the fear die down. He sees the news. He knows the city is on the alert."

"That's true. Did you learn that today?" Quinn asked him.

"No, pure conjecture on my part. I can tell you that much."

"Aha!" Natasha said. "Father Ryan is trying to tell you something he's not supposed to."

They were standing just to the side of the entrance to The Cheshire Cat. They heard the tinkle of the bell as the door opened and Danni stepped out.

"What's going on?" she asked.

Natasha laughed softly. "Father Ryan is wrestling with his conscience."

"Oh, someone went to confession," Danni said.

"Seems to be the case," Quinn agreed, smiling as he looked at her but wincing inwardly. He loved her. And she was becoming her father, dedicated to solving strange mysteries and saving lives. It was so different working with her, though. Quinn had spent most of the time with Angus more worried about coming out alive himself, rather than worrying about Angus. He'd been a hell of a highlander, massively muscled, a tall man, as sturdy as the rugged cliffs of the highlands himself.

Whereas with Danni . . .

He was so in love with her. It was impossible to work on the kinds of cases they handled and not be worried about her. And yet, he couldn't change things. She'd inherited not only the shop but Angus's mission and passion, as well.

He remembered one of his mom's magazines that had a monthly article called "Can this marriage be saved?" He wondered what they would think if he wrote in and asked the "experts" about him and Danni. *The love of my life inherited a calling to solve crimes with paranormal undertones. Oh, yeah, and I died on the operating table but was brought back to life, and ever since I've had a similar calling. The problem is, I'm always afraid something's going to happen to her, and I wish she was somewhere safe and not in harm's way . . .*

"I bet Shamus was in to see him," Danni said. "Nice Irish boy, likely to be Catholic. And since we've just learned that Gus owns a Glock 19 that might have fired the 9 millimeter rounds during the robbery, I'm guessing he went to confession because he's worried about something his bandmate said or did, so now he wonders if Gus might have something to do with the murders."

As she spoke, Father Ryan turned and started walking away.

"Hey! Where are you going?" Natasha called after him.

"For a drink! Even a priest is allowed a

372

drink now and then."

"Wait up — I'll join you," Natasha said, and hurried after him.

Quinn was left to look at Danni with a combination of amazement and amusement. "I think he's feeling torn now," he told her.

"But he did the right thing, and he didn't really say anything," she said, smiling. Then she frowned. "Could it really be Gus?"

"It could be anyone," he said gently. "But we have to follow whatever leads we get, Danni. This killer has to be stopped."

She nodded. "Yes," she said softly.

She was so beautiful, he thought. Auburn hair flowing around her shoulders, blue eyes crystal clear as they met his.

He didn't need to write to anyone about Danni. He loved her. What he had to do was learn to let her stand on her own, to take on the role she had been born for.

"It's almost time to go. I thought we'd drive Brad and Jenny down to Magazine Street. Larue will have a man watching over them tonight," he said.

"Ready when you are," she told him.

And she was. She looked great. She could front any band, he thought. She was striking in dark leggings and a leather jacket.

Hot, he thought.

"What are you grinning at?" she asked him.

"The idea that I'm going to be at La Porte Rouge tonight."

"That's not news. So . . . ?"

"I'm just glad," he told her. "That's all."

It was almost time to be at work. What he was doing was definitely dangerous, but then, desperate times called for desperate measures.

She hadn't been part of the in crowd or the Survivor Set — as they had ridiculously called themselves — but she still deserved greater scrutiny.

He'd watched her, so he knew her routine. She was secretive; she didn't let even those closest to her get truly close. He knew where she lived, knew that her mother lived in the second half of the duplex, making it easy for her to watch the child. Funny, none of them had ever seen her son, either.

It seemed impossible, but he was a fan of Sherlock Holmes. Once you had eliminated the impossible, whatever remained, however impossible, had to be the truth.

They were watching him, so he had to change. He had no choice. But he still needed to blend in, even in costume. Luckily, in this city that could mean almost anything.

Today he was a robot. He was good at the mechanical motions. He attracted an audience as he moved through the streets of the French Quarter. He played with the kids. He posed for pictures.

And he reached her house.

He rang the bell. He heard someone moving. Heard the old woman say, "Hold your horses. I'm coming."

She opened the door. He paused for a moment; she had to be at least fifty, yet she remained almost as beautiful as her daughter.

He was stunned by her appearance.

She was equally stunned by him, a perfect robot, right out of a sci-fi flick, standing in her doorway.

They both froze.

Luckily for him, his senses returned first. With his metal-gauntleted fist, he struck her a hard blow to the head, sending her flying back against the far wall.

She crumpled to the floor with barely a whimper.

He stepped into the house, surveying the parlor. There was a piano near where she lay on the floor. He saw sheet music on the piano, but there was no sign of any other musical instruments. He would have to take further care of the old woman. He didn't have much time and couldn't afford to be interrupted. The drapery cords would work as tethers to keep her still in a nearby armchair. He could use her own scarf as a gag.

But just as he was reaching for the drapes, a little boy walked in and said, "Memaw?"

He paused, stunned once again. The kid was a cherub. Innocent, sweet — and looking at him in complete awe.

" 'Obot!" the boy said, delighted.

Frozen, he just stood there. And then, in a state of shock, he panicked. Somewhere in his mind, he knew he needed to stay and finish the job.

But with the kid staring at him that way, he just couldn't. He turned and ran.

CHAPTER 14

Jessica had given Danni a list of duets intended for two women. Danni had listened to all of them in search of the easiest ones — which meant none of them.

But when she got to the club that night she was able to tell Jessica that she had learned two of them, anyway. "I mean, I don't know them well, but . . ."

"Which two?" Jessica asked her.

It was still slow at the bar; only a few patrons were sipping drinks and listening to the canned music that drifted through the air. Eric controlled the music while waiting for the band to come in and take over, and he seemed to be in an energetic mood. Bon Jovi was playing, almost too loudly for conversation, Danni thought.

" 'Me Against the Music' by Madonna and Britney Spears and that song from *Jekyll & Hyde,* 'In His Eyes.' "

Jessica's eyes brightened. "Really? We can

do them both?"

"I don't have your vocal register, you know," Danni told her. "I'm not even sure why you want to do duets when you're phenomenal on your own. You should sing with the band every night, and *I* should be waiting tables."

"That's sweet," Jessica said, smiling. "And I really appreciate it. But I make good money on the floor. And I need it. Hey, want to go to a back corner and run through them quietly together?"

"Sure," Danni said, though she wasn't sure just how quiet they would have to be; the music was pretty loud, and though there weren't many patrons, their conversations were animated, not to mention that the band was setting up, and there was plenty of noise coming in from Bourbon Street.

"Let me just check on my tables first," Jessica said.

As Danni leaned against the bar, waiting, Eric came over to chat.

"She's pretty amazing, isn't she?" he asked.

"Absolutely," Danni agreed. She remembered seeing him with Jessica and the others at the cemetery. "It's none of my business, but are you two a duo?" she asked.

"Me and Jess?" he asked, seeming surprised.

"Yeah, you and Jess. At the cemetery I thought, well, you two seemed to be together. More or less."

"I guess *more or less* would define it," Eric said. "I'm more into Jessica than she is into me. But I'm biding my time. She worries because she has a baby. Or a toddler? I don't know. We never see him. I tell her I like kids. She tells me she doesn't want her son having anything to do with Bourbon Street. I remind her that I work on Bourbon Street, and that I'm nowhere near it when I don't have to be. I try to walk her home every night, even though it's only seven blocks, but sometimes one of the others takes her instead. Gus or Shamus. Or Max, best bouncer in the Quarter. No one's going to mess with him. I know she cares about me, just . . . not like I care about her. Not yet."

"What about Sharon?" Danni asked.

"Sharon — or Sharon and Gus?" he asked.

"Are they a couple?"

"You'd have to ask them. Today was kind of an accident."

"You went to the cemetery by accident?"

"Not exactly. Sharon had been talking about wanting to go. I talked to Gus and

379

said we could go with her then have dinner somewhere nicer than usual and still make it to work on time. He was the one to suggest calling Jessica. Maybe he saw it as safety in numbers or something."

Safety in numbers? she wondered.

"Danni!"

She turned around to see Jessica waving her over, a smile a mile wide on her face. "Coming," she said.

As she walked over to join Jessica, she saw Sharon come in.

Sharon smiled at her and said, "Hey, Jessica told me she was hoping to sing with you, so I thought I'd pop in on my night off and cover her tables so she wouldn't have to worry."

"That's really nice of you," Danni said.

"The band's ready," Jessica said, joining them. "They said to do the Madonna first, then *Jekyll & Hyde.*"

"So we're crashing right in, trying out both songs?" Danni asked.

"Tyler said it's the way to do it," Jessica said. She smiled. "We'll be fine. I know them both backward and forward. I won't let us fail, I promise."

"Okay, then."

The two of them hopped onstage. Danni suddenly felt as if something was chewing at the pit of her stomach. She wasn't Jessica. It wasn't that she lacked confidence, but her talent was for art. The thought of ruining something Jessica was so excited about was daunting.

Quinn was already onstage. He smiled and gave her a thumbs-up sign. She smiled back, studying him. At six-four, he seemed to tower over everyone else, and his eyes, she thought, were heartbreakers, his smile enough to give her the courage she needed.

Then she remembered that they were only there at all because people had died, and a murderer was still on the loose.

The music started, rousing her from her dark thoughts. Jessica sang the leads, and Danni did her part, glad she didn't have to carry the songs on her own.

Jessica's voice soared.

Danni missed a few notes and skewed the melody a bit here and there, but her confidence grew as she kept singing, and she was sure most of the audience didn't even notice her mistakes, not with Jessica covering for her so beautifully.

And Jessica was clearly delighted to be doing what she loved. She seemed to be shining. Danni was sure she'd never seen her so happy.

The place had grown more crowded as

they sang, and when Jessica stepped down from the stage, people rushed to her.

It was a truly gratifying moment, seeing Jessica so happy. Danni beamed, and when she looked at Quinn, she was expecting him to be smiling, too. But he wasn't. He was frowning and looking toward one of the tables.

She turned to look in the same direction and saw that Jeziah had come into the bar. He was speaking to Father Ryan; Natasha was nowhere to be seen.

The band had moved into a number with Tyler on lead vocals. Danni hurried off the stage and over to the table.

"What's wrong?" she asked anxiously.

"I found a kid roaming in the street. Just a toddler, really. Maybe two years old," Jeziah said. "I'd just closed up, and there he was, wandering down Royal. I thought maybe he was from the French Quarter, and since Natasha knows everyone, I brought him here. She's out on the street with him now."

Father Ryan set a few bills on the table to pay for their drinks then stood. "You coming?" he asked Danni.

Quinn was watching them as he played, clearly ready to put down his guitar and lend a hand if necessary. Danni raised a hand to tell him that he didn't need to worry. Then she hurried out with Father Ryan.

Natasha was a pillar of stillness as the Bourbon Street crowds swept by, people laughing, carrying their drinks, ready for a night of fun.

She appeared to be heedless of all of them.

She was holding a little boy in her arms. He was beautiful. His skin was a light golden copper, his eyes were green, and his hair was rich and thick and curly, a darker shade of gold. He was well dressed in little denim overalls and had sneakers on his feet. He'd been crying, Danni thought, but Natasha was crooning to him, and that seemed to please him.

"Natasha, do you know him?" Father Ryan asked.

"No, I've never seen him. We have to call the cops. His parents must be somewhere going crazy."

"Did he tell you anything? His name, maybe his address?" Danni asked, walking over and smiling at the little boy.

"Hi, I'm Danni. This is Natasha and Father Ryan. What's your name?" she asked him.

"Gram," he said.

"He said his name is Gram," Danni murmured.

"No, I don't think so," Natasha said.

The toddler was shaking his head. "Gram fall down," he said.

"He fell down?" Father Ryan murmured.

"Oh, come on, John!" Natasha said. "He isn't Gram. Gram has to be his grandmother. She was probably watching him and fell down. She's probably hurt somewhere."

Danni already had her phone out. She could have called 911, but she dialed Larue instead.

Even as she was trying to explain the situation to Larue, she heard a startled yelp from inside La Porte Rouge. Turning, she saw that Jessica was staring at them all, stricken.

For a moment she appeared to be frozen in time and place. Then she let out another strangled scream and came racing toward them.

"Mama!" the toddler cried, his little arms reaching out.

Larue, still on the phone with Danni, heard the noise and asked, "What's going on?"

"Um, we've found the mother," Danni said.

And yet she knew there was something

more going on.

Jessica sounded hysterical as she shouldered past Max, grasped her child and asked, "What . . . where did he come from? How did he get here? He was with my mother. What's happened to my mother?" Still clutching her son, she took off running.

"Larue, please get to Jessica's house. I don't know the address, but someone at the club can get it for you. I'll see you there," Danni said. "And send an ambulance!"

She was already running as she hung up. It was the only way to keep up with Jessica.

Once he heard Jessica scream, Quinn knew that Danni had been wrong. Everything was *not* fine.

He did something he'd never done before in his life. He leaped off the stage midsong, leaving his guitar behind, and ran out to the street.

"What happened?" he asked.

"Turns out that was Jessica's kid," Max said.

"Kid? What are you talking about?" Quinn said. "And where the hell is Danni?"

"Sorry," Max said. "That Jeziah guy showed up with some kid he found wandering the neighborhood. Asked me to hold him for a minute while he ran in to get Natasha. Turns out it was Jessica's kid. She went nuts when she saw him, yelled something about her mother and started running. Danni took off after her, and the others followed *her*."

"Which way?"

"Toward Jessica's house," Max told him.

"Which is where?" Quinn demanded.

Max told him the address, and Quinn started running himself, dodging the groups of tourists and locals walking — and stumbling — along the street. He turned off Bourbon as soon as he could and increased his pace.

As he rounded the corner near Esplanade, he heard a heart-wrenching scream.

He reached Jessica's house in time to see the door wide open and Jessica on her knees just inside, Father Ryan, Natasha and Jez at her side. Natasha was holding a toddler, who was sobbing and looking scared. As Quinn drew closer he saw Jessica try to calm her son, but then she began to sob herself.

His breath stopped. Where was Danni?

A moment later he started breathing again when he saw Danni kneeling on the floor beside the limp body of a woman. Older, blonde, still slim and beautiful, eyes closed, forehead bloody . . . dead? Danni, he realized, was searching for a pulse.

She looked up at Quinn. "She's alive!"

Quinn could hear sirens drawing closer even as he pulled out his phone to make sure an ambulance was on the way. Within a matter of minutes Larue arrived, followed by the emergency medical personnel.

Danni left her position by the woman — who had to be Jessica's mother, he realized — so the professionals could work on her. Danni shot him a quick smile then put her arms around Jessica, comforting her, assuring her that her mother was alive. Natasha still had the boy. Seeing things under control, Quinn stepped back, surveying the house, noticing that nothing seemed to have been disturbed. It looked as if someone had decked Jessica's mother then left, which made no sense at all.

His phone started ringing. Tyler. Everyone at the bar was going crazy. Eric was getting ready to close up for the night, and screw the owner if he didn't like it.

"There's nothing any of you can do here, so tell him to stay open," Quinn said. "It looks like someone attacked Jessica's mom, but she's breathing, and the medical personnel are here. So are the cops. Just tell Eric to ask Sharon to stay on. Jessica won't be back tonight."

He rang off and watched the scene unfold. Larue was trying to talk to Jessica, but she kept bursting into tears then hyperventilating. Danni was trying to help her and help Larue get through to her. She led Jessica to a couch and had her sit with her head between her legs, a paper bag ready for her to breathe into if necessary. One of the EMTs called out that they were ready for transport to the hospital. Jessica refused to let her mother go alone, but she also wouldn't let go of Danni, so Larue was arranging for both of them to ride with Jessica's mother.

Jessica suddenly leaped to her feet. "Wait! What about Craig? What should I do? I need to go with my mother, but I can't just leave him here."

"I've got him," Natasha said. "No worries there, none at all."

"What if . . . what if whoever did this comes back?"

"We'll all go to Danni's place, Jessica," Quinn said. "Don't worry. There will be lots of people there to protect Craig. He'll be fine, believe me. You go with your mom. I'll be at the hospital soon myself. Everyone will be all right. I promise."

"Thank you," Jessica breathed then turned

and raced after the med techs and her mother.

Danni glanced quickly at Quinn. He nodded to her and was amazed at how easily they could read each other's minds. He smiled as she followed Jessica.

He intended to join her at the hospital as soon as he finished talking with Larue.

"Not to be rude," Larue told the others, "but find what you need for the kid, then get out of my already-compromised crime scene."

Quinn dialed Bo Ray quickly to let him know what was happening and that more company was on the way.

Bo Ray asked him, "The kid walking?"

Quinn wondered for a moment what the hell that had to do with anything, then gave up and asked.

"I'll get things out of the way he might get hurt on," Bo Ray said.

"That makes sense, thanks." Quinn said goodbye to Bo Ray and immediately called Billie, who picked up right away. He explained about Jessica's mother and said none of them would be back. "Make sure you tell everyone not to leave alone — not under any circumstances."

"I'll get the word out, and I'll make sure

no one goes home alone," Billie assured him.

By the time Quinn got off the phone, Natasha had found what she needed for Craig, and they were getting ready to go. As they were starting out, Quinn caught Father Ryan by the arm. "I think you're safe right now, but keep the house locked up tight, and keep Wolf inside with you."

"What about the band?" Natasha asked. "They're still at the club."

Larue overheard her and said, "I'll send an officer to keep an eye on things there."

After that it was just Quinn and the cops.

"He left her alive," Larue said. "Assuming this was the killer, why the hell would he have done that? And the kid . . . the kid was just wandering the streets?"

"From what I've understood, Jez found him. Natasha knows half the neighborhood, so he figured she might know who he was, and they could get him home before his parents went crazy. But then Jessica saw him . . . and here we are," Quinn said. He walked to the door. "Here's what I think. The killer knocked on the door. Jessica's mom answered it. He burst in and slammed her across the room. She fell. And then . . ."

"And then he stopped and left. I'm not sure he even came in," Larue continued.

"He turned around and left, and left the door open. Why?"

"He saw the boy," Quinn said.

Larue shook his head. "With this guy's disregard for human life, I'm amazed he didn't just kill the woman and then the kid, too," he said.

"No," Quinn said with a certainty he couldn't explain. "Seeing the boy freaked him out."

"Why?" Larue asked. "If he knew Jessica, he knew she had a kid."

"He didn't know *whose* child," Quinn said.

"What do you mean?"

"The kid. He's Arnie's. We knew that Arnie was hooked on someone. We should have realized it before. Jessica's son is Arnie's son, too. The killer finally thought of looking around Jessica's house — except that he didn't know the boy was Arnie's, either. Not until tonight. I don't know how he figured it out, but he did. I'd stake my life on it."

CHAPTER 15

Danni didn't have to ask Jessica anything.

Once they reached the hospital and were left to sit in the emergency waiting room together, Jessica began to talk, and once she started, she didn't seem able to stop.

"We should have been honest, from the beginning. We should have told everyone we were seeing each other again. But we'd both been through a lot, you know? We'd been in love before and it hadn't ended well, so we both wanted to make sure things would last between us, you know? And what if it didn't work out but we were still trying to work together at the club? It would have been so much worse if everyone knew we'd been seeing each other. It all started a long time ago, really. I was the one who started flirting first. I know you knew him, but I wonder if you ever *really knew* him, though. He was so kind, so sweet. He knew all along that he was going to enlist, though. We used to talk

392

about it a lot. He didn't believe the US should police the world, but he also didn't believe that people have a right to attack us or anyone who has different beliefs. The first time he killed someone he was horrified. I mean, he was meant to be a musician, not a war machine. But he felt he owed this country. He wanted to do his duty. And he didn't want us getting too serious and telling our parents until he got back, because what if he didn't make it back? And then he did make it home, but things were different. He was different. So we took it slow — *I* took it slow, anyway. He was a lot more certain about how he felt — but things were going okay. He was getting to know Craig, and I was starting to hope we . . . And then he . . . he was . . ."

She trailed off, clearly unwilling to talk about Arnie's death.

"Jessica, did anyone at La Porte Rouge know your child was Arnie's child, too?" Danni asked.

Jessica shook her head. "No," she said softly. She looked at Danni, her eyes tear-filled. "No, we weren't going to tell anyone until we were certain we were going to stay together. Even our families didn't know. Well, I'm pretty sure my mom guessed . . ."

She began to sob softly. Danni held her

and patted her, soothing her as best she could. "So you never told your families?" she asked. "Not even when you were first seeing each other years ago?"

"We were afraid."

"Why?"

"Because of the race issue."

"In New Orleans?" Danni asked. "Jessica, half the people I know are some mix of white and black."

"It's — it's getting easier," Jessica said. "But it's still hard. Oh, everyone tells you it doesn't matter to them what color someone is. But then you do it, you tell people, and they look at you funny, like they just figured out it kinda does bother them after all. I didn't care as much as Arnie did, though. He was worried."

"His parents are the nicest people in the world."

Jessica nodded. "Yes, they're wonderful," she said in a whisper. "And we were talking about telling them. About introducing them to Craig. Craig was Arnie's grandfather's name, and Arnie admired him so much . . ." She stopped speaking and winced, and then tears welled in her eyes again. "Then Arnie died. And I wanted the world to know that it was a lie, that he wasn't on drugs and that he would never have committed suicide.

But if I said anything, then everyone would know, and, well . . . I'm embarrassed to admit it, but I was afraid. Afraid of being judged. Afraid no one would believe me about Arnie, anyway, so I wouldn't have done any good at all." She straightened, as if forcing herself to act braver than she really felt. "So I kept my son away from everyone associated with Arnie. I was so afraid for him, because what if the person who killed Arnie came after him? What about Craig, Danni? Is he in danger now? And my mom. Danni, I did this to my mom. Oh my God, she could be dying!"

"Your mother is going to be okay," Danni promised her, silently praying she was telling the truth. She pulled Jessica close again, looking over the younger woman's shoulder.

They were safe, at least for the moment. Larue had seen to it that two officers were on duty at the hospital. Right now one stood at the door to the ER, while the other sat nearby in the waiting room, watching over them. There was, of course, hospital security, as well.

"It's going to be okay," Danni assured her. "Just think of what this will mean to Arnie's family."

Jessica straightened and stared at her, frowning. "What do you mean?"

"They have you now, and Arnie's child. They'll love you and your son."

Jessica looked at her doubtfully. "Are — are you sure?" she asked.

"Of course! Jessica, he's a beautiful boy. He'll be a ray of hope for them. You can never trade a life for a life, but they'll be so happy that Arnie left a legacy, his little boy."

"You — you don't think they'll see me as some lowlife who was just playing with their son?"

"No!"

This time Danni knew she was telling the truth. Earlier in the day, when they'd all run into one another at the cemetery, Amy had liked Jessica just fine.

It was Sharon she hadn't trusted.

Why?

Dr. Lassiter, part of the team taking care of Jessica's mother, walked into the waiting room. He was a man of about fifty, his hair graying but his eyes kind.

Jessica leaped to her feet. Danni stood, too. Jessica clung to her, waiting and watching with dread in her eyes as the doctor reached them.

"Miss Tate, your mother is hanging in. She lost a lot of blood and suffered a serious concussion, but she's stable now, and we're hopeful that she'll make a full recovery."

"Oh, thank you, thank you!" Jessica cried. She started to collapse, and Danni eased her back down into her chair.

"When can she see her mother?" Danni asked.

"The nurses are finishing now — give it about ten minutes," the doctor said. "Someone will be out to let you know." He sighed softly. "The police need to speak to her, too, of course, so don't tire her out. That could be dangerous. So no long conversations. Just be there, okay?"

Jessica nodded. "Yes, of course. I'll just tell her I love her." Tears were filling her eyes again.

"Cry it all out now," the doctor told her, "then be happy and confident when you see her." He nodded to Danni. "We were all lucky today," he added with a grim smile.

As the doctor left, Danni saw Quinn and Larue arrive. Their timing couldn't have been better. Quinn looked at her, and she smiled. It felt like her first real smile in hours.

It had all gone down just as Quinn had imagined.

The only thing he hadn't nailed was the way the killer had dressed this time.

As a robot.

He and Larue let Jessica have a few minutes with her mother first, but when they did go in to speak with Victoria Tate, Quinn discovered he admired the woman very much.

When Larue asked her if she was up for a few questions, she told them to please come in then told them how stupid she felt for answering the door to a robot, of all things, and how incredibly grateful she was that her grandson was fine.

"When I think of what might have happened . . ." Her voice trailed off, and she looked at Jessica, who sat in a chair by her side, holding tightly to her hand.

"Mom, it's okay. Craig is fine."

"He's at Danni's house," Quinn told her. "Protected by a half dozen people and a giant dog. Now," he said gently, "tell us about the robot. Can you describe the costume?" He wondered if it was going to do any good even if she could. The killer would simply change costumes next time, anyway.

"He was a robot," Victoria said, not blinking as she looked at him. "Just a big robot."

"What kind of a robot?" Danni persisted gently. "Like a *Lost in Space* robot? Or one from *Star Wars*?"

Victoria seemed to brighten. "Tall, thin

and gold. Like the one from *Star Wars,*" she said.

Quinn glanced over at Danni. A common costume, they both knew. Available at costume shops all around the city, parish and state.

"Thank you, Victoria," Quinn said.

"I wish I could tell you more," Victoria said.

"You've been a tremendous help," Quinn told her. They needed to get back to the house, he thought.

A very crowded house at the moment.

Glancing at his watch, he saw that four hours had passed since he'd gone running after Danni and the others from La Porte Rouge. The bars would be closing for the night; Billie and Tyler would be heading back to the house.

He rose, looking at Larue and Danni.

Danni rose uncertainly, a question in her eyes.

"Miss Tate, will you be staying here with your mother?" Larue asked her.

"I don't want to leave her," Jessica said. "But I have to take care of my son."

"He'll be fine with us," Danni said. "I'm sure he's sleeping now." She still looked as if she were uncertain about leaving.

"The officers will stay on duty through

the night," Larue said. "You'll be fine, Miss Tate, and, as Danni said, your little one will be fine, too."

"Rest and get better," Danni told Victoria. "And, Jessica, please don't worry about Craig."

Jessica nodded then stood to tell them goodbye. She thanked Larue and Quinn, but she hugged Danni and held her tightly for a long moment.

Outside in the hall, Larue sighed. "We're going to need more cops. We're trying to protect musicians around the city while keeping an eye on our suspects. Now we need to watch the hospital, too."

"It's going to end soon," Danni said.

Quinn and Larue both looked at her.

"If this guy is going to go after every sax player in the city, a lot more people could die," Larue said.

"But he didn't kill Victoria Tate," Quinn said. "He knocked her across the room, but then he ran." Studying Danni, he added, "And you know why, don't you?"

She nodded. "Jessica *was* the woman Arnie told Kevin about. Her child is Arnie's child. You'll see when we get to the house."

"Already did," Quinn said. "But why did she deny the relationship when we asked?"

"Fear," Danni said. "She and Arnie were

still working out their relationship. She was dragging her feet a lot more than he was."

"But what were they afraid of?"

"I think Arnie was afraid of commitment while he was in the service, afraid he might not make it home," she said. "But then their son came along, and he was out, and they were trying to figure things out when Arnie was killed. And then Jessica didn't want to tell the truth in case that put Craig at risk."

"Well, I'm sure the Watsons will be ecstatic," Larue said. "Now come on. I'll get you all home."

The Watsons were already ecstatic, as they discovered as soon as they got home. According to Natasha, Amy had known the child was her grandson the minute she'd seen him. She'd cried for an hour and then started getting to know him, playing with him, singing to him then convincing him to go to sleep. The Watsons and Bo Ray were sleeping; Jez, Natasha and Father Ryan were standing sentinel in the kitchen. Jez volunteered to stay up that night while the others got some sleep.

The situation had changed tonight, Quinn thought, and he was still trying to get a handle on what that meant. It was interesting that the killer had apparently been as much in the dark about Jessica and Arnie's son as they had been themselves. And he had been so stunned by the discovery that he had abandoned his attack.

He had changed things up, as well. He'd attacked during the early evening instead of the very early morning when his preferred targets were on their way home.

They would need to be even more vigilant in the days ahead. He'd never been a profiler, but even Quinn could see that things had changed for the killer. He would be growing more desperate.

And even more dangerous.

They were both exhausted; it felt as if they had been exhausted for days. So Quinn was surprised when Danni began peeling off her clothes the minute they reached her bedroom, leaving a trail on her way to the shower.

"You could wait till we wake up," he said gently, and teased, "You don't smell that bad."

"Hospitals, beer, smoke, Bourbon Street? Ugh!" she called back to him. She disappeared for a moment then peeked out from around the door. "You're welcome to join me."

He was so tired, and the bed was so

tempting.

But Danni was more so.

It was amazing, he thought a moment later, what standing beneath the hot spray did to sharpen his senses.

She looked as if she were trying to scrub away the clamp of fear that had settled over the city. But she needed to be held, as well. To touch him and be touched in turn, to curve into him and feel his arms around her.

The shower was for foreplay; his height made making love there tricky. Drying off became more foreplay, and crashing into bed, feeling the heat of her skin against his, breathing in the scent of her, clean and sensual, created the kind of desire that transcended the world around him. He'd thought they would be gentle, playful. But instead their lovemaking was heated and volatile, passionate and, finally, sating. At last, exhausted, he lay next to her. She rested her head on his chest, so he began running his fingers through her hair. He didn't want to move, but finally he did. He got up and donned a pair of boxers. Danni was half-asleep, but he managed to get her into a long sleep-shirt. There were just too many people in the house for them to sleep the way they liked, flesh touching flesh.

Four hours later, he was glad he'd urged her into the T.

He felt her move and was instantly awake. He realized that she was sleepwalking, so he let her go and followed her downstairs, where she headed toward her studio. As they passed the kitchen he saw that Amy and Woodrow were there with Craig, feeding him cereal and playing with him. Woodrow instantly looked up, ready to come to the defense of his family. Quinn smiled and motioned for him to stay then followed Danni into her studio.

She flipped a page on her drawing board, picked up a pencil and sat down on her stool then began to sketch.

It was the same scene she had sketched before — but with a crucial difference. The B-Street Bombers were all there. Tyler, seemingly unaware of anything but the music, was playing the saxophone, clearly transported by the music. Shamus was idly tapping on his drum set and looking toward the bar. Both Jessica and Sharon were at the bar, empty trays resting on their hips as they talked to the customers, smiling, relaxed and friendly.

Gus was also standing at the bar. Quinn himself was standing nearby, watching Gus. Billie was at a table with Father Ryan and

Natasha. They were all there; they'd just moved around from her last drawing.

But this time there was more.

Craig was sitting on the bar, and while everyone in the room seemed to be doing something else, they were all really watching the little boy.

Danni finished the sketch and sat back. In a matter of minutes she had created detail and life. It was amazing, and yet . . .

Damned if he could figure out what it meant.

Other than that the killer had to be someone connected with La Porte Rouge, and they'd already been 99 percent sure of that.

He set a hand on her shoulder. She blinked and looked at him, and just like that she was awake again.

"Hey," she murmured. "So . . . what does it mean?" she asked, studying her own work. "Do you think anything would have been different if we had known? If the Watsons had known? Or even if Jessica and Arnie had sped things up a little and gotten married?"

"We'll never know, but things could be worse, too. Jessica and Craig could be dead, too."

As he spoke, he heard Wolf barking. He and Danni both rose and hurried back into the hallway; the sound was coming from the main door to Royal Street, and they headed through the shop to see what was going on. Wolf was jumping excitedly and continuing to bark. Quinn took a look through the peephole.

Jessica was standing outside, accompanied by a police officer.

"Larue told me to deliver her directly into your hands," the officer told Quinn as soon as he opened the door. The officer was grinning broadly.

Quinn realized he was standing there in boxer shorts. They were as well designed and more concealing than a lot of bathing trunks, so he just shrugged and thanked the man.

"Oh, and Larue asked you to call him as soon as you can."

Jessica looked even more exhausted than he'd felt the night before, Quinn thought, and quickly ushered her in. Wolf greeted her as a friend.

"How's your mom?" Danni asked, stepping up from behind Quinn.

"She's good, but they're going to keep her another night, or maybe two. She got a really good knock on her head when she crashed against the wall." Jessica swallowed and looked around anxiously. "Where's

406

Craig?" she asked.

"Right here, darling girl, right here," Amy said, coming from the kitchen with the toddler in her arms. "We've just been getting to know our grandson."

Jessica turned white and looked at Danni reproachfully.

"The Watsons have been staying with us," Danni said. "They figured things out on their own."

Jessica looked as if she was about to crumple right to the floor. Quinn started to reach for her, but Danni pushed past him. "Come on into the kitchen, Jessica. You can sit down, see your son, have some coffee."

Amy swept back into the kitchen with Craig, and the rest of them followed. Jessica fell into a chair, tears welling in her eyes. "We wanted to tell you," she choked out. "We loved each other, we really did, even though we had our ups and downs. But we were careful. We used birth control. I didn't know I was pregnant until he shipped out — and then I didn't tell him until I could see him, face-to-face. And now, well . . . now we were working it out together. We were going to tell you. We just weren't quite ready yet."

"Jessica, you had your reasons. You don't owe us a thing," Woodrow said. "We're just grateful you and little Craig are fine, and we want you to know we're here when you need us." He didn't try to hug her, only offered her a warm smile that was so genuine that Jessica started to cry again, at which point Amy, still holding Craig, went to put an arm around her.

Danni smiled at Quinn and slipped out to the hall, catching his hand as she went.

"Let's give them some time," she said.

"Good idea. Besides, I think we ought to get dressed," Quinn said.

"You have to call Larue," she reminded him.

"As soon as I have clothes on."

Billie walked in from the shop at that point, staring at them. "New look?" he asked.

"No, we're running up to get dressed right now. How'd you and Tyler do last night after we all ran out?" Danni asked him. "Did Sharon stay and fill in for Jessica?"

"We were all right. Things seemed odd, though. The whole room just seemed tense to me all night," Billie said. "But maybe that was natural. I mean, the bunch of you lit out like bats out of hell. Jessica screaming like that . . . it put everyone on edge."

"We'll be back tonight," Quinn said. "This afternoon we — What the hell time is it, anyway?"

"Two o'clock," Billie told him.

Quinn turned quickly to Danni. "We'd better get moving," he said.

Danni was dressed by the time Quinn finished speaking with Larue.

She walked up to him with a questioning look.

"Larue is frustrated," he told her. "He was talking to Grace, and she's frustrated, too. She isn't getting fingerprints, and everything that was used to bind and torture the dead men came from their own houses. We know the killer shot 9 millimeter bullets when he attacked Rowdy, Lily and Jeff, and that's about it. They've had men watching Gus's house, but Larue doesn't have the manpower to follow his every movement. Same with Steve."

"We know he's changed his pattern, coming out earlier at least the one time," Danni reminded him.

"I know," he said.

"Costume shop records might let us know about a spike in purchasing if he's using a certain place," she suggested.

"Larue's already tried that. No credit card records to tie either of our suspects to the costumes the killer's used, and no one shop has sold all three recently. Whoever he is, he's smart enough not to go to the same shop every time. Anyway, I'm going to run surveillance today."

"Surveillance on who?" Danni asked.

"Gus Epstein."

"I'm going with you."

"Danni . . ."

"I'm going. And you won't have to be worried about me, because I'll be with you."

He smiled. "Actually, it has nothing to do with me being worried. I was going to tell you that it's usually the most boring job in the world."

"And I'm not going to start an argument, but I suggest we drop in on Shamus. He was the one who went to confession, so we should see what we can get him to confess to us."

"Good idea. We'll stop by his place on the way to Gus's."

He'd fucked up. He'd fucked up big-time last night. He should have known. Fucking Arnie, he always had everything. First he had the magic sax, and now it was obvious that he'd also had Jessica. And when he found her purse one day and saw pictures of the kid — well, he'd known. He'd known then. Even so, he'd followed Jessica, just to be sure.

He'd barely kept his facade in place, he'd been so stunned. No wonder she'd never brought the damned kid around. No wonder she'd never shown pictures around. He was angry — and anxious. He needed that sax. Needed it *now*.

For a moment frustration almost overwhelmed him. This was a big city. It was filled with musicians. Any one of those bastards could have the sax.

No. It had to be someone with a connection — a strong connection — to Arnie.

He pulled out the picture again and studied it. Who else had Arnie known? Who else had he played with over the years?

It should have been one of the big guys, one of the top guys, but . . .

He studied the picture more closely. The Survivor Set, huh? Well, they weren't all survivors anymore, were they?

He drew a deep breath and willed himself to be calm. It was all in the facade.

He had to choose a new facade.

And he had to get that sax.

Quinn called Shamus to tell him they were on the way over. Danni watched him as he spoke into the phone. He glanced her way as he repeated what had obviously been

411

Shamus's question. "Why? We just want to catch you up on last night."

They could see Shamus watching through the window as they arrived. He opened the door as they reached the front steps, looking nervously up and down the street. A boy was riding a skateboard past his house, and an old woman was walking by with her groceries.

"Get in, get in," Shamus said, sounding stressed.

The minute they were inside, he quickly closed, locked and bolted his door.

"I may get caught by this guy eventually," Shamus said, "but I'll be damned if I'm going to make it easy for him."

"It's always smart to be vigilant," Quinn said.

"You guys want coffee or tea?" Shamus asked.

"Sure," Quinn told him. "There's never enough coffee to keep me awake these days."

Shamus led the way into the kitchen. He lived in an old shotgun house; the parlor led right into the dining room, which led into the kitchen, where two bedrooms broke off to the side. The decor was Bohemian and retro hippie. He had drapes for doors and strings of Mardi Gras beads hanging from archways. A drum set took up most of the back bedroom. Danni could also see amps and mikes, along with several guitars set in stands.

"I don't even own a sax," Shamus said, reaching into a cupboard for mugs. "So while Arnie and I were friends, I don't know why anyone would think I have his sax. But this guy is crazy, so I'm not taking any chances. I mean, why the hell attack Jessica's mom then leave her alive and let her kid out and all?" he asked. "They're both all right, aren't they? Nothing's happened to them since Billie filled us in last night, has it?"

"No, not that we know of," Danni said. She perched on one of the stools by his counter. "Shamus, do you have any idea who could be doing this? Are you suspicious of anyone — did anyone ever say or do anything odd around Arnie before he died?"

"We all teased Arnie. We all said we could be just as good as he was if we had magical instruments, too," Shamus said.

He already had a pot of coffee ready. He filled mugs for them and topped off his own. Then he reached up and pulled a bottle of Jameson Irish Whiskey from the cabinet and offered it to them. They shook their heads, but he added a liberal portion to his own mug then took a sip.

413

"I don't. I don't know anything," he said.

"But Gus and Arnie didn't always get along, right?" Quinn asked.

"Who told you that?" Shamus asked, frowning. "They got along fine except for . . ." He stopped and lowered his head to avoid meeting their eyes. "It was just the one time."

"They had a fight?" Quinn asked.

"Yeah, sort of a continuing argument," Shamus said. "But that can't have anything to do with this. Gus has a temper on him, sure, but it's because he cares so much about the music. He wants everything just right. All musicians hear things just a little differently or have their own ideas about how an arrangement should sound."

"But something is wrong. Something *is* bothering you about him, right?" Danni asked.

"I promise we'll never say that you were the one who felt something was off," Quinn said. "If he's innocent, we'll find that out, too. Why do you think he could be doing this?"

"I don't!" Shamus protested.

"Then what is it?" Quinn asked.

Shamus looked down, shaking his head. "Jessica," he said quietly.

"What about her?" Quinn asked, and

added, "Please, Shamus, if the man is innocent, we have to start looking elsewhere. Tell us what you know."

Shamus sighed. "Gus and Arnie fought over Jessica. Gus saw how they flirted, and he told Arnie that if they wanted to be together, they'd better both get new jobs. He didn't have any right to say it, but the thing is, he was into Jessica, too, and he could have made things unpleasant for them if he wanted to. And then, the morning after the Watsons' house was broken into . . ."

"What, Shamus? For the love of God, just tell us," Quinn said.

"He came here — to my house. He was wound tight, upset. He had a cut on his hand. And he — he had a gun on him. He told me it was legal, and for as long as someone was running around killing musicians, he was going to carry it. He's my friend, you know. He and Blake and I hang around together, we see each other home at the end of the night, and I've tried to dismiss it, but . . ." He paused again. "I had to talk about it. I went to confession. Me mum back in County Cork would be proud. I went to confession because I needed to talk about it, but I didn't want to betray a friend when I still can't believe it's him."

"I understand, Shamus, I do," Danni said.

Shamus lowered his head again. "He's my mate, my friend. But — and God help me for this — I always find a way to be dropped off first. I leave him alone with Blake." He looked up at them. "Do it — do whatever you need to do to find out the truth."

"Excuse me," Quinn said. He walked into the other room, and Danni knew he was calling Larue and telling him that they needed to go ahead and pick up Gus for questioning.

"He'll never forgive me if he finds out," Shamus said.

Danni's phone rang just then, saving her from having to make a promise she wasn't sure she could keep, and she excused herself to answer it.

It was Steve, according to her caller ID.

"Hey, Steve, what's up?" she said.

He didn't reply and her phone went dead. She looked over at Quinn as she tried calling Steve back. He didn't answer.

She tried to tell herself that he had butt dialed her. If he was in trouble, he would have hit 911.

But anxiety ripped through her. "Quinn, tell Larue to get to Steve's place. Have him send the closest officer there, too, and . . . let's go, okay? Shamus, thanks," she said.

And then she and Quinn were heading out to the car.

CHAPTER 16

Quinn pulled over to the curb just as the first patrol car arrived.

He jumped out and headed for the door, leaping up the steps leading to the house.

The door was open.

An officer came running from the patrol car. "Mr. Quinn, wait!"

But Quinn was armed and ready and through the doorway even as the officer reached him. Danni burst in behind them. "Steve!" she cried out desperately.

There was no one in the living room.

They heard a noise from the back, a scraping sound. Quinn followed it, pausing for a split second at every arch and doorway, even though he was certain the killer wasn't there anymore.

He hurried forward, anxious to find Steve before Danni could.

He was in a back room.

He was tied to a chair, his head hanging

down. Quinn feared the worst.

Trying to stop Danni was like trying to change the weather. She burst past him, sliding to her knees at Steve's feet. "Steve!" she cried.

And Steve lifted his head, making it obvious why he didn't reply; a kitchen towel was tied around his mouth, gagging him.

He tried to say something, but it was unintelligible.

"Hang on, we'll get you out of this," Danni said, searching for a way to release him.

Quinn knelt down beside her, pulling out his pocketknife. Steve had been secured to a wooden kitchen chair with a belt, two neckties and what looked like his cell phone charger. Quinn quickly ripped his way through the bindings and the gag.

"Just left . . . out the back," Steve gasped.

"As what? What's he dressed as?" Quinn asked.

Not that it mattered; the costume would be off by now, and tossed or stored where they would never find it.

"Woman," Steve said.

"A woman?" Quinn repeated.

"Dressed . . . dressed as a woman."

Quinn turned to head out in pursuit.

"Mr. Quinn, you need to wait for backup,"

the officer said.

"We've already lost him," Quinn said in disgust as he stopped at the open back door. He could hear sirens from the street and knew the place would quickly be filled with police.

He left Danni to calm Steve and stood in the doorway, looking out. It led out to a back lawn, slightly overgrown and filled with pieces of broken furniture Steve was apparently working on. There was a short wire fence at the back, a higher wooden barrier to the left, and bushes and trees to the right. He was heading to the rear then noticed something and turned toward the bushes. Part of a hedge seemed to be flattened; he walked out that way then passed through the neighbor's yard and reached the sidewalk.

No one of either sex was running, or even walking, down the street. There was, however, a group of children playing in one of the yards. There were about seven or eight of them, and they were taking turns throwing a ball at a net attached to the family garage.

He trotted over to them. "Hey, kids," he said.

They stopped; the kid holding the ball surveyed him gravely and then looked down the street to where several police cars were now pulled up on the sidewalk and the lawn.

"Did you see anyone running along here? Or walking? Did you see anyone at all who you don't know?"

"Just the lady," the kid holding the ball told him.

"The lady? What did she look like, and where did she go?"

"She was tall," one of the other kids offered.

"Of course she was, moron. She was wearing heels," a slightly older boy said.

"She had dark hair — long, down her back," the first boy offered.

"She was funny-looking," another said.

"Fat legs!" one said, laughing.

So their killer was a tall, funny-looking woman with fat legs — or a man in disguise.

"Thanks. Which way did she go?" he asked.

They pointed around the corner. Quinn began to run, his feet pounding hard on the pavement and then the grass as he cut across a lawn. As he ran, he heard the loud revving of an engine moving down the next street.

He kept running, hoping he could catch the license tag.

But it was no good. The car was gone,

undoubtedly turning onto the highway beyond the next block. He stopped, doubled over as he caught his breath, and damned the fact that they'd missed the killer again.

Once he was untied, Steve seemed to be fine, at least physically. Danni kept a comforting hand on his shoulder as he trembled in reaction then finally looked at her and said, "Sorry. Guess I'm not hero material, huh? Asshole material, yes. I know it was stupid, but I opened the damned door. But it looked like a woman. In fact, at first I thought it was Jessica."

"Jessica Tate?" Danni asked, frowning. "Why would she be here? Her mom is in the hospital, and her son —"

"I know. I thought she might have needed something — help, maybe, a shoulder to cry on," Steve said.

"How well do you know Jessica?" Danni asked.

"I met her at the club, or I thought I did. But you know what? I'd run into her before. I realized that when we all had a night off and met up to see what was going on along Bourbon. We got to talking, and she reminded me that we'd met at a parish competition years ago."

"And you really thought it was her today?"

Danni pressed. It wasn't surprising that people in the city knew one another. It just seemed odd that he'd thought she would come to him at a time like this.

"She looked kind of like Jessica," Steve said. "I just saw a woman with long dark hair standing at the door. I admit, both my libido and my curiosity made me open it."

Danni heard a commotion at the door and realized Larue had arrived.

He walked in, commanding, "Anyone touching anything, stop now. We've got to get something on this guy from someone." He saw Danni sitting by Steve. "Of course you got here first," he muttered.

"Steve was just telling me what happened after the killer got in."

"He'd just gotten a knife out of my kitchen when you and Quinn got here. Without you guys . . ." Steve said dully. He shook his head, humiliated.

"Let's go back to where you were," Larue suggested. "You opened the door and . . . ?"

"I opened the door, and he got me with a right to the jaw. I went down, and the next thing I knew, I was being tied up with my own stuff."

"Why did you open the door in the first place?" Larue asked.

"It was a woman," Steve said softly.

"The killer is a woman?" Larue said.

"I know some tough women," Steve said, "but none with a right hook like the one that downed me. No, it was a man dressed as a woman. And he looked pretty damn real, at least through the peephole."

Larue pulled out his notebook and asked Steve to go over everything that had happened. Grace Leon had arrived with her crew by then. She suggested that Steve might need medical attention, but he said he was fine for now and promised to see a doctor later.

Quinn walked back in then, and Larue ceded the floor to him. Between the two of them, Steve was asked nearly every possible question.

When they asked what color the "woman's" eyes were, Steve was thoughtful for a moment and told them that they were yellow. "Like demon eyes," he said.

"Seriously?" Larue muttered.

"Contacts, maybe?" Quinn asked.

"Probably," Steve said.

Larue swore. "Bastard changes like a chameleon. He'll be something else next time he strikes. We're getting nowhere," he said in disgust.

Quinn caught Larue's eye and nodded toward a corner. Before he turned to speak

424

to Larue privately, he said to Steve, "I'm sorry, but we need to know everything you can think of about what happened. Would you mind talking to us down at the station?"

"Not at all," Steve said. "The truth is, I don't want to hang around here alone."

"We'll get going, then," Larue said. "Grace, I'm saying a prayer you'll get a print."

"He wore gloves," Steve said. "Black lace gloves."

"Of course," Larue said drily. "Grace —"

"I'll see what I can get, anyway," she finished for him. Then she turned to Steve and said, "Before you go, I need to know where he was, anything you can remember him touching, anything at all that could help us find even the most infinitesimal bit of forensic evidence."

"I'm all yours," Steve told her earnestly.

Larue headed out to join Quinn, and a minute later Danni followed. When she stepped outside and joined them, they were already talking about Gus Epstein.

"We don't have a single piece of real evidence," Larue said. "The best I can do is ask Epstein if he'll come in and tell us anything he can think of for the record. I can tell him we're talking to everyone who knew any of the victims."

"Why not just stop by and visit him? Make it look casual, less stressful," Danni said. "Plus we could look around his place on the sly."

"Good idea," Quinn said. "Though if he is our guy, he'll find an excuse not to let us in, not if he has any kind of evidence lying around."

"Worth a try, though. You two stop in and see him," Larue said. "It won't look as suspicious if I'm not there. Meanwhile, I'll try to figure a way to get a search warrant. Because if we don't handle this legally, any evidence we find will get thrown right out of court."

"If we don't handle this some way," Quinn said, "we'll just have more bodies piling up." He looked at Danni. "Let's go," he said grimly.

"I know why we can say we're dropping in on him," Danni said.

"Really?" Quinn asked her. "Why?"

"We're worried about him. Steve was just attacked, and after the killer's targeted so many people we know, we can tell him we're trying to check on everyone we know and make sure they're all doing okay."

"Sounds good," he told her.

When they pulled up in front of Gus's

house, Quinn saw that a patrol car was parked on the block. Larue had been doing his best to keep eyes on both suspects and possible victims.

Quinn pulled up directly in front of the house. He noted that Gus's SUV was in the drive, just where it should have been.

He went around to Danni's side of the car, but she was already out. "Be careful," he warned her. "He does have a gun."

"I know." She patted her shoulder bag. "So do I."

He nodded. "Yeah, you do, don't you?"

He knocked on the door. There was no answer. He looked at her with a frown then pounded harder on the door. Still no answer.

The patrol officer down the street got out of his car. "He's in there — has to be. I never saw him leave," he called, hurrying toward them.

"Unless he went out the back," Quinn pointed out. "Or someone went in."

At least the cop had the grace to blush.

"I'm going around back. Be careful and stay covered," Quinn said to Danni, who pressed herself tightly against the wall, out of range of the windows and doors.

Gun drawn, Quinn hurried around the side of the house, trying to see through the windows as he went. The house was dark; Gus could be sleeping, getting ready for another late night.

But he wasn't, and Quinn knew it.

When he reached the small yard, he found that, as he'd suspected, the back door was open. Using his hip to avoid contaminating evidence — not that he expected there to be any — he nudged the door open farther. He moved quietly inside, finding himself in the kitchen. Muted daylight showed dust motes on the air. Nothing was on the stove; the room was as clean and neat as if it hadn't been used in weeks. He moved through an archway into the dining room.

He thought, when he reached the parlor, that he would find Gus tied to a chair and likely dead. But what he found instead was chaos. Furniture thrown everywhere, the buffet drawers open, upholstery ripped to shreds. He quickly checked out the two bedrooms. They, too, were destroyed — but there was no sign of Gus.

"Coming out — house is clear!" he shouted before opening the front door. "No Gus, total destruction," he said briefly.

Danni walked in, while the officer waited outside.

"Watch what you touch," he told her then holstered his gun and called Larue, watching as Danni moved deeper into the house.

"Damn it," Larue said as soon as Quinn finished describing the state of the house.

"This doesn't make any sense," Quinn said. "His place is trashed, his car is here. I'm hoping he isn't dead, but I have no idea, because he isn't here. Why the hell would he have trashed his own house?"

"To put us off the scent?" Larue suggested.

"Quinn!" Danni called from the front bedroom.

"Hold on," Quinn told Larue. He headed toward the bedroom.

Danni pointed under the bed.

He knelt down to look, and there, almost hidden in the shadows, he saw a *dottore* mask.

He stood up and looked at Danni, his heart sinking. He hadn't wanted it to be Gus. He hadn't wanted it to be anyone they knew. He'd wanted to find out the killer was a total stranger.

"It gets worse," Danni whispered. She pointed to a framed picture hanging on the wall.

The picture Danni's father had taken of the Survivor Set.

Arnie's face was scratched out. So were Holton Morelli's and Lawrence Barrett's.

There were slashes over Jeff's, Brad's and Jenny's faces.

And there were checks on Tyler's face — and Danni's.

His stomach knotted, and he put the phone back to his ear. "Larue? You still there?We have to find Gus — and find him fast," he said. "You've got to put out an APB, and you've got to say he's armed and dangerous. He owns a Glock 19."

It wasn't easy convincing bar and restaurant owners to close down in NOLA — even when lives were at stake.

Even the owner of the Midnight Royale Café didn't want to close, despite the fact that one of his house musicians had nearly been killed. His arguments were solid: no one had been attacked in a restaurant or a bar. Closing down was giving the killer just what he potentially wanted: the destruction of the local music scene. His final point, that there was no musician out there who couldn't be replaced, earned him less sympathy. But eventually he agreed that a one-night shutdown might be in order.

It wasn't as difficult with La Porte Rouge, where Eric Lyons ran the establishment for an absentee owner.

"Gus? I can't believe it," he said when

Danni called him. "I mean, he's got a temper on him, yeah, and he has a thing for Jessica, but . . . I still can't believe it. As for closing for the night? Yeah, already got a request from the cops, and it's no problem. The band needs time to get their heads together, anyway. You take care, okay?"

Danni promised that she would and told him to do the same. "Don't forget, the killer went to Jessica's house. Her mom is still in the hospital."

"Speaking of . . . how's Jessica doing?" he asked. "We all care about her, you know?"

"I *do* know. And she's fine."

"She's not alone, right?"

"No, no, she's not alone," Danni assured him. She hesitated. "What about you and Sharon? Can you guys hang together, watch out for each other?"

"We'll be fine," he said. "I'll try to reach her."

When Danni hung up, Quinn was watching her, the light coming through her studio window casting shadows across his face. "Okay?" he asked.

"Not a problem," she assured him. "But . . . what if the police can't find Gus? We can't ask people to close down forever. And I'm not sure that it does do any good. No one has ever been attacked in public or inside a club."

"The street is public, and that's where the killer went after Jeff, Rowdy and Lily," he reminded her.

"I can't help wondering . . ."

"Wondering what?" he asked.

"What if it's *not* Gus?"

"The evidence at his house was pretty damning. And I think he might be going over the edge. No matter how sane a face he's been portraying to the world, what he's doing has to take its toll. That puts him at risk for making a mistake, and that can only be to our advantage. Unfortunately, it also means he's liable to do anything. Anyway, I'm taking Wolf, Billie and Father Ryan and going back to Gus's house. We're going on the hunt. If Wolf can pick up a scent, we'll be able to follow Gus's trail."

"I'm coming, too," Danni said.

"I'd rather you stayed and watched out for Jessica, Craig and the Watsons. You'll have Tyler and Bo Ray, along with Brad and Jenny. I don't like leaving the house un-guarded with the dog gone. Larue is leaving an officer out in front, but I want someone I can count on inside, too," he told her.

Danni raised her eyes, challenging, then realized from the look in his that he recog-nized the fact that they were in this together, and that he couldn't make his every move with the idea of protecting her.

The truth was, what he was saying made sense. She had a houseful of people who did need protecting. And if Billie was with him . . .

"All right, I'll stay here and watch the house," she said.

She got up and walked over to him and stood on her toes to kiss his lips. "Just be careful out there, okay?" she said softly.

He put his arms around her and pulled her close for a moment. She felt the whisper of his breath over her hair, and she wanted to hold tight and refuse to let him go.

She realized after a moment that he was actually looking over her shoulder, and she turned and studied the picture she'd sketched during her last sleep-drawing session.

"What is it?" she asked.

He shook his head. "I don't know. The picture . . . everything looks so normal. Except for the kid on the bar, of course."

Danni looked at her own art. "We're all there, Gus playing with the band as usual." She hesitated. "I looked at the picture up on Gus's wall, and the first thing I thought, before I saw what he'd done to it, was why did he even have it? He wasn't one of us, wasn't part of the Survivor Set. Do you think he just hates everyone who was? Or was he just convinced Arnie Watson would have given someone in the picture that sax?"

"I don't know," Quinn said. "Maybe, when we find him, we'll be able to find out just what was going on in his mind."

"I wonder if we'll ever find the sax," she said.

"Maybe. Let's pray we do. God knows when the idea of a magic sax could cause someone else to go mad," he said.

He was still looking at the drawing.

"What?" she asked.

"It's telling us something we just aren't seeing."

"Something we should know?"

He shrugged, shook his head as if to clear it and turned to her. "Okay, we're off. Bo Ray and Tyler are closing up the shop, and they'll set the alarm. Woodrow is at the kitchen table with his shotgun, a cop is outside — and you have your gun."

"We're good," she said then added, "*I'm* good."

He started to leave then came back suddenly, pulled her to him and kissed her hard then turned to leave again.

And that time he really did go.

Cops were combing the city. They were on foot and horseback in the Quarter, and driving in the surrounding districts. Larue had called in every available man for overtime, and the mayor had approved it. News alerts were out.

With so many people looking for him, Quinn would have thought there was no way for Gus Epstein to hide, except that his powers of disguise seemed to be just this side of supernatural.

Billie, Father Ryan and Wolf were tense and quiet as Quinn drove to Epstein's house, but he knew that inside they were alert and ready for anything.

Grace Leon and her team were still going through the house when Quinn arrived with his small posse. She found a piece of clothing for Wolf to sniff; the dog caught the scent and barked enthusiastically then raced for the back door.

They already knew Gus had gone out the back. The true test of Wolf's abilities was yet to come.

Wolf led them through Epstein's backyard and then the neighbor's, and finally out onto the street. He ran for several blocks, with Quinn on the other end of the leash, and Father Ryan and Billie right behind.

Wolf ran for two blocks, and then he stopped, sat on his haunches and began to howl.

"What in God's sweet heaven does that mean?" Father Ryan demanded.

"It means the scent ends here," Quinn said. "He got into a car or on a bus."

The dog began to bark again then headed back toward Gus's house.

"What does this mean?" Father Ryan asked.

"I'm not sure," Quinn said.

"I can't believe he's making us run back the way we just came," Billie said breathlessly.

"Take it more slowly, then," Quinn shouted, carried along after the dog.

"Like hell — Sorry, Father," Billie said. "If Wolf is on the move, it means something!"

And it did, Quinn knew.

But what the hell was it? What were they missing?

What was right there in front of their faces that they hadn't seen?

CHAPTER 17

Danni was still in her studio, studying her most recent drawing, when Jessica tapped at the door.

"Hey," Danni said. "Come on in."

"You sure?" Jessica asked.

"Of course."

Jessica walked into the studio as if she were stepping on hallowed ground.

"How's Craig? *Where's* Craig?" Danni asked her.

Jessica offered her a broad smile. "He's just fine. His grandma is doting on him. Oh, Danni, I feel like such a fool. How could I have had so little faith in the people who raised Arnie? They're wonderful. I just have to hope everyone else will be, too."

"I guess we have to be cautiously optimistic."

"That's what they said about my mom when we got to the hospital. I think that's going to be my new approach to life, cautious optimism," Jessica said. Then she walked over and looked at Danni's drawing.

"What's Craig doing on the bar? I never brought him to the club, Danni."

"I know that, Jessica. I just draw people, and sometimes my imagination gets a little carried away, I guess."

Danni's phone rang. She answered it to find Shamus on the other end.

"Danni?"

"Yes. What's up?"

"Did they get him yet?"

"I don't know, Shamus. They're looking everywhere. If they haven't found him yet, I promise you they will."

"I'm frightened, Danni. What if he knows? What if he knows I said something?"

"There should be a cop out front of your house."

"There is, but there have been cops around before."

She hesitated. "Have you spoken with Blake? Has he seen Gus?"

"He's gone, Danni. Blake took off. He went to Florida. He said he'll be back when this is over."

Shamus really was afraid; Danni could hear it in his voice. "Do you want to stay here, Shamus?"

"Hell, yes! I mean, you're not alone, right?

There are a lot of people there?"

"Yes, there are a lot of people here."

"You got guns?"

"We have guns."

"Will the cop bring me?"

"I'll call Larue. I'll tell him that you don't want to be alone and ask if the officer can drive you over."

"Thank you, Danni."

"No problem."

She hung up, called Larue and made the arrangements.

"Shamus, huh?" Jessica asked. She smiled. "He's a big sweetie. I'm glad he's coming. I hope you don't mind, though. There are so many people here already."

"A full house is a good thing right now, right?"

Jessica nodded. She turned away from Danni's sketch and said, "I'm going to check on Craig."

"I'll go with you, see what everyone's up to," Danni agreed.

Everyone seemed to be doing their best to make time pass in as normal a fashion as possible. While Woodrow wasn't about to abandon his position, he was more than willing to play gin with Bo Ray and Tyler, who had joined him at the table.

Natasha and Amy were taking care of

Craig, laughing with him as he assembled the pieces in a little Busy Bee block game.

Jenny was cooking, with Brad awkwardly helping her. She'd insisted on preparing lasagna for dinner.

It was almost a party, Danni thought drily. "Shop locked up tight?" she asked Bo Ray.

"Yup. I locked up and set the alarm right after Quinn and the other guys left with Wolf," he assured her then grinned and announced, "Gin!"

"I'll be damned," Woodrow said.

Danni's phone rang. She excused herself and went into the hall to answer. It was Quinn.

"Any luck?" she asked anxiously.

"No, but Wolf is following a new lead," he said.

"Wolf?"

"Hey, I trust the dog, okay? I just wanted to make sure everything there was all right."

"Everything is fine," she assured him. "Shamus is joining us. Blake left town, and he's alone and afraid."

"Yeah, I just talked to Larue. The cop watching his place is bringing him over, and then he's going to stay for a while. That puts two cops with you, which seems good to me."

"Okay, so . . . keep me posted, yeah?"

"Yep, absolutely. And call me, if anything comes up."

"I will."

"Danni?"

"Yeah?"

"I love you," he said.

She smiled. "I love you, too," she said and hung up.

She looked back into the kitchen. All really was well. Everyone was busy doing something. If she hadn't known better, she would have thought everything was normal. But she *did* know better. And so did they.

Because every so often, one of them would pause, looking around. Reassuring themselves. And waiting . . .

Because it was in the air. Something was going to happen.

Wolf was running around Gus Epstein's house. He was picking up a scent, Quinn knew; he just didn't know *what* scent.

"I think your dog has gone nuts," Grace told him. "And I'm not finished here, Quinn. Not that we've found a damn thing or expect to, but still, there's procedure. And having your dog lose it in the middle of my crime scene isn't helping."

"My dog doesn't lose it, Grace," Quinn said. "He's onto something. But don't worry about it, because he's done with your crime scene."

Wolf *was* done; he was standing by the door, whining. He was ready to move.

"We're going to follow Wolf *again*?" Billie asked.

Quinn nodded. "Maybe I should have someone get you back to the house, Billie."

"Hey!"

"You're not exactly a kid, and you still seem winded from earlier."

"I'm not keeling over yet, either, young man. If we're following the dog, we're following the dog."

"And I'll be right here with him — just in case we need last rites," Father Ryan teased.

"Watch yourself, Father, or you'll be the one in need of last rites," Billie threatened with a smile. "Come on. Let's follow Wolf."

The dog lit out the minute Quinn opened the door and started toward the Quarter.

He finally stopped by a hedge on Rampart Street and started barking. Quinn looked closely.

There was blood on the leaves. And as he carefully moved the branches aside, he spotted a bit of fabric. Denim. He pulled out his phone, got hold of Larue and told him to get Grace down to the hedge. "I don't know whose it is, but we've got blood and fabric," he said.

"On it," Larue promised him.

"And we're moving," Quinn said.

Wolf was barking insanely. He wanted to cross Rampart, but the traffic was too heavy, and Quinn held him back.

Father Ryan moved into the street as soon as there was a slight break in traffic. He held up his hands and brought cars screeching to a halt. "Go!" he shouted. "Thank God I've got the collar on. Even atheists think twice about hitting a priest."

Danni automatically excused herself when her phone rang again. She was anxious, but she wanted to hear what was happening before she told anyone else, whether it was good news, bad news or no news at all.

She was stunned, glad she had stepped out of the kitchen, when she heard the voice on the other end.

"Danni?"

"Gus?" she said incredulously.

"Danni, I didn't do it. I'm being framed."

"Gus," she said, thinking as quickly as possible, "Gus, if that's true, you've got to get to the police. Tell them —"

"Tell them? What makes you think I'll have time to tell them anything. They'll shoot me down like a rabid dog!"

"No, Gus." Was that the truth? she wondered. "Gus, Quinn is out with Father Ryan, Billie and Wolf. If you call him and find a way to meet him, he'll make sure you get to the station safely."

"He came to my house. The killer came to my house. I ran, and the next thing I knew, I was being hunted by the cops. Danni, I didn't do it. I saw the news on my phone, and I'm being set up. I'm being framed by the real killer. I barely got out. See, I ran, panicked, then went back — I was running blindly, probably in circles half the time, because I thought the killer was still there. I cut myself, and I'm sore from crawling over fences. Danni, please, you have to help me."

"If it's not you, Gus, who is it?" she demanded. "Did you see him?"

"Her."

"No, Gus, it was a costume. So you don't know who it was?"

"Well, he looked like a dark-haired woman."

The same disguise he'd used at Steve's house.

She'd never believed it could be Gus. Of course, this could just be his way of tricking her.

"Gus, you've got to go to the police."

"Danni, I'm scared. If he sees me before I

can prove my innocence, I'm dead. He's magic or something, Danni. He gets in."

"How did he get into your house?"

"He had a key! I heard my door opening. I looked out a window and saw the woman. I ran out the back."

Looked at logically, she had to admit that the story sounded preposterous.

"Where are you, Gus?"

"Danni, you have to believe me," he insisted.

"Then you have to trust me. Where are you?"

There was silence for a long moment.

"I'm here, Danni. I'm in the house. I slipped into the shop with some customers, and then I sneaked into the house and hid. It's the only place I feel safe."

It was too easy. Ridiculously easy. In the end he hadn't even needed a costume, because he was invisible. Invisible in plain sight. He stepped right up to his friend.

"You're scared out here, too, right?"

"Yes. There's safety in numbers, right?"

"Safety in numbers."

At the courtyard gate, he hit a buzzer. A female voice answered carefully. Danni, he knew.

"Can we come in and stay with you and

everyone else?"

"Hang on," she said.

He smiled. So many of them were there . . .

The precious Survivor Set. Amy and Woodrow Watson. Jessica . . .

And Danni.

He was invisible. But tonight they would see him.

Danni had frozen when she heard the courtyard bell, but now she was glad of the new arrivals.

Her gun was in her bag, which was in the kitchen.

Gus was in the house. But where, exactly?

He must have come in after Quinn had left with Wolf, because the dog would have barked his head off if he'd known a stranger had come in unaccompanied.

He claimed he was innocent.

She hurried into the kitchen to see that Shamus had arrived, along with Eric Lyons.

"Hey," Eric said to her. "I couldn't get through to Sharon, but her roommate told me that she went out of town to see family after I told her we were closing. And I . . . well, I decided that I didn't want to be alone. Not when we know that Gus is still out there."

"You're just in time for lasagna," Jenny told the newcomers cheerfully.

"Hey, guys," Danni said. She wasn't sure why, but she suddenly felt even more uneasy.

Gus was in the house somewhere. Gus, with all that evidence against him.

Claiming he'd been set up.

And now she had even more people to keep safe.

"Hey, where are the rest of the troops?" Shamus asked.

"The rest of the troops?" Danni said. Then she realized that Jessica wasn't there, and neither were the Watsons.

"Craig needed changing," Tyler explained.

Danni heard a voice coming from her side. "Danni?"

It was Gus. She'd forgotten he was still on the phone.

"Excuse me," she said, and fled to her studio. "Gus, where are you — exactly? And why the hell should I believe you?"

"Because it's true, and I'm begging you. And I'm right here."

She turned around. And there was Gus, filthy, his clothes marked by several tears, standing in the doorway of her studio. He brought a finger to his lips, begging for her silence.

Then he closed the door.

It was easy, so easy. Because he was magic. Invisible in plain sight.

He took out Tyler first, because he was the biggest, the strongest and the most capable of putting up a fight. He pretended to compliment Jenny on her cooking as he slammed the butt of the gun down on Tyler's head so he fell without a sound. Spinning around, he caught Bo Ray with a hard thwack to the jaw. After that he pointed the gun at Jenny, and warned Shamus and Brad that she would be dead before they could move their lips if they didn't listen.

They listened then did as he said, tying up the fallen and then each other. After that he moved up the stairs and took old Woodrow by complete surprise. All he had to do next was threaten the kid to get the old woman to do anything he wanted.

And then he had Jessica . . .

Downstairs now for Danni and the sax, and then the fun of killing them all, one by one.

Wolf had led them to Bourbon Street and then to La Porte Rouge.

It was locked up, of course, but Wolf stood

at the door and barked without stopping.

"Great. Now what?" Billie demanded.

"I don't know. I don't know what he wants, but Wolf is always right on," Quinn said.

"We can break the door in," Father Ryan suggested.

Quinn looked at the old, heavily bolted door then at the windows, whose shutters had been drawn down and locked.

"Wolf really wants in," Billie said.

"We could call Larue and get the cops to open it," Father Ryan said. "Or go back to plan A and break it down."

"We may have to — if we can," Quinn said.

But as he spoke he heard the heavy inside bolt sliding open.

The door opened, and Max, the bouncer, stood there looking down at them. "What's going on? I heard we were closed tonight."

"Right. So what are you doing here?" Quinn asked him suspiciously.

Max shrugged sheepishly. "I lost my apartment. I've been sleeping here. No one knows, but with what's going on . . . well, I looked out from upstairs, saw it was you and figured I had to open to you."

Wolf rushed past Max and stood at the bar, barking.

449

"What the hell?" Billie muttered.

"Okay, what's going on?" Max demanded.

"I don't know," Quinn said, following the dog. "There's no one else in here with you, is there?"

"No, sir, I'm alone," Max said.

Quinn walked around and behind the bar. The cash register was closed. He couldn't begin to understand what was making Wolf so crazy.

Then he noticed a locked drawer beneath a row of call brand 285 rums. "Max, what's in here?" he asked.

"Stuff. Stuff that belongs to the employees," he said. "I don't know. I don't keep anything in there. Don't really have anything worth locking up. Guess the girls leave their purses or wallets or whatever when they're working."

It was just the bar itself that seemed to have Wolf worked up. But Quinn was curious about the drawer. "You got a crowbar or anything anywhere?" he asked Max.

"You want me to break the lock?" Max asked him.

"If you will."

"You'll be responsible?"

"I will," Quinn said.

Max joined him behind the bar, opened another cabinet and took out a toolbox. He

450

took out a hammer and a screwdriver, and used them to force the drawer open.

There were just a few papers — invoices.

Father Ryan called his name to get his attention, and Quinn turned. In the drawer where the tools had been there was a cigar box. Father Ryan took the box out and opened it.

"Sweet Jesus, I guess now we know," Billie breathed. "I guess now we know the truth about the killer."

"I didn't do it, Danni. I swear I didn't do it. Please don't scream."

"Gus, let me call Quinn."

"Yes, call Quinn. Don't tell him I'm here, but call him and make him get back here. Please. Because if the killer's not here already, he will be soon. I know it. I just know it."

"All right, Gus. Let me get back out there before people start to wonder where I went. I'll call Quinn, but first let me —"

She stopped speaking as a muffled squeal came from the kitchen.

Gus winced. "Oh, God, he's here," he whispered.

Damn it! Her gun was still in the kitchen, Danni thought, praying that her instincts were right. "Gus, get back behind that stack of canvases, and stay there until I call you."

He obeyed her instantly.

She opened the door and jumped. Jessica was standing there, holding her son tightly in her arms. Her eyes were wide with fear and horror.

And, Danni realized, she wasn't alone. Eric Lyons was standing behind her, a gun shoved into Jessica's back.

"Hello, Danni. How nice to see you. Here we are. Most of us, anyway. Tyler, Bo Ray, Shamus, Brad and Jenny are all nicely tied up in the kitchen. Poor Mr. and Mrs. Watson are knocked out upstairs, but I'd hate to have them wake up to find out what I did to their grandson when you didn't give me the sax. I know you have it. It's what you do. You collect things. It took me a while, but I finally figured out that skinny bastard Billie has been playing it. Where is it, Danni? Where's Arnie's special sax?"

Danni couldn't have been more stunned. She didn't know why. Eric had said that he played; he'd said that he wasn't very good. She knew she had to think fast, but she had no idea what to do. Quinn and Billie and Father Ryan could come walking back in any minute, completely unaware. And while there would be three of them — and there were cops right outside — someone in the house could die if she didn't play this just right.

"You think *Billie* has been playing Arnie's sax?" she asked.

"Don't mess with me. Just shut up and get it for me from wherever it is," he said harshly. Jessica let out a little yelp as he shoved the gun harder into her back. "I'm in control here, and I'll kill one of you for every minute you make me wait."

"Okay, okay. I'll get you the sax," she said. "It's up in Billie's room."

To her surprise, he was looking past her.

He was staring at the picture she had sketched of all of them at the club.

He shoved Jessica hard, sending her flying into the room. She clutched Craig close to her to keep from dropping him as she fell to her knees with a sob.

"Shut up!" he warned her. "I'd be happier than hell to kill that bastard's illegitimate brat. I tried so hard, Jessica. I would have done anything for you. But you were sleeping with *him,* slinking away, the two of you, to screw like rabbits!"

"I didn't know!" Jessica cried. "I didn't know you cared!"

Eric's eyes shot back to the drawing. "There we are, just like always. All of you there, and not one of you noticing me.

Arnie's not in the picture, so the attention is all on the bastard's kid."

Danni gasped, realizing then what she should have seen all along. "You! You're the one by the tree in my dad's picture."

He swung on her, pointing the gun her way. "Yeah, I'm in the picture. Not one of you ever saw me back then. I was just a kid. I wasn't 'special.' I couldn't sing or act or draw. I was just there. And not one of you ever saw me. You, Danni, you were just like Jessica. Sashaying around and never seeing me, never speaking to me, never hearing me when I tried to speak to you. Well, that's going to change for the rest of my life. I'm going to have the sax. I'm going to play so well that the whole world hears me, and then everyone will see me."

"You weren't in my graduating class —" Danni began.

"No, I wasn't in anyone's graduating class, because I left that damn school. You just made my point for me, Danni. None of you saw me, so none of you noticed when I wasn't there anymore. When I started at the bar — which I own, by the way, not that any of you ever bothered to find that out — not one of you knew me. You passed me in the halls, sat next to me at assemblies, but not one of you saw me. But that's all over."

He suddenly reached for the drawing on the board, ready to tear it to shreds. As he did, Gus came flying out from behind the pile of canvases.

But Eric was too fast. He swung in time and fired. There was very little sound, but Gus crumpled to the floor, his temple bleeding.

Craig began to cry. Jessica was still sobbing herself as she tried to soothe him.

"A silencer. Clever," Danni said, trying to remain calm — trying not to rush to Gus's side.

"Get up," Eric told Jessica. "And you!" he said, spinning on Danni. "Get me that sax, and don't try to fool me. Make it the right one!"

"I told you, it's upstairs," she said.

"Then we go upstairs," he said. He indicated with the gun that she and Jessica were to precede him. "And no sudden moves or the kid dies first."

All she could do was play for time. Quinn would come back soon. Or he would call, and when she didn't answer . . .

He would send the cops or come rushing in himself, and someone would die. Someone else. Gus was already bleeding out his life on her studio floor, if he wasn't already dead.

"Move!" Eric told her, waving his gun. His Glock 19, modified with a silencer.

Danni had no choice. She moved.

"Why don't you call the cops stationed out front?" Billie shouted, running behind Quinn.

Quinn was running hard, determined — and afraid.

"Because he's in the house!" he called back.

"You can't be sure," Billie said.

"Wolf is sure," Quinn said, and he knew it was true. The dog had barked insanely while they were at La Porte Rouge then suddenly lit out again.

"If he feels he's cornered, he'll take down everyone he can before he goes down himself," Quinn said.

"The cops could go in en masse before he could do anything," Father Ryan panted.

"I can't take that chance. If he's got a full clip in his gun . . ." Quinn said. "I have to get in myself. Without him knowing."

They kept running.

None of them spoke again.

Passing the kitchen on her way to the stairs, Danni saw the bodies on the floor, bound and gagged.

She was shaking as she headed up the stairs, aware that Jessica — holding Craig — was right behind her.

And that Eric was right behind Jessica, his gun trained on her.

She entered the attic apartment shared by Billie and Bo Ray. It had a kitchenette/dining/living area and two bedrooms.

She didn't have to go into Billie's bedroom.

The sax he'd been playing was right in the center of the room.

"There it is," she said, turning and desperately hoping that inspiration would seize her, that she would suddenly see something she could use to save them all.

There was nothing. Just the sax on the stand where Billie lovingly kept it, and near it, the stand for his precious bagpipes.

"How do I know it's the real one?" Eric demanded.

"I swear to you, it's the one Arnie's family gave Tyler, and he gave it to me for safekeeping," Danni said.

"Prove it. Play it for me," Eric said.

"I can't play any instrument!"

"If it's the magic sax, you'll be able to play it."

"First off, Eric, you're wrong. There never was a magic sax," she said.

"The sax is magic. *I* am magic. Invisible. And when I play that sax . . . Show me. Show me that it's the real deal."

She had no choice. She picked up the sax. She didn't even know how to hold the thing correctly.

"You're going to have to show me how to . . ."

She tried to sound as confused as possible. As hare-brained as she could.

She walked toward him.

And when she was close enough, she used the sax as her weapon, slamming it against him as hard as she could, striking his shoulder and head.

He cried out, staggering.

But he didn't lose hold of the gun.

"Run!" Danni shouted to Jessica.

Jessica didn't need to be told twice. Her son gripped tightly, she made it out the door. Danni could hear her running down the stairs.

Eric was between her and the door. With little choice, Danni threw herself at the man, trying to bite his arm, to get him down so she could slam him against the floor — anything to make him lose his grip on the gun.

But he was strong. He threw her off. She tried to scramble up and tackle him again.

But he was too quick. He stood over her, the gun pointed at her face.

"Now you know me," he told her. "Now you see me. And now you'll die."

She heard the sound of a bullet being fired and waited to die then was stunned when she didn't.

Eric was staring at her, his expression stunned as she knew hers must have been.

A red flower began to blossom on his chest.

And then he fell to his knees, still staring at her in surprise.

Finally he crashed to the floor, and when she turned she saw Quinn standing in the doorway, lowering the weapon he had just fired.

Shaking, she stood then walked over to him, trembling.

They didn't speak. They didn't need to. They just held each other.

And then they heard the sirens, footsteps on the stairs.

In seconds the night was filled with chaos. But it was over.

The sax was just a sax. Not magic.

And Eric Lyons hadn't been magic, either. He had simply been a man.

Three days later there was a party, and it

was a nice one, Danni thought. She had planned it well.

Victoria Tate was out of the hospital. Gus had only been grazed by the bullet, and he was grateful not only to be alive but also that the world knew he hadn't been the killer.

They were at the house on Royal Street; The Cheshire Cat was closed, and dinner was being served.

Natasha had cooked a Creole dinner for them, with shrimp and cheese grits, crawfish étoufée, red beans and rice, turnip greens and salad, and bread pudding for dessert.

Jenny had said she wasn't about to cook, and that she didn't want to see lasagna again as long as she lived.

They talked a lot about Eric; maybe they all even felt a little guilty, Danni thought.

Guilty that they really hadn't known him. That they hadn't remembered him. That they'd never recognized him as the boy looking on in the picture her father had taken so many years ago.

"Did we make him a monster? Or was he always one and we were just the excuse he gave himself for what he did?" Brad asked morosely.

"We were never mean," Jenny protested.

"We just didn't notice," Tyler said. "And

maybe that's worse."

Hattie had joined them, and she told them determinedly, "Don't go taking blame on yourselves. We are all responsible, in the end, for our own actions."

"Amen," Father Ryan said.

"There's another question we really do need to answer," Quinn said.

"Where is the real sax?" Danni said.

"Well, I've been thinking. And thinking," Amy said.

"And?" Danni asked her.

"There was a bag of Arnie's things . . . He said that if anything ever happened, he wanted to be buried with them," Amy said.

"But I thought he was playing the sax the night he was killed?" Tyler said.

"Maybe not. Maybe he was playing a different one. He owned several," Amy said.

"You mean . . ."

"She means we buried our boy with a bag of his belongings, just like he asked," Woodrow said.

"Oh," Father Ryan said thoughtfully. "We could arrange to — to look," he said. "Have another graveside service."

Jessica spoke up immediately. "No! We are not tampering with Arnie's grave."

"No," Tyler agreed. "A sax is a sax, and Arnie's sax . . . If there was any magic, well,

Arnie and the way he touched our lives with his music, that was the magic. He made the sax magic, not the other way around."

"All right, then," Woodrow said, looking at his wife and smiling. "We will not disturb the grave. Our new daughter says no."

"And I agree," Amy said.

"Then that's that," Quinn said. "Tonight we'll remember him and all the magic that was his life, and we'll thank God we all still have our own lives. It's over."

"Well," Hattie said, "hold on. It's not quite over."

"Oh?" Quinn said.

"I have a plan to end this sad chapter on a happy note that honors Arnie quite nicely. If you're all willing, of course."

"Do tell," Quinn said.

So she did.

EPILOGUE

There were two saxophones being played that day.

A few numbers had been chosen to allow for the bagpipes, as well. Billie was beyond delighted by that. He'd suggested that military men and women in attendance might enjoy the inclusion of the bagpipes, and the others had agreed.

The B-Street Bombers were together with a new member — a female lead singer with a voice like a lark.

Quinn was playing rhythm guitar; Danni was singing backup and performing two duets with Jessica, as well. Tyler, Gus, Shamus and Blake were playing music they knew like the backs of their hands, but still, the occasion was important and they were nervous.

It was probably, Danni thought, the best they had ever sounded.

She realized — glancing at Hattie, who

sat with Natasha, Father Ryan, the Watsons, little Craig and Kevin Hart — that she might never know just what strings Hattie had pulled to arrange for the band to play at Walter Reed from 11:00 a.m. till 9:00 that night. Hattie was like a lovely fairy godmother.

She wasn't a spring chicken, though, so it was a good thing the others were there, along with a host of Arnie's old army buddies, to make sure she was comfortable and ride herd on Craig, who had learned that he could do more than walk, he could run. He was happy and laughing, and he was also perpetually all over the place. He kept the adults hopping, but none of them minded. He was a beautiful reminder of the past, of Arnie, and he was hope for all good things to come.

His smile was Arnie's smile, and he had his mother's faith that good things were everywhere.

Kevin Hart had obviously spread the word that they were coming, and that they were friends of Arnie's. The cafeteria was full all day, and they were greeted with applause for every song. It was wonderful, but it was even more wonderful to see the way Jessica basked in the pride the Watsons showed in her.

They weren't her parents, though they should have been her in-laws. But neither birth nor a piece of paper seemed to matter to them. They smiled at her and beamed with pride. She was the mother of their grandchild. She was family.

And they smiled just as proudly at Tyler as he played the sax.

It wasn't Arnie's precious special sax. But like that sax, it was magic when played by a man who loved it — and loved where he was playing.

When they finished playing for the day and said their thank-yous and goodbyes to those who had served their country, their families, the doctors and nurses, and everyone else who'd come, Amy walked up to Tyler and gave him a hug.

"Any sax is magic in your hands, son, as it was in Arnie's," she said, giving voice to Danni's thoughts. Then she turned to Quinn and Danni, winked and told them, "Magic can always find a way into the world when there's enough belief, enough longing." She scooped Craig up into her arms and held him close. "Magic." She offered them a wry grin. "And you two will always find it, wherever it might lie!"

Quinn was standing behind Danni, holding her tightly to him. She felt his whisper against her ear as he said, "Ah, yes. Magic. My magic is your arms, Danni."

She turned and kissed him.

Yes, that was magic.

ABOUT THE AUTHOR

Heather Graham grew up in Dade County, Florida, and attended the University of South Florida at Tampa, majoring in theater arts and touring Europe and parts of Asia and Africa as part of her studies. After college, she acted in dinner theaters, modeled, waitressed, and tended bar. After the birth of her third child, she was determined to devote her efforts to her writing: her dream. She sold her first book in 1982.

Today, this author's success is reflected not just by reader response and the over 20 million copies of her books in print, but in many other ways. In addition to being a *New York Times* bestselling author, Heather has received numerous awards for her novels, including over 20 trade awards from magazines such as *Romantic Times* and *Affaire de Coeur,* bestseller awards from B. Dalton, Waldenbooks, and BookRak and several

Reviewers' Choice and People's Choice awards.

Heather has appeared on *Entertainment Tonight, Romantically Speaking,* a TV talk show that aired nationwide on the Romance Classics cable channel, and *CBS Sunday News.* She has been quoted in *People* and *USA Today,* been profiled in *The Nation,* and featured in *Good Housekeeping.* Her books have been selections for the Doubleday Book Club and the Literary Guild. She has been published across the world in more than 15 languages and has published over 70 titles, including anthologies and short stories.

Somehow, this prolific author manages to juggle it all — family, career, and marriage — while reaching a level of success to which few can aspire.

The employees of Thorndike Press hope you have enjoyed this Large Print book. All our Thorndike, Wheeler, and Kennebec Large Print titles are designed for easy reading, and all our books are made to last. Other Thorndike Press Large Print books are available at your library, through selected bookstores, or directly from us.

For information about titles, please call:
  (800) 223-1244

or visit our Web site at:
  http://gale.cengage.com/thorndike

To share your comments, please write:
  Publisher
  Thorndike Press
  10 Water St., Suite 310
  Waterville, ME 04901